THE ULTIMATE
WRITERS OF
SCIENCE FICTION

John Barnes	Jack McDevitt
William C. Dietz	Alastair Reynolds
Simon R. Green	Allen Steele
Joe Haldeman	S. M. Stirling
Robert Heinlein	Charles Stross
Frank Herbert	Harry Turtledove
E. E. Knight	John Varley

penguin.com/scififantasy

ACE RoC

Ace Books by Anne McCaffrey

The Tower and Hive Series

THE ROWAN
DAMIA
DAMIA'S CHILDREN
LYON'S PRIDE
THE TOWER AND THE HIVE

The Freedom Series

FREEDOM'S LANDING
FREEDOM'S CHOICE
FREEDOM'S CHALLENGE
FREEDOM'S RANSOM

LYON'S PRIDE

ANNE MCCAFFREY

ACE BOOKS, NEW YORK

THE BERKLEY PUBLISHING GROUP
Published by the Penguin Group
Penguin Group (USA) Inc.
375 Hudson Street, New York, New York 10014, USA
Penguin Group (Canada), 90 Eglinton Avenue East, Suite 700, Toronto, Ontario M4P 2Y3, Canada
(a division of Pearson Penguin Canada Inc.) • Penguin Books Ltd., 80 Strand, London WC2R 0RL,
England • Penguin Group Ireland, 25 St. Stephen's Green, Dublin 2, Ireland (a division of Penguin
Books Ltd.) • Penguin Group (Australia), 250 Camberwell Road, Camberwell, Victoria 3124, Australia
(a division of Pearson Australia Group Pty. Ltd.) • Penguin Books India Pvt. Ltd., 11 Community
Centre, Panchsheel Park, New Delhi—110 017, India • Penguin Group (NZ), 67 Apollo Drive,
Rosedale, Auckland 0632, New Zealand (a division of Pearson New Zealand Ltd.) • Penguin Books
(South Africa) (Pty.) Ltd., 24 Sturdee Avenue, Rosebank, Johannesburg 2196, South Africa

Penguin Books Ltd., Registered Offices: 80 Strand, London WC2R 0RL, England

LYON'S PRIDE

An Ace Book / published by arrangement with the author

PUBLISHING HISTORY
Ace/Putnam edition published 1994
Ace mass-market edition / February 1995

Copyright © 1994 by Anne McCaffrey.
Cover art by Danny O'Leary.
Cover design by Lesley Worrell.

ISBN: 978-0-441-00141-5

ACE
Ace Books are published by The Berkley Publishing Group,
a division of Penguin Group (USA) Inc.,
375 Hudson Street, New York, New York 10014.
ACE and the "A" design are trademarks of Penguin Group (USA) Inc.

PRINTED IN THE UNITED STATES OF AMERICA

23 22 21 20 19 18 17 16 15 14

ALWAYS LEARNING   **PEARSON**

This book is dedicated to

MATTHEW HARGREAVES

for all the hard work, effort and time that he
expended in nailing down an excellent bibliography
of all the works by this grateful author

(except this one which wasn't written yet!)

PROLOGUE

THE first incursion against the Nine Star League by the Hive entities occurs at Deneb, where Jeff Raven and the undeveloped Talents of his planet stave off a vicious attack by three alien scout ships orbiting Deneb IV. Calling for assistance from the Earth Federated Teleport and Telepath Prime, Peter Reidinger, Jeff Raven encounters the Rowan, Callisto's Prime. In a mind merge, two of the three invaders are destroyed and the third sent back, as a warning, to whence it had come.

Three years later the Mother Hive ship, a spherical leviathan, appears at Deneb heliopause. The Talents once again merge to defend the planet: the Rowan, pregnant with her second child, Cera, is the focus for the feminine minds which then immobilize the female Many Mind that governs the Hive ship. The male merge, with Jeff Raven as focus, then teleports the Hive ship into Deneb's primary.

Nineteen years later, while recuperating on Deneb,

Damia Gwyn-Raven, another T-1 Talent, and Afra Lyon, a Capellan T-2, have "dreams" which they realize are being implanted by the alien figures which appear in these dreams. Contact is made with these visitors, who call themselves the Mrdini. Through dreams the Mrdini explain that they have been defending themselves and their colony worlds against the incursions of the Hive for centuries. They had followed the Hive ship to Deneb and been fascinated by its destruction without loss of life on the part of the defenders. They offer an alliance.

In order to establish meaningful relationships, young 'Dinis are placed with Human children, in the sound belief that early exposure to another species facilitates understanding. Among those selected for this experiment are the children of Afra and Damia, now Tower Prime for Iota Aurigae, a mining world. Their eight children all have 'Dini pairs.

At sixteen, the eldest daughter, Laria, is sent to the 'Dini homeworld of Clarf to teach 'Dini Human language and to expand her own understanding of the adult vocabulary. At about this time, Mrdini scouts observe three Hive ships which separate before the 'Dini can catch up. But the ion trails left by the three are strong and can be followed on their disparate ways.

The Alliance of Mrdinis and Nine Star Leaguers decide on a four-pronged expedition. The first element of six ships is to backtrack to see if it cannot locate the elusive homeworld of the Hivers. The other three elements are to follow the Hive ships to their destinations, preferably to destroy them if at all possible before they can colonize another world by first sterilizing it of all existing life forms.

Isthian Lyon, Laria's brother, is seconded by FT&T to the AS *Vadim* to act as Prime with the tracking mission of six ships, four Human, two Mrdini. It is his job to improve communications and relations between the Allies, and to receive supplies to keep the ships moving toward their objective. Thian has always been interested in naval matters so he is well suited by the assignment. Thian is accompanied by his 'Dini pair, Mrg and Dpl (Mur and Dip).

When the *Vadim* encounters a lifeless stationary derelict, it is identified as a Hive ship, though larger by another third than any previously encountered. It appears to have been destroyed by the heat of an expanding nova. Three escape pods seem to have been used, though others were destroyed *in situ*. An exploration detail of both 'Dini and Human is to examine the wreck. Encountering hostility from a crewman, Thian is nearly killed on the Hive ship, where he discovers undamaged Hiver eggs. These are sent to be studied by the Alliance xenobiologists. Recovering from his injury, Thian elects to continue with the Mrdini ship, the *KLTL*, as the Mrdinis insist on being certain that a nova has destroyed the Hive homeworld.

Two of the ships in Thian's element are required to start the derelict on its way to a point at which both Mrdini and Human specialists can examine it thoroughly. The remaining three ships decide to track down the three escape pods. It is essential to capture the pods, for just one queen is sufficient to establish a new colony.

While Thian continues with the *KLTL* on toward the site of the nova, the search for the three large ships, as well as the escape pods, continues. Attempts are also being made to reassemble from its shattered parts as much of the big Hive Sphere as is possible to reconstruct, in an effort to learn more about the enemy.

One of the escape pods, bearing a live queen, is discovered by the *Beijing* and captured, and is safely in tow behind the ship. Afra and his son Rojer are sent out to 'port the pod to the Heinlein Moon Station where it can be safely examined in great detail. There is considerable debate and many factions: some wishing to summarily execute the queen, others wishing to approach her in an effort to establish communications with and knowledge of a species never before captured. The Mrdini are particularly against keeping the queen alive. Rojer, with his father acting as focus, easily transfers queen and pod.

Back on Earth, the captured queen pod is secured and placed under twenty-four hour survelliance. When she finally emerges, she is seen as a mantis-type creature, ten-limbed, and egg-heavy. Since no one has had much luck in incubating the eggs discovered on the derelict ship, it is decided to deposit these with her.

There is considerable objection to keeping the creature alive, but those who insist that knowing more about the enemy may be a deciding factor in a final victory over its incursions manage to win the argument. She is kept alive. Food of all varieties is supplied and she is seen to prefer vegetables or fruits. Her actions, when there are any, are monitored and shown to all interested.

Zara, the fourteen-year-old sister of Laria, Thian and Rojer, becomes emotionally involved with what she sees as the queen's dreadful plight and imprisonment. In a remarkable adventure, Zara arrives at the Observation Station and, distraught by the queen's condition, 'ports herself into the facility and realizes that the queen is freezing, being accustomed to a much hotter temperature in her parturitional stage. Zara's intercession saves the queen's life although, despite a hope that there has been some empathy between Human and Hiver, this bizarre incident is not repeated, nor can Zara explain why she acted as she did. Her parents realize with some regret that Zara is not Tower material, even though a Prime. Elizara, the T-1 medic for whom she was named, and her great-grandmother Isthia decide she may have healing Talents.

Meanwhile, one of the escaping Hive ships has been tracked to a star system where it is obviously slowing down. Rojer is sent to the *Genesee* to expedite messages for Squadron B—two Human ships and one Mrdini ship—which is hovering, undetectable, within an asteroid belt of the system.

The crew watch as the arriving Hiver ship is attacked from moon bases and planetary surfaces. When the ship's ammunition is exhausted, the queens flee in escape pods which are disintegrated. This shocks those on the *Genesee*. As much as the 'Dini have observed of their enemy over the centuries, they are as surprised and stunned as their Human allies. It is new territory for them, too.

Instead of being allowed to go in blasting, Squadron B and the *Genesee* are ordered to hold a watching brief, utilizing as many probes as possible, with Rojer's help, to gather information. It is thought that Thian, on his way back to "civilization" on the *KLTL*, which has now definitely established that the Hiver homeworld was destroyed in the nova, will join or replace his brother on the *Genesee*.

Two squadrons are still in pursuit of the remaining two Hive spheres while Squadron A, Thian's original group, is searching for the other two pods which evacuated from the Great Sphere before it was hit by the nova shock wave. A waiting game is played on several levels and ethical problems of great magnitude must be addressed by both Human and Mrdini civilizations.

CHAPTER
ONE

DURING the course of the next few weeks, while Rojer waited for his older brother, Thian, to replace him on board the *Genesee*, he spent a great deal more time on the bridge than he had originally thought he would. Not only was Rojer Lyon the FT&T T-1 which linked Squadron B with its homeworlds and was the means by which the three ships were kept supplied by twice-weekly importations of supplies, he was also able to provide other services to the Squadron not in his original brief. If he was referred to as "the boy" or "the civilian," he couldn't deny "boy" as he was not quite sixteen, although tall and well-muscled from an active life on his home planet. He also had inherited the family lock of silver hair which made it difficult for some to believe he hadn't yet reached his majority. Most times these references to his age or status were jocular. Sometimes envy or disparagement tinged these epithets—until he 'ported in the next supply drones, when he was again in favor with all. Sometimes it appeared to him that his 'Dinis, Grl and Ktg, were more acceptable to the *Genesee* officers and crew than he was, but he encouraged them to continue teaching their language to any on board who wished it. At night, in his cabin, he could enjoy the consolation of his friends and they were very good at diverting him with amusing shipboard incidents and their own special companionship. When he was particularly upset, they would "dream" the tension away.

Since the Squadron was on orders to hold a watching brief and to take no direct action against the ancient enemy which occupied the system, tedium became a problem. Even escape pod drills became a welcome variation of daily routine. So, when Captain Osullivan asked Rojer if he could 'port the newly developed and undetectable probes to discover what they could about the moons' defenses and the three spherical ships in docking orbit around the planet, he was quite willing to oblige.

The activity was one he was well able for: in fact, it gave him no little satisfaction to know that "the boy/civilian" had an ability no one else in the B Squadron had. He was also just as curious as anyone else in the Squadron to learn as much as possible about the Hivers' world. He had discreet knowledge from Gil and Kat that Captain Prtglm of the *KTTS* would have preferred direct action to surveillance and had been extremely upset by the "surveillance" order from the High Council which had originated from the Human Supreme Commander, Admiral Tohl Mekturian, and the Mrdini High Councillor, Gktmglnt.

The Squadron had been given a stunning display of the planet's defenses when they had observed the attack on the refugee Hive ship which they had followed to this system. Their three ships would have been totally outgunned and unable to inflict telling damage on planetary installations. It was a different matter entirely to survey as much as possible of this enemy planet. Rojer enthusiastically entered into dispersing disguised monitors to the material clustering about the three sphere ships which were in a construction-level orbit about the planet. Certainly any ground-based sensors wouldn't notice him tucking a few more "pieces" amid the clutter that spun in disarray round the world. Frankly, Rojer thought tossing such garbage into space was an appalling way to discard rubbish.

Neither Captain Quacho of the sister ship, the *Arapahoe*, or Captain Osullivan of the *Genesee* had expected that the refugee Hiver ship would be attacked by its own species, its queens driven to escape in the pods which had then been summarily disintegrated by the planetary batteries. Captain Prtglm had announced that it was no more than could be expected of Hivers.

Since Rojer's first assignment was to inspect the three sphere ships in their docking orbit, tensions were defused further when the monitors proved that only one looked to be spaceworthy. Quite possibly it had been the ship which had transported the original colonizing group. One of the other two was near completion, though it had significant gaps, probably left open to receive equipment, while the other was only partly hulled. That gave rise to further speculation as to why the planet's defenders had "holed" the refugee ship, rendering it unusable.

Somewhat reassured by that investigation, which he had Rojer relay in his daily message to Earth Prime, Captain Osullivan requested Rojer to make a geographical survey of the eight land masses, the biggest one spreading from pole to pole. An opportunity like this, to gain firsthand knowledge of a Hiver world, should be utilized to the fullest extent possible. It also provided occupation during the tedium of a watching brief.

The Hive culture appeared to be totally land-based and

every centimeter of land was cultivated. Rojer's guided sensors showed that mountainsides were terraced up to the snow-line with what Commander Metrios, the engineering officer, considered amazing techniques and, although some fields were fallow, the majority sprouted with vigorous, if unrecognizable, flora. Narrow tracks bordering the fields provided access for the scurrying life forms involved in agricultural occupations. Their constant presence made it dangerous to attempt to 'port in a sample-collecting probe. Another variety of beetle-like creatures specialized in irrigation, trundling water, held in body sacs, which was carefully dribbled along neat rows. What surprised Lieutenant Istvan Mrkovic, the science officer, who had made due note of the teeming marine life, was that the Hivers had not made any attempt to harvest nutritious seaweed and plankton so abundant and easily obtained.

"So they're vegetarians? Seaweed's a vegetable," he exclaimed.

"They seem to be single-minded in many respects," said Anis Langio, the astrogation officer whom Rojer admired at a distance. She was the prettiest of the female bridge officers and he was old enough to appreciate her presence. "A stagnant culture determined to replicate itself ad infinitum."

"That may alter," was the captain's crisp remark.

"I'd give anything to see a weed among all that perfection," remarked Anis Langio in a tone bordering on disgust. "Talk about purpose bio-engineering. A purpose for every critter and a critter for every purpose. Appalling. Specialization ad absurdum!"

"Look at these," Rojer said, focusing his sensor at its finest magnification where gatherers were stripping rows of a globular green vegetable form. Finishing the collection, the gatherers turned from the rows into neat triple ranks and trundled toward a central installation into which they disappeared.

Thousands of these installations had been scanned. They varied in size, evidently depending on the volume of crops, but not in shape, all being square buildings covering three to four acres, four or five stories in height with interior access at ground level along each side. Rojer had whizzed a sensor close enough to see that the entrance sloped downward. Activity continued night and day, for the creatures apparently did not require illumination for their tasks.

"And we thought this duty was boring," one yeoman was heard to mumble, eliciting widespread grins and a mild reproof.

"Those buildings have to be the access to tremendous subterranean networks," Istvan Mrkovic said thoughtfully. "There isn't enough space inside any of them to store the amounts brought in on a daily basis. Do they pick for daily use, since I noticed they do leave immature vegetables on the vines and bushes, or just to process for storage? Yet I can't pick up any trace of smoke or heat to account for cooking."

"Vegetarians eat a lot of raw foods," Anis remarked. "Or maybe they have a critter with heat-resistant paddles to stir the stew."

Istvan shot her a reproving look for such levity, though even the captain smiled. "Certainly we haven't seen anything coming back *out* for distribution so that has to be taken care of underground. Wow! What an organization! You gotta give 'em that."

"The workers *have* to be fed something at some point to continue at the pace they go," Anis Langio said, no longer bantering. She had her head propped on one hand and, as she watched the screen, was idly twirling a dark, springy curl around one finger. It seemed oddly out of character for someone of her rank and expertise. "You don't see any of them lying down on the job or expiring from lack of care."

"All mining must be done subterreaneously, too," Mrkovic decided. "I haven't seen anything remotely resembling an adit but those ships required a variety of metals. I've noted the presence of all the ores that we use but only that one finished ship in the construction orbit has been covered with their special coating. And if they have every centimeter producing food, the planet must be full up."

"The last harvest before blast-off," Anis quipped.

"Not if they've only one spaceworthy ship."

"Maybe the agricultural workers are multi-tasked and once the harvest's in they turn on their construction mode," was Anis's rejoinder. Istvan gave her another of his disgusted looks.

"She could be right," Metrios said. "The palp that pulls the pepper could also manipulate delicate equipment."

"And the trundlers shift struts and panels . . ." Anis went on.

"While the irrigators fill the fuel tanks," Doplas said, joining in the fun.

"That is when we must be most cautious," the captain said, and turned to Rojer. "You can withdraw the monitors quickly?"

Rojer nodded.

"Commander Yngocelen and I are still trying to include a small self-destruct unit, sir, just in case," Metrios said. "Small enough not to create much flare but enough to fuse the innards to an unrecognizable slag."

The captain nodded approval. "Our relief ships are not that far away."

Rojer held his breath in surprise. Would he actually be

in on the first invasion of a Hive world? He had heard the gunnery officer, Lieutenant Commander Yngocelen, and some of his staff discussing what would be needed to "take out" the moon batteries but no one had sounded very optimistic about success in that direction. Despite all they had seen of this Hive world, there were many unknowns.

From their Mrdini allies and once firsthand on Deneb, Humans did know something about Hive colonization practices. The creatures preferred G-type stars, M-5–type planets, worlds similar to Earth, or Clarf, the Mrdini homeworld, which meant that the three species were in competition with each other. The Hive method was to send one of their Sphere ships, managed by the Many Mind of ten to sixteen queens with specialized workers doing whatever crewing was needed. Each Mother ship was equipped with scout vessels which it sent on ahead to investigate appropriate systems. The Hiver then "cleared" the planet of all life forms, using as a fumigator first one, then other, viral infections, until the world had been cleared of its indigenous life forms. Then the Mother ship landed its queens and propagated its species until the new world, too, was overpopulated, when the process of exploration and colonization was repeated.

"But we've seen no activity at the ships at all," Anis said. "Or has the arrival of the refugee caused panic . . ."

"Hivers wouldn't know panic if it bit them . . ." Metrios interjected drolly.

". . . Well, then a rethink? I don't understand why they haven't done anything to repair the refugees' ship for use if they're about to send off a colonial expedition!"

"They also haven't restocked their moon installations," Yngocelen remarked. "They pumped out a bodacious amount of ordnance in that attack . . . even if most of it fell short. Surely they'd have to replenish it unless they

have almighty storage facilities up there." He glanced
hopefully at Rojer, who laughed.

"Sir, there's no way I can get a probe in those moon
emplacements. Not a niche or a crack and I've no idea of
what space is available inside. I can't 'port blind."

"No, no, of course you couldn't, Rojer," the gunnery officer replied, but his expression remained wistful.

"Been no messages sent there. No communication on
any frequency," Doplas said, glancing down at his control
console as if it had capriciously malfunctioned.

"Told ya the refugees didn't have the right password,"
quipped Metrios, a grin on his narrow sardonic face. Then he
suddenly sat up alert. "Lookee here. Activity in the shipyard." All attention was instantly focused on that screen.
"Can you hold that monitor stationary for a bit, Rojer?"

"Sure thing," and he complied, trying to see what had
attracted Metrios's attention. A wide hatch had swung
open at the end of the one uncultivated area on the whole
planet—its space facility.

"Doplas, magnify," Captain Osullivan said and paused a
beat before he added, "Pods! The units they're carrying look
the right size and shape to be made into escape pods."

"To replace the ones they blew up!" Anis added unnec-
essarily and glanced anxiously at the captain.

His strong-featured face showed only keen interest in
the surface activity as hundreds of low-slung many-legged
creatures, loaded with sections, trundled slowly across the
flat surface and deposited their burdens at sixteen separate
places before they scuttled back to the aperture, which
sank back into the ground.

"Are the *Arapahoe* and the *KTTS* receiving these trans-
missions, Doplas?"

"Aye, sir, on automatic relay."

Before the captain could ask Doplas to open a channel,

both Captains Quacho of the *Arapahoe* and Prtglm of the *KTTS* called in.

"They begin to refit," Prtglm said. "Time takes. Talent informs Alliance."

"They don't seem to be doing any work to complete the other two ships," Quacho remarked dubiously, his heavy brows nearly bridging over his roman nose.

"Those are already fitted with escape pods," Osullivan reminded him.

"Always queens are first," Prtglm said. "Time takes."

Rojer dutifully made contact with Jeff Raven to report the activity and was told to relay further developments as they occurred. Once the ground entrance closed, no further activity was seen. Excitement waned and Rojer was allowed to retire from the bridge at the end of his watch. Rather than have to evade questions on this new development, he spent the evening quietly in his cabin with Gil and Kat, watching more of the *Genesee*'s huge library of old tri-Ds until the red alert had him 'porting himself and his friends to the escape pod assigned him. He and the others who occupied his pod were nearly asleep again when the "all-clear" hooted.

The next morning he overslept and had to 'port himself to the bridge to be on time. Looking somewhat as grumpy as Rojer felt, Commander Metrios duly noted his hurried arrival but issued no reprimand. Casually Metrios told Rojer that no further activity on the space field had been noted.

"Maybe they have to *hatch out* the assemblers?" Anis Langio suggested and then yawned, wiggling her fingers in welcome as Rojer stepped up to his couch. He grinned back at her.

"Any corrections needed, Commander?" Rojer asked Metrios, gesturing to the screens and the roving sensors.

"No, Roj," Metrios said, with a wry grin. "They're where we need 'em right now. We're just lucky there's so much space flotsam that our sensors seem just like one of the boys out there."

"You know, for a planet that's spotless," said Eri Gander, the morale officer who often dropped by Rojer's station, "they've made a right mess of space."

"Haven't developed a form to gobble up their garbage, that's all," Metrios replied.

"Vegetarians get their iron and minerals from their food," Anis remarked with an overly innocent expression on her face. "Which reminds me, Eri, we could use some new tri-D's. There's nothing I haven't seen a zillion times."

Eri and Anis both looked queryingly at Rojer who held his arms wide, mimicking Anis's expression. "Look, I'm just transport. I have nothing to do with loading."

"Which reminds me why I'm here," Eri said, turning to Rojer. "I've four to ship back this week." He raised his eyebrows queryingly.

"No problem. My 'Dinis told me that there're two 'Dini pairs to go as well."

Anis heaved an exaggerated sigh. "I'm always glad to know they are not as po-faced and stiff-upper-lipped as Prtglm pretends they are."

"The 'Dinis're going to hibernate," Rojer said and grinned to defuse any criticism as he added, "That's not considered a weakness in 'Dinis."

"At least you save them from going on the line," Metrios said, nodding his head approvingly.

Anis gave a convulsive shudder. "I don't care what euphemism they apply to the process, it's still cannibalism."

"Term it exigency during long space hauls and accept that interpretation," Mrkovic said, but his expression indicated he was in complete agreement with the astrogator.

"At least we have Rojer here. Man and Mrdini's best friend is the local FT&T Talent."

Rojer grinned back, relieved that the subject of 'Dini traditions was not pursued. On the bridge, at least, he wasn't quizzed to the point of aggravation by pruriently curious crewmen and women. He had had to make the point that he might have lived closely with "immature" 'Dini, but he didn't know much about the adults.

"So what's to be done today, Commander?" he asked Metrios.

"Close watch on the shipyard and those pod elements. We've got a little self-destruct package in the new probes I ordered up in case we need to put more in action."

"Don't I just wish we did have some action," said Yngocelen as he stared glumly at the static scene on the screen. "Aren't they putting the cart before the horse? I mean, assembling escape pods when they haven't repaired the hole they put in the refugee ship? Never did understand why they plugged it. Especially after they had already conned the queens into leaving in their escape pods."

"Puzzling indeed," Metrios admitted, "since it damaged a perfectly spaceworthy craft which would have nicely increased their existing fleet."

Because he now knew these officers well enough, Rojer decided to voice his thoughts.

"Commander, I don't think that torpedo hit a cargo or docking area," he said.

"You don't?" Metrios's expression encouraged him.

"No, sir, I think they holed the life support systems. Because it was a hole, not a shattering blast."

"Show me." Metrios was not the only one who perked up with interest.

Rojer 'ported one of the monitors into the appropriate position. Unfortunately the entrance point was in deep

shadow. What was visible were the clean edges of the torpedo's entrance. The damage would be easily repaired. At
least it would on any of the Alliance ships.

"Maybe there was something in that torpedo they sent
up," Rojer added quietly, steeling himself for dispute.

"Yeah, but what and why?" Yngocelen asked in a caustic tone. "We know from even the partial reconstruction of
the Great Sphere which A Squadron discovered that they
can seal off decks and areas just as we can."

"Yes, but the queens were evacuating and there'd be no
one to issue orders to the workers to close anything. I
think," and Rojer paused so as not to sound as sure as he
was of his theory, "this lot wouldn't want the workers
spawned by other queens. They'd want to get rid of them
before they filled the ship with their personal workers."

"So the torpedo delivered a gas or something noxious to
fumigate it, huh?" Yngocelen asked, mulling over that theory.

"Boy's got a good point," Metrios said, over Rojer's
head, but his tone was approving.

"I could send a probe inside the ship to find out," Rojer
volunteered, since no one had discredited his theory. Although Captain Osullivan had not taken part in the conversation, he had been listening.

"Then do so, Mr. Lyon," Captain Osullivan said, nodding
to Yngocelen. "And program it for a full scan, Mr.
Yngocelen. It's about time we learned what's going on in
there, since Mr. Lyon's Talents allow us to be discreet."

Although Rojer sent the tiny probe through ventilation
ducts and up and down dark and empty corridors, nothing
was going on inside the hulk. Nothing apart from a haze
which still hung like a miasma in the interior, and especially heavy in the center of the vessel.

"Could be a combination of gases," the science officer

said, "because there sure aren't any workers of any description left and there are signs of corrosion on the few organic substances the monitor identifies. The Hivers seem to specialize in lethal doses. I wouldn't want to send anyone in to investigate. Despite the hole in the hull letting vacuum in, the stuff's lingering. It's going to take time to flush all that out."

"Sections weren't closed off either," Yngocelen said, tapping Rojer approvingly on the shoulder. "Yup, and that junk even cleared out the tubes where larvae are stored. Clean sweep!"

Rojer could not entirely suppress his delight that his theory had been verified, but everyone was smiling so he felt it wasn't inappropriate for him to do so, too.

"Good thinking, Rojer," Osullivan said to cap his moment of triumph.

Nonetheless Rojer heard—not from the direction of the officers—less grateful sentiments from one or two of the ratings on duty.

"It *was* only a theory, sir," Rojer said, altering his grin to modest self-deprecation. It was awful hard to please everyone all the time no matter how carefully he conducted himself.

"How long will it take for that gas to clear, Mr. Mrkovic?" Osullivan asked.

"Can't say for sure, sir, it's heavy stuff. All systems are dead on the ship. If they were activated . . ." and he shrugged. "With respect, sir, the *Genesee* doesn't have eva suits on board that would protect us Humans against a corrosive gas atmosphere."

Nor did the Mrdini when the options were discussed at a captains' conference. Although the derelict Great Sphere was being subjected to the most exhaustive scrutiny by both Humans and Mrdini, the emphasis had been on establishing what powered Hive ships and what fuel was used, and analyzing the peculiar composition of the hull material. Ventilation and life support systems were a low priority.

"Captain Prtglm would like us to figure out a way to get in that ship," Captain Osullivan reported to his staff officers. Rojer was also sitting in, as he had attended the captains' meeting as translator. "It has an idea," and Osullivan's smile was amused, "of boarding and bringing a relatively undamaged Hive ship back to Clarf. I gather Prtglm is to be retired at the end of this mission and it would like to do so in glory, as it were."

There were murmurs of understanding for such ambition.

"I didn't think Mrdini did things like retire," Anis Langio remarked.

Osullivan cleared his throat and smoothed back his hair. "I believe it's a question of size."

"Yeah, it is the biggest 'Dini I've ever seen," Yngocelen said thoughtfully. "If it gets much bigger, it won't fit in its own ship. It has to bend over to walk our companionways and this ship's built for tall." As the gunnery officer was just under the two-meter mark, he was sympathetic. "But you know," he went on off-handedly, "maybe Rojer could 'port a small boarding party directly into the torpedo hole. *They*'re obviously waiting until the gas disperses. Of course, we'd have to figure a way of doing *that* first."

"What *do* we know about the Hiver ventilation systems?" Osullivan asked rhetorically.

"No more than what the probe could see, sir," Metrios replied.

"Any idea of where or what the controls would be?"

Everyone turned in Rojer's direction.

"Me? I know as much as you do but . . ."

"But what, Mr. Lyon?" the captain prompted in an encouraging tone.

"Well, sir, when I first came on board, I believe I mentioned that groups back on the homeworlds are trying to reassemble the innards of the Great Sphere? We know what the main investigative team is working on—the fuel and engines—but maybe somebody else might have a clue to the life support area. I could make a discreet inquiry."

"Of whom?"

"The T-8 engineer at the Aurigae Tower."

Metrios looked considerably more receptive the moment Rojer mentioned "engineer."

"Please contact him then. Discreetly, of course," Osullivan asked Rojer.

"Certainly, sir," Rojer replied. He had determinedly not fallen into the habit of naval parlance of responding with the usual "Aye, sir." That was his subtle reaction to "boy" and "civilian."

Metrios grinned. "Would you need much power?"

"Not for a query," Rojer said, grinning back. Xexo would be as up-to-date as possible on what was being assembled, either by the naval or the "civilian" piece jiggers. "And he might even have some informed guesses. Thing worries me, though, is that that explosion might also have taken out the ventilation control system."

"That's a distinct possibility. Sure wrecked the area," Metrios said.

Rojer held up one hand, indicating he was initiating his query, but he sensed a definite eagerness in the atmosphere of the bridge. Clearly Captain Prtglm was not the only one who wanted to secure a trophy out of this encounter. Of course, the *Genesee* and the *Arapahoe* would share any honors with the *KTTS*. Everyone in the Alliance would rejoice to have purloined a nearly operational ship from a Hive colony. He suppressed the chuckle that threatened to overset his composure and sternly focused his mind on the gestalt to send the message.

Familiarity with Xexo's mind made the 'pathing easier. Rojer elected to make it an informal query because nothing might come of it and there was no point in getting hopes up only to dash them down.

Xexo was surprised to hear Rojer.

Coming through loud and clear, lad. But shouldn't you . . .

No, this is between you and me, Xexo, about our piecing. They don't have a set on board here and I need your help on one aspect of the reconstruction.

Oh, well, in that case . . . Xexo had always been more interested in the mechanical aspects of Tower than protocol so he made no further objections. *Whaddya need to know?*

What Xexo knew about the ventilation and life support systems was incomplete. In fact, Rojer realized that his probe had accumulated more cogent information, which he then shared with the T-8. Xexo could then confirm that the main environmental control systems had probably been demolished by the torpedo.

Queens seem to have had an independent emergency supply. Get that started and you might flush a lot of the gas out, 'specially with a hole already in the hull. Hey, you guys bring that ship back and you will be real heroes! Xexo added, excitement coloring his usual imperturbable manner. *Too much of the ship Squadron A salvaged has been damaged beyond guess or gosh.* Then Xexo "showed" Rojer what diagrams existed, incomplete as they were.

"Since the queens abandoned ship," Metrios said when he had a chance to study what Rojer transferred to the screen, "that area would not have been secured. But it appears," and his finger wandered off the diagram, "that one could flush the system of the gas quite efficiently from the main circulation point."

"If we knew how to work such controls," Rojer said. " 'Dinis keep telling us that the queens developed specific workers for various ship operations. What would a life-support worker look like?"

Metrios shrugged. "That'd be a problem. They seem to produce all kinds of workers."

The other officers on duty on the bridge had been following the conversations.

"The 'Dini records have reconstructions of some definite types, from corpses that were found after space battles," Anis Langio said and keyed in a program. They all watched as the sketches were accessed. Langio gave a snort. "Take your pick."

"That queen they've got at Heinlein Moon Base? Have her eggs hatched yet?" Metrios asked.

"They're growing and she's eating," Rojer replied with a shrug. He was still of two minds about his sister Zara's interference even if it had saved the queen's life from hypothermia.

One of the three pods to escape the Great Sphere had contained a live and egg-heavy queen. Conveying the pod to the Heinlein Moon Base had been Rojer Lyon's first official duty as a Prime, though his father had been the focus of the kinetic energy of that teleportation. An Observation Module had kept close track of her activities since she had emerged. She was, in fact, the first living specimen of the Hive race that either Human or Mrdini had seen. Her continued existence had elicited controversy, and sometimes strain, among the Allies. Fortunately some of the more liberal Mrdini leaders also felt that the need to know more about their enemy was of greater importance than a very public and summary execution, no matter how psychologically satisfying. Others found some beauty in her mantis-like appearance: the maudlin were deeply concerned about her total isolation and incarceration.

"I'd heard that each queen lays several different types of workers," Anis said. "Maybe she'd been programmed for the type we need right now." She turned an impudent gamine grin on her audience.

"If we knew what sort we needed," Metrios said, gloomily. He leaned forward across his panel. "If we could somehow clear enough of the gas to put a salvage crew aboard . . ."

"Ah, we're much too far away to use tractor beams . . ." Yngocelen said and then turned brightly to Rojer.

"Hey, don't look at me. That's *mass*, Commander," Rojer said, fending off that suggestion with raised hands. "It'd take a whole Tower crew to shift that one."

"Then it'd have to be a landing party. . . ."

"With Hiver ground batteries trained on it?" Yngocelen asked sarcastically. "They'd blast it out of the sky once they saw it moving away rather than let us have it."

"But they don't *know* we're here," Langio reminded them.

"And they're not supposed to," Metrios said, heaving a sigh.

"Rojer, you couldn't just inch it out of their surface-to-air missile range?" Langio asked plaintively.

"No, I couldn't. Not even to give Captain Prtglm its moment of glory."

"Now wait a minute," Metrios said, and turning to his console, accessed another program. "To get the Great Sphere back, two Galaxy-class ships acted as tows, and a shuttle was attached to control directional thrusters. . . ."

"So?" Yngocelen asked.

"If we could mount thrusters on the hull . . ."

"That would mean we'd be seen from the surface . . ."

Yngocelen interjected. "Oh ..." he added, and turned, as Metrios had, to Rojer.

Rojer shook his head. "Look, *sirs*," and he paused to give the courtesy address emphasis, "I'm glad to oblige with a lot of things but if anyone ... anything ... down there is monitoring space—and they sure knew when the refugee ship arrived—thrusters big enough to move it out of orbit would be very very visible, even if putting them there wasn't."

"What do we know about Hiver eyesight?"

"They probably have a specialist for that, too," Anis remarked in a caustic tone.

"Possibly," Metrios agreed and then went on, "but why would they be watching a ship they know is disabled and uninhabited?" Clearly, he wanted to defend his strategy. "They *don't* know we're here. They certainly wouldn't expect *anyone* to come robbing them of a ship. Surprise is a big plus. . . ."

"Our orders, gentlemen," Captain Osullivan reminded them in droll reprimand, "are to hold a watching brief." Then he gave them a wistful smile. "The Council has not given us any latitude. We are especially not to engage the enemy at this point in time." He heard their murmurs of discontent and disappointment. "If we can follow their ion trails, they can follow ours."

"True enough, sir, but they don't have another operational vehicle," Metrios pointed out.

"We have our orders, gentlemen, and we will obey them," Osullivan said and strode to his command chair, where he remained the rest of that watch.

It was the next morning that the captain asked Rojer to report to the bridge before his usual watch.

"It occurred to me, Rojer," Osullivan said at his most

relaxed and genial, "that we shouldn't miss a golden opportunity."

"Which one, sir?" Rojer asked dubiously, glancing at Metrios, Doplas and Yngocelen, who were ranged behind the captain.

Osullivan grinned, as did the others. "Only that one area of this vessel is destroyed? Right?" When Rojer nodded, the captain went on, "You seemed to have no difficulty 'porting that monitor around the interior."

"It was a small one, with a limited detection capacity. . . . Oh, I see . . ."

At Rojer's sudden comprehension, Osullivan turned to the other officers. "He catches on real quick. Good lad. If we can present coherent diagrams of every level of *this* ship, the crews restoring the Great Sphere will have a template to work from. Captain Prtglm informed me that the design has not altered in all the centuries they've been dealing with the Hivers."

"Except for the size of the Great Sphere . . ." Metrios interposed.

"Would you oblige?" Osullivan said, gesturing at Rojer's couch and grinning with invitation.

"I don't see why not, sir. I've been everywhere else I could 'port a device. But what about the corrosive gas . . ."

"You can use as many probes as you need," Metrios said expansively. "When the captain made his suggestion, we found a coating that will somewhat retard corrosion . . . I think! I hope. First one you have to bring back, we'll run an analysis on and see if we can't identify the combo used."

"I've altered the visual schematics," Doplas said eagerly, "so that we can get dimensional readout and identify any gross design alterations."

Rojer found the process more time-consuming than tiring but he was very glad when that watch was over. Five probes had been affected by the gas and he had deposited them in a gas-proof container in the ship's lab. Although this ship was not as large as the Great Sphere, his first day's investigations had delineated only a very small segment of the total ship. But there was enough to cause every science and specialist officer on all three ships to spend the rest of the day analyzing and rendering drawings. The gas had done its work thoroughly: only such stores as had been encased in metal survived.

As Rojer 'ported the probes further inboard, printouts became blurred where the gas was thick. There came a point of no input. Sufficient data had been gathered to give the squadron some idea of the interior layout of the vessel: someone called it a "spaghetti-macaroni network of tubes, tunnels and conduits." There were features in the ceilings and along the floors of the queens' quarters which gave rise to considerable speculation. Was each of the queens responsible for one aspect of the ship's operations? Or were the controls mutual?

"The Rowan said she met a 'Many Mind,' " Rojer said, trying to sound impartial while reporting his grandmother's action, "a nexus of the queens which is what she immobilized when she was focus for her merge."

"So it's likely the queens moved in concert?" asked Osullivan.

"That's consonant with the hive mentality: all working for the same objective," the xenob officer replied. Lieutenant Sedim Mehmet had been asked to sit in on a primarily engineering conference.

"Those control panels are undamaged," Metrios said, switching the screen to that set of printouts. "But I'd need a ladder to reach 'em and which would control what!"

"Don't seem to be any touch-type arrangement,"

Yngocelen remarked. "But perhaps when back-lit we'd identify controls."

"The queens' palps are odd-shaped," Mehmet reminded them. "Palps end in different-sized triangular joints."

"The problem," Osullivan said, "is not so much the shape as the function."

On that they were all agreed. Captain Prtglm seemed to sink deeper onto its stool, spreading its bulk noticeably. Rojer thought it was depressed by this current impasse. Gil and Kat said their Great Captain had already achieved many battle honors but it wanted one more significant award to add to a career that had spanned over a hundred Human-length years. Rojer could sympathize with that wish, knowing that Prtglm's color would bask in glory for centuries more if it could bring back to Clarf an empty Hive ship.

Rojer and some of the lesser staff members were politely thanked and dismissed from the conference. Since it was likely he'd be called to send back a report at the conclusion of the meeting, Rojer took the opportunity to grab something to eat. The sort of mental work he did made him ravenous. Rather than appear to eat more than was considered polite on shipboard, Rojer often secreted food in his cabin for emergencies. He always had something for Gil and Kat, too, and so they were indulging in an illicit feast when his com unit clicked on.

"Require Talent assistance return," said Prtglm's unmistakable tones. "Talent to return, too."

"WE COME, TOO?" Gil asked, and Kat was hanging on Rojer's response.

"RJ SEES NO REASON NOT. PRTGLM NEVER NOTICES YOU ANYHOW." While Rojer knew Prtglm was a Great One, he had been slightly peeved that it was too great a personage to notice his dear friends. He took Gil and Kat across to the *KTTS* whenever possible because they did enjoy visiting among their own kind. "WE USE BIGGEST CARRIER ANYWAY. YOU HIDE IN DARK."

Knowing it would take the 'Dini captain time to make its ponderous way from the bridge area to the transfer pod in the cargo bay, Rojer stripped out of his rumpled shipsuit and donned a clean one, buckling on the formal belt and pouch he rarely bothered to wear. He was in awe of Great Captain Prtglm and a "uniformed" appearance bolstered his morale.

Gil and Kat were so excited they squirmed in his arms as he gathered them up for the 'port. Actually, he landed neatly right at the hatch to the cargo bay, and in an empty corridor. He could, however, feel the vibration in the deck plates of a heavy tread.

"QUICK, YOU TWO," he urged, adding body language to his words, opening the hatch and thrusting the two warm furry bodies ahead of him. "THE GREAT ONE COMES. FEEL IT?" His two friends scurried to the large pod that would be used. They opened it and were disappearing inside as Rojer explained to the deck officer that he'd be taking the captain back to the *KTTS*.

"You sure know when that biggie's coming, doncha," Ensign Menburia said as the vibration through the deck plates was even more discernible. "No disrespect intended, but it can barely get through that hatch. Oops!" And the ensign ducked back to her engineering board as the massive figure of Prtglm appeared.

The captain required time to settle itself in the pod while the cargo bay crew appeared extremely busy at their stations. Finally Rojer could enter.

"Is power up, Ensign?" Rojer called, and received a thumbs-up from Menburia. He closed the hatch and tried to compress himself so as not to touch the captain. A Great One did not appreciate tactile contact.

Rojer picked up the pulse of generators he was now as

familiar with as Xexo's at Aurigae Tower. He knew where he was going and 'ported them on board the *KTTS* so lightly he was sure that Prtglm wasn't even aware the transfer had taken place until the hatch was opened by one of its own officers, and it was officially welcomed back on board. Prtglm rattled several phrases off so quickly that Rojer didn't follow the sense of them. Something about "new probes" and "decision."

"COME," Prtglm said curtly to Rojer as soon as it had its back legs on the deck. Rojer scrambled out to see Prtglm making its way to an opening that led to the interior of the 'Dini ship, not to the bridge as Rojer had expected.

It was as well Prtglm made its way without a backward glance for Gil and Kat suddenly clung onto Rojer's hands.

"WHAT'S WRONG?" he asked, but each made the sudden quick head movement that told him to keep quiet. He could feel their digits trembling despite the strength with which they held on to him.

They were alone as they followed Prtglm down the corridor, which was just wide enough to accommodate the massive body of the captain. Then a hatch slid back and Prtglm entered, pausing to gesture to them to hurry. Rojer obeyed despite the fact that both Gil and Kat seemed to impede his forward progress.

"What's wrong?" he muttered, bending down to their ear holes.

Kat managed a quavery noise and, taking a breath as if steeling itself, stepped over the hatch and into the big hangar facility. Rojer and Gil followed. Rojer knew his dear friends were awed by any proximity to Prtglm, but there was some new quality in their manner now that began to infect him with doubt and anxiety.

The hangar was dark, but Rojer could make out racks of long slim shapes that had a metallic shine: many of them.

Light came up and Rojer blinked to adjust to the glare. Gil and Kat audibly moaned.

These were not probes, Rojer instantly noted: they had a deadly precision of line that made their purpose unmistakable even before his horrified stare took in the deadly bulb of a warhead on the pointed end. And there were an awful lot of them.

Prtglm's digits flashed over a terminal and the multiple screens above it flicked on, each with a different view. Three depicted the orbiting sphere ships, another the flat surface of the space field, and the rest were split, sometimes in three separate scenes, showing the largest of the square buildings his probes had found.

The sick feeling in Rojer's guts developed rapidly into a certainty that was no precog. If he had not been so immobilized by fear and shock, he would have 'ported himself and his friends out of the hangar. But he couldn't move. He couldn't *believe* that Prtglm would make such a devastating unilateral decision. Somehow he had to stop it from happening.

"TALENT!" Prtglm turned and it had never appeared so massive or forbidding in aspect.

"GREAT ONE," Rojer managed to say before he had to swallow convulsively to wet his dry mouth and throat.

"YOU SEND MANY THINGS TO WORLD BELOW. YOU SEND THESE. TO THESE PLACES! THEN SQUADRON TAKES SPHERE AND RETURNS WITH TRUE HONOR."

"Sir, these are bombs?" Rojer forgot all 'Dini.

"OF COURSE," and the captain's body made the massive surge from bottom to top that was an angry reaction to the question: indeed, to any questioning.

"I am not permitted to destroy, sir." Rojer concentrated on speaking clearly and firmly.

"YOU 'PORT MANY THINGS. BOMBS ARE BEST!" Most 'Dini

voices expressed little emotion but Prtglm's intonations were rich with satisfaction and righteous vengeance.

"I AM NOT PERMITTED TO DESTROY, SIR. MY ORDERS ARE STRICT." Rojer fell back into 'Dini, hoping he could make his point better in that language. "YOUR ORDERS ARE TO WATCH, NOT DESTROY. ORDERS WHICH CAME FROM COORDINA-TOR GKTMGLNT AND ADMIRAL TOHL MEKTURIAN. THIS LOW PERSON CANNOT DISOBEY ORDERS."

"LOW PERSON RJR OBEYS THE ORDER OF PRTGLM NOW! OBEY."

Prtglm began to pulse and expand, a frightening aspect that rooted Rojer to the deck but did not alter his determi-nation to disobey.

"I am not permitted, Great One," he repeated, dropping to one knee in an attitude of respectful subservience.

"GREAT ONE PRTGLM, RJR IS FORBIDDEN BY HUMAN GREAT ONES TO DESTROY ANYTHING," Gil said, inching forward with the greatest respect it could display.

"THE HUMAN IS TO OBEY OR HUMAN WILL BE ON THE LINE."

Rojer could not believe what he heard.

"I CANNOT OBEY CAPTAIN PRTGLM!"

Fury engorged the captain now and, in a movement so swift Rojer could have done nothing to intervene, Prtglm's top arms descended on Gil's poll eye and smashed its im-mature body to the deck.

"OBEY!" roared Prtglm and, lifting its great gory fore-arms, began the downward swing that would have also killed Rojer.

" 'PORT," Kat cried, shoving Rojer to one side and tak-ing the blow meant for him, which crumbled it beside the mangled body of Gil.

'Port Rojer did, out of the *KTTS*, and to the one place au-tomatic reflexes could take him without conscious thought!

CHAPTER
TWO

"WHERE the hell could he get to?" Captain Osullivan said, scowling with annoyance. "He knows the time he's due here for the daily report."

"Sir?" Doplas said from his com station, "Ensign Menburia says that Rojer 'ported Captain Prtglm back to the *KTTS* at 1130. She logged that and saw them depart."

" 'Porting doesn't take Rojer more than thirty seconds. Where'd he go then? Did the ensign see?"

"Sir, log says that Rojer accompanied the captain. At its request evidently. He had his 'Dinis with him."

"So?"

"Com officer of the *KTTS* says that neither the Human Rojer nor his 'Dinis are on board."

"Is there a record of when Rojer 'ported back here?"

"According to their records, the captain's pod is still in place and the Human Rojer has not approached anyone on the *KTTS*. The big pod did not return here."

"Aw, now wait a bleeding minute . . ." Metrios began in

total disgust. "If the pod is over there, on the *KTTS*, Rojer has to be there. Talents don't generally 'port themselves about in a space vacuum. Dangerous. And what's he been doing there for over eight hours anyway?"

"I should very much like to know," the captain said in a tight controlled voice.

"This isn't like Rojer," Anis Langio said.

"Dammit, Anis, I know that," Osullivan said, shifting about in his command chair, his face grim. "Metrios, any power use consistent with a long-distance 'port?"

"No, sir," the engineering officer said with only the briefest of glances at his station printout. "And there's no way Rojer could 'port all the way back to Aurigae, or even Clarf, which is spatially nearer."

Osullivan stared grimly at the digital time display as the seconds and hundreds turned over rapidly. His fingers rattled an agitated tattoo on his hand rest.

"Sound a yellow alert. Ship's crew to locate Mr. Lyon. This ship is to be searched stem to stern. Alert Captain Quacho. Doplas, I want to speak to Captain Prtglm."

"It hasn't been available, sir," Doplas said in a semi-apologetic tone.

"It'll be available to me, Doplas!" Osullivan's icy tone made Doplas's fingers skip over the touchplates.

"Prtglm is not available for speech," the 'Dini com officer said. "PRTGLM IS NOT AVAILABLE," it repeated in its own language to be sure the information was understood.

"We search for Rojer Lyon," Doplas said.

"RJR LN REPORT IMMEDIATELY TO THIS SHIP," Osullivan added to be sure the 'Dini officer also understood.

This time the 'Dini officer shook its upper body and then directed its poll eye fully at the screen. "NO HUMAN ON THE *KTTS*." The screen went blank.

"What's all this about young Lyon disappearing?" demanded Captain Quacho, his image illuminating the main screen. "We've supplies to come in and I've two crew needing to go back on the carrier. I've been waiting for Rojer's signal to bring them over."

"A full ship search is under way, Quacho. I understand Lyon's disappearance no better than you do. And he's not on the 'Dini ship!" Osullivan grimaced and he rubbed his jaw. If the boy had gone to the 'Dini ship, why hadn't he come back aboard the *Genesee*?

"Sir?" an excited voice immediately captured his attention. "Sir, one of the escape pods is gone."

"Which?" Osullivan snapped the query out in such a hard voice that even Doplas recoiled.

"One-oh-eight, starboard, sir. And the controls were altered to make it appear to still be in place."

No one on the bridge needed to remark that the one-oh-eight pod was the one assigned to Rojer Lyon.

"Has there been *any* activity *towards* the planet?" Osullivan demanded. When he received a negative reply, "Or toward that damned empty hull?"

"No, sir. And I'm scanning for a recent ion trail."

"The boy wouldn't have had to use the escape pod engine, Metrios," Osullivan said, puzzled, angry and half-despairing. He had grown quite fond of young Lyon. The boy had conducted himself extremely well and been as helpful as he could, way beyond the scope of his original assignment.

"Something happened while he was on board the *KTTS*," Metrios said in a quiet, intense tone of voice.

"His 'Dinis went with him?" Osullivan knew that they had but he grasped at that one possibility of finding out what happened.

"Yes, sir, Ensign Menburia now reports that they slipped on board the probe before Prtglm or Lyon did."

"They often went with him," Anis said softly.

Osullivan waved his hand to cut off discussion. The boy had used an escape pod after a trip to the *KTTS* in Prtglm's company. The 'Dini was determined to return home in honor. Suddenly, Osullivan jumped to a conclusion he did not like, not any aspect of it and not for any reason.

"Let us hope he can reach his family safely."

Everyone on the bridge turned to stare at their captain and then began to exchange shocked glances. Metrios propped his head in his hands and stared down at the lights running their normal patterns on his board. Just then, they gave him little consolation.

Captain Osullivan, this is Jeff Raven. Why is my grandson not in touch with us?

Etienne Osullivan had been expecting some form of contact from the FT&T Prime ever since the time for the usual daily call had passed, and still more seconds ticked by.

"Earth Prime, he is no longer on board the *Genesee*. We had hopes that he has made his way back to you, or his homeworld." Osullivan spoke aloud so that the bridge crew would understand that he was communicating with the Prime.

Surely you realize, Captain, that Rojer is not able to make such a long distance 'portation without assistance. What has happened to my grandson?

"We do not know, sir, and we are extremely worried." The captain then detailed the known sequence of events leading up to the discovery of the missing escape pod. Then he cleared his throat. "Prime Raven, it is my belief, unsupported though it is, that Captain Prtglm may know either where Rojer is or why he left so abruptly. But the captain is unavailable. I request formal permission from Gktmglnt to board the *KTTS* and investigate."

That will be unnecessary, Captain, though the offer is certainly appreciated. I am informing the High Council of Prime Lyon's disappearance. You may expect assistance shortly. Have the courtesy to await it.

"Of course, Prime Raven." Captain Osullivan inclined his head in obedience to that directive and then sighed.

Ask your medic for an analgesic, Captain. A direct send to a non-empath will produce an intense headache. Raven's advice was kindly, and something unknotted in Osullivan's midriff.

"Someone's coming," he added, remembering no one else on the bridge had heard the message.

"Soon?" asked Anis, her pretty face flushed with concern.

"Can't *be* soon enough," Metrios said in a growl.

"Aye!" The single word of accord came from many directions around the bridge.

The sound reverberated with acutely felt echoes and Osullivan retired briefly to his ready room to find a painkiller before his brain burst through his skull.

Precisely three-quarters of a very long hour passed before a glad message was relayed from the cargo deck.

"Passenger pod aboard, sir."

"Escort the passenger to the bridge immediately, Ms. Menburia."

"No need, Captain," said a curt feminine voice, and the Rowan, a large dark grey 'Dini beside her, and Afra Lyon with a smaller 'Dini pair flanking him appeared on the bridge upper level.

Osullivan shot to his feet and was halfway to the Rowan when she held up her hand to restrain his impulse. Once again he felt a mental touch and almost recoiled from a second experience.

"Sorry, Captain," the Rowan said with a fleeting smile. The pain went as quickly as it had begun. "It was the quickest way for me."

"We apologize for taking so long getting here," Afra went on. "We stopped at appropriate intervals to listen."

"Ohhh," and Osullivan breathed one single despairing note of denial.

"My grandson *is* alive," the Rowan added, her expression severe. Afra nodded a brief reinforcement of her statement. "We would know if he was not, if that affords you any consolation."

"It does."

"We must go aboard the *KTTS*. Do you have any pictures of its bridge configuration?" Afra asked.

"Here," Doplas said, pointing to his screen.

"That's enough," the Rowan said and turned toward the engineering position. "You are Commander Metrios? I thought so. We will need a touch of power."

"All you want," Metrios said, throwing his hands up in exaggerated relief at being able to do something. Their air of competence and determination revived him from the despair which had engulfed him since Rojer's disappearance became known.

The generators surged briefly and the group was gone. Someone breathed a "Wow!" of awe.

"The Rowan?" Yngocelen asked in a low voice.

Osullivan nodded.

"I thought she never left Callisto."

"Not often, but she's the clout needed," Osullivan said, encouraged in spite of his pessimistic fears.

"Sir?" Ensign Menburia's voice sounded almost apologetic. "They brought the supplies, too."

"That boy *must* be found, safe and unharmed!" Osullivan said, bringing both fists down hard on the armrests. He had personal as well as professional reasons, and a few which would have repercussions that he didn't want to think about, even clear-headed.

"Aye, aye, sir!"

The Rowan had been angry before with the stupidity of people, or things, or avoidable accidents, but she had never been so frighteningly angry before. Even as Jeff had been receiving information from the *Genesee*, he had Gollee Gren contacting the Mrdini High Council representative stationed on Earth. Mrtgrts was not only a grey, Captain Prtglm's color, but it was the High Councillor's chief liaison official and had served two decades as manager of the 'Dini colony world, Sef. It immediately volunteered to accompany whomever the Earth Prime sent to investigate.

The Rowan had informed Earth Prime that none other than herself would be the FT&T representative, having forcibly overruled her daughter, who felt she had the right to discover what had happened to her own son. *Aurigae may not be without its Prime, Damia, and that's that.* But the Rowan had then relented sufficiently to ask Afra to accompany her. *You can manage without Afra and he is the boy's father. But Aurigae can't manage without you.*

Then how is it that Callisto can do without its Prime? Damia had demanded caustically. *He's my son!*

And my grandson and I carry more clout. Callisto's in occlusion or we'd've had to send Jeran.

I'd rather you went, Damia had said, subsiding.

We will find Rojer, dear girl. We will. You know he's alive.

Yes, I know he's alive. . . . and Damia's tone had dwindled off while leaving her mother with the full impact of her shock and despair.

Now 'port your husband and your 'Dinis. We'll need them almost as much as we'll need me.

The Rowan had almost balked at waiting for the cluster of supply pods destined for Squadron B but the handlers at Callisto had the pods attached with such alacrity that she didn't have time enough to voice an objection.

I'd hazard that the supplies are needed for the morale value if nothing else, Jeff said soothingly. *Rojer seems to have been very well liked and Captain Osullivan is genuinely and deeply upset by his disappearance.*

And so he should be. A good lad. Not too cocky, either.

The Rowan did not, however, wait until the encircling pods were removed by the *Genesee* cargo handlers but 'ported herself and her companions directly to the bridge. She heard Captain Osullivan's apologies and a reiteration of the circumstances. Then she and Afra 'ported with their 'Dinis to the *KTTS*, where they were met by the next in command, another grey 'Dini of good size but one who instantly made deep obeisance to Mrtgrts.

"THE PRESENCE OF PRTGLM IS REQUIRED," Mrtgrts said, its tone coming from deep inside its strong large body.

The poll eye of every 'Dini on the bridge was turned respectfully in its direction.

"I, PRIME OF CALLISTO, REQUIRE THE PRESENCE OF PRTGLM *NOW*!" the Rowan said, drawing herself up to her full height. Despite being dwarfed by almost all the 'Dini bridge staff, she was so imperious in manner that she received equal respect and attention.

"I, FR, SIRE OF RJR LN, REQUIRE THE PRESENCE OF PRTGLM," Afra said, and he towered above everyone. Though he knew the 'Dini were not empathic, he allowed himself the luxury of radiating the anger and indignation that consumed him despite all his attempts to suppress such unmethody emotions.

Trp and Flk, the 'Dinis who had lived with Damia and Afra for the past eighteen years, suddenly began to swell.

"WE KNOW, WE GO," said Trp, and with no further explanation, it and Flk ran, as nearly as their body shapes allowed them, to a bridge exit and disappeared. That precipitous departure caused some of the lower crew members to moan and prostrate themselves.

Mrtgrts took charge, flicking one set of digits in a warning to the two Humans. The Rowan bridled, incensed to be ignored.

Don't, Rowan. Let Mrtgrts handle this. I've never seen such behavior from 'Dinis before and we must be patient.

Patient? When we don't know . . .

We know that Rojer lives. If we can find out what caused him to run like that . . .

A Gwyn-Raven doesn't run, the Rowan began, her mental tone a vivid purple-red, she was so incensed.

"There has been a command failure," Mrtgrts told them suddenly and now it, too, made a humble inclination of its upper body to the Talents.

"A what?"

"Prtglm has attempted unilateral action that would not be approved by Admiral Mktrn or Gktmglnt." Mrtgrts bowed again, its color paling to exhibit a degree of embarrassment that Afra had seen only in very young 'Dini miscreants.

"What sort of action?" the Rowan demanded imperiously.

"The Talent offspring of Afra Lyon became so deft at sending unseen probes that Prtglm saw the opportunity to destroy the function of this world forever."

Damn! The word exploded with ferocity in the Rowan's livid mind and included the actions which she desired to inflict on Prtglm's person.

"How dared it!" Afra's fury matched the Rowan's and Mrtgrts swayed back from them as if it felt the impact as a personal blow. "That was not the assignment my son accepted and that I, as his parent, approved, Mrtgrts. I do not know what punishment can be meted out to a personage of Prtglm's rank and color but this is an unacceptable perversion of FT&T services and a gross affront to the pacific nature of FT&T personnel."

"All FT&T services will be withdrawn from . . ." the Rowan began, suddenly white and trembling with reaction.

Flk and Trp returned, their pelts almost colorless.

"THERE ARE MANY PUNITIVE MISSILES IN THE CARGO BAY. GRL AND KTG DIED ON THE LINE."

The Rowan's face mirrored the horror both she and Afra felt.

No wonder Rojer disappeared, she said in the saddest tone Afra had ever heard from her in all their long association. She swayed and he stepped close to support her.

"ESCORT ME," Mrtgrts told the bridge officer who had met them. Its whole body shuddering, it turned to another of the exits from the bridge facility, Flk and Trp falling in behind it.

The Rowan made a move to follow but Afra restrained her and eased her onto the nearest stool before her knees buckled. Keeping one hand lightly under her arm to comfort her, Afra blanked out the flood of emotions she continued to broadcast. Far better for all if she dispersed as much of her feelings as possible where it could not be felt or heard before Mrtgrts returned.

Why would Rojer's 'Dinis be killed, Afra? Why? They were young, blameless.

Rojer would have refused outright to 'port weapons of any kind, Afra said wearily, for he now had a sense of what had probably taken place. *He oughtn't really to have sent probes either, but certainly the knowledge that has been amassed is more than worth that slight deviation from his orders. But . . .* Afra shook his head.

We started these operations to clear the stars of Hive incursions, didn't we? the Rowan began, and Afra was relieved by the healthier indignation of her mind.

It was also mutually decided by the Alliance not to promulgate any attack against an entrenched Hiver position because we bloody well couldn't succeed.

The least that should be done is blow up those ships so this group will be planetbound for a long time to come, and her eyes flashed with determination to wrest that much of a concession from those who preferred nonaggression. *We'll never be able to communicate with that species. I certainly don't want to have to meet any mind of theirs again, single or many!*

Afra certainly understood her hostility and resentment of the species but he had been raised on a methody planet which did not approve of violence of any kind, even in self-defense. "There are always alternatives: keep talking" had been the guiding rule about confrontations that might lead to force and bloodshed.

Until we can find the weaknesses of this species, we cannot arrive at a solution which will produce success without needless waste of life, he said as gently and persuasively as possible. He didn't wish to aggravate the Rowan, and he knew her sentiments in depth, but he also had the right to his opinions and the right to express them.

Even when Rojer has been the first casualty of such an attitude? The Rowan's grey eyes flashed at him and she shifted herself away from his gentle support.

He sighed, but he expected nothing else.

A door whooshed open and Mrtgrts stood there a moment, its poll eye aimed directly at the two Human Talents. As it stepped onto the bridge, Flk and Trp followed.

"PRTGLM EXCEEDED ORDER AND OBEDIENCE. A CARRIER IS CURRENTLY AVAILABLE. IT MUST BE TRANSPORTED TO CLARF IF SUCH A TASK CAN BE REQUESTED OF TALENTS, KNOWING THAT A YOUNG OF YOURS HAS BEEN BASELY ABUSED. THERE WILL BE NO GOOD GREY DREAMS."

The Rowan gave a little shiver. *I'd like to consign Prtglm to this primary, not to Clarf.*

That would be sparing Prtglm the ultimate humiliation, Rowan, Afra pointed out. *I can send a carrier that far if you would rather not deal with the send.*

Oh, and her eyes blazed at him, *in that case I myself will bump him back to Clarf and half bury the capsule . . .*

Afra signaled her to wait as he turned to Flk and Trp. "WHAT HAPPENED TO GRL AND KTG AND WHY?"

"THEY PRESUMED TO INTERFERE WITH PRTGLM'S ORDERS TO RJR. PRTGLM PUNISHED SUCH PRESUMPTION."

The Rowan hid her eyes for a moment and a sob racked her. Afra sent the gentlest soothing thought he could, though his heart pounded bitterly at the sacrifice, at the terrible shock such a loss would have dealt his son. Rojer was no older, in either 'Dini or Human terms, than the two who had tried to help him. Afra could and did allow himself a brief surge of pride in a boy who would not be coerced into doing something against training and conscience.

"*THEY,*" Flk continued, drawing itself up straight, "DO HONOR TO THEIR COLOR AND THAT OF YOUR DWELLING."

"THEY HONORED MY SON MORE," Afra said, though his voice cracked uncertainly. He bowed his head and let his tears flow. The 'Dinis didn't understand weeping but he scarcely cared at that moment what their reaction would be.

"Put your erring person in the carrier," the Rowan said

in a steely voice. "Which station handles power generation?"

Every 'Dini pointed and she moved to that station, its attendant stepping respectfully back.

"Who is to be informed of the reasons for Prtglm's crime and return?" the Rowan asked Mrtgrts.

The big 'Dini inclined its body to the Rowan. "This one will inform Gktmglnt personally of this terrible misconduct of Prtglm who now submits to retribution. Details will be forwarded to you."

The Rowan responded to that with a curt nod of her head. Gktmglnt was one of the high-placed 'Dinis who accepted Human reasoning and logic in the Alliance campaign to restrict Hiver incursions. A pall of tense silence was maintained until it was announced that the carrier had been loaded and was ready for transfer.

Afra followed the Rowan's thrust. She did not quite plow the capsule into the concrete of the Clarf landing field. She gave the Clarf Tower Prime, her granddaughter Laria, quite a shock to feel a carrier being brought in so precipitously.

Grandmother, I just had the most extraordinary orders not to touch that personnel pod. There's a crew swarming over it, painting some kind of message I can't understand. Is there someone or something inside? The sun's boiling here today. Anything enclosed like that will bake in its own juices.

Then follow your orders, Laria, the Rowan said. *The creature in the carrier killed your brother's 'Dinis.*

WHAT?

As Callisto Prime I speak to Clarf Prime, the Rowan went on in a flat voice.

As Clarf Prime, I listen, Laria said, though her grandmother could sense the quickly suppressed quaver of uncertainty in the mental message as she expressed the formula of total discretion now required.

Briefly the Rowan related what had happened. She caught a brief flare of Laria's regret that the Hivers had not been bombed.

Clarf Prime, such an action would have been totally beyond the parameters of your brother's position. He has acted properly, and bravely. Had he complied, he could never have been trusted to run a Tower.

Yes, Callisto Prime, of course I see that. You'll let me know the moment you find Rojer? And it was a caring sister who asked, not a Tower Prime.

He did not contact you directly for assistance then?

No, Grandmother. He could have reached me. He's gotten very strong, you know. I'd say he was stronger than me . . .

Than I, her grandmother corrected absently. *I doubt you'll need gestalt to hear when we do find him. Have you any ideas where he might go? Could he possibly have gone to Deneb? You children were always keen to visit Isthia.*

Laria was astute enough to catch the wistfulness in the Rowan's voice. *She would have informed you the moment she was aware of his presence on Deneb. And she would be.*

Yes, she would be.

Laria hesitated, surprised by the tinge of despair in her indomitable grandmother's tone. *You'll find him, Grandmother, I know it. Especially if Dad's with you. You two could hear to the farthest arm of the Milky Way.*

You have a ridiculous tendency to exaggerate, young woman.

The contact was broken, but not without Laria's sensing that her "exaggeration" had somehow cheered the Rowan.

* * *

She's right, you know, Afra told the Rowan, since the exchange had been open to his mind, too. *We could make ourselves heard a long, long way. Farther than Rojer could have thrown that escape pod. But he hadn't turned on the engines so he didn't use them in gestalt.*

Which means he's nearby, concluded the Rowan and allowed an audible sigh of relief to escape her lips.

"WE STAY HERE A WHILE," Flk and Trp told Afra. "MRTGRTS, TOO. ALL COLORS ARE FADED."

"THE MISJUDGMENT BELONGED ONLY TO THE CAPTAIN AND ITS NEED FOR HONOR," Afra replied.

"NO. THEY WERE REQUIRED TO MAKE THE BOMBS. THEY WERE GLAD TO THINK THAT IT WOULD BE PERMITTED TO BRING DESTRUCTION TO THE HIVE PLANET WHEN 'DINI PLANETS HAVE SUFFERED SO MUCH."

They have a point, the Rowan said, but before Afra could argue, she added, *I can't stay another moment on this ship.*

"CONTACT ME WHEN YOU WISH TO RETURN TO THE *GENESEE,*" Afra told the 'Dinis, who bowed in acknowledgment.

Reporting formally to Captain Osullivan in his quarters, the Rowan and Afra were immediately offered refreshment.

"I knew old Prtglm was up to something," he said, "but it's still hard for me to interpret some of the more obscure 'Dini body language. Commander Yngocelen came to me—oh, two weeks back—when the *KTTS* requested some unusual ordnance supplies from our stores. I didn't think much of such oddments and we *are* under orders to comply with any reasonable requests. The *KTTS* had been making probes for Rojer. . . . Any word on his whereabouts, Callisto Prime? We are most worried for his sake."

"We appreciate that," and the Rowan sighed again.

"I'd've given anything to have spared him such a shock

and the loss of his 'Dinis. They, too, are ... were well liked by all the crew and officers. Gave lots of their time teaching us pronunciation and vocabulary." Osullivan shook his head.

"I do not think he has gone far, Captain, but we," and the Rowan gestured to Afra, "would like to go in deep gestalt to locate him."

"A shock like that to a sensitive young man ..." Captain Osullivan said sadly. "He may not wish to be found and, knowing what caused him to disappear, I can't say that I blame him."

"Nor do we, which we shall make paramount in our thoughts," Afra said. "But the reason for his disappearance has now been removed."

"I needed that," the Rowan said, finishing the last of the small sandwiches and the wine in her glass. She stood. "Let's find the missing, Afra."

"If I might make a suggestion," the captain said, his expression startled by the thought that came to him. "It's always the last place you look. I mean, if you're looking for something or someone." He glanced from the Rowan to Afra, hoping they followed his illogical rationale. "The last place anyone would look for Rojer—because of the danger—would be on that refugee ship!"

"How so?" And then, impatient with slow speech, the Rowan plucked the details from Osullivan's public mind. "Ah, yes, I see your point. The escape pod would be sufficient protection from any residual gases and he'd know the interior spaces to the square centimeter." Her face lit with a smile that almost made the captain reel from its sudden brilliance. He was full of envy for Jeff Raven, and indeed, anyone who was close to such a vivid personality.

He caught the wry smile on Afra's face and felt himself blush at having been quite so transparent. The barest shake of Afra's head, and an increase in his smile, suggested to Osullivan that his reaction was rather common when the unsuspecting dealt with the Rowan.

Commander Metrios immediately ushered Afra to his chair while the Rowan settled on Rojer's couch.

"We may not need to draw much on the gestalt," she said with a quiet confident smile that put heart in the engineer's uneasy mind. Metrios had been excoriating himself for not having kept closer tabs on Rojer, on the messages recorded, or not, on his own station.

"We suspect he has parked the escape pod on the refugee ship," Afra said by way of explanation.

"Of course! Why didn't we think of that!" And Metrios wallowed for a moment longer in guilt.

"Not that it would have done you much good, except relieve your apprehension, Commander," Afra said, radiating conciliation. He glanced at the Rowan and the pair immediately went into a mind merge, the focus of which stabbed in the direction of the deserted ship.

The pod is there! In a cargo hold on the perimeter of the ship, which is in full vacuum, clear of the gas. I believe we could dissipate the rest of it throughout the ship. That might solve transport problems.

So it might. But we know that the ship is within range of the surface-to-air missiles.

That can be altered. Ah!

Rojer, said his father very gently, touching the mind of a boy so deeply sunk in despair and shock that only a flicker was palpable.

Daaaaad? Unexpected joy/immeasurable relief/then shame followed.

No shame, Rojer, no shame! the Rowan quickly responded. *You were honorable.*

Are Gil and Kat honorably *dead then*? The anguish/ shock/loss/hatred/fury in Rojer's tone had to be fended off by parent and grandparent.

Laria is correct, the Rowan said on a tight aside to Afra, *Rojer has strengthened significantly.*

More the pity that his tour should end on such a tragic note.

We will make positive out of the negative, old friend. Swiftly, the Rowan told the boy what had ensued.

I could have, SHOULD have, *stopped Prtglm. I could have, using force,* Rojer said, still grieving and accusing himself.

NO! both the Rowan and Afra said so fiercely that Rojer recoiled from them.

Sorry, son, Afra said. *I know you feel the loss of Gil and Kat very very deeply. Trp and Flk do, too, and with an implacable hatred I have never heard from any 'Dini before towards one of its own kind.*

Prtglm is, I believe, roasting in its personnel carrier on Clarf, the Rowan added with some relish, *in the noonday sun.*

Despite the appalling consequences, Rojer, his father added, *you behaved exactly as you should.*

Going AWOL, Dad? I should have called *you! That's what I should have done. Thian got to Granddad when he needed help. But I just . . .*

Both could hear the sobs that he had been able to choke back until now.

Now, there, love, a good cry is what's needed most, the Rowan said in an uncharacteristically gentle tone, *but you are not the only one, I assure you.* She paused for a long moment, ending with a deep sigh. *We all grieve for your friends, Rojer. We can feel your loss as if it is our own, Rojer, and you have only to reach out from the focus of your grief to realize that.* She felt his hesitant contact and let him see how deeply she, and beyond her, all his kin, joined him in mourning. That seemed to astonish the boy out of his self-absorption. So she went on in a brisker tone. *Now, will you need assistance to bring that escape pod back to its proper position?*

You're tired, son. Let us help you.

I got myself here, Dad. I'll get myself out.

The Rowan approved of his attitude but, in a tight aside to Afra, she proposed that they surreptitiously assist him.

Grandmother, I'm not being cocky, but this I will do myself. All by myself, Rojer surprised them both by saying. Before he had completed the mental sentence, Commander Metrios jubilantly announced that the pod had been reconnected to the *Genesee.*

The Rowan abandoned dignity and 'ported a very weary grandson directly into her embrace on the bridge.

Don't embarrass him, Rowan, Afra began until he saw how tightly the boy clung to his grandmother before he turned to his father, and Afra knew that her instinct had been correct.

A cheer cut through their private reunion and Metrios was the first to grasp Rojer's hand and pound him on the shoulder, forgetting every protocol regarding the Talented in his relief at seeing the boy. Rojer was too exhausted to be offended and much too gratified by Metrios's genuine response. Doplas, Anis Langio, Yngocelen, even the yeomen and women on duty, all crowded around to welcome the boy back. The captain's approach made them step aside.

"Rojer, it is such a relief to see you unharmed . . ." the captain began, pumping Rojer's hand in his turn. "No, you're not exactly *un*harmed, lad, are you, after such an encounter, but you have our sympathy for your losses and our appreciation of your courage. I should have been hard-pressed to stand up to Prtglm when it was so obviously deranged."

The captain's admission surprised Rojer so much his mouth dropped open.

Close your mouth, boy. Learn to accept praise with proper modesty, the Rowan said, but her tone was kind.

Rojer immediately closed his mouth and managed a smile.

"He's out on his feet, Captain," Afra said, putting a protective arm about his son's shoulders. "I'll take him to his cabin." Which Afra did, with as much tenderness and affection as he thought would not rob Rojer of his new manliness.

Then the Rowan indicated to the captain that she wished to speak with him privately and he led her back to his ready room.

"What Rojer had no authority to do, I have," she said, gracefully seating herself. With no subtle prompting from her, he offered wine which she accepted with relief. They both sipped, organizing their thoughts. The Rowan had acutely experienced Rojer's trauma, which went deeper than she had expected. But then she had not had close 'Dini relationships. The boy's attachment to his 'Dinis went far beyond that of the unusually deep familial bonds of the Talents, so his loss was far more profound. They'd have to deal with that on his return. She had another, more immediate matter to attend to.

"We must, of course, discuss the proposal I have in mind with Gktmglnt and Admiral Mekturian," she began, and Captain Osullivan gave her as good a double take as she had seen in many a year. She allowed a slight smile to put him at his ease. "That refugee ship must never be used by Hivers. Nor the other ships in orbit. We have enough of this species loose in the galaxy right now." She held up her hand when Osullivan opened his mouth. "I certainly cannot condone—much though in essence I approve of Hiver containment—what Prtglm had planned nor its proposed delivery. As you may be aware, controversy rages over whether we, the Alliance, have the right to inflict the atrocity of destroying occupied Hiver worlds. That's the sort of barbaric retribution which we Humans have outgrown. Yet we cannot, by the same token, permit them to continue to exterminate life forms on the planets they wish to colonize.

"It has been put forward that perhaps they recognize only their own species as intelligent and sentient and are unaware that they are slaughtering developing sentient forms. Be that as it may, certain actions have been discussed and this situation here allows us some leeway. I will propose to Gktmglnt and Admiral Mekturian, subject to their agreement, that Squadron B demolish the three orbiting ships to prevent the obviously imminent colonial expedition. I shall myself 'port the missiles so expediently available: an action in which T-2 Afra Lyon cannot be expected to take part, since he is methody by training and choice."

Now it was Captain Osullivan's turn to drop his jaw and stare at her in amazement, tinged with a certain equally gratifying relief and delight.

"First, however, it will be necessary that the refugee ship be surreptitiously removed beyond the range of planetary missiles. Then it should be easy enough to tow it back to where the Great Sphere is being examined." She grinned with wicked delight. "How much more we can learn from an intact vessel than a melted hulk."

Osullivan's expression brightened considerably.

"Prime Rowan, it went severely against the grain to know that those Hivers would have four colony ships available to them."

She chuckled, twisting the stem of her wine glass, her grey eyes sparkling at him over its rim.

"Soon there will be none. I'm delighted you find yourself in tune with this plan."

" 'Delighted' isn't strong enough but it will suffice," Osullivan said. "I'm certain that Captain Quacho will concur. I assume," and he hesitated, "that the *KTTS* will release the missiles to us."

"The *KTTS* will insist on taking part as well, Captain. Their honor needs some restoration."

"Shall we confer with Captain Quacho?"

"Of course," said the Rowan, and Osullivan turned to his console to key in the signal.

Afra joined them sometime after the Rowan, having obtained Quacho's enthusiastic cooperation and Mrtgrts's agreement, had relayed the proposal to her husband, who put the matter before the two Alliance commanders. Captain Osullivan had ordered dinner and when Afra appeared, asked for service. First he poured Afra a glass of wine.

"My own special favorite, Mr. Lyon," the captain said, hoping by his courtesy he managed to convey what he could not express to the Aurigaean T-2.

Afra tasted the wine with due solemnity and a little smile of appreciation.

"Rojer is all right?" the captain asked.

"He's asleep," Afra replied, "with Flk and Trp to ease him with good dreams."

"May I say how heavily this despicable incident rests on my mind?"

"You have in many ways, Captain," Afra said solemnly, "and we have been aware of each, even if we have not properly thanked you for the depth of your concern. Rojer will recover. He certainly bears you no rancor. Ah," he said, changing the subject as stewards entered with steaming dishes, redolent with delectable aromas. "I hadn't realized how hungry I am."

"You were very considerate to bring in those supplies or, I can assure you, my cook would have been hard put to present you a decent meal."

"This is a feast," the Rowan said, holding up her glass for more wine. "Where *does* this vintage come from?"

"You can't guess?" Afra asked in polite surprise.

"Then it has to be Capellan," she said with a mild grimace. "It has always amused me that such a methody planet produces such fine vintages."

The next morning Afra and Rojer left for Deneb where Rojer would undergo such ministrations as his great-grandmother, Isthia Raven, thought advisable to ease his mind. The large carrier also left with the 'Dini pairs needing hibernation and the four crew members whom the morale officer had ordered to take furloughs. The Rowan remained aboard the *Genesee*. She had not discussed the punitive proposal with Afra although she supposed he had picked up references to it from the captain—who was full of the prospect of some action—or any of the elated officers and crew. He said nothing beyond telling her that he would inform Rojer if he felt the knowledge would be therapeutic.

The Rowan also awaited the decision of the High Council, though she had some assurance from Jeff that there was little doubt the proposal would be accepted. It would salve the conservatives that the planet would be left unharmed and placate the militants that all space capability was destroyed.

The decision was affirmative but she would have to await

the arrival of Thian Lyon as FT&T replacement and an additional T-1 to assist in the seizure of the refugee ship. Even the Rowan had to admit that the sphere ship had too much mass for her to move, even with the assistance of more gestalt power than Callisto Station ordinarily provided.

If it makes you feel any better, my dear, her husband informed her, *the T-2s replacing your good self at Callisto are working their balls off and desperately awaiting your return.*

Do 'em good, the Rowan replied smugly.

Does you good, too, m'darling, to find that you cannot, after all, move mountains all by yourself, Jeff teased her.

Ha! Who are you sending?

Let that be a surprise. It'll cheer you up, I know.

He gave her a phantom hug and an enthusiastic kiss and a figurative pat on the head for the work she had cut out for herself but he didn't budge on the identity of the third T-1.

I suppose it's as well that Thian wasn't here when Prtglm had its brainstorm, she said, knowing she couldn't tease the information out of him.

Prtglm would have gotten no more help from Thian than he did from Rojer. Less. Thian would have seen the missiles and immediately 'ported out of danger. Possibly even despatched Prtglm back to Clarf with a blistering note about exceeding orders.

He'd've been exceeding his if he did, the Rowan replied tartly.

Honey love, you can't have it both ways.

I can *try!*

Until Thian on Squadron A's 'Dini *KLTS* had reached a point where he could be 'ported to the *Genesee*, the Rowan busied herself reviewing the fascinating tapes Rojer had gathered by probe. Before, the Hivers had been featureless creatures in a death-dealing sphere; now they were still featureless—as humans reckoned such matters—but the work ethos, the discipline, the minutiae of daily life in some of the orders of Hiver creatures, were depicted, and at least one of the worlds the Hivers had chosen to populate. The Rowan spent more time than she intended on such records. Then, resolutely, she planned how to destroy the planet's space-faring capability. The two half-finished ships would be easy to demolish, but the third ship was tightly sealed. Commander Yngocelen pointed out that the weapon ports would do nicely: there were sufficient of them to allow the Talents to penetrate into the ship and then a simple matter to 'port in sufficient explosives to disintegrate it.

Several conferences on the disposition of the refugee sphere decided that dispersing the lethal gas was not an urgent matter. Rojer had suffered no harm in his escape pod and another would handily accommodate the Rowan, Thian and the third T-1 while they surreptitiously eased the refugee ship out of its holding orbit and beyond the range of the ground batteries.

Permission was also given to destroy any pursuit vessels that the Hiver world might launch. The biggest they would have, according to all information the 'Dinis had amassed, would be surface-to-orbit shuttles. The scout vessels might be stored on the closed sphere and blown up along with the ship, but if they were available as deep space pursuit, the Squadron received permission to destroy them, too.

Assuming that there was, indeed, no intercolony communication, this Hiver world could not call for reinforcements which might follow the Squadron's ion trail. By the time a suitable deep-space vessel could be constructed on this world, any traces would have dissipated.

With plans and material in place, Thian's arrival was

keenly awaited. His grandmother thought he looked a trifle gaunt but she caught a remarkable energy exuding from him, once he recovered from a stunned surprise at finding her on board the *Genesee*.

"Where's Rojer then?" he asked, glancing about him, having looked forward to a reunion with his brother. His 'Dinis, Mur and Dip, were also looking about for they had been eager to see Gil and Kat. He was perplexed by the minute shock he read from his grandmother. An indefinable sadness darkened her eyes.

Then, with a nod of greeting to the 'Dinis, the Rowan unexpectedly hooked her arm in her tall grandson's and walked him from the cargo bay, Thian's 'Dinis following discreetly. As they moved slowly in the direction of the captain's ready room, she told him what had happened. She managed to time her report so that they were within the ready room by the time she had to relate the sacrifice Gil and Kat had made to protect Rojer from Prtglm. She soothed Thian with what mental easing she could while he held his grieving 'Dinis tightly against him. When they had regained some composure, she explained what action was now proposed. Thian had no reservations about what he obviously considered necessary destruction, only determination and an eagerness to assist her in any way possible. She was well pleased with a mental attitude that did not emanate any vengefulness or malicious delight; feelings which she had sensed in some officers and many crew members. She preferred to think of their coming actions as deterrent rather than vindictive.

Know that your father is not of a militant disposition, the Rowan said, honor requiring her to mention the fact.

Dad won't find me a hardened militant for all my months on board a 'Dini ship but that would not be why

I find this course of action justifiable, Grandmother. Until we can communicate with the Hive species . . .

That *we'll never be able to do,* the Rowan said flatly. *I know!*

But I understood that the captive queen . . .

Is understood at only a very basic level and on the one or two occasions when a Human has been in her presence, the visitor has been totally ignored, as if the Human didn't exist. I'm beginning to think that they don't recognize any species but their own.

Thian gave a wry grin. *You sure do hate 'em, don't you, Grandmother.*

No, Thian, I wouldn't waste such a powerful emotion on them. *At the same time, I will* not *tolerate any depredations when I can prevent them. That's the distinction which I don't think your father is willing to appreciate. No matter. By the way, did your grandfather mention the identity of the third Prime?*

No, and Thian grinned down at his diminutive grandmother, looking more like a slender young girl in the lavender shipsuit she was wearing. *He likes his little surprises, doesn't he? When he can pull them on you.*

The Rowan scowled and then had to break into a laugh because Thian was enough like his father to ignore what Afra had always called her fits and starts.

"Rowan, ma'am," the ship's com system began, "please return to the cargo bay for an incoming personnel carrier."

"Damn," the Rowan said, spinning on her heel to retrace her steps, "he could have warned me."

"I'd say he wanted to give you time to brief me, Grandmother," Thian said, not at all put out.

"Do you have to stick up for him?" she asked irritably.

"As grandfather or Prime?" Thian asked, but he had a sense of eager anticipation. His grandfather was subtly providing a diversion from what had been a large dollop of bad news.

"Never mind," she said and walked all the faster back to the cargo bay.

They had reached the facility just as the generators lifted briefly and then a shiny new single carrier landed smoothly on the cradle. The ensign on duty shot a glance at the Rowan and Thian, but she nodded for him to lift the hatch.

Oh, am I late, Callisto Prime? was the quick concern of a feminine mind, touching them both.

Thian narrowed his eyes down at his grandmother, who was genuinely surprised. *He'd mentioned her to me several times but certainly not for* this, the Rowan added before stepping forward to greet the girl nimbly leaving the capsule. She smiled graciously at Ensign Tollert who had offered her assistance.

"T-1 Flavia of Altair requests permission to board."

"Permission granted," Tollert replied, grinning broadly.

"A pleasure to meet you, Flavia," the Rowan said, stepping forward in turn to touch fingers briefly with the girl. *Don't gawk, Thian,* she added tightly.

He took two long strides forward as if he had merely given his grandmother precedence. In fact, he had been nearly as stunned as Tollert. Flavia wasn't beautiful in a classical way, not as Laria or some of his cousins were, but she had large and startlingly vivid green eyes and long straight blonde hair which she wore simply pulled back by green combs from her oval face. Standing next to the too-slender Rowan, she appeared well-fleshed and her pale green shipsuit emphasized a very womanly body.

"Thian of Aurigae," he said, exerting control not to touch her fingers longer than Talent protocol dictated. Mint/green/rose was her touch.

"I believe Jeff said you are the grandchild of Bastian

and Maharanjani," the Rowan said. "I worked with them, Thian, in the Tower on Altair."

Flavia nodded briefly with a becomingly reserved smile.

"The duty has been explained to you?"

She nodded again. "It is an honor to work with Callisto Prime for any reason."

"Humph," the Rowan said.

Tollert cleared his throat loudly. "Ma'am, the conference is waiting on the Primes."

"You have a carisak, Flavia?" the Rowan asked and when the girl nodded, Tollert cleared his throat again.

"I'll take care of that, ma'am. Prime Flavia's quarters are next to yours."

"Hmm, that's as well," the Rowan remarked obliquely. "We shouldn't keep this conference waiting any longer than necessary." *We'll 'port once we reach the corridor,* she added and led the way.

"How are your 'Dinis called, Prime Thian?"

"I'm just Thian," he laughed, disclaiming any title, "and these are Mur and Dip."

"FLV TRUSTS THAT YOUR DREAMS HAVE BEEN GOOD," she said in excellent 'Dini.

Score one for the child, the Rowan said privately to her grandson.

And Granddad, Thian said with a sparkle in his eyes as he opened the hatch for the women.

"Do your 'Dinis mind 'portations, Thian?" the Rowan asked.

"Not any more," he said and closed the hatch behind him.

He clasped Mur and Dip against his legs, nodding to the Rowan that he was ready to 'port. They all did, arriving in the corridor outside the *Genesee*'s conference room. The Rowan tapped the panel for admittance and a yeowoman smartly opened the door. All within stood at her entry and throughout her introductions of her grandson and Flavia Bastianmajani of Altair.

Thian kept his expression bland as mixed comments reverberated from minds keyed up in anticipation of action. "He's bigger than Rojer." "That young slip of a girl's a Prime?" "Quite a family resemblance to Rojer with that same white lock of hair." "Wouldn't mind Priming with her." "Carries himself well." "She's a bit young for this sort of operation, isn't she?" "So this is the fellow who spent over a year on a 'Dini ship alone! That took guts." "Why on earth did he bother to save Hive larvae? Sometimes I don't understand these Talented people." "Two women and one male barely into manhood to move *that* mass?" "I wonder will Rojer turn out as well."

And Thian identified the thinker of that remark as the pretty dark-haired astrogation officer, Anis Langio. There was nothing subtle in his grandfather's seconding of Flavia to this mission, and she was certainly a lovely young woman, but Thian was *not* going to settle quite so quickly into the family pattern of an early marriage.

Captain Osullivan formally made Flavia, Thian and his 'Dini companions welcome. Then, with the Rowan on his right side, and Flavia on his left with Thian seated beside her, he opened the official final planning conference. The captain was certainly not in on any of his grandfather's machinations, but Thian was extremely conscious of Flavia's proximity, aware of the delicate scent she wore, of the pulse of her very finely tuned and attentive mind. After a year on the *KLTS*, he had mastered the art of concentration.

"This is, as I'm sure you're all aware, the first time the Alliance has taken action against a Hive world. You have all seen tapes of the ground-to-air missile attack on the refugee ship but we also know the extent of its range. However, we must not be for a moment lax in vigilance against any unsuspected retaliatory strikes."

Mrtgrts nodded in verification of that caution.

"As you also know, the Rowan has already 'ported explosives into the assigned positions to destroy the orbiting ships. Heat-seeking missiles are ready in each ship of the Squadron for use in destroying any shuttle craft lifting through the mess they leave in orbit around their planet. Operation Snatch," and Osullivan grinned, his gaze ending on Flavia's attentive face, "can begin as soon as our Primes are in position. Once the refugee sphere is out of range of surface missiles, the other ships will be blown. We will then seed additional space mines in case the Hive do still have scout ship capability that has not been detected by Rojer Lyon's intensive probing." He nodded briefly at Thian for his brother's accomplishment. "Are there any questions?"

After a brief pause, Thian raised his hand. "Grandmother, Flavia, may I escort you to our vehicle so we can get this show on the road?"

"You may be mixing metaphors, Isthian, but if Commander Metrios's engines are ready to support gestalt . . ." She turned to Mrtgrts and Captain Quacho. "Are you ready to return to your own ships?"

"Ready indeed, ma'am," the engineer said, but his last word was spoken to empty air for all five had gone. "I wish they wouldn't do that!" he murmured, giving a shake.

"Stations, everyone," Captain Osullivan said, rising. "Red alert!"

"This must be the captain's own," Thian said as the three T-1s made themselves comfortable in the escape pod. "It's a lot roomier than the last one I was in."

"For three, yes, it's roomy enough," the Rowan said. "Shall we?" and she nodded at both young people.

"Of course," Flavia said and Thian murmured consent. This would be a brief rehearsal for the longer, harder merge they would have to make.

He'd never worked with his grandmother but he was accustomed to merging with his parents and was very pleased when Flavia deftly slipped in behind him as if she had similar hours of practice.

The Rowan-Thian-Flavia merge did not need to touch the power available to it from the linked generators of the three ships of Squadron B in this initial push. The cargo area to which they were 'porting could have held a hundred escape pods. Merely the slightest bump gave them notice that the pod had settled on its broad base in the Hive ship exactly as planned: close against the hull, facing the direction in which it was to go. They were immediately assailed by the most intense sting-pzzt that emanated from Hive metals, a sensation peculiarly limited to the Talented.

Flavia gave a visible shudder, looking about her, a grimace marring her features. "What is *that?*"

"I do beg your pardon, Flavia, we should have thought to warn you," the Rowan said, casting an accusatory glance at Thian. "Talent is susceptible to a resonance from Hive metals."

Flavia worked her mouth, producing saliva, and shuddered again.

"Unpleasant taste in your mouth, too?" Thian asked helpfully.

She swallowed. "Yes, at the back of my throat. How can you stand it?"

"I," the Rowan said rather loftily, "ignore it." When Flavia looked astonished, the Rowan relented. "It is particularly strong since we are inside a Hiver, but shortly we'll

be busy enough to be able to put it out of our minds. We'll only have to endure it for a very short space of time."

"Thank goodness for that," Flavia said, pursing her lips and rubbing her tongue against her cheeks and teeth in an attempt to hydrate her mouth.

The Rowan initiated the merge then, ever so slowly pushing the ship out of its orbit and the gravitational pull of the planet. Since the maneuver was also being performed as night fell across this section of the planet, the stealthy movement was unlikely to be immediately discernible no matter how sensitive the Hive instrumentation might be.

Breathe, Isthian, his grandmother said once and he grinned at her as she sat in the padded seat as calmly as if she were in her Tower at Callisto, her silver hair shining in the pod's lights.

Gradually the merge increased its strength, three pairs of eyes also watching the special instrumentation installed in the pod that expressed speed and relative distance from the planet. Slowly they reached the mark on the dial showing when they had passed beyond the known range of surface-launched missiles.

Stop hunching your shoulders, you two, she added at a later point. *Any missile they could launch would have to penetrate the diameter of the ship to reach us. If, that is, they had any idea we are here.*

That made both Thian and Flavia smile. He rotated his shoulder blades because he had indeed been unconsciously hunching himself against an attack from the rear. He grinned at Flavia who was rubbing her neck and still trying to swallow the sting-pzzt away.

"Good. Now we can speed up and complete this snatch," the Rowan said, absently licking her lips and swallowing against the concentration of sting-pzzt.

He felt the intensity of the merge now and surrendered

himself to her guidance at the same instant that Flavia did.
He hadn't even thought to be capable of moving such
mass but, with the merge and the gestalt capability, it was
abruptly accomplished. He did feel the drop in his energy
level when his grandmother released them from the merge
and then the slight jar as the tractor beams from the squadron latched onto the sphere.

"I do hope something down there was watching," the
Rowan said with a mischievous smile more compatible to
his sister Morag's age and habit than his grandmother's.
"First the ship was there. And then," her smile deepened
with great satisfaction, "it wasn't! Well done, Isthian.
You've been well-taught, Flavia, and my pleasure to merge
with such fine strong minds. Now, let's get out of this Hive
sink of contamination and put the pod where it belongs.
Then we can find out what else has been happening."

"I feel like I need a good long soak to rid me of that awful reek," Flavia said, making another grimace of revulsion.

"Later, when our work is done, my dear," the Rowan
said. "We will have time, however, for a drink to take the
taste out of our mouths."

"Something sharp, Grandmother, like orange juice."

"Does this ship have something like that?"

Thian "provided" the juice in long cold glasses to
Flavia's obvious relief and his grandmother's only marginally less fervent thanks.

"You were far enough away not to have felt any shock
waves," Captain Osullivan said when they joined him on a
bridge that was packed with officers and crew, and ringed
with additional screens so that every view of the theatre of
operations was accessed. "Ah, that's our first casualty,"
Osullivan added, pointing to a screen which had just ceased
broadcasting. "One of the probes Rojer hid in the flotsam."

"The ships?" Thian asked, rapidly checking the secondary screens.

"Reduced to the debris you see floating in a band around the planet," the captain said with quiet satisfaction. "What the bombs you placed, ma'am, didn't fragment, the mines you sowed did. Mind you, there is a time lag between the event and our visuals of it . . ."

"Do any monitors need replacement?" the Rowan asked. "Now that we've completed Operation Snatch, we are at your disposal. Thian? Flavia?"

The Rowan took the couch, Commander Metrios vacated his seat with alacrity to Flavia and another chair was brought for Thian.

"Well-timed, ma'am," the captain said, pointing in turn to the three central screens which scanned the space field. "They may now retaliate."

"Indeed," said the Rowan with an almost primitive surge of adrenalin as she recognized the tapered prow of a Hive scout ship emerging from an underground hangar.

"Mrtgrts here, Osullivan," said the 'Dinis' liaison officer's unmistakable voice over the Squadron link. "Is the second wave ready?"

"It is," the Rowan answered. "Isthian, you will use the missiles on the *KTTS*, as you're more familiar with 'Dini ships. Flavia, have you located the *Arapahoe*'s? Good. It's as easy for us to work from here as on the separate ships." She waited until she could feel the young Talents "reaching" the missiles on the other ships, her eyes never leaving the screen as first one scout ship, then another, and a third became visible. "Three. The normal complement of a Hive colonial ship. They'd be a much more interesting challenge if they changed their tactics," she added almost ruefully. "Isthian, take the right-hand one; Flavia, the one that's just emerging;

and I'll dispose of the one that made it to the field. I believe it's about to launch. At my count . . . three, two, ONE!"

Each Prime 'ported the heavy torpedoes easily to the recommended range. Then, before the Hiver world's warning systems could alert defenses, launched them at the correct velocity for devastating strikes.

There was, as Captain Osullivan said, a time lag before the screens would register the result, but all three Talents had followed the missiles to their targets and knew their strikes had been accurate. Until visible proof appeared, Metrios toyed with a stylus, his eyes darting from one screen to the next. Though Captain Osullivan appeared completely at his ease, his fingers beat a tattoo on his arm rest. Minutes later, the explosions were recorded.

In what appeared to be a leisurely fashion, each of the three ships exploded, parts arcing up and then showering down on the trundling Hivers that had been massed on the space field. The debris fell almost gracefully to the now riddled surface and lay smoking and burning in a circle of destruction that spread well beyond the perimeter of the space facility.

"Someone's left the doors open," Thian remarked.

"In that case," the Rowan said with a shrug, "let us take advantage of such carelessness."

Even as additional missiles were armed and sent on their way by the three Talents, more hangar doors punched upward out of the debris on the field, revealing the squat forms of shuttle craft. These emerged at speed from the protection of the hangars, but not swiftly enough.

"Fire as ready," the Rowan ordered Thian and Flavia and they lobbed missiles at the shuttles and then into an aperture that could be seen through the smoke and raging fires.

"Is this their only space facility?" Thian asked when no

more targets were visible. "There are other substantial buildings on the planet."

"They seem to be agricultural collection depots," Captain Osullivan said.

"Such is not a target," the Rowan said, glancing sternly at Thian, who shrugged.

"Did the probes not discover where the queens are housed?" Mrtgrts asked.

"No," Osullivan replied. "We were limited to observational probes, not reconnaissance."

"The queens are effectively planet-bound," the Rowan said. "Further action has not been authorized."

"We will remain on orange alert," Osullivan said, touching the arm plate for intership communications. "Captains? Any queries?"

"A successful attack," Captain Quacho said, his brows drawn together in what seemed to be a satisfied scowl.

"Do not rule out the possibility of reprisal," Mrtgrts said. Behind it on the bridge, 'Dinis could be seen waving their forearms about, expressing their triumph at the success of the mission. Only Mrtgrts appeared dissatisfied and pessimistic.

"Reprisal with what, Mrtgrts?" the Rowan asked caustically, surveying the destruction on every screen. Then, putting both hands on the arm rests, she pushed herself to her feet. "If we are needed, call us," she said to Captain Osullivan.

Thian caught the surprised expressions of Langio, Metrios and Yngocelen but he, too, rose, indicating that Flavia could join them. He paused by the captain's chair.

"Permission to leave the bridge, sir?"

"Of course," Osullivan said, eyes widening at Thian's formality even as he shrugged as the Rowan disappeared.

"She'd be the last to admit it, sir," Thian said, leaning

confidentially toward Osullivan, "but Grandmother had to expend more energy as focus than we did."

"Yes, yes, of course."

There is absolutely no reason for a T-1 to apologize or explain any *action, Isthian Gwyn-Lyon!*

Thian, catching Flavia's startled expression as she also heard the fierce reprimand, grinned at the girl. *No, Grandmother, but it is only courteous to observe ship protocol. And you* are *tired.*

The bridge door whooshed shut behind Thian and Flavia.

I might be but you are never to presume . . .

Grandmother, your husband gave me specific orders on the care and feeding of his favorite wife . . .

His only wife . . .

And the only Prime who can rule Callisto and you ARE tired.

Fighting a war at any age is tiring.

Flavia's little gasp of surprise caught Thian unawares. "Was that a war we just fought?"

Thian stuttered in surprise. "Well, a battle, certainly. What did you think you were going to do here?"

"Keep the Hivers from leaving this planet."

"And that's not war?"

"It's analogous to clearing out vermin."

"On rather a large scale," Thian said, wondering at her curious calm.

"We have to do so often enough on Altair when there's been prolonged and heavy rains in the swamplands. Otherwise the towns and settlements would be overrun," Flavia said quite matter-of-factly.

Your grandfather did *know what he was doing,* said the Rowan in a tight tone to Thian and added a snort of amusement.

CHAPTER
THREE

*D*AD? There was the special note in his daughter Laria's voice that brought Afra sharply to attention. He was alone in Aurigae Tower, making some minor in-system shipments. Damia was out hunting with Morag, Ewain and all the 'Dinis.

Yes, Laria?

Dad, just between us? The unusual note of exasperation and self-doubt was one Afra had never thought to hear from the nearly twenty-three-year-old, confident and poised Tower Prime of the Clarf FT&T installation. On completing her training at Callisto, Laria had taken up her duties with a competence that even her perfectionist grand-mother couldn't fault. Yoshuk and Nesrun, the T-2s who had originally run the Clarf Tower, had been shifted to Sef, the most major of the four Mrdini colony worlds. Laria had recently been assigned Clarissia Negeva as her assis-tant, a T-2, who had been trained by David of Betelgeuse. Clarissia was replacing Stierlman, who had not achieved the necessary rapport with Laria. She'd had no trouble at all with the other members of her Tower staff; Vanteer, the T-6 engineer, or Lionasha, the T-7 station manager and expediter. Although there had been 'Dini-Human pairings on her home planet, Clarissia was unaccustomed to working with them and never gave direct orders to the six paired with the other three Station personnel who happily doubled as cargo handlers or whatever other functions could be done by non-FT&T personnel.

Clarissia's not working out either? Afra asked.

I do better running the Station on my own, Dad, was the tart reply. *She's been here nineteen weeks and she still turns pale when more than* our *'Dinis are present and you know that 'Dinis notice color changes. And she's been moaning about that carrier ever since it got here. Not,* and Laria's mental tone altered, *that I enjoy the sight, or more recently, the stench from it. Prtglm is definitely deceased. I'm beginning to think they don't intend to move it, leaving it there as a reminder that a Human was responsible for Prtglm's ignominious end.* Laria's voice had a grim edge to it, then confusion colored her thought. *There's ideographs all over it now. They're ancient ones and I can't recognize more than the slashes for dishonor. Tip and Huf won't translate: won't even answer me when I ask what they mean.*

Yoshuk's a scholar of their ancient forms. What does he say? Or have you discussed this with him?

I have and he says it's too obscure for him but he's still trying to find references. He does reassure me that they're not anti-Human.

This is one of those occasions, Afra said firmly but soothingly, *when you know that Humans don't interfere with 'Dini customs.*

The custom I can ignore if I wish, even if the reek is om-

nipresent, but I have to be very careful about transfers. Originally, Prtglm's carrier came down—hard—on the middle cradle. I was told not to move it to one side, but I didn't, for one minute, realize it was going to take up such permanent residence! I could have used that cradle a hundred times. Once again her tone altered to one less assured. *Daaaad, does anyone there know why it's being LEFT? I almost don't blame Clarissia but I also need to understand what's going on about it—Prtglm, I mean—so I can deal with the reason it's been left there so long. Is it a subtle way of punishing me because I'm Rojer's sister . . .*

I doubt that! Afra replied stoutly. *'Dinis don't think in those terms.*

I sure hope so, Laria replied, exhibiting some of the distress she had been covering.

I can ask Jeff . . .

I already did and he doesn't know but he doesn't have 'Dinis. Do yours know anything?

We never did get any more answer to queries about Mrdini penal codes than that the miscreants were apt to be shipped out . . . Afra paused, since Laria would know what that could mean on a long trip. The cynical said that saved time, space and money and was an admirable use of expendables, but the thought made him shudder. He forced himself to more positive thinking for Laria's sake. *Remember Prtglm is, or was, guilty of several . . . errors of judgment even in the 'Dini lexicon, and certainly several against Humans. They don't want a repetition and that may be their way of driving home the lesson.*

When one's own son had nearly been a victim of Prtglm's coercion, it was very hard, indeed, not to take a judgmental stand. Once Afra knew that Rojer was responding to the discreet therapy of his grandmother, Isthia, on Deneb, he felt less bitterness, a most unusual emotion for him, toward the misguided Prtglm. The latest report was that Rojer could now mingle with both Humans and 'Dinis without the intense grief/loss/deprivation reactions he had initially experienced. He was becoming more and more engrossed in his practical engineering studies. His uncle, Jeran, Deneb's Prime, was going to insist that when the Hiver ship that had been "appropriated" by the Rowan merge reached the investigation orbit at the Mars space facility, Rojer would have a place on that study team. Of course Rojer needed to meet the qualifications, but that had given him a definite goal and he was studying with good purpose and diligence to satisfy the requirements.

I know that, Dad, but to have that grisly reminder on my Tower field . . .

Afra could feel the anger flaring within his daughter's mind, an unfocused anger and so ambivalent that it was no wonder that she was under great stress.

You feel that Rojer should have obeyed Prtglm?

No, I mean, yes but . . . *Prtglm just ought not to have required Rojer* . . .

Who was the only one who could have carried out Prtglm's plan . . .

Prtglm is—was—an old and revered captain and should have been obeyed. That planet should have been just . . . *wasted.* Her tone was riven with intense animosity. *When I know how much damage the Hivers have done to 'Dini worlds, and hundreds of others, that* . . . *that Xh-33 really should have been* . . .

When Laria could not find an adequate fate, Afra couched his suggestions in an ironic tone he rarely used with his children.

Exterminated? Fumigated? Wiped of life forms? Scorched beyond use?

There was a long pause. *Something like that, so that that planet could never be able to colonize, to massacre innocent life forms on any other planet.*

So? We must emulate their methods?

Well, just look what they did! Forcing queens of their own species out of that ship and then blasting them, without ever trying to find out why the ship came? Indignation now colored Laria's anger.

That's very much a 'Dini viewpoint, Laria.

It's not that I'm ignoring other *opinions, Dad. Aren't I transmitting messages backwards and forwards every day?*

You are, but are you listening to the content or just the context?

What do you mean by that, Dad? And what group do you support? Her tone was aggressive as if any other than the position she espoused would be suspect.

Along with many other thinking folk, I find the data insufficient and most theories have at least one fundamental flaw. We may never have *answers to half the questions we've asked because there is no communication. Observation is as open to interpretation as any other method of recording, since invariably the observer translates from his or her own experience.*

There hasn't really been that much useful observation either, Laria said caustically.

Afra smiled, keeping his amusement well away from his argumentative daughter.

I disagree, Laria. The material recorded from Rojer's probes is still being analyzed ...

All it shows is that the Hivers have not changed their methods or the dominant drive of their species in the centuries the 'Dini have known them.

The 'Dinis never got close enough to a Hive world to make observations, or attempt contact, Afra said patiently.

Laria's feelings were quite pent-up, by which he guessed she had had the tact not to discuss this with her Tower staff.

But we know what they do to planets. We know they've been doing it for centuries. Laria sounded querulous.

We know what the 'Dinis have reported for the centuries of their struggle to avoid being "exterminated" and that was limited to destroying Hive ships in space. The planet Xh-33 is the only world which they, and we, have seen populated by Hivers. There is a lot more we don't know than what we do . . . even by extrapolation, Laria. What exactly *upsets you, my dear?*

I wish I knew, Dad, Laria confided in what Afra recognized as a wail of conflicting loyalties.

It is not up to us to dispute the 'Dinis' right to punish their own, he said gently. *We must not let our own moral integrity be weakened by conflict with theirs. We can expect that 'Dini reactions will not mirror ours. For one thing, Humans have not fought a sustained battle for centuries, a condition which certainly alters perceptions in a way we can't yet evaluate. That we have managed to pursue the joint purpose as far as we have and with as little friction as there has been . . .*

You've reduced Prtglm to the status of "friction"? Laria sounded appalled.

. . . is a matter of no little achievement. Prtglm caused its own downfall by exceeding orders from the High Council of Alliance: orders in which it and our captains had been thoroughly briefed and in agreement. Do you not see that much?

That's the easy part. What bothers me so is that Gil and Kat are dead, defending Rojer, when none of them should have been put in jeopardy in the first place. But Prtglm is still there*! I can't escape seeing its carrier and* knowing *what's inside and* . . .

Suggest in your most off-handed manner the next time you have occasion to speak to either Plrgt or—who's its main assistant now—

Flgtm, and Plrgt's now Plrgtgl.

Plrgtgl has been very efficient. I hear its name mentioned more and more. Suggest that the carrier is impeding the full use of the area available to you and is there not somewhere else that it can be placed for even more effect?

Out of sight, out of mind, huh, Dad?

Well, out of your sight at least if it is distressing you to the extent that it has . . .

It's not just the carrier . . .

Ah yes, the matter of Clarissia? If she's not working out, my dear, request her transfer . . .

But Granddad's going to be furious with me, and there was a quaver of uncertainty in Laria's voice. *I couldn't get on any sort of terms with Stierlman, and now Clarissia . . . I never had any trouble with Yoshuk and Nesrun! I've excellent relations with Vanteer and Lionasha.* Laria's tone rose to the level of guilty confusion and doubt.

Laria, dear, and Afra couldn't resist chuckling, *the tales that are told of your grandmother's search for suitable Tower personnel are not exaggerated!*

Until you came along, Laria said smartly, and then descended into disillusionment again, *but you're you and she's the Rowan and* . . .

You have exactly the same right to . . . ah . . . dismiss unsuitable personnel—though I hope you won't need to go through as many as she did to get a comfortable "fit" in your Tower. Furthermore your situation on Clarf is far more sensitive than Callisto or Altair ever were, so it's even more important that you are totally comfortable with and can rely on each member of your staff.

A tone of hopefulness entered the *Do you really think so, Dad?*

I know so. As Prime to Prime, inform Jeff Raven of Earth FT&T that T-2 Clarissia is unable to integrate or accept the special requirements of Clarf Tower and you must . . .

I can't say "must" to Grandfather . . .

Possibly not to "Grandfather," dear, but certainly to Earth Prime Raven! Make the distinction and request a replacement. And keep in mind, too, that you haven't had a vacation from your duties at Clarf Tower in over a year. You might benefit from a respite.

Not right now and not if I have only Clarissia to mind the shop while I'm away, Laria said brusquely. *And when did you and Mother last have a break from Aurigae?*

Ours is a slightly different situation, my dear child. We're not dealing with an alien culture . . .

'Dinis are not alien. I've known them all my life!

nor living on a planet where such a brilliant primary produces stress you may not realize until you are away from it. A little distance might help you resolve some of the ambiguities that bother you. You are not the only one—of us or in the Human-settled worlds—to have them.

Oh, Dad, I don't consider me unique. Her tone held the quaver of a laugh but immediately altered. *Sometimes . . . sometimes I don't know what to believe. Then I do, and then something shakes me up again. I really ought to know my own mind by now.*

Your mind you know, Laria, my dear, Afra said with an affectionate chuckle. *It's your emotions and changing perceptions that cause problems. I'd hate to think your ideas were graven in granite at not quite twenty-three.* Briefly

Afra remembered instances of his Damia's captiousness which her eldest daughter certainly had not inherited. *And change IS a constant we must all bear with. At least,* and he let a grin color his mental tone, *we are not locked immutably into a cultural pattern as the Hivers are.*

Gee, thanks for that, Dad!

You're welcome, he said with equal mockery. But he also caught the steadier quality of her mental tone. She'd talked out some of what bothered her. If he and Damia had trouble rationalizing the matter, how hard it was on Laria, a Prime who had not yet found a personal companion to sustain her in arduous, and so often, deeply troubling times. *Now inform Earth Prime of the fact that Clarissia's not working out and why. Either inadequacy is ample cause for replacement.*

Actually, Laria was as strong a T-1 as the Rowan had ever been: a T-3 or even a good T-4 would be adequate support if they were compatible. One never knew until one tried different combinations. He'd always been slightly amazed that he, Afra Lyon of Capella, had been acceptable to Callisto Tower Prime Rowan. Maybe . . . He cut off that thought. He had had parents interfering with him: he and Damia had taken great pains not to repeat such manipulation.

When Laria signed off, he made his muscles go slack from the unconscious effort of such long 'pathing. He told himself it had more to do with the nature of the exchange than age, since the Rowan was older than he, and still going as strong as ever. That was when he also felt a bit of the framework on the left side of the couch, coming through the cushioning. How long had the couches been in use now? Nearly four decades. About time to replace the padding.

He reached out for Damia's mind but she was joyfully

retrieving the scurriers she'd brought down with her accuracy with her slingshot. He smiled as he felt Morag's envy and Ewain's amazement at their mother's casual skill. They could discuss Laria's conundrum later. Bringing her home for a brief respite from all those pressures and conflicting theories would certainly rest her mind and buffer her when she returned to duty.

They might be, as so often Talents said between themselves, only a thought away: but that was not precisely accurate. Contact, yes, but similarity or mutuality or harmony of thought was another matter: so was a cuddle when one was depressed.

Afra found himself at odds with his older son on many points on the issue of the Hivers, and even more puzzled by the bizarre actions and notions of his daughter, Zara. Fortunately her grandmother and Elizara, the T-1 medic for whom she was named, were coping with her and she had passed through a difficult hormonal transition to young womanhood and stability. He knew Rojer was still fighting a private battle with grief, and a harder one with the guilt at having put Gil and Kat in fatal jeopardy. Laria could not escape being sympathetic to the Mrdini interpretations, even if these were considered biased by other, less involved citizens.

Afra swung his long legs off the Tower couch, feeling again the worn place—worn by just this action—where the framework was no longer adequately padded. Just like the framework of long-held ethics and morals was—in some minds—prodding minds through the once comfortable habits of generations.

Afra was also fully aware of other pressures at the highest level—for the Rowan and Jeff often used him as a sounding board and, as often as not, followed his advice. The intransigence of Prtglm and the deaths of Gil and

Kat were having a more far-reaching effect on Human-Mrdini relations than that carrier left on Clarf's Tower field. A strong faction of high-ranking Mrdini were of the opinion that, if Rojer Lyon had been old enough for the duties of a Prime, then he should have complied with Prtglm's plan to devastate the planet Xh-33, regardless of the fact that Rojer was a non-combatant, a minor, following the orders he had been given by his superiors. He had only been on the *Genesee* as a substitute until his older brother was available. The fact that Thian also would not have complied with Prtglm's orders was irrelevant. But Thian already had "hero" status in 'Dini eyes which would have given him the stature to reason with the 'Dini captain and helped him defuse the incident tactfully. It was also quite likely that Prtglm would never have tried to coerce Prime Isthian Lyon.

Yet, since the Mrdinis had allied themselves with Humans, Afra mused, they must often have had dreams, and delusions, of using the human kinetic abilities to produce a grand rout of the Hive species. The fact that the Talents had defeated a Hive colony ship without suffering a single casualty was a frequent theme of 'Dini dream-projections and story-telling. When the Mrdini and Humans had finally made contact, the Humans had enthusiastically embraced 'Dini aspirations and followed their guidance, since obviously the 'Dini had far more information about the Hive predators than Humans did.

In total, such information boiled down to a painfully intimate knowledge of Hive ordnance, its range and destructive abilities: of the number of suicide ships needed to penetrate and destroy any Hive intruders; enough of the Hive mode of colonial expansion to know it was fatal to any planetary life form. Deneb IV was remarkable as the only world where Hive tactics had been unsuccessful.

Since these tactics had been effective so long, the Hive species had not altered them, or its ships and armaments, in the centuries that the Mrdini had been defending themselves. The Mrdinis had, on the other hand, improved spaceships and peripheral technologies, and created more effective unmanned missiles. They had managed to protect their own colony worlds, all the time searching for allies, the Hive homeworld and new resources to help them win the final victory.

Humans had far too long eschewed wars: naval strength being deployed more in the search for colonial worlds, or as deterrent against the occasional renegade privateer. Consequently minor incidents of friction were bound to occur between a war-honed species and one which had been at peace, where the only casualties had occurred in space accidents which were then so ruthlessly investigated that repetitions were unlikely.

On the positive side, since the Alliance had been formed and great efforts made by both species to improve communications and appreciation of each other, there had been significant developments that ought to have had a morale building effect. The fortuitous discovery of the ion trails of three Hive ships had given the Alliance the splendid opportunity to send an expedition to backtrack and locate the Hive homeworld. The trail had led first to the hulk of the biggest Hive ship ever seen by the Mrdini: a hulk which had been partially destroyed by a searing nova explosion. To discover if the nova had indeed destroyed the system which had spawned the Hive species, one resolute 'Dini ship, with Prime Isthian Lyon on board, had driven to the origin of the fading ion trail.

Discovery of the damaged Hive ship disclosed that three escape pods had managed to leave the Mother ship shortly before the nova shock wave hit it. The Human-manned ships had gone in search of the pods to prevent even a single queen from surviving to start a new colony on a hospitable world: a circumstance that the Alliance wished to thwart. One pod had already been captured and it contained a live queen. She had been "decanted," as someone termed it, at the Heinlein Moon Facility, from which escape was unlikely. Her apprehension made her the first live specimen of this engimatic species for both Human and Mrdini. Shortly after her arrival at the Moon Facility, she had laid a huge mass of eggs.

The other two pods had also been accounted for: or rather the remnants of the one which had collided with an asteroid and the other whose occupant had died when its supply of oxygen had given out.

The *KLTS*, through Thian, had reported the absolute surety that the Hive home system had been incinerated by its nova-sun.

Squadrons C and D were still in pursuit of the other two Hive ships, going further and further from their home-worlds. One lobby urgently wanted the squadrons to return on the grounds that the two Hive ships were light-years beyond any Alliance system and therefore no further threat.

"No immediate threat," another faction rebutted, and urgently wanted the squadrons to explore the significant number of G-type star systems with M-5 planets that had been identified during the pursuit, to see why the Hive ships had ignored them. Were these already infested with the Hive species? But investigation was certainly in order to discover if these primaries had generated planets suitable for colonization for either species of the Alliance.

The quandary of continued pursuit now obsessing the High Councillors was ethical in substance. Was it right to let the Hivers continue, knowing that once the Hive ships found the sort of world they needed to colonize they would exterminate whatever life form might exist? Certainly one of the avowed aims of the Alliance was to seek out and identify worlds that had been taken over by the Hive species and prevent them from developing to the stage where their population expanded to the point of recolonizing.

Twenty eggs of the captive Hive queen had hatched, producing creatures who were apparently limited to attendance on the queen, cleaning her, bringing her food, or sent scurrying down the empty corridors of the Heinlein Base: useless errands, since there was nothing but unfurnished rooms, offering only more empty space.

Of more immediate, and perhaps helpful, value was the refugee Hive ship which the Rowan-Thian-Flavia merge had purloined. It would soon be back at the main Earth naval base, totally free of the gases that had destroyed all organisms.

Human and Mrdini naval specialists were impatient to examine an undamaged queens' quarters which contained the control systems for the ship. The most important discovery would be navigational records or star charts that might identify which worlds were Hiver-occupied.

Ever since the Rowan mind-merge had subdued the Many Mind on the Leviathan Hive ship attacking Deneb, it had been assumed that the queens managed all aspects of control on the ship, formulating tactics and forwarding orders to their specialized minions. Whether the duties were equally distributed among them or whether each of the ten to sixteen queens on board a colony ship had different responsibilities had yet to be discovered: hopefully from the type of controls in each queen's quarters. Engineers, astronauts, and technicians, Human and Mrdini, were eagerly awaiting clearance to board this entire ship and begin their investigations.

The Prtglm episode had somewhat eclipsed the positive activities of the Alliance: such as the tapes Rojer had taken, unique in establishing the culture, or rather agriculture, of the Hive species.

Destroying Xh-33's imminent colonization project was a controversial choice from the several solutions that had been available. Most 'Dinis would have preferred to see the planet devastated in retribution for those innocent worlds which had been fumigated by Hivers. Human opinion was virtually solid that destroying the Hive ability to get off that planet was a legitimate and the most acceptable deterrent. There would have been a massive Human outcry had the affair been carried further.

To reassure both apprehensive Humans and the aggressively vindictive Mrdini majority, Captain Quacho of the *Arapahoe* had remained behind on sentinel duty until a discreet space facility could be 'ported to the nearest of Xh-33's moons. Any activity in Xh-33 space could be recorded. Should any occur, unlikely though that seemed, the Alliance could then vote on more lasting punitive action.

Meanwhile there were other enigmas to interpret: if there was no communication between Hive worlds or ship-to-surface contact, how could the Alliance hope to establish any interface with the Hivers? If no communication was possible, there was no hope of arriving at any mutually satisfactory, non-aggressive cohabitation of a galaxy which had sufficient M-type systems to accommodate all—with some control on over-expanding populations.

Afra sighed. Being of a methody upbringing as well as Talented, he eschewed violence: didn't really know if he would even defend himself. He would, he thought, defend his children, but probably not himself. Except that that would leave Damia unsupported. So he might even defend himself, much as he would abhor the necessity. Humans had grown beyond that exigency. Association with the 'Dini had, unfortunately in Afra's estimation, revived "war." If only there were some avenue of interface available . . .

Every attempt to get the captured queen to communicate—or *notice* that other intelligent beings were in her presence—had so far failed. How his daughter Zara had known that the queen was suffering from hypothermia, on the verge of extinction, was a matter no one had been able to establish—especially Zara. She had also had no further empathetic contact with the queen. No one had. The queen had ignored any visitor, even a Mrdini: even the very large Mrdini which towered above her not inconsiderable form.

That she could see and hear had been established by adroit remote testing. Various frequencies and combinations had elicited no more response from her than a twitch of discomfort. Those settings were kept on record.

It must be an amazing mind-set, Afra thought, to consider one's self the only being of worth in the galaxy. There had been Humans who had had such delusions. They had generally died because of them and remained as small paragraphs in the greater history of Humankind.

In an oblique fashion, it followed that, in the Hiver extermination of all life forms on any planet they had chosen to colonize, they were totally unaware that they were eradicating entities which might feel they had the inalienable right to live.

The Hivers must also have been surprised by Mrdini resistance, though only the most determined attacks by Mrdini squadrons and fleet units had deterred the creatures.

Did other Hivers *know* of Mrdini resistance? If the

Raven-Rowan merge had not sent the one survivor back to the Mother ship, would it have *known* that Deneb would resist?

His musings solved nothing and he could "hear" his family returning from a very successful hunt. He left a note for Keylarion, the Tower's T-6, to investigate recovering the couches and went back to the house to start dinner preparations.

Laria followed her father's advice immediately and contacted Earth Prime Jeff Raven to say that the T-2 was unable to tolerate the Mrdini, an essential requisite for duty at Clarf Tower. She had been about to add an apologetic note when her grandfather cut it short.

All we need is unhappy Mrdinis, Jeff said, but in such a genial tone that Laria began to relax and wonder why she'd delayed so long in broaching the problem. Nearly five months was a long enough period to allow Clarissia to integrate and the girl hadn't. Laria did not mention some of the young woman's other less admirable characteristics which had enraged Vanteer from time to time and certainly annoyed Lionasha.

I'll have a word with Gollee Gren and see if he's got any promising candidates. And stress 'Dini adherents. . . . Of course, it would be best to have a 'Dini-raised kid like you. That solves most of the problem Clarissia posed.

How many 'Dinis were paired out, Grandfather?

Gren's got such figures. I seem to remember there were about a thousand in the first adoptions. Not all to Talented families, of course, and spread about the old Nine Star League worlds. And then as many as the 'Dinis could spare for placement. There'll be someone. And, mind you, miss, you keep after me until a proper match's been made. That's more important than you may realize and it is cer-

*tainly MY function to make sure any Prime has the right
support group. Hear me? You put up with Stierlman far
longer than you had to. As my old mother used to say, if
a shirt's dirty, it's dirty.*

Whaat?

*And don't tell me you've never heard how often your
grandmother switched Callisto staff about until she
latched onto your father!*

All right, then, I won't. Laria giggled.

*That's better. Gollee's already on it. As soon as he finds
a likely suspect, I'll ship it out and you can ship Clarissia
back.*

Oh, good heavens!

Sooner the better, pet.

Before Laria could start to temporize, Earth Prime was
gone. As immensely relieved as she was not to have to put
up with Clarissia much longer, Laria hoped that she'd have
time enough to warn the girl. It wasn't exactly Clarissia's
fault that she couldn't abide 'Dinis ... No, it *was*
Clarissia's fault because she'd made absolutely no attempt
to see "good" in the Mrdinis.

In fact, all latent sympathy Laria had for the girl dispersed two minutes later when Clarissia contacted her.

*There is a delegation of those creatures on its way
across the field, Prime* ... Clarissia's tone reeked of distaste.

Laria looked out her Tower window, though the Clarf
"tower" was no more than a four-sided plasglassed cupola,
raised eight feet above the rest of the complex, and saw
that the delegation contained the large form of Plrgtgl, two
medium-sized assistants and six lesser, smaller 'Dinis.

*Vanteer, Lionasha, full honors. Clarissia, can you at
least assemble the proper refreshments?*

Yes, came so curt an acknowledgment that Laria could

almost see the repugnance on the girl's long face and the twitch of her slender hands, indications of the revulsion the young Talent felt at having to deal with the "creatures" in any capacity. Another twinge of pity racked Laria, for the girl had been so eager to be assigned away from her homeworld. Her xenophobia had not then been apparent to anyone, even Gollee Gren, but it developed speedily enough on Clarf.

Vanteer, a stockily built mid-thirties native of Procyon IV, with the heavy bones of that planet's Human adaptation, and the dark-eyed, dark-haired, dark-complected Lionasha, the "lithe" (which was Laria's special designation for her T-7 expediter), could be counted on to divert 'Dinis from approaching Clarissia. It was as well, Laria thought with a sigh, that native 'Dinis did not read Human countenances as well as the Tower 'Dini contingent did. Nor did any of them really notice that Clarissia conveyed no body language at all—standing stiff and straight as if lacquered in position. That was a mercy since she would have made the true depth of her revulsion all too easily readable in movements.

Once Plrgtgl announced its mission, Laria had no further time to fret over Clarissia's possible misdemeanors. Plrgtgl had a huge job for the Tower, requiring it to organize and expedite the timetable for a considerable amount of cargo to be shifted: to the other 'Dini planets and to the satellite space docks. Without its being stated, Laria and her staff realized that a goodly portion of the 'Dini space fleet was being refitted and resupplied in the shortest possible time. Such activity provided her with the perfect reason to remove Prtglm's carrier.

"WITH SO MUCH TO BE SHIPPED TO DIFFERENT PLACES, ALL CRADLES WILL BE NECESSARY," she said as she riffled through the documentation. "THE CARRIER WHICH HAS

RESTED ON THE FIELD COULD PERHAPS NOW BE MOVED TO A
SOUTHERN LOCATION TO DISPLAY ITS MESSAGES THERE TO
GOOD EFFECT." She pretended total disinterest in Plrgtgl's
reaction to the request and quickly moved to another topic,
adding body language to augment the praise of her words.
"SO MUCH OF THIS YEAR'S HARVEST TO GO OFF-WORLD, TOO. A
CREDIT TO THE COLORS."

Plrgtgl rolled its poll eye, attractively covered by a
crown of lace which had recently become a 'Dini fad.
Laria was well accustomed to such scrutiny and continued
to scan the cargo waybills for the red ones that indicated
live 'portations.

"IT WILL BE GOOD TO SEE THE *KLTL*," she added as noncha-
lantly as she could, since she was overjoyed to see the ship
listed as an arrival. Laria kept very good track of what
went to the *KLTL*, since her brother Thian had spent so
much time on board. And saved so many 'Dinis from the
ultimate sacrifice of their kind. Thian was now FT&T on
board the *Genesee* and they exchanged news whenever she
had a shipment for the Squadron.

"YES. THE *KLTL* HAS HONORED ALL MRDINI3 AND EVERY
COLOR THAT SERVES ON IT," Plrgtgl said, shifting its lower
limbs, body language she had come to read as "pleased."
"THN LN HAS SERVED THE *KLTL* TO THE HONOR OF YOUR
HOUSE."

As she bowed in acknowledgment of such praise, Laria
kept her expression neutral despite an intense desire to
grin. Plrgtgl had used another human idiom. High-ranking
'Dinis, like Plrgtgl, were gradually sprinkling their conversations with more and more Basic terms. If only that usage
could also alter some of the 'Dini minds and methods.

First things first, she said to herself.

Hey, said Vanteer, his expression bland though his voice
was triumphant, *another score for Basic!*

Keeping count, are we, Van? asked Lionasha, whose eyes twinkled.

And thank whatever gods there be that you're getting rid of that monstrosity. If you're downwind, the stench is appalling. Vanteer added a flash of himself holding his nose and gagging. *Even my 'Dinis are complaining.*

Laria dared not react or even shoot him a warning glance. All her attention must be on Plrgtgl. She signalled for Lionasha to take the documentation and begin organizing a timetable for the 'portations.

"THERE WILL BE A GREAT RECEPTION CEREMONY FOR THE ARRIVAL OF THE TRIUMPHANT *KLTL*," Plrgtgl said.

"AS THERE SHOULD BE FOR A SHIP THAT HAS DONE SO MUCH," Laria replied formally and made the necessary body gestures that signified pleasure, honor, delight and acceptance. She could carry on high-level communications now with just body language, though more and more 'Dinis had become fluent in Basic and prided themselves on using it in the presence of Humans. She flicked her eyes to where Tip and Huf were standing respectfully to one side of the great Plrgtgl and caught their approval of her expertise.

"IS THERE TIME TO REFRESH WITH COOL DRINK?" Laria asked, gesturing toward the table and its array. Clarissia had—unobtrusively at least—backed herself against the wall. Tip, Huf, and the other 'Dinis—all too well aware of her dislike—took over the hospitality duties, bringing forward 'Dini seating while Vanteer and Lionasha served the fruity juices which Laria imported from Earth, knowing how much 'Dinis liked them.

I'm not telling you your business as Tower Prime, Vanteer said on a tight private level, *but we're going to have more 'Dinis in and out of here and* she's *becoming more and more of a liability.*

We'll back your decision in that, Lionasha added.

Your Prime's already initiated the appropriate steps for her transfer, gang, Laria replied, focusing her thought to the two, though Clarissia was so tight in her xenophobia she wouldn't have been aware of a telepathic shout in her vicinity.

Hallelujah! was Vanteer's response in an archaic term that surprised both women.

Despite Clarissia, the official visit went off very well and Plrgtgl was so excited in its own fashion with such imminent traffic—Plrgtgl was rather possessive of the Tower as its special project—that her reserve went unnoticed.

"We'll be busy, kids," Lionasha said, having had a chance to estimate how much Tower time and energy would be required for the material and animate objects scheduled to be 'ported and received. She grinned around the room but her grin faded at Clarissia. The thin girl stepped forward then, swallowing convulsively.

"I do not wish to abandon Clarf Tower at a time of maximum activity, Prime, but I request as immediate a transfer as possible." She swallowed again and the others noticed that her pale complexion had turned yellowish.

"Oh, you won't leave us short, Clarissia," Laria said airily. "Prime Raven has already promised us additional assistance. As soon as you like, I can 'port you back to Blundell."

Both Lionasha and Vanteer were too self-possessed to show any surprise at Laria's abruptness and were kind enough to make appropriate sounds of dismay.

"No, really, I must go," Clarissia said, her fingers twitching at her sides and without another word, actually 'ported herself out of the room.

"Well!" said Lionasha and turned to Laria, hoping for an explanation. Vanteer's grin got broader and he winked at the Tower Prime.

"As I said, I've been working on the problem," she said casually. "I just got the official permission today. We may have to work harder . . ."

Not if you'll meet me halfway and bring me in, said a male voice that Laria did not recognize.

She glanced from Vanteer to Lionasha to see if the 'path had been audible to them. Apparently not, so she continued her sentence.

"But not for long, it seems." *So where are you so easily retrievable?*

Not precisely "easily." I'm currently with C Squadron, and his spatial coordinates tagged on to the 'path. *T-2-ing on the AS* Strongbow *as courier and pack mule.*

Laria could almost see a wry grin on the speaker's face. She also caught the sense of terrible fatigue and ennui that his flippancy was trying to conceal. Pack mule? Well, that was better than "stevedore."

When can we expect you?

I have my orders, I'm packed, and I'll get into the capsule as soon as you tell me to.

You really aren't wasting any time, are you?

Frankly, Clarf Prime, I'll be very glad to leave this ship. I've . . . I've been gone a long, long time.

There was that in his tone of voice that touched an echo of deep empathy in Laria.

"Tower generators up, please," she said, taking the stairs to her aerie two at a time. *What is the Squadron going to do about resupply,* she asked, *if you're here?*

I've been reliably informed that my replacement will follow swiftly.

And you are? Laria asked, suddenly realizing that al-

though she would now recognize his mental touch anywhere in the galaxy, she didn't know his name.

Oh, and she heard him chuckle, *I* have *been on board
too long. I'm T-2 Kincaid Dano, Altairian bred.*

You'll be very welcome, Kincaid.

Thanks. And a laugh again echoed in her head. *My
'Dinis are ecstatic at the posting, never having touched
down on their homeworld.*

Laria let an exaggerated sigh of relief escape her lips.
He had volunteered the answer to her most important
question.

*That's probably the only reason I got promoted, Clarf
Prime,* he said with another dry chuckle which told her he
had at least heard, and understood, her sigh. Another plus
which he couldn't possibly know—she'd had to *explain* so
many casual references to Stierlman, and Clarissia had always been so worried about how to respond to any attempt
at levity, Laria had found her sense of fun was atrophying.

Why on earth hadn't she been assigned someone of
Kincaid's caliber in the first place? Then she recalled how
long the two Squadrons had been traveling. But surely . . .
She took herself sternly in hand: she had been able to run
Clarf Tower quite capably with Yoshuk and Nesrun. Then
Vanteer had been sent to help until the Sef Tower had been
commissioned and her T-2s had been sent there. Lionasha
joined her and Vanteer, and Stierlman was sent as her T-2.
A Tower Prime did not need to find exactly the "right"
personality for a good rapport—those complementary
qualities which her grandmother had found in Afra after
trying to adjust to many incompatible personalities.
Kincaid's 'Dini affiliations would now be essential, to
counter any harm Clarissia's short tenancy might have
caused.

A totally wayward thought made her choke back audible

laughter: what if Clarissia was to be Kincaid's replacement? A shipful of long-voyage officers and crew might just be what the girl needed.

Being 'Dini-paired is certainly an advantage here, she 'pathed, *but that would scarcely be the deciding factor, Kincaid.*

The Tower generators were reaching the necessary whine as she asked Lionasha to put the relevant space charts up on the screen for her. She triangulated the position and, settling into the couch, reached out with her mind for the unmistakable mass of metals and Humans which had been vivid in his peripheral identifications of his current position. She felt for the equally identifiable mass of a carrier, Kincaid and his two 'Dinis within.

Ready?

You have no idea how ready! was his devout response and she picked him up, feeling once more the definite and deep fatigue in his assistance to her contact. What under the suns had the Squadron required of this courier–pack mule to bring him to this level of exhaustion? She lowered the carrier gently into the cradle nearest the Tower, hoping the wind blew the stench of Prtglm away from him. *It is also very important,* he added in an aside that she wasn't certain she was supposed to hear.

Vanteer, do the honors, will you? She could sort out this "important," when they were face to face. *He's Kincaid Dano of Altair, our T-2 replacement, plus 'Dinis. Clarissia,* she added in a direct 'path to the girl, *a personnel carrier has just arrived and is available to take you to Blundell—if you'll give me an estimate of how long it will . . .*

I can go right now!

Clarissia was hysterical with either relief or joy, or both, at the serendipity of release. By the time Laria had risen from her couch and gone to the window overlooking the field, she saw Vanteer shaking hands with a tallish man whose back was to her. Her sense of his fatigue was reinforced by the sag of his shoulders. When he and Vanteer turned back to the carrier to assist two well-grown 'Dinis to alight, the lid hid his face from her. Clarissia, with a welter of luggage following her, half raced across the plascrete. The two men then helped her and her gear into the carrier. Laria grinned as Vanteer closed the lid with a definitely firm shove.

She's ready to go, Laria. I'll bring Kincaid, Npl and Pls up to the Tower.

Laria nearly 'ported herself back onto the couch, she was so eager to send the girl *away!* She could also feel Clarissia's assistance in getting the generators back up to launch. First time the girl hadn't waited for orders.

I wish you well wherever you go, Clarissia.

Don't be so magnanimous, Laria, the girl answered in a snarl. *You know perfectly well you've been wanting to get me out of your hair since the moment I got here and you discovered I'm not a weasel-lover like you. You'll soon find that the popularity of you collaborators is on the wane and your family will be replaced. That I can promise you.*

Laria stifled the dismay such animosity caused her. She refused to respond to silly mouthings and threats. And the service her family gave could scarcely be considered sinecures. She forced herself to respond with dignity.

You are a competent T-2, Clarissia, and as that I can recommend you to your next post with no hesitation. Goodbye!

You haven't heard the last of ME!

Laria ignored the virulently delivered rejoinder but she flipped the carrier as fast as she could back to the huge Earth landing field at the Blundell Cube.

Gollee!

Open to you, Laria.

Clarissia's a good T-2, but watch her.

I had that intention if she couldn't work out with you, Laria.

In Gollee's tone was an anodyne for Clarissia's parting venom.

Are you coming down, Laria? asked Vanteer in an "I think you should" tone.

You bet I am.

Clarissia launched a choice parting shot? asked Lionasha with a trace of anxiety.

Laria did not respond but came down the stairs with a far lighter tread than when she had ascended. She shouldn't be so naive, but she had hopes for the newcomer, if only because of his humor.

Kincaid was tall, his 'Dinis nearly as big as her Tip and Huf. Despite being of different colors, Npl and Pls were being most affectionately ringed by the six resident 'Dinis, all wriggling and nattering in the most fervent of welcomes imaginable.

Kincaid was whistling a very old tune that Laria only recognized because her Denebian grandmother had sung it to put her younger siblings to sleep on summer holidays. "If you go down to the woods today, you're in for a big surprise."

After the strains of the morning, Laria burst into laughter and knew that she couldn't fail to like Kincaid. He advanced toward her, his thin, very pale face alight with pleasure that she'd identified the tune. He couldn't ever be called "handsome," not the way Yoshuk was, but he *was* attractive, despite a ship's pallor and a dry skin that gave him more facial wrinkles than he ought to have. She didn't think him older than Vanteer. Rangily built but far too thin for the big bones of him, he held out to her a big blunt-fingered hand, palm sideways so she could merely brush it, for the touch that Talents preferred as casual contact, or shake it.

She was so glad to see him, a confirmed 'Dini person, a man who laughed easily and obviously had an outrageous sense of humor, that she grasped his hand and took full advantage—as he did after a moment's polite hesitation—of the complete contact. He was piney/green/oddly velvet, very very tired and, though he didn't try to hide the fact from her, she caught the hesitancy and realized that he was homosexual. If he made a good T-2, that wouldn't matter. It would almost be better if they were friends, as her grandmother and Afra had been, rather than lovers. Still . . .

"The first thing you do, Kincaid Dano of Altair, is get some extended rest," she said briskly, twisting her hand in his and starting to lead him out of the main Tower room to the living area. "You'll have to be careful of the sun here, Kincaid, you've been confined too long in a ship . . ."

"Don't you just know it . . ." he said ruefully. *Look, Laria Prima,* he *said on the most private level which their* joined hands provided, *there is something exceedingly important . . .*

"I'll get some of the strongest blocker," Lionasha said, "and goggle glasses to reduce Clarf's dazzle. Even peripherally it's going to bother you."

"Go on ahead, Laria, and darken the room . . . the best guest, Clarissia's left hers in a welter," said Vanteer, picking up one of the duffels that Kincaid had brought with him. "You're to sleep!"

"Look, I'm here to help . . . ." *Laria Prime, I must . . .*

"You're in no state to be help in any form, Kincaid,"

Laria said firmly, in answer to both voiced and 'pathed messages, "until you've had some rest."

You don't realize . . . He was insistent and gripped her hand to express his urgency.

A couple of hours won't make that much difference, will it? she asked, as if his admission of his sexuality would matter to her. Or maybe he didn't realize that his fatigue had made it very easy for her to reach to the more private areas of his mind. *Even with my help you couldn't 'path much beyond your nose.*

A few hours, no, I guess not. But, and he added aloud, "Nil and Plus *have* to contact their . . ."

"Ours can manage that courtesy while you're grabbing a few hours' sleep," Laria said placatingly, dropping his hand as she pushed open the door out of the Tower. Lionasha grabbed up the second duffel as they all maneuvered the long man where they wanted him to go. Raising his arms in surrender, he allowed himself to be guided.

Laria marched straight to the nearest and largest guest bedroom, palming the blind controls to complete darkness, and lowering the room lighting to a suitable dimness.

"Ah!" Kincaid exclaimed as he took in the spacious surroundings. "A real bed, too!"

Laria laughed. "Yes, you wouldn't fit on a bunk too well, would you?"

He did a shoulder roll onto the extra wide and long bed and lay there, sighing with intense relief, arms and legs spread out to the edges. For a beat, the other three Talents waited for another comment from him.

Laria covered her mouth and her giggle.

"He's asleep?" whispered Lionasha.

"Out like a light!"

The three left the room, Laria palming the lights off and carefully sliding the door shut.

"Not that I think a torpedo would wake him . . ." Laria said as they returned to the Tower complex. Halfway down that corridor they could hear the excited 'Dini voices. Their gang were already taking care of the arrivals.

"They can all have the day off," Laria said as they entered the main complex. "Nothing's due in now."

"You're right," Lionasha said, glancing at the topmost waybills on her desk. "None of Plrgtgl's shipments will arrive until tomorrow but here," she added, tearing a slip from the printer with a flourish, "are the coordinates you can send that misbegotten carrier to." She handed Laria the slip.

"Prayers have been answered all round today. Rev up the generators, please, Vanteer," Laria said, and settled herself in the nearest chair. "I have the oddest feeling I've already done a full day's work with only one catch and one send. This one is the bonus." Print-out in hand, she concentrated and, catching the rhythm of the generators, flipped Prtglm's carrier to the coordinates given. "And that is that!"

Vanteer sniffed the air about him. "Yes, a definite improvement."

"All round," Lionasha agreed. "Don't know how you stuck her so long, Laria. You've the patience of a saint."

"What's a saint?" asked Vanteer.

"Oh, you!" Laria said, for Vanteer's fey humor broke out at the oddest times. This might be one of the times he was trying to catch her out.

Lionasha had taken Vanteer's query at face value and, being keen on history, explained the concept thoroughly while Laria listened. If this Kincaid fit in with these two half as well as she rather thought he would, they were finally a real Tower Team. Vanteer was as hetero as she could wish—she could also wish for a bit more from

Vanteer but there was no way she could initiate things, not with Van's personality and the fact that he liked spreading himself around, which inhibited her. There were several others in the growing Human community who might find Kincaid companionable.

"TLP, HGF, ALL OF YOU, PLEASE TAKE NPL AND PLS TO SEE CLARF. DO NOT FORGET ANY OF THE SIGHTS THEY SHOULD SEE AND DO NOT WORRY ABOUT REPORTING UNTIL TOMORROW MORNING FOR WORK."

The darker-pelted of Kincaid's two sable-colored 'Dinis turned most politely to Laria. "KNKD HAS TIRED WITH TOO MUCH STRAIN. YOU WILL LET HIM SLEEP, LR LN?"

"UNTIL HE WAKES, MOST EXCELLENT NPL."

There was a moment of excitement between Nil and Plus, for neither had been formally introduced to Laria, and her being able to identify one from the other pleased both immensely.

"LR LN KNOWS MRDINIS WELL," said Tip with as much pomposity as a 'Dini of its longevity could manage. Huf, Vanteer's Dig and Nim, as well as Lionasha's Fig and Sil, were convulsed in 'Dini giggles. It took all three Humans to herd eight wriggling 'Dinis out the main Tower entrance. They were still reeling with laughter until they reached the outer gates, when suddenly all eight assumed the usual dignified postures of 'Dinis of reasonably high rank.

Laria Prime?

The summons must have been repeated on gradually increasing levels of urgency before Laria woke, unable in her sleepiness to identify the caller.

Who? She was surprised as well as slightly annoyed to have a deep slumber broken into.

Kincaid. I apologize but I am rested sufficiently now

to make an extremely important and top secret report to Earth Prime. There was a hesitation that Laria interpreted as both embarrassment and necessity. *I am unable right now to make so long a 'path and ask for your assistance.*

What he did not say, and which alerted Laria as nothing else could have, was the fact that the secrecy of the communication was crucial. None of the Tower staff must know of the 'path, the generators must not be used.

Kincaid might say he was sufficiently rested but Laria knew by the edge on the words he spoke that he was by no means as rested as he would like her to believe.

I'll collect you on my way to the Tower, she said, and slipped into the loose light long robe that most of the Humans living on Clarf preferred.

He was standing at his closed door, still wearing the shipsuit he had arrived in although he was barefooted. She nodded approval and led the way. It was four in Clarf's morning and the floor under their bare feet was almost cool. She took the stairs two at a time and realized that he did so, too. Another nice change from Clarissia who had been prim to the point of the worst excess of methody. Laria pointed to the couch which, she also noted, they would have to lengthen to fit his frame comfortably, but he sank onto it now without a murmur.

Have you merged often enough to be comfortable with the procedure? she asked. There was a great deal she would need to learn about this man before they did many 'portations.

More with other T-2s and T-3s than with a Prime . . .

It's as well you're still too tired to resist then, she 'pathed, and firmly took control. Deep inside, she wondered again what the Navy had been doing to the man to reduce him to this level of nearly total mental and physical exhaustion. Then she caught edges of anxieties, deep loss and disillusionments. So he'd had a rough emotional time on the *Strongbow* as well as overwork. Despite that, the merge was as easy as slipping a hand into a perfectly fitting glove. More to admire in the man.

Laria-Kincaid merge to Earth Prime, urgent.

I'm here and I've been expecting Kincaid's contact, Laria. Just support him, will you?

That was surprise enough for Laria and she immediately assumed the secondary position of the merge, deft enough with all the practice she'd had with her parents at Aurigae Tower, bolstering the strength of the merge.

I had my orders, as you know, sir, but there were other ways in which I was asked to assist the Squadron and since there was no specific limitation, I used my own judgment when the matter was presented to me.

Properly done, Kincaid. Proceed.

Laria tried to keep herself from tensing: this sounded suspiciously like what had happened to her brother; no *specific* orders *against* an action which had disastrous consequences. Judging by what she had empathed of personal distress, even Kincaid's maturity and a wider scope of experience had not prevented a trauma with which he was trying to cope.

*I was asked to send the new design plastic probes to those M-5 planets which we were passing when at a feasible distance for my ability. Captains Steverice and Hsiang were most anxious to establish some reason for such bypasses. The first had once—*and Kincaid paused significantly—*been occupied by Hivers, for the colony ship was in orbit and sufficient of the now identifiable Hive buildings and agricultural workings were visible— though the world did not show the same concentration of effort that was visible on the Xh-33. No activity was observed during the forty-eight-hour parabolic surveillance.*

The second world examined was completely devoid of life or vegetation but there was a ring of debris which both Captains Steverice and Hsiang decided was similar to the one observed by Squadron B. The third M-5 world was not yet dead but in such ecological imbalance that only immediate action could reverse the process. I have the coordinates and I suggest that an expedition be mounted—joint if that is politically sound—to save what could be a habitable world. Hivers were there; two small buildings remained, but in ruins. The fourth world is being colonized by Hivers.

Was that probe seen?

Negative.

Thank you, Kincaid. You've done more than you were required and we very much appreciate your efforts. Prime Laria, you are to be certain this man is completely recovered before he is required to take his position in the Tower.

You can count on me, Earth Prime.

I know I can, dear child. Now both of you get back to your beds. Especially you, Kincaid.

Laria, still merged with Kincaid, felt him starting to reach out with another sentence and deftly, and as painlessly as possible for even the merge had caused his mind distress, eased away.

"You heard my grandfather. Enough is enough."

Kincaid had swung himself sideways on the couch, burying his head in his hands, body sagging.

"Glutton for punishment, aren't you?" she said, a trifle annoyed with such dedication even as every ounce of her heritage approved it.

"You realize how important the messages are."

"Yes, indeed. But, now, my friend . . ." and she paused just long enough to cause him to make eye contact at her use of the word. She smiled down into his tired eyes.

". . . Friend Kincaid Dano of Altair, you're going to sleep yourself out."

Then, without asking, she gently 'ported this long man friend back to the bed in his quarters, amused at her maternal attitude but keeping that amusement well screened. He made neither protest nor resistance to such manipulation. Too exhausted to, she thought. When she passed his room on her way back to her own, she "peeked" in. He had turned on his left side, cradling his head on one arm. She flipped the light cover over him. Dawn brought a cool breeze no matter how hot the night had been or the day would be. She didn't want him coming down with a ridiculously Humanoid cold.

Kincaid roused late the next evening and was instantly served a nourishing meal which Laria and Lionasha had spent some time concocting.

Thanks, whoever sent this, he said when he had finished every scrap of the tray. He was asleep again before anyone working in the Tower could respond.

"Whatever *did* they do to the poor guy?" Lionasha asked.

"More than a T-2 should be required to do, I'd say," Laria replied with some asperity.

"Like your brother, huh?" Vanteer asked.

Laria shook her head. "For one thing, Kincaid *is* a T-2 and didn't have the capacities either Thian or Rojer have, but he did a lot more than he should have. Pretty far off even for just normal catch and shove."

Vanteer looked up at the tri-D galactic globe that was being updated almost monthly by the various squadrons, Human and Mrdini, exploring in every direction. "Yeah, he would have been dangerously close to his limit, even with the generators those Galaxy class ships have."

Lionasha gave a sigh. "We *are* going to need his heist soon, Laria," she said, patting one sheaf of the heavier materials to be sent to the moon spaceyards. "Those are big daddies."

Laria had tested the state of Kincaid's sleeping mind and was reassured by the return of a healthy resilience.

"Another twenty-four hours and he won't know himself."

"Then we can schedule the party for the day after tomorrow?" asked Lionasha, with just a hint of the eagerness she had for the project.

Vanteer and Laria laughed, knowing just why she was eager.

Since the early days of the Clarf Tower, when Yoshuk and Nesrun had managed however they could in the strange environment, many more Humans had moved to take up administrative or consultancy posts on Clarf, and on the two Moon bases. Close to three thousand Humans, some with varying degrees of Talent, though that was not a prerequisite, now formed a loose but agreeable social unit. Specialists came, integrated briefly, or stayed on as their work required them. The Tower facilities had been enlarged several times and into several levels to accommodate transients. A large tract of land, near the sea, had been allotted the more permanent Human colony. Lately Lionasha had been seeing a young Denebian servomechanics engineer, Buzbeth Hawk. While he was a T-5, he was only just marginally empathic with Humans. Lionasha didn't mind: she got through to *him* with no trouble. Vanteer preferred to "mingle" as he put it, though he was already contributing to the support of two children from different mothers of minor Talents. He was certain the girl was already a receiving telepath. Laria often wished that Vanteer would "receive" a little more from her than he did. But you don't force Human relationships, especially among Talents. She knew *that* much from the story of her father and mother.

Twenty-four hours later, looking refreshed and certainly relaxed, Kincaid joined the Tower staff for their early morning meal. He had obviously found time to discover the working schedule to know that Clarf Tower liked to get as much of its heavy work done in the dawn hours as possible.

"Am I fit, Prime?" he asked as he pulled out a chair to sit opposite Laria.

"Yes, or I wouldn't have allowed you out of your quarters," she said, passing him the coffee pot.

Appreciatively he sniffed the steaming aroma and grinned. "It's real! The Navy has some brew they insist is coffee but, believe me, it isn't!"

"We do have certain perks in this Tower that even the Fleet can't manage," Vanteer said, passing him over the dew-fresh fruit which 'Dini farmers regularly left at the Tower gates.

"Clarf is certainly an improvement." Then he gave a sudden jerk to his shoulders and looked about him frowning. "Where are Nil and Plus?"

"Helping the others," Vanteer said, jerking his thumb over his shoulder toward the still shadowy Tower field. "We got big daddies to move. They've integrated so well you'd think they were the same color."

Kincaid looked immensely relieved and began to eat his breakfast. "They've been ... well, they were incredibly understanding on our tour with Squadron C."

Lionasha leaned slightly across the table to Kincaid. "Don't be surprised if they keep their poll eyes elevated a while. They've been given heroes' welcomes. Their color kin mobbed the Complex the first morning and they've been out every night since."

"They need to be with their own. Both are close to hibernating."

"Yes, we noticed, and Plrgtgl made very prestigious arrangements for them," Laria said with a grin as she rose. "Bring your coffee up to the Tower, Kincaid. We've got to get started."

He swallowed the fruit he was chewing, splashed more coffee into his cup and made for the stairs.

"Refills, whenever," Lionasha said as she settled at her station.

"You've worked a Tower before?" Laria asked.

"Hasn't my file caught up with me?"

"Oh, it's in the banks all right, but I'd rather work with you," she said, with a slight emphasis on "work." "You had no trouble merging, even dead on your feet, and that's the hardest part of Tower work. Some never get the knack."

As she chatted to put him at his ease, she settled herself on the couch.

"Hey, this one's new, isn't it?" he asked, running fingers along the suede-like covering and noticing the length of it.

"Well, you'd hardly have fit on Clarissia's old one."

"Well," and he mimicked her tone exactly, "it's much appreciated," he said, sliding onto the couch and giving a sigh as his legs were supported beyond his long feet.

"With the stuff we'll have to shift today, Kincaid, comfort is as essential as placement. Lionasha," and she raised her voice, "what's first?"

"The big daddy for the moon base . . ."

Laria pointed to the placement tri-D on the screens above the couches. "We've more inner-system traffic than most Towers."

She saw Kincaid listening to the rising whine of the generators, then felt his mind touch hers.

"It's all of us today for one of these, Kincaid," she said, and took first Lionasha and then Vanteer into the merge with the T-2 as backup. The generators reached the required strength and Laria pushed the merge to 'port the cargo carrier deftly to the cradle awaiting it on the moon base.

Kincaid turned his head to grin at her. "So that's how a real Tower handles mass."

"The first of many. And thank goodness we've got eight 'Dinis for ground handlers. They really are the best!"

Kincaid fell into the rhythm as if he'd been a part of the Tower complement for years. Neither Vanteer nor Lionasha would have commented on how easily he fit in but Laria could nevertheless feel their relief. Almost before they knew it, they had swung the significant volume of outgoing traffic and were beginning to haul in the out-of-system. By the time Clarf's sun reached zenith Laria called a halt. Despite the air-conditioning, the Tower room was becoming uncomfortable.

Hey, came the cheery voice of Yoshuk from Sef Tower, *anytime you want to send that guy here, he'd be welcome.*

That goes for me, too, added Nesrun.

Don't either of you dare poach now I've got someone who fits in, Laria said firmly.

Yes, ma'am, no, sir, Yoshuk replied so cockily she could see the grin on his face.

Kincaid was stretching and relieving the tension of muscles which had been automatically responding to the day's "lifts." His mind had lost the morning's resilience and Laria hoped she hadn't pushed him too far.

"Lunch, and then with this sort of heat pushing down on us, we all take a siesta," she said, certain that both Vanteer and Lionasha would fall in with her scheme. "That gives the 'Dinis time to rest, too. And don't look out on the bright of the day without glasses!" she added as Kincaid strolled to the windows to look down at the 'Dinis scurrying about. Two were lagging somewhat behind the pace of the others. "Nil and Plus'll notice the difference for a while but they all adjust more quickly than we do."

Blinking vigorously with tearing eyes, Kincaid managed a half-sided grin. "Who was it told me that Clarf was an easy Tower?"

"Oh, it is," Laria said, on her way down the stairs. "We're just a little busier with all the rearrangements. Next week, we'll hardly have a snitch to switch."

Sensibly they ate as lightly at midday as the 'Dinis. Nil and Plus needed some judicious eye care but when Kincaid would have performed it, the other six 'Dinis pushed him out of the way and had a great time fussing over exactly how to effect the most result in the fastest time. The three long-term residents of Clarf Tower smiled proudly at the concerted effort.

"I've been away longer than I realized," Kincaid said, slowly peeling one of the meltingly sweet bogpears that the others had recommended.

"How long were you on that cruise?" Vanteer asked.

Kincaid paused, frowning before he answered, "Nearly five years, I think. Basic."

"That long?" Laria tried to remember exactly how long Thian had been out, but it was no five years.

"Oh," Kincaid said with a diffident flick of his fingers, "I'd been sent out with Squadron C long before those ion trails were discovered. We picked 'em up in our quadrant. Then it was even more important for the Squadron to have a Talent."

"Were they *trying* to burn your mind out?" Vanteer demanded with heated indignation before Laria could speak.

"No, and they didn't," Kincaid replied, though he began to rub his forehead in an unconscious gesture. "I'd more than enough latents among the crew personnel to draw on when I had to . . ."

Waiting for some clue to his personal distress, Laria caught it. So, the long cruise had had many complications for the Talented homosexual.

"How long have you been getting headaches like that?" Laria asked, trying to keep both dismay and concern from becoming evident.

He dropped his hand from his forehead and met her eyes. Then managed a chuckle. "Comes and goes."

"Fine Prime I am," she said, pushing back her chair and coming around behind him. She placed her fingers lightly, like a net, around his skull and gently supplied the inhibitors that would reduce both the ache and the minute swelling of the cerebral area which governed all psionic activity.

"I'll be fine, Laria, really I will," he said, reaching up as if to disengage her fingers.

"Don't you dare," Lionasha said, waggling a finger at him. "Laria's one of the best at healing."

What Laria also felt, because Kincaid had no way to prevent it, was that his emotions were in a turmoil, more of the brew of hurt, loss, disappointment, and, yes, physical pain, that had not been resolved by the sleep and relief of bodily fatigue. His participation in today's merge had almost wiped out the remedial affect of several days' much-needed sleep. Considering his state, he'd been a real trooper.

"Headache gone now, friend?" she asked casually, removing her hands since she now knew more than he did about his condition.

He gave her as searching a stare as he could without calling attention to the exchange. Then his taut lips relaxed into a brief smile. She resumed her seat and took another bogpear from the bowl, as if her treatment had been no more than a simple pain block.

"Yes, *friend*, much better. Thank you," he said and finished eating his own pear.

"Lionasha, it's just the lighter stuff for the evening pushes, isn't it?" Laria said and managed a very convincing yawn. "Won't be that much to do when it cools down."

"Right-o," Lionasha said.

"I want to check that ping I heard before I get my nap," Vanteer said, moving toward the stairs that led to the Tower's machine level.

And that was how Clarf Tower managed to deceive Kincaid until the worst of both the physical and mental fatigue began to heal.

CHAPTER
FOUR

WHEN Rojer's profound emotional trauma began to ease, Isthia advised that he be allowed to enroll in an engineering program which he had been so keenly interested in prior to the tragedy. He must learn to shift his concentration from his loss. She offered her beloved cottage, not so isolated any more as Deneb City was spreading ever closer to her lakeside retreat, and flattened arguments that too much solitude for the grieving boy might have an adverse effect.

And you think that one or another of us won't be subtly aware of his state of mind at all times, Damia? Isthia had snorted with disdain. *We are always but a thought away, yours, mine, Afra's ...*

Jeff's, added Earth Prime.

The cottage worked for you and Afra, didn't it? Isthia went on, ignoring her son's interruption. *We all know he needs to grieve. Let him. Right now companionship is not high on his agenda. In fact, it would only serve to remind*

*him of his loss. We've done as much metamorphically as
we can. Now he needs to be diverted and, if it's engineering that he has a passion for, let's fan those flames and put
his mind to work.*

Damia and Afra drew Xexo into the discussion and the
Aurigae T-8 had no hesitation in supporting Isthia's suggestion. Rojer had a natural engineering bent and he was
in the right place to get his qualifications. There were
other engineering candidates on Deneb, so he could have
as much, or as little, social intercourse as he wished. After
all, how many Towers were there for Primes to run? Xexo
went further and, after a long and useful discussion with
Commander Metrios of the *Genesee*, developed a curricu-
lum, meticulously tailored to beguile young T-1 Rojer
Lyon into studying himself out of grief.

After a desultory and half-hearted start, Rojer began to
respond to the cleverly devised study program and to
spend hours on the terminal, competing with himself on
Engineering Teach. His progress was duly noted. If Xexo
grinned fatuously as he tended the generators at Aurigae
Tower and adopted a smug smile whenever Rojer was
mentioned, no one contested him when he'd allude to
Rojer's progress as one of his own better "engineering"
accomplishments.

Occasionally, his uncle Jeran, Deneb's Prime, called
Rojer to assist in the Tower, "to keep his hand in." There
he met cousins with varying degrees of Talent who were
also pressed into service. Though he had never much liked
his cousin Rhodri, he found himself drawn to the youngest
of the Eagles, the shy and self-effacing Asia, who was also
in the Engineering program.

He was constantly receiving invitations from the cluster
of relatives, Eagles, Ravens, Sparrows, but he rejected all,
with the excuse that he had to study, keep up the garden

and keep down the fish population in the lake. At first he had railed at what he considered their tactless disregard of his loss. Except for Asia, whose deep blue-grey eyes always saddened whenever he caught her looking at him in the monthly tutorial sessions. But that attitude was difficult to maintain when, empathic as he was, he sensed a supportive presence when the black moments descended on him. Never the same person, and never an intrusive one, but someone *there* when something sharpened the pain of his loss. Damia was most often *there*, or his father; once it was his grandmother, several times Elizara, particularly at the beginning; but mostly his great-grandmother Isthia, or his aunt Besseva, supplied the solace. Once he was sure it was Asia who reached him one very black night, but then definitely the presence was his grandmother. He could not avoid knowing how deeply they were willing to share his pain, his sense of loss—especially when their thoughts became inadvertently specific in their own personal experiences with loss and grief. While he was left to himself to heal, he was never truly *alone* and that, all by itself, was the greatest balm.

Then, about six weeks after his installation in the cottage, either Isthia or Besseva—both women insisted he drop the familial titles—started taking him out to dinner and an evening's company. At first he suspected some sort of "kind" conspiracy when he noticed no 'Dinis present but his female relations, having so many homes to choose from, adroitly picked those which had no Mrdini associations. He often rode with Asia to her house because she'd listen to him sounding off on engineering theories. She often had some very adroit suggestions.

"Why don't you speak out at the tutorials? Anyone would think you were just being tolerated in the class?" he asked one day when she startled him with her grasp of jo-junctions.

"Oh," and she waved her free hand nervously, "I might be wrong and then they'd all laugh at me."

"You haven't been wrong once with me," Rojer said, annoyed at her diffidence.

"Yes, but you're different from everyone else in my family," she replied. "You listen to me."

Rojer kept his annoyance to himself, remembering all too well how much of a bully Roddie had been: probably the reason his sister wouldn't speak up for herself.

"Would you care for a fish dinner? Say tomorrow night?" he asked her several weeks later. "Only," and he grinned broadly at her, "you have to catch your own fish."

She had a rippling kind of laugh and, rather than send her scuttling back into herself, he grinned back.

"I am, however, a very good cook so you don't have to cook it."

"I really ought to study the quantums . . ." she said, already retreating from that moment of amusement.

"So do I. We'll make it a work evening: catch fish, eat fish and discuss quantums while we eat."

He knew Asia was a T-4—she'd been tested—but it didn't hurt to reinforce her and he was deft enough to do so. Like so many Denebians, she was lackadaisical about honing the ability she had. That made it all the easier for him to make a few adjustments, to help her think better of herself.

"You do understand the quantums better than I do . . ."

"We'll find out whether or not I do tomorrow. Right? Gotta get on home now," he said, as they came to her turn-off. He kicked his pony, Koto, into a lope and waved one hand in an airy farewell.

They got together once or twice during the next few

weeks. By then his studies had begun to intrigue him into making voluntary forays into the various aspects of spatial engineering. Such problems were the best meat to feed a healing mind. Many Ravens had been of an engineering bent and Rojer had caught his share of it, as well as a keen sense of spatial relationships. The math was soothing, too, and, over the next four months, he advanced as fast as the computer Teach would let him. When he and Asia shared tutorials, he realized that her grasp of the fundamentals was as firm as his own, because she would volunteer answers if he was the only other student present.

Some days, when he had worked to total mental fugue, his great-grandmother would suddenly require some item of hers from the cottage and he'd have to ride Koto to wherever she was. He knew, and she knew that he knew, that either of them could have 'ported the item to her if she needed it urgently but they both knew he was the better for the exercise. He submitted to her careful bullying with good grace. Isthia never had cause to call him a cocky boy and she approved of his friendship with Asia.

But, oh, in the night, how he missed the feel of warm 'Dini bodies snuggled against his. And oh, how often he was about to ask Gil's opinion or share a wry notion with Kat. He'd still wake to find his pillow damp but Isthia insisted that tears were well spent.

I'm over five times your age, Rojer Lyon, and I still cry! Isthia had told him rather forcefully the first time he protested that he was too old for weeping.

It gave him a headache but he'd usually feel better inside.

Then there was the morning when Jeran required help to bring in a large ship of Mrdini specialists who wanted to prowl through all the bits and pieces that Denebians had found of the original two Hive scout ships. As Jeran had no 'Dini language skills, Rojer had to perform the landing courtesies. That gave him his first contact since the tragedy and, to his surprise, he slipped easily into the required formalities of body and language. Then, too, these were 'Dinis he'd never met before nor would be likely to meet again so there was no real personal involvement.

Isthia had been right, Rojer decided on his return home. Time did heal. He recognized that he had taken one more large step out of mourning. He began to spend more time with Asia and managed to teach her to fry her own fish without burning it.

Rojer? His uncle Jeran's voice was unmistakable. *'Port yourself here.*

Rojer had also learned over the last year not to expect explanations from Jeran, so he saved the problem he was working on the Engineering Teach and checked to see if his clothes were clean enough for a Tower appearance. He'd depilated his face that morning and had had a recent trim, though today's scrutiny in the mirror made him realize that the Gwyn silver lock seemed to have broadened. Finger-combing it back from his forehead, he exhaled a deep breath and 'ported himself to the plascrete apron at the foot of the Deneb City Tower.

It was as well he picked the spot he did, for there were quite a few vehicles parked just beyond him, and several of the ubiquitous Denebian ponies in the turn-out field. He wondered what was up.

By the time he had assessed the population of the large Tower room and "felt" the agitated presence of his cousin, Asia Eagle, he decided that today was Test Day for the several engineering students of Deneb City. He took the Tower steps three at a time. Jeran welcomed his breathless nephew with a solemn nod—his uncle could be more methody than his father ever was—and pointed to the one free workstation. There were six, back to back and arranged so no one could see into another. Asia was in the workstation opposite him. He gave her an encouraging grin because her complexion had an odd green tinge to it.

"Maybe he shouldn't have sprung the test on you so suddenly?" he whispered as he sat down.

"He *knows* how I'd fret," Asia said, looking sicker than ever.

"You'll do grand, Asia. You're faster'n'me in jojunctions and quantums."

She cast him a dire look. "No one's faster'n you at quantums, Ro . . ."

NO TALKING! "Of any kind," Jeran added aloud. "I'm the monitor."

Asia made a sorrowful grimace.

"Your stations will display the test questions in precisely one minute four seconds. Two hours are allowed for the first section, to be followed by a break of fifteen minutes during which you may move about or relieve yourselves. There are four papers, with a half-hour break for lunch. You may, of course, leave the test station whenever a paper is finished." A mixture of groans and guffaws met that statement. Jeran permitted a small smile. "It has been known to happen. Is everyone prepared?" Deeper groans greeted that query.

The dark screen before Rojer suddenly lit and the initial page of the first paper presented him with a problem he *knew* he could answer easily. That gave him considerable self-confidence. He'd show them all . . .

"There's no way I've passed," Rojer heard Asia groan in a tone of abject defeat at the end of the examination day.

"Don't come on like that with me, Asia," he said as sternly as he dared. Even with him, she'd sometimes retreat into a silent unresisting victim. "I've been working with you too long. I know your abilities. And I won't have you belittling yourself." He did a little "tinkering" to encourage more optimism. "There wasn't a single problem we haven't gone over and you know all the structural ones because we've gone over them together. So, we'll just wait and see if I failed, too."

Shocked out of her self-denigration, her ripple of laugh bubbled up, slightly hysterical with disbelief.

"You? Fail? Rojer, you couldn't!"

"Since I know as much as you know, then you couldn't either. Or we both did. Pick your choice!" he added airily, grinning. Somehow he could usually make her smile back at him. It was a tired and tentative effort on her part, but it was a smile.

He gave his head a shake to clear the tension of a long day's concentration and exhaled sharply. He really didn't think he'd done too badly, so there was no way she had. Certainly not on the spatial equations and the jo-junctions. They'd been snaps. He'd seen Commander Metrios work them often enough while on the *Genesee* . . .

He pushed himself back from the workstation, compressing his lips. He hadn't thought of Gil or Kat all day—even at the lunch break when they'd all been exchanging complaints about the severity of the testing.

That is as well, Rojer, for you must move on now, he heard Jeran say softly, and not because there was anyone who would listen but because Jeran wanted to convey more than sympathy and approval. "Softly" expressed such multiples better.

"You're dismissed now, candidates," Jeran said out loud. "The results will be tabulated and sent to your personal terminals later this evening. You've been diligent and I am certain that all who should qualify will."

"He says that every year," murmured one of the boys Rojer did not know.

"Rojer," Jeran went on, though he surely had heard the cynical remark, "Raini asked if you'd care to stop by before you leave the City."

Rojer grinned at the implied invitation to dinner. Jeran's wife was an extremely good cook and tonight would be one when he'd appreciate having a meal he didn't have to prepare. He could even put up with the proximity of his cousin Barry's 'Dinis.

Jeran also caught that and nodded once again, his eyes so like grandmother Rowan's, brighter with approval.

"Not the fatted calf, but that casserole you're so fond of," Jeran said, after the others had departed. He was closing down the station, switching the messaging system to his house unit.

"Can I help?" Rojer asked.

"This doesn't take long. Get a breath of fresh air, lad," Jeran said and gestured for his nephew to leave.

Just as Rojer reached the bottom of the stairs, he was astonished to hear the generators turn on.

Find yourself a carrier, Rojer, a voice told him. *You have five minutes to gather up any things you need from the cottage. Mother'll send on the leftovers under your bed.*

Granddad?

Speaking as such, let me congratulate you on the high scores you achieved on your exams. Honors, even. There was a chuckle. *Speaking as Earth Prime, you're to get your lazy butt to the Mars Moon Base. The refugee ship has just now assumed its assigned geosynchronous orbit and the technicians are thronging to get inside it. High*

Council has insisted that I assign Primes to assist in this venture into alien territory.

Father, Jeran interjected, *Rojer's had an exhausting day. And you know perfectly well that we Primes can't bear proximity to Hiver metals. The reaction on a tired mind will be all the more intense. . . .*

Jeran, you fuss more than your grandmother over the boy. And it's Rojer's choice. Care to come?

Suddenly mental fatigue vanished as the adrenaline of challenge swept through Rojer. Even the Moon Base had food dispensers. And sleep? At this moment?

I got honors, Granddad! If he had, then Asia had.

High enough to make Xexo impossible, according to your mother, and certainly Earth Prime wants one of his own there to keep an eye on things. You won't be required to go "in" the vessel: just maneuver lights and rescue those who step into Hiver tubes.

Rojer wasn't certain if it was making Xexo proud or the challenge of investigating, even at a remote distance, the undamaged Hive sphere, that was causing his elation.

Hell, Granddad, I could even manage going inside it—if I didn't have to stay too long, Rojer replied.

Then move it, lad, or the post'll have to go to someone else.

Granddad, did Asia Eagle pass?

Asia Eagle? There was a pause. *Yes. But don't waste time.*

Rojer did not consider it a waste of time to try to give Asia that reassuring news but when he tried to reach her mind with the good news, she'd closed up tight as a pod in a misery of anxiety. Just like her, the silly clunch! She'd know soon enough and he'd tease her—gently—about her lack of confidence. Then he focused his mind on his room in Isthia's cottage and started 'porting tapes, disks, oddments, belatedly remembering to snatch a carisak into which he dumped these belongings.

You'll need at least one change of clothing, lad, Jeran said with an amused snort and himself plucked several items of clothing from the cottage, more neatly folded than Rojer had left them. These were added to the carisak.

Closing it, Rojer sprinted for the nearest single personnel carrier. As he stretched himself out on the narrow couch inside, he reached out a long arm to haul the lid down. He heard a brief second thump and grinned that his uncle bothered to check that the latches had caught. So methody of him!

Please thank Raini for me, Jeran. I'm sure I won't eat as well . . .

Good luck, Rojer, the brisk kindly voice of his great-grandmother cut in.

Thanks for ev . . . and then Rojer felt the indefinable sensation that told the experienced traveling Talent that he was no longer where he had just been. He heard a chuckle.

Granddad? Now I'd call that cocky!

Would you? And his grandfather's chuckle renewed with a certain pleased edge to it.

"Okay in there, sir?" a slightly less confident voice asked.

"Fine!"

The hatch opened to reveal a double domed darkness, well sprinkled with stars, but Rojer was too familiar with Callisto to believe that's where he'd been 'ported. He sat up and saw the naval rating peering in at him.

"Rojer . . ."

Prime . . . his grandfather corrected him firmly.

". . . Lyon, Prime. Am I expected?"

"Yes, sir, you are, sir."

Rojer grimaced a bit at the "sirring" since it evoked

memories which still caused him to wince. He hitched himself out of the carrier, slung the carisak over his shoulder and gestured for the rating to lead the way.

As he came round the carrier on his way to the air lock that joined the carrier depot with the gigantic Moon Base facility, he stopped abruptly. There, above him, half-lit by Sol, was the complete sphere of the refugee ship he was here to explore. She was appropriately equipped with regulation buoy lights.

"She's a beauty, sir, even for an alien craft," the rating said with a odd ring of pride in his voice. "We were lucky to snag her to Mars Phobos Base even if now there's as many 'Dinis here as there would be if she'd been sent to one of theirs."

" 'Dinis bother you?" Rojer asked, bridling at the hint of intolerance in the rating's tone.

"Me, sir? No, sir," was the almost startled reply as they entered the first of several lift shafts on the way to their destination. "Cute little bu . . . beggars, most of 'em. Better manners'n some I could name not too far from here. To starboard now, sir,"

A quick scan of the rating's mind showed Rojer that the man was honest enough—so long as he was not required to be much in their company.

"Don't they keep that Hiver queen here?"

The rating visibly flinched and shot Rojer a nervous look. "No, she's down on Earth's Moon Base. Heinlein Buildings. No way she or anything she can make out of her eggs can get out of *that* place."

"Oh? Has she hatched more of the larvae?" Surely someone would have mentioned it to him, Rojer thought, if the matter had been noteworthy.

"A couple of oddies. Small scuttling things," and the rating gave a snort of disdain. "Vents got checked again, thinking she might be trying to send 'em outside. No way she can!" The man had pride in his service's security measures.

As they traversed several corridors and took one more long ride upwards, Rojer wondered how soon he could wangle a chance to get down to the Moon and observe her. If, as the experts were now fairly certain, the queens controlled all ship functions, he ought to see her for himself as well as the attendants and other varieties she had finally allowed to hatch. As far as he knew, his cousin Rhodri was still on duty there.

"Here you are, sir," the rating said, stopping by a door and pointing to a palm-pad. "If you'll just do the necessary . . ."

Rojer obliged by placing his hand on the pad and felt the tingle that registered the quarters to his imprint. Then the door whooshed open on a good-sized, attractively furnished lounge area: a good few notches above the usual naval base interiors. Peering about, he saw that he also had separate sleeping and sanitary rooms. The rating was more concerned that he know how to operate the internal com unit, where emergency life support equipment was stored and which numbers to dial for which services. He had no sooner finished this briefing than the com unit blinked a message light.

"I'll leave you to it, sir," the rating said and, with another smart salute, left.

Rojer depressed the "deliver" button. A mellifluous voice—much kinder to the ear than the usual "service" computer voice—informed him that Commandant Enarit del Falco would like to see him as soon as he was settled. A directional node dropped out of the message slot.

Rojer checked the digital on the wall and decided, as he reset his wrist unit to the local time, that "as soon as

he was settled" included attending to the rumbling in his
guts. It was mid-morning here and he was far too hungry
to wait till lunchtime.

The dispenser unit was standard Navy; the menu that
scrolled past Rojer's incredulous eyes was anything but.
Delighted, Rojer watched long enough to discover many
favorite and esoteric dishes before he ordered the most unusual item he saw—a high protein described as "genuine
beefalo steak" which tasted succulent enough to *be* genuine. *Then* he contacted the commandant's office that he
was now settled in.

Donning the button which had been forwarded by pneu-
matic slot to him, he let it guide him through the maze of
corridors and lifts. He knew that the Phobos Moon Base
was as many levels deep in solid lunar rock as above it
and equally as wide. He figured by the upward progress on
which the rating had led him that he was housed in "exec-
utive territory" but he made another upwardly mobile short
journey to an even more prestigious level, encountering
more and more officers of high rank as he progressed—
inward now, he thought. Though he was an obvious civilian, he was more often accorded a salute than a smile.
Then, as he turned to a set of wide double doors, the node
informed him that he had arrived.

The commandant's suite of offices was imposing—on a
par with his grandfather's level of the Blundell Cube. He
sensed many minds not far away and wondered if stopping
to eat a meal had made him late for an important meeting.
The handprint pad was conspicuous enough to suggest that
everyone put his hand there, so he did. One leaf to the
door swung inward to a huge but empty foyer, walls and
ceilings impressively decorated with naval ships, sea and
space, down the ages.

Damn, Rojer thought, *I should have made some attempt*

to find out this commandant's status in the table of Alliance organization.

He's not quite as important as Grandfather, said a very welcome voice, *but he thinks he is.*

Where are you, Thian? Rojer looked at the many doors leading off this foyer.

Come now, brother, surely that's elementary!

Rojer chuckled and confidently turned to the right-hand one of two double-doored entries. It opened to a huge, well-populated "operations" area, dominated by screens wrapped round the walls, with horizontal plotting boards at various locations on the floor space and two transparent spheres, one of which was fitted out with some internal components. All around the room workstations were occupied and equations and displays flashed their messages to those seated before them. He spotted five with engineering configurations. The room was full of Humans . . . and Mrdinis . . . and no one paid his arrival any attention whatever.

Hi there, bro, said Thian, his voice buoyant with cheerful welcome. *Did you like the beefalo? Smart of you to eat while you had the chance, because the admiral is unlikely to take into consideration that you've done a full day's work already.*

Once his brother began speaking, Rojer located him at the far end of the chamber in a group of evidently high-ranking naval officers, to judge by their static positions and somber expressions. About them, like satellites, other uniformed personnel hovered, either busily checking notepads or awaiting assignment.

As Rojer made his way toward his tall, self-assured brother, he noted the obvious fact that, while Thian wore a Navy shipsuit, there was an FT&T insignia on his shoulder and the Prime tab on his collar. He also thought his brother looked a lot older than he had when they had last met. Whenever that was. Ah, yes, when Laria had come home for her birthday. There were subtle changes in his older brother's face and bearing.

Watch the one who's jabbering at me, Thian added as Rojer made his way across the cavernous room, although Thian gave every outward appearance of total concentration on what was being said to him by a shorter, black-haired man with a strangely taciturn face. *If Prtglm had had the sense to get Human support to destroy Xh-33, Admiral Enarit del Falco, our base commandant, is the man who'd've given it and rejoiced. Del Falco is also extremely shrewd, intelligent and capable. There isn't a thing that happens on this Base that he doesn't know about within seconds. He's got absolutely no Talent so we're safe to say all the things we want right in front of his face. On the other hand, he's got a natural shield as impregnable as a Hive sphere, which is very inconvenient. Even Granddad and Grandmother can't winkle in.*

The admiral turned slightly just then and Rojer gave an inadvertent shudder at the closed face and took the final steps to his brother under the admiral's scrutiny.

"Ah, Admiral, speaking of the devil . . ." Thian said, as if he'd just noticed his brother's arrival. He raised one arm which he then placed about Rojer's shoulders, squeezing his hand in welcome. And continued a mental briefing while he effected the introductions. "Here's Prime Rojer Gwyn-Lyon, Eng. Mec., top honors—*Yes, you did get top honors today, which is exactly why you got snatched from the quiet of Deneb and Grandma's cottage and thrust into this situation without a chance for a day's rest*—who's assigned along with me to help you penetrate the interior of the Refugee—*That's her official designation, bro. Don't let his manner get under your skin, Roj. He tries that one on everybody, even Granddad and Grandmother. Got nowhere with them so we have to keep up the family tradition. He doesn't like Talents but he needs the help only we can give him. Fortunately both you and I are independent of his authority even if we are assigned to help.* Good to see you, bro." And Thian dropped his arm, smiling down at the Admiral in his charismatic way, much as their grandfather might have done in a similar situation.

Having Thian in physical and mental support with so much coming at him all of a sudden made all the difference. So Rojer could smile, too, summoning up what Isthia had called the deplorable tendency of her male relatives to charm as easily as they breathed. Adopting a casual confidence, he inclined his head courteously to del Falco. The commandant did not offer his hand to the young Talent. Instead del Falco gave him such a piercing stare—he had the sort of large black eye that appears to see through to the soul—that Rojer was very glad of his brother's warning.

"Privilege to be aboard, Admiral del Falco."

"I thought you were younger than your brother."

"We're not far apart age-wise, sir," Rojer replied.

Perfect response, Roj. He hasn't had time to read your transcript because we had to wait to see if you passed the exams before we could snatch you here. The team that's going on board the Refugee requires stiff qualifications. You got more than some, less than most. He won't take long to assess you. He's got an info-plant. And he's accessing your file right now. His eyes flicker when he's listening to it. Updates on demand. Don't know why he isn't schizo. Oh, and our birth years are not *given. Granddad's had dealings with this bird. Just as well you don't* look *seventeen.* That last was said in a rueful tone, acknowledging Rojer's bereavement and its tragic circumstances, and accompanied by an affectionate mental hug. *Steady on. He's coming up with "the look"!*

The admiral was, and in spite of Thian's warning Rojer very nearly rocked back on his heels at the intensity of that black and penetrating gaze. So he smiled as equably as he could until del Falco broke the eye contact, having evidently heard sufficient from his info-plant to place Rojer in the pertinent category.

'Dini coming up behind you, Roj! his brother said, his tone colored with apprehension.

So Rojer had just enough warning to be prepared when a 'Dini voice spoke.

"RJR LN, YOU WILL NOT MIND TO WORK WITH GREYS?"

One of the good guys, Thian added, smiling at the newcomer.

So Rojer kept the smile on his face as he turned and almost committed a solecism as he began to drop his eyes to the usual 'Dini height. But the 'Dini who had spoken was nearly as tall as Rojer. And not at all like the grey Prtglm.

"GREY HAS ALWAYS BEEN AN EXCELLENT COLOR," Rojer said, using the body language that expressed honor at being in its company while inclining from the waist with the bow deserved by a 'Dini of such size. The memory of Prtglm, or its color, no longer had the power to distress him. "WHAT NAME, PLEASE, IS ONE TO USE IN ADDRESS?"

"THIS ONE IS KNOWN AS GLMTML."

"I'm glad that you two Primes have the chance to meet Glmtml," the admiral said, observing the exchange. "It leads the Mrdini team that's going to reveal Refugee's secrets for us." A smile that was not a smile but nearly a threat spread his lips just slightly. "Prime Lyon has just arrived, Glmtml, so he hasn't been briefed. . . ."

"Not that Rojer needs it," Thian said in a bland tone and a shrug of his shoulders. "Straight transfers of carriers to the Refugee airlock, and then we act as guiding lights. And we rescue when required. You know how many tubes a Hiver ship has!"

Rojer nodded solemnly while the admiral, unaccustomed to being interrupted, hesitated for one beat before smoothly continuing. ". . . Then there is no further need for delay, is there?" He turned to Glmtml. "Your team is now assembled for transfer?"

"All are," Glmtml said, deferentially switching to Basic, since the admiral apparently was not fluent in 'Dini.

"Then let us proceed with Operation Illuminate," and the admiral turned his basilisk stare on the two Talents. He snapped his fingers behind his back and one of the waiting ensigns leapt forward.

The very gesture raised Rojer's hackles. Maybe an admiral had prerogatives a space captain didn't, but the implied absolute obedience to such a discourteous summons rankled.

Why do you think I enjoy baiting him so much, Roj? Thian said.

"Escort the Primes to their ready room, Ensign."

"No need for such ceremony, Admiral," Thian replied. "I know where we're stationed," and he shot Rojer a mental picture of where they were going—a small room with three Tower couches. The room already had one occupant.

More surprises, Thian?

Thian grinned. *This evaluation operation is going to take all three of us and wish we were more. Let's go. I love 'porting away from him. He hates it and there's not a thing he can do about it since 'porting expedites troop movement.* "My compliments and best wishes, Glmtml."

Rojer had only time for a similar courtesy before his brother 'ported away. He followed.

That admiral had better watch himself, said the very

pretty occupant of the room as Rojer and Thian appeared. *He has female officers. Why do I have to creep about the place like an anathema, Thian?*

"I told you that you should flaunt yourself, Flavia. This is, obviously, my brother Rojer, who will remember his manners when he stops gawking at you."

Completely surprised by the sight of such a lovely woman, Rojer willingly held out his hand to touch hers. Green/minty/velvet. Flavia smiled quite gently back at him and then turned with a businesslike attitude to Thian.

"They've got the right sort of beams now, and I think every single marine and Mrdini is festooned with more light cells than Noel trees," she said as she slipped gracefully onto her couch.

Thian directed Rojer's attention to the huge transparent three-dimensional screen that dominated the wall facing their couches. At the point which Rojer also identified as the main hangar deck of the Refugee, there were three colored globes: blue, green and yellow. Concentrating briefly on that area, Rojer also sensed a large number of Humans and 'Dinis.

"Rojer, I'm supposedly in nominal charge of our part in this operation," Thian said. "That board'll light up with each centimeter we cover so we'll know where we've been. I know you had a little look round the Refugee . . ."

"Through a glass darkly, bro, since the inside was still fogged with gas . . ."

"Since you're so full of engineering honors, you get to hunt for the engine room . . ."

"I found it before—I think."

"In the southern hemisphere, yes? Good. My priority is the life-support system which the boffins think might surround the central axis."

"Are they suited up?" Rojer asked.

"No, the Navy flooded the ship with enough oxygen to fill a volume of enclosed space equal to the size of the Great Sphere, and there's an auxiliary system as backup stuck off in the corner of the hangar. Plus, everyone's packing an emergency breather. The sooner we get the integral life-support system going, the better. The other priority for you is finding out what sort of fuel the Hivers use that'd also be stored in the southern hemisphere of the ship. Flavia," and Thian grinned at the girl, "is going to penetrate into the queens' quarters and we might need you to switch there, too, Rojer, to figure out how to turn the power on. Mostly we gotta keep track of people who get into trouble, slipping off into tunnels and getting stuck in the small tubes."

"Like you did on the Great Sphere, huh?"

Thian gave his brother a mock scowl. "*I* was following orders when I found the larvae."

"Still comes down to baby-sitting," Rojer said with a spurious groan.

"I wouldn't let any of the marines hear you put it like that, Rojer," Flavia said in mock warning.

"Marines can break legs just like anyone else," Rojer replied flippantly.

"Not with this admiral," Thian said tartly. "Everybody comfortable? Good, then," and he pointed to the red light blinking on the com unit, "the boffins are all loaded. Let's hoist 'em up there."

Rojer turned his attention then to three large carriers, each filled with excited men and Mrdinis, cradled and waiting to be 'ported up to the ship.

"Okay?" Thian said, looking from one side to the other.

Flavia and Rojer both nodded and simultaneously the three Primes lifted the carriers and deposited them in a neat line on the Refugee's hangar deck where once the deadly Hiver scout ships had been housed.

What'n'ell is that? A smell or an emanation? The voice was female, the tone disgusted and uneasy.

"They've sent Talents up there?" Flavia asked in surprised indignation.

"Admiral doesn't believe in the sting-pzzt," Thian said, "although I explained it quite carefully and so did Granddad and Grandmother."

"So who's the speaker? Can we reassure her?" Flavia asked.

Thian had closed his eyes briefly. "I think that's Lieutenant Commander Semirame Kloo, head of the naval exploration team. According to her file, she's a T-5 sender, with little or no training. She opted for a place in the Naval Academy."

"So we don't know if she can receive?" Rojer asked.

Commander Kloo?

Huh? Who?

Primo Thian speaking. You are experiencing what we Talents call the "sting-pzzt" of Hive metal.

That wasn't in my briefing. She sounded both relieved and annoyed.

I don't believe the admiral accepts this reaction as valid. As you are currently surrounded by Hive metal, you'll be pleased to know that such a reaction confirms the possession of latent Talent.

Thanks! was the droll response.

Anyone else in your team seem affected in a similar fashion?

So far I'm the only one complaining, Prime Lyon, and her tone was resigned.

Thian, please, Rame.

*How'd you know my nickname? Nemmind. Of course,
you would. How do I get rid of this sting-pzzt sensation?
Or reduce its effect somehow or other. It's rather . . . dis-
concerting.*

*It won't hurt you but continued exposure might make
you rather short-tempered.*

*Ha! I've already got that reputation so now I've a good
reason. So long as it doesn't bite me, I'll just get on with
the job. Shall we?*

*My brother, Rojer, is your guide, Rame. He can dampen
the reaction to some extent. Let him know if you notice
anyone else affected or if it begins to affect your judgment.*

*Thanks. Hey! That's better. And hey, I didn't know I
could receive.*

Rojer took over. *Primes can manage two-way communications with much lower than a T-5, Rame. Now, I've ig-
nited my guide globe and, if you'll just have your group
follow it, we'll begin Operation Illuminate on its way to
the engine room.*

*I've got enough ladders to climb us back down to Mars.
And hey, this beats staying on the com button.* Rojer could
almost see her grin. *Let's move it,* and by the additional
depth to her tone, they knew she was speaking aloud to
her detail. *Follow the yellow-bright light! Forries, you
take left, Maumu, take right and plant those cells . . .
whoops, just lost Maumu down a tube. Oh, hey, that's
great!*

Rojer retrieved the faller, who was as shaken by the unexpected and almost instantaneous rescue as he was by an
equally unexpected descent.

Well, slap a light beside the damned tube, sailor, was
Rame's testy comment. *And if you were stopped before
you hit the bottom, be glad we've got the Talents on our
tails. Beg pardon, lighting our way!*

As the various teams proceeded, the sphere slowly filled with details. Oval tunnels of varying circumferences riddled the periphery and evidently provided access for Hiver specialist life forms from one area to another. Few were comfortable for those exploring them but gradually, over the next week, a network in each quadrant and hemisphere began to emerge.

Rojer found the engine room and the incredible clutter of components that, when activated, gave Refugee its propulsion. Fuel was discovered in sealed tanks, each fed by intricate coils into one section of the vast engine mass. More powerful light units were requested by those who had had a harrowing trip down smooth, cramped oval tunnels. The engine room was not all that spacious either and seemed to be accessed by conduits much too small for either Human or 'Dini bodies.

"A combinant fuel," was one expert's immediate theory.

"Then why is the mixture apparently run over that large crystalline object so carefully bracketed in the housing?"

Opaque pipes around the chamber suggested some sort of lighting: a theory that was supported by the fact that the various feed lines and coils were color-coded. To prove it correct, the sphere's power would need to be on.

"You'd have to be an acrobat to service this bloody affair," said a propulsion specialist from Earth. He was attempting to get on top of the main unit for a better perspective.

Several fascinating boards, of a control type, were discovered at floor level. They were segmented into different colors and were touch-controlled. Another few sections covered one of the lower ceilings of the large oval chamber. Judiciously removing some of the floor plates showed that these panels led directly either to the engine mass or the fuel tanks. Getting diagnostic machinery into the cramped engine room required both Rojer's assistance and the removal of nearly a dozen specialists. "Removing" them back to the main cargo bay where food was being served and remote screens had been sited did much to reduce their disappointment and anger at not being right on the scene.

Flavia's group penetrated rather more easily than expected to the twelve queen quarters which formed a circle around the inner axis of the ship. Four of the twelve were larger than the others, suggesting that there was some order of precedence among the queens. Once again, controls were situated in awkward—for Human and Mrdini—positions: depending from ceilings, angled up from the floors and in the narrow ends of the oval-shaped quarters.

"No one's found the starting button yet," Rojer remarked to his companions. He was halfway to canceling a random thought as too ridiculous when his brother started to laugh.

"They may yet have to do just that, Roj."

"Do what?" Flavia demanded, half turning her head in their direction while she kept most of her attention on her work.

We've got a queen, Thian said softly. *Presumably she'd know how to start up . . .*

Flavia's eyes went round. *Let her aboard that ship?*

She can't take it anywhere but if all the king's horses and all the king's men can't figure out how to turn the power on . . . Thian said and shrugged without adding the obvious conclusion.

"Oh!" Flavia mulled that problem over. "Surely someone . . ."

"Hope so!" Rojer said but he couldn't be very encouraging as he watched his group clambering over the machinery, following colored leads, attempting to fathom the unusual composition of the Hive drive. It was apparently much more efficient than it looked.

There were only so many viable forms of space drive, or so Humans and Mrdini were agreed. Perhaps they should have tried to capture one of the Xh-33 scouts or shuttles when they had the chance. But, according to what Rojer had been told, that had been impossible as well as unlikely. The kidnap of Refugee had been thought to be enough of a coup as well as a solution.

Wasn't this more of an academic exercise anyway, Rojer wondered. They didn't really need to know how the Hive ship worked, or who did what where and when. The Navy did need to discover exactly where to aim what sort of missiles to destroy a Hive ship, or render it helpless.

Thian had located the life-support area, just above the queens' level. The gas had destroyed whatever plant types generated oxygen although emergency supplies in tanks were carefully racked in adjacent storage space. Thian's second find was the round cases of foodstuffs: all color-coded, though whatever glyphs the spheres bore were undecipherable. The semantic experts were delighted with this much to work on. The ship seemed oddly devoid of signs of any type, though illumination proved that certain colors must be recognizable to various queen workers. Why else would they bother coloring anything?

One of the 'Dini xenobiologists suggested that a sample of each of the food cases be sent to the Heinlein Base. The queen had been quiescent far too long and the theory was that she might be missing some vital nutritional elements. Surely that could be remedied by supplying her with home-grown sustenance.

On the main schematic board, tubes, halls, oval access conduits, pipes and tunnels were appropriately colored to match the originals. Save for the irising air locks, hangar and cargo bays, there were no doors.

There didn't seem to be "crew" quarters either but there were more of the larvae tubes, all spiking out from the various queen quarters, similar to the ones Thian and Lieutenant Auster-Kiely had discovered. Empty, of course.

After two full watches of exploration—and the kind of vigilance required of the three Primes—Thian sent a message to Admiral del Falco that the Primes were going off duty.

"Don't let him argue you out of it, Thian," Rojer said, the inexorable fatigue of nearly thirty hours' of intense activity making itself felt in his mind and bones. "I'm bushed."

"That is quite obvious," Flavia said, but she spoke with such kind concern that Rojer couldn't resent it. She swung her legs to the side of her couch. "They've more than enough to keep them going with the main objectives found. *They* have enough personnel to swap round but we don't have that option. I'm quite hungry! Those sandwiches they sent up—oh, hours ago now—have left a larger gap."

When contacted, the Admiral grunted and frowned. "And what happens if there is an emergency requiring a Prime's abilities? Had you thought of that?"

"Indeed we have: Earth Prime has delegated a capable T-2 for such duty," and right on cue, someone rapped on the door. "Here is Clancy Sparrow now."

Another cousin? Rojer asked in amazement just as the door to their ready room slid open.

"I know. I keep trying to live it down," Clancy replied with a grin which widened appreciatively when he turned to Flavia. "Boy, you guys lit the great white way!" He swallowed then, eyes rounding in concern. "Let's just hope I don't get more than one emergency at a time with such an area to cover."

Thian laughed and gestured for Clancy to take his couch. "Call on Beva Margellis if you do get pushed. She's a T-3 Healer but she can 'port independently or in merge. You met Beva, didn't you, during the briefing?"

"Yup, got her touch. See you. And, hey, Roj, congratulations."

So much had happened that day that Rojer couldn't remember why Clancy would be congratulating him.

"Oh, yeah, thanks. How did Asia do?"

Clancy grinned. "Li'l coz was only two points below you!"

"I told her she'd passed. Asia's not stupid!"

"Oh, hey, I know it," Clancy said, recoiling from Rojer's fervent partisanship. "We all know it back home on Deneb. We just can't seem to get *her* to know it."

"Go to bed, Roj," Thian said, and Rojer wasted no more time, using the last of his energy to 'port himself to his quarters. He took time for a shower and a nutrient drink. When he gratefully stretched out on the excellent and comfortable bed, he had time for one guilty thought: he'd've had plenty of room for Gil and Kat in with him.

"Those are emergency repair ways and it's the scuttling critters that were used for 'em," Thian was saying the next day when Rojer reported for duty. He was speaking on screen to a scowling, grizzled naval officer with commander tabs on his collar. "If you've plumbed 'em with remotes, that's the best that's available. Doesn't that help? Or do you want to borrow one of the scuttlers the queen hatched?"

Hi, Roj! Boy, do you feel a hundred percent better this afternoon.

You shouldn't have let me sleep so long.
You needed it and we need you alert.

"Permit one of those . . . those vermin . . . into the Refugee?" The commander turned brick red with outrage.

Flavia waggled fingers at Rojer as she lay on her couch, without turning her head about. Rojer could see that she was directing a remote node down one of the narrower tubes.

To judge by the colors that criss-crossed the sphere map, the internal investigation of Refugee was proceeding well.

"The 'vermin,' Commander, were designed to maneuver in those spaces as mobile repair units. The wiring seems to be coded by an imbedded design, since there wouldn't be sufficient light to see color. Since neither Humans or 'Dini come in the appropriate size, it was just a suggestion!"

"And totally unacceptable! Totally! You may be a Prime but you're here to do just one job. Now stick to that!"

"As a Prime, let me remind you, sir, that I would be in complete control of the critter," Thian replied and Rojer had no trouble 'pathing how much Thian enjoyed the present exchange.

No one's found the power switch, Flavia said, her mind alive with laughter though her expression was serenely polite. *The Navy's having knicker attacks. The 'Dinis are sulking and it's all* our *fault.*

Sipping from his third cup of really fine coffee, Roj sat on his couch to listen to both levels of Thian's conversation. Interesting that his brother had had much the same notion that had occurred to him. The only beings who could operate that ship were those for whom it was designed. For all the consultants, advisers, experts and technicians swarming about in the Refugee, not one of them had the shape, height or digital equipment that was required to power up the ship. No complete investigations could be essayed.

"Just forget that asinine suggestion, Prime, and I'll forget you made it."

Thian shrugged. "As you wish, Commander, but I feel obliged to mention that there would be no risk. The creatures are purpose-built, as it were, and can do no more than they were designed to do—run those small access ways to make necessary repairs."

"Repairs are NOT the problem, Lyon. IF," and the commander's pause was significant, "and when you come up with any more such bright ideas, use the proper channels." The screen went blank.

Flavia then doubled up with a fit of the giggles.

You were marvelous, Thian, she 'pathed, since she was physically incapable of speaking intelligently through her laughter. *Oh, Roj, that man's been impossible since we came on duty. To begin with, he doesn't like Talents and resents having to work with us. And the stupid things he wanted Clancy to do . . . The only one on this watch with any sense is Rame Kloo. SHE thinks we should make a device like the palps of the queen and see if the board can't be activated by using those.*

Pressure-operated? A sequence needed? What? Which?

Thian had turned away from the blank screen, his facial expression one of disgust and frustration.

"Okay, engineer, you got any ideas? I sure would like us Primes to start up that bloody ship of theirs. Hell, we've done *all* the work on it so far, following it, capturing it, stealing it, and bringing it back. Lighting the whole damn thing up so *they* could see where they were going. And now we're supposed to turn it on. *They're* the naval experts. We're just lousy T&Ts." Then Thian let out a long breath and apologized to them for sounding off.

"You got the right, bro," Rojer said and then cocked his head. "You got the right idea, too. Only putting one of the queen's scuttle bugs on the ship isn't going to solve anything. If I remember correctly, Grandmother Rowan was under the distinct impression that the queens gave all the orders so if the scuttle hasn't any orders, it'll just sit there."

Thian regarded his brother, flicked his grey eyes to Flavia and a smile started to curve his lips.

Now, just a minute, Thian, Rojer said with more intensity than he intended, *I got in trouble . . .*

YOU didn't get in trouble, Roj, Thian said; his eyes sparkled with sudden anger as he corrected his brother. *And you had enough smarts to recognize Big Trouble when you saw it. So did Gil and Kat.*

The unexpected reminder brought tears to Rojer's eyes. This was the first time any one in his family had spoken so bluntly about the incident. But Thian was wound up and Rojer forced himself to ignore that painful reminder and concentrate on what his brother was saying.

But I think we all have the same idea. Flavia? She nodded. *I'll clear it with Grandad,* Thian added. *Besides, we'd need his help and Roddie's at the Observatory. But it could be done.*

The Navy'd have apoplexy, Rojer began, although the idea was taking firm root as the only way to many objectives, not the least of which was confounding people like Admiral del Falco who fundamentally did not *like* Talents and made their distrust and hatred as obvious as the commander had.

Okay, Thian, how would we go about it? Rojer asked.

Thian crossed his ankles, dangling them off the side of his couch, his hands clasped between his thighs. *Well, it'd take a fair amount of timing. One, getting Roddie to falsify the recorders in the Observatory so no one knows the queen is gone. Two, we gotta have the queens' chambers on the Refugee cleared of people and right now technicians are crammed into them, each thinking he or she'll find the switch-on. Three, we need the right sort of personnel on duty, both 'Dini and Human, so no one panics when the ship turns on.*

How can we be sure the queen'll cooperate even if we could get her there? Flavia asked.

If you'd been locked up away from all that was familiar to you, and you were suddenly in a ship you could operate, wouldn't you try to escape? Thian asked.

I would, being a Human, Flavia said.

A 'Dini would, too, Rojer said. *But would a Hive queen?*

I think so, Roj, Thian said thoughtfully. *You said they didn't waste any time scramming from Refugee when they were threatened. I think survival is the highest priority of queens.*

But if it takes twelve queens to crew a ship, Flavia put in, *and that's what our experts believe now . . .*

So, if she just stands there as she's been doing, we won't have lost anything, will we? Thian said. *But look how survival-oriented she is—hatching attendants to tend to her needs first, then the tiny ones she obviously hoped would be able to get out of the facility. She hasn't done a thing since they failed. Common sense suggests she'd try.*

And that's all we need her to do, isn't it? Try? Flavia said. *Show us how to start that wretched ship up. Then we can leave this installation and do something more appropriate to our rank and skills.*

Thian and Rojer both regarded Flavia with surprise.

I'm Tower-trained, Flavia said with a touch of asperity, *and while I've certainly enjoyed a break from my usual duties, I do not appreciate being belittled by persons like that commander.* She pursed her lips and regarded the brothers with a slightly defensive expression, as if daring them to reprimand her.

Thian smiled, and Rojer rolled his eyes as his brother soothed Flavia. "Yeah, it could get under your skin. But then, you have every right to be annoyed at the treatment we've been getting. I've been serving on Navy ships so it doesn't bother me as much but that commander's attitude needs adjusting." He winked at Flavia and then Rojer. They'd been reasonably sure that their ready room conversations were being recorded, a standard operating procedure. *So, do we put this bright idea through the proper channels?*

Granddad? What if he doesn't like it? Conflicting emotions which obviously didn't worry Thian at all besieged Rojer. But then Thian . . . Rojer canceled that line of thought.

So, we get our heads handed back to us by one more authority. Thian shrugged. *I think it'd be kind of fun to* try! *Hell's bells, Roj, it was your notion to begin with.*

Yeah, but . . . Then Rojer stopped to ponder the ramifications.

Yeah, but, Thian dared him, *if it's young Engineer Prime Lyon who shows the Navy boffins just how easy it was to determine where to turn the power on . . . It'd shake a lot of people and 'Dinis up and certainly give us Primes a minor triumph.*

I'm game, Flavia said with a laugh, her eyes twinkling as she was caught up by both mischief and a possible triumph. Then her expression sobered. *CAN we transport a Hiver?*

We've never run across anything we couldn't 'port, Thian said, *and both Roj and I have handled some pretty odd packages. Hell's bells, Flavia, you were in with me and Grandmother stealing that sphere. We just steal the queen—for a few minutes. Okay?* And before his fellow conspirators could restrain him, Thian sent a finely tuned message to Earth Prime.

Are you available, Earth Prime?

To you, Thian, always.

We've an idea which needs your clearance, sir, and your help.

Let me have it. When Thian finished the explanation, all three young Primes held their breath throughout the seemingly endless silence from their superior. *As the naval operation seems stymied, obviously an unusual step must be taken to break the impasse. Yours makes more sense than any others I've heard. And certainly poses no danger to anyone. Of course, the queen might not be docile once she realizes where she is. Can you cope with that possibility and be able to restrain her?*

All we'd have to do is 'port her back to Roddie.

But should she start the ship up . . .

Sir, Rojer said, *a ship this size takes time for its engines to warm up to take-off power. We'd have her back in her quarters before she'd get that far in a countdown.*

Look, I'll hedge that possible problem with a little safety net of my own, Jeff Raven said. *I'll contact Roddie myself to see how we organize the . . . ah . . . excursion from his end. I gather she's in one of her immobile states now.*

Lieutenant Rhodri Eagle was only too happy to conspire to "loan" his prisoner to the scheme.

I've kilos of recordings I can set in place. But you are sure *she can't just scuttle out of the queens' quarters and get loose in the ship?*

That possibility's being handled, Thian assured his

cousin. There had been so many minor injuries of personnel falling into tubes, tunnels and crawl-spaces that grills
had been placed over apertures not in use. The ones leading from the queens' quarters could be telekinetically
"locked" down.

*Sort of mean of us, though, isn't it? Giving her false
hope?* Roddie asked, showing an unexpected sympathy for
the Hiver queen.

*Hey, man, you need a change of duty if you're starting
to think like that,* Thian replied.

*Well, you know, maybe I ought to apply for a transfer.
This duty was exciting—for a while. But the glamour has
long since worn off. Any chance of you guys speaking up
for me?* Roddie asked.

*Sure thing. Who to? Earth Prime or your c.o.? What
sort of duty did you have in mind?*

*ANYTHING. I've even learned enough 'Dini to get
along with them!*

*We'll tell you when to switch tapes. Get one picked out
and ready to substitute because we'll have to move fast
when we do.*

Getting a chance to speak privately with Lieutenant
Commander Semirame Kloo might have presented some
problems but she solved that by appearing at their table,
tray in hand, during the next meal break. They had chosen
this end of the officers' mess room because the next table
was empty.

"Can I join you? Or are you off naval types?"

"Why would we be?" Thian said, surprised at her query.

"Baldwin!" she said succinctly, sliding her tray into the
surface and seating herself. "I heard how strong he came
on today, the xenophobic pea-brain. He hates having to
work with mixed crews, and that means you as well as the
'Dinis. He also wants to take all the credit for any progress

made on his watch as he's a little overdue for promotion, you see."

Thian grinned at her. *This mess hall bug-free?*

Rame Kloo rolled her eyes and grinned at Thian.

"Sure is. Whatcha got to say?" While her eyes began to sparkle with curiosity and her body tensed ever so slightly with anticipation, she started on her meal, acting in a perfectly normal manner. "But remember to say something out loud so no one'll wonder why this corner of the room's gone silent."

So Thian began one of the double-talking conversations he was becoming adept at. "Chow's good today and we sure need the break." *We have an idea that we could get the queen to show us how to power up the Refugee.*

"Hmmm, so it is." And Rame chewed with evident relish. *Tell me more, you delightfully devious man!*

All three Talents took turns explaining the plan, sprinkling innocuous comments now and then. When all was made clear, Rame looked wistfully down at her empty plate.

"I know that was a good meal but I've absolutely no recollection of what I ate . . ."

"You nearly choked once . . ." Rojer said, keeping his face straight with an effort.

"And had two coughing fits . . ." Flavia added helpfully.

"But we can do it," Rame said. "Only it will have to be on the next watch. I'm on, so is Glmtml. . . ."

"It'd go along with this?" Thian was surprised.

"Oh, you'd be surprised," and she switched to covert speech, *at what old Glmtml'd do, it's so fed up with some of the brass on this project.* She blotted her lips with the napkin, rose and picked up her tray. "Thanks for the company. Like to do it more often while you're here." *I may need your discreet help in rearranging the duty roster?*

Like having the less cooperative types sent to check out ordnance? She grinned with sheer malevolence. The Refugee had racks of missiles but no launchers set in installations clearly awaiting them: yet another sign of how rushed the Hivers had been to leave their system and its decaying primary.

"Any time," Thian said. "See you around?"

"Yup!" and Semirame Kloo strode confidently toward the disposal slot, slipped in her tray and left the wardroom.

Slightly more than an hour later, Kloo gave a polite rap at the Talents' ready-room door before she slipped quickly inside, a grin plastered on her face, as she flattened herself against the wall.

Got some tinkering for you to do with the duty roster. Gotta get it done in the next five minutes. Can you?

Throw it up in the air and I'll catch, Thian said without moving from his couch.

Rame hesitated a moment, shrugged and tossed a folded piece of film up in the air. It disappeared.

I can have everyone crucial to this operation of yours in position fifteen minutes before this watch ends. Okay? she added.

Couldn't be okayer.

She was gone as smoothly as she'd arrived. Thian spread the film on his thigh and smiled.

Cover for me, will you, Roj, Flavia? I'll have to get myself into the main . . . ah, here. Hmm. That gal's pretty clever. There, that should do it. Roddie?

You rang, coz?

Thian gave him the time.

Uncle Jeff agreed? Ohohohoho! I take back half the things I've said about my illustrious relative, Rhodri Eagle chortled with gleeful anticipation. *If he's going to cover your asses, he'll cover mine, too. Wow! Why is it that you can never brag about the really neat things you've done?*

Because then *they wouldn't be the* neat *things,* Flavia said unexpectedly. "I do believe they have the life-support system on line," she added out loud. "D'you think *sgit* leaves *will* make a difference . . . to the quality of the oxygen, I mean?"

"They do on all the ships I've been on which added *sgit* leaves to their plant banks. And the 'Dinis never have foul air."

"In'trusting," Flavia said, drawling. "Well, it will save the drain on the Moon Base supplies, of course."

Because the Talents were more on a stand-by basis now that the Refugee's interior had been diagrammed, the rest of the watch seemed to drag almost interminably.

My crew's in place, Thian, Rame said. Then over the com unit, "Ah, Prime Thian, this is Lieutenant Commander Kloo. Can you stand by? We're effecting a decontam drill."

"We heard you, loud and clear, Commander. Work away."

Rojer caught a shadow out of the corner of his eye and, turning to investigate, nearly fell off his couch.

Granddad's here, he tried to whisper to Thian.

Thian didn't turn his head but grinned broadly.

Sort of thought you might, sir.

Since I might have to save your asses, as Roddie so inelegantly put it, I thought I might as well be in on the fun.

And as backup, too. Don't you trust us, sir? Thian said, only half in jest.

I trust you all right, Thian. It's that elongated insect that worries me. We know so little about their psychology.

Ready when you are, came Rhodri's cheerful voice.

Your plan. Go ahead, Thian, Jeff Raven said, folding his

arms and standing approximately where Rame had earlier in the watch.

Merge, Roj, Flavia, Thian said.

The three minds linked neatly, just as if this wasn't the first time they'd made such contact. With Thian in the lead, Rojer was more aware of the strength of both minds than he'd been during their more or less solo workings on the Refugee. He was also conscious of another potency which both bolstered and encouraged, yet was not a part of the triple merge.

They had no difficulty finding the Hiver queen where she nestled in her shavings bed, her attendants polishing her body parts and smoothing the fine hairs of her limbs. The sting-pzzt from her was unbearably acute as the Thian merge made contact but the hesitation lasted only that brief second of surprise and then they neatly placed her in the now darkened queens' quarters of the Refugee: in one of the larger chambers.

Somehow Rame had rigged "night" lighting which showed the watchers the queen's form. She had been in a semi-recumbent position in her shavings, but the Merge had placed her upright and she had to adjust her limbs for the standing position. That done, she remained motionless.

Hell's bells, Thian said, *we don't have* days *for you to decide where you are and what to do.*

Stay calm! said the confident watching potency.

Abruptly the queen moved into action with such speed they nearly missed her first movements. Palps reached ceilingward, seeming to slide across the panels. She had also rocked back on one set of nether legs, freeing the front set to dance across the floor panels. Instantly orangey lights came up around the room in the tubes that had been theorized to be Hiver lighting. Next the panels lit, decorated with odd symbols and different shadings.

We got power all over the fucking place, Rame said, in choked amazement. *I'm not sure I can explain this.*

Don't bother.

Oh Lord, engine room's going crazy. Hey, I think this has gone far enough, Thian! Panic colored Rame's tone.

Don't worry, Commander, Jeff Raven said. *This ship's anchored so tight not even full speed forward could break her loose.*

I know the sequence to turn the power on, Rojer said.

I've got the pattern of how she activated everything, Flavia said.

Sorry, gal, your parole just got canceled, Thian said, and the Merge replaced the queen in her prison.

What'd you guys do to her? Rhodri complained. *She's going wild!*

Can't say I blame her, Jeff remarked placidly. *I'd be a bit pissed off, too, if I thought I'd just seen the way home and it disappeared.*

Your decontam drill just finished, Rame, Thian told her. *Queen's back in stir and doing a mad dance.*

Wheeee! But can you start it all up again when we *want you to?* the commander asked, doubt coloring her tone.

Any time we want to.

For all the good that does, Jeff remarked. *Well done, Primes, not an ass in jeopardy. I'll leave you to the fun of explaining it all to the admiral. But I'll be listening, so don't say anything I'll have to apologize for.*

Granddad!

CHAPTER
FIVE

"ADMIRAL, it was a concerted effort," Rojer repeated, an edge on his voice now because he was growing weary of the barrage of naval doubts and, particularly, del Falco's aggressive interrogation. He was sorry that, as the engineer of the three Talents, he had volunteered to answer any technical questions. "Any" had turned into an incredible "many." And none of his answers pleased xenophobic Baldwin who was as close to sulking as a grown man should get. All three Talents had been particularly careful in answering his stabbing questions since his suspicions were so clearly "heard" in his public mind. "Given the height of the queen," Rojer explained patiently, "the positions of her manipulative limbs and her optics, the upper panel was the logical main control, while she received status information from the lower one. The three of us merely fiddled with variables until we hit the right combination. I think it was Flavia who actually got the lights turned on."

"The queen's upper limbs have triangular-shaped

palps," Flavia said, her voice falling into a "rote" pattern as she repeated her part of the explanation, "so that was the form of pressure I used."

"Why did you call a decontam drill at that time, Commander Kloo?" Baldwin demanded, abruptly switching to the other "culprit," the duty officer.

"Sir, if you will remember, you yourself suggested that we start emergency drills on the Refugee, due to the fact that the life-support system was only just on line," Semirame said in an earnest tone, leaning slightly toward him, not quite apologetically but with an air of gentle reminder. *Actually, he gives so many orders, he'll never remember he didn't. A drill is s.o.p., especially with a new installation. If he hadn't ordered it, he should have.*

I don't know about you and Rojer, Thian, Flavia said with considerable vexation in her voice, *but I find their attitudes suspicious, disagreeable, ungrateful and positively spiteful. What difference does it really make who found out how to turn on the power in that wretched old ship? It's never* going *anywhere. But it IS now powered up and I do not like being accused of "going behind their backs for personal glory," or "overstepping" the parameters of our "assigned functions." We kept their personnel safe and we made the ship just that bit more safe when we turned on its lightning system. We've explained and explained and diagrammed as much as we know, so I think it's time to leave this merry-go-round.*

With no brass ring. And I concur with your analysis, Flavia, Thian replied. *I'm fed up with such a catechism. We have finished our "assigned functions." Therefore we can* leave. *Rame, will our stalking out in indignation put you in jeopardy?*

Don't know how you've stood it as long as you have. As I was busy overseeing a decontam drill and nowhere near the site of your crime, they can't even pin dereliction of duty on me. 'Sides, del Falco's not after me. I'm crew. He's after you because you're not.

Flavia, do you wish to make the statement aloud or should I?

You'd better do it, Thian, Flavia replied. *I might lose my temper.*

Thian and Roger exchanged surprised looks.

"Mr. Lyon!" del Falco said, obviously having had to repeat the call to attention, for he was scowling with annoyance. Both Mr. Lyons regarded him.

He asked you why you chose that precise moment to try out your theory, Rame supplied.

Thian rose, the signal for both Flavia and Rojer to follow his example.

"We chose that moment because the queens' chambers were empty and we would not be jeopardizing anyone's safety in case we hit the wrong buttons," Thian said. "Now you can turn the panels on and off at your discretion. The ship is thoroughly and safely explored, independently lit and supplied with oxygen, so our assignment has been completed. Earth Prime has just informed me that we must return immediately to the Blundell Cube. It has been our pleasure to assist in this project for the Navy on Mars Phobos Moon Base, Admiral, Commander Baldwin, Commander Kloo, Glmtml, and sirs." Thian bowed to the panel of Humans and Mrdinis that had been interrogating them for the past three hours; then he strode from the room.

The courtesies that Rojer and Flavia gave their inquisitors were as polite but briefer and then they were in the corridor.

Let's blow this joint, Thian said.

They all heard the commotion inside and 'ported to their

quarters, where they collected their possessions in deft sweeps of closets and drawers.

Where away? Rojer asked Thian.

Blundell, of course, Thian replied as if there could be no doubt. *There's a large enough carrier on the transport deck.*

They met there moments later, Flavia looking attractively flushed by their dramatic and precipitous exit.

And we won't even have to use the Base generators, Thian said, chuckling, last to enter the carrier. He pulled the lid firmly shut. *Okay?*

At Rojer's mirthful shout and Flavia's giggle of acknowledgment, their minds merged and they propelled themselves off the Moon Base and down to the headquarters of Federated Teleport and Telepath on Earth.

You're a cheeky lot, said Jeff Raven, but he, too, was chuckling. *Report to my office so you can repudiate the blast I'm getting from Admiral del Falco.*

The man is not only ungrateful, Flavia said firmly, *but unmannerly. He never so much as thanked us for solving his problem for him.*

'Port right up to my office, kids, I've cleared the way for you, Jeff said as the lid of the carrier was opened by the head expediter of Blundell facility.

"Boss wants you pronto," but he was grinning broadly.

Is the word out all over the world yet? Rojer asked Thian on a very thin line.

No, nor will it be, Jeff answered, having no trouble at all insinuating himself into his grandsons' link. *Hurry up. The admiral's just getting to the part about gross insubordination, exceeding orders, and I suspect mutiny will figure in there soon.*

"Sorry," Thian said to the expediter and 'ported himself as ordered, Rojer and Flavia a nanosecond behind him.

Knowing Jeff Raven's office well, all three made sure to arrive at a point out of range of the occupant on the screen. Admiral del Falco, Commander Baldwin visible on his right, was waxing eloquent about the "antics" of these "unruly, undisciplined and unprincipled Talents."

"I thought you kept more control on your people, Raven. You told us they were well trained, skilled and capable of the assignment. They walked out of a half-finished debriefing with many questions unanswered. I don't mind telling you that I, Commander Baldwin here, and . . ." He turned to his left and his scowl deepened before he gave a snort of displeasure and faced directly into the com unit again. "We will not recommend that those three receive assignments from any Navy unit again."

"Oh, really?" Jeff said. "How odd. Because I've had twenty urgent requests," and he lifted a pile of message flimsies from his desk into plain view of the Admiral, ". . . from naval exploration groups, Squadrons C and D, now refitting at Clarf, and from Captains Osullivan, Ashiant, Cheseman, Quacho, Prl, a priority urgent one from Captain Spktm of the *KLTS* and another top security assignment which I don't believe you are cleared to know."

Hey, Granddad, that's a low blow, Thian said, chuckling.

Hit 'em again, harder, Rojer suggested, delighted.

Admiral del Falco glared and his impassive face settled into an even more threatening blandness. "They may change their minds when they see the report I shall insist be attached to their NE-440 forms."

"Really? That they prevented serious injury by rescuing seventy-five crew members, Human and Mrdini, during the course of your exploration of Refugee which was completed in less than the scheduled time? That they were also able to discover and turn on the ship's independent power system? That, by the way, was not in their assignment's parameters but Talents pride themselves on doing *more* than they are required to do. Part of the dedication of our personnel, Admiral. And don't go filling out NE-440 forms on FT&T personnel: a waste of time as they're not under your jurisdiction. Thank you for your perceptions on this mission and good luck with your operational enemy ship." With a peremptory wave of his hand, Jeff blanked the screen. "And that makes the Phobos Moon Base low man on FT&T job priorities." He rose from his chair, still taller than his grandsons, vigorous and obviously amused by recent events. "I don't think they gave you anything to eat during that three-hour grilling, did they? Name your pleasure," he added, gesturing for them to take seats in the lounge area of his spacious office.

"My guts wouldn't've let me eat any more of their food anyhow," Rojer said and, turning his head to the dispenser, called out the elements of a sustaining meal. Jeff chuckled at the choice, then urged Flavia to send her order.

Thian realized that his stomach was unknotting as well and shortly had as comprehensive a spread of dishes as his brother.

"Hope you haven't taken a dislike to Navy life, Flavia," Jeff said when he had ordered a salad and all were sitting about the beautiful Altairian fruitwood table, now laden with succulent comestibles.

"No, sir. I had no trouble with the lifestyle, sir. Both Thian and Rojer have told me a little bit . . ." She shot Rojer an anxious glance until she realized he was applying himself diligently to his meal and only half listening. ". . . about the services they performed. I'd have no apprehensions of serving as a Talent on a ship. Taking an objective viewpoint, I did feel that Admiral del Falco's internal conflicts and ambitions were the source of much of his behavioral pattern."

"Well said," Jeff muttered with a laugh and roguish grin at his grandsons.

"Were you considering another naval assignment for me, sir?" she asked.

Watching Flavia delicately consuming a pasta dish, managing a neat twine of strands of hot cheese around her fork, Thian could well imagine the impression she'd make on any crew. Maybe he'd read more into Granddad's choice of her as a mission member than existed. Except he knew Jeff Raven wanted his grandchildren to marry into Talented families to produce yet another generation of gifted children.

"Several situations have come up for T-1s so I'll spread the lot of them on the table," Jeff said. "Squadron C's been brought back for refitting and resupply, as well as a change of personnel. C's been out longer than D."

"Then they're going to follow the other Hive ships to their destination?" Thian was excited as well as relieved. He hadn't liked the idea of that ship loose and preying on an unsuspecting planet.

"That's what I hear," and implicit in Jeff Raven's voice was the caution that what he had heard might be altered. "Squadron A replaces elements of C and D and will continue the search with augmentation and would very much like you back, Thian, especially Captain Spktm. Squadron B will now consist of four human and four 'Dini ships; if you'd consider that assignment, Rojer, you'd have no prejudice, believe me." Jeff glanced reassuringly at Rojer. "The *KTTS is* one of them but the ship has a new captain, officers and crew. Captain Quacho's finally been relieved at Xh-33, but the *Arapahoe* will need refitting. There's to be some other reshuffling of units in B, but I don't know what. The Squadron's been ordered on a mission to survey the M-5 planets the Hiver ships bypassed. The xenobiologist lobby is rabid to get to those damaged planets, as much to see what went wrong as to see if anything can be salvaged from Hiver occupation. I'm also not sending any T-1 on these long cruises without a personal support team, and with such augmented squadrons, I'd be happier to have two T-1s, or a T-1 and a good T-2 as backup. There are also some shorter-term exploratory cruises in the Xh-33 quadrant of space, if you don't care for the longer journeys. Having Talents aboard has been of great assistance. Don't know why I didn't think of it before, except that FT&T has been mainly planet-based. Think about your options. And there are always dirtside openings if you want a complete change." Then Jeff grinned. "One more matter, just before del Falco got on to me, I had word from Heinlein Base that the queen's been energized." He grinned, cocking one eyebrow, his deep blue eyes twinkling. "I don't know if it's the food you sent over from the Refugee or what, but Roddie reports that she's minutely re-examined every single one of the Great Sphere larvae that were sent there and she's done something to more of the eggs she herself laid—in between having a good munch-out on three of the nine containers. The others she hasn't opened."

Flavia gave a little sigh of regret. "Maybe it was truly unkind to raise her hopes when we never intended to let her escape."

"I don't think the Hive psyche has evolved sufficiently to recognize kindness," Jeff said gently to Flavia.

"They've sure shown none," Rojer said, remembering the destruction of the queen pods by their own species at Xh-33.

"Isn't it a good thing that she's active?" Thian said to Flavia. "Better for her."

"Samples of what's in those food containers have been sent to the Heinlein Labs for analysis, haven't they?" Jeff asked.

"Sure have," Rojer said. "There were more than enough containers with the same markings to allow us to 'port one of each to every biology and xenob group active in Hiver study. That didn't even make a noticeable dint in the amount still in store in the cargo holds."

"Good thinking," Jeff said, nodding approvingly.

"Wasn't me, sir. Roddie suggested it. He thought her own sort of food might contain basic elements she isn't getting in the diet they've provided her."

Thian grinned broadly. "Now wouldn't the right food cause the queen to activate?"

Jeff's grin was just as broad, with just the slightest hint of malicious delight about it. "I think that will certainly be the official position and supported by the resident xenobs."

"Granddad," Rojer began, "backtrack a bit, would you? You mentioned M-5 type planets where the Hivers didn't make colonies work?"

"Ah yes, you wouldn't be up to date on that, would you?" Jeff said, tossing his napkin to the table before pushing his chair away. Cocking his knee against the edge of the table, he leaned back. "We'd a T-2, Kincaid Dano. Name's not familiar? No matter. It was fortunate that he was with Squadron C. I'd only just initiated the program of Talents on long-cruise missions. When the Hive ship C was chasing didn't investigate any of the M-5 systems they were passing, the High Council asked me if probes similar to the ones Rojer used couldn't be deployed to investigate. Clearly those two Spheres were looking for a place to colonize, so why did they keep passing likely systems by? We shipped Dano probes. He'd enough other low Talents on board to help him 'port them on a parabolic course. In and out. Rather interesting details emerged. Of the four planets investigated, two had obviously been colonized by Hivers because there were the ruins of the sort of installations the Xh-33 has."

"Ruins?" Thian asked.

"Ruins. Hive ruins. Including the same sort of space garbage as around Xh-33 and, in one case, an orbiting sphere ship. Another planet is ecologically on the point of ruin, presumably because the Hiver extermination policy eliminated something vital to its ecosystem. The point is that there are more M-5 type worlds out there that the Hivers never bothered with. Why? is one of the questions asked. Do they have records of all the systems their species have colonized? Another question is, obviously, can one of the Alliance species use any of these abandoned worlds? And there're more out there—as we've always known there were—to be investigated. C Squadron is being recalled. While the expanded Squadron A picks up where they left off, Squadron B will do evaluations of the abandoned colony worlds . . ."

"And knock out the inhabited one the way we did the Xh-33?" asked Thian, with a certain eagerness in his voice.

Jeff gave him a long look. "I've no specific directions as yet. I'd rather one of us didn't start another battle. The Navy feels that that's *its* prerogative." Then he grinned. "Even if certain Talents do seem to lend a helping hand when least expected. However, I've had my wrists slapped by the High Council, so orders are to be followed this time."

Each one felt him gently prod their minds.

"Granddad," and Thian waggled a finger at Earth Prime.

"Sorry," Jeff said, lifting his hands in a gesture of compliance, "force of habit." His grin had not a vestige of apology in it.

"That means, sir, that the Squadrons will continue to hunt down the remaining Hive ships?" Flavia asked.

"I repeat, that's the current," and he lightly emphasized the word, "plan. These chasings off into unexplored regions of space keep lasting longer than anyone anticipated . . ."

"A lot that's happened couldn't be anticipated," Thian said, thinking of the Great Sphere and the dead star that had once shone on the Hive homeworld.

"You can say that again," Rojer murmured, remembering the unexpected events in which he had taken part. "Where are your 'Dinis, Thian?" he asked suddenly.

Thian shot him a glance, adding a mental touch blended of compassion, affection, pride and relief that the question had been asked. "Hibernation. They should be out in another week."

"Oh!"

"Mur and Dip would like a chance to see you, if that's all right with you, Roj." Thian turned to the Earth Prime. "That is, if Granddad hasn't shipped us off to the different ends of the galaxy."

"Not in the next two weeks," Jeff said affably. "Your parents have expressed a wish for your company," and his eyes twinkled as his mobile face suggested he couldn't understand why they would, "and you all require leave after running those naval hazards." He turned to Flavia. "My wife and I would be delighted to have you stay with us at Callisto, Flavia. Damia has also extended an invitation to you to return to Aurigae with the boys if you'd prefer."

"Old home week's fun on Aurigae," Rojer said. "Do you ride? We've great ponies and good hunting."

At that prospect, Flavia brightened. "I haven't had a decent hunt in ever so long. What sort of game do you go after? I'm afraid that I don't know much about Iota Aurigae."

"Any chance of Laria getting home leave, too?" Thian asked his grandfather.

Jeff smiled and nodded before he folded his hands behind his head, leaning back in his chair at an almost dangerous angle. Relaxing with his young relatives around him was a good way to get perspective on completely different problems.

"Give a think to the various assignments, Squadrons A and B, or a dirtside assignment, or one of the shorter exploratories. Talents don't have to ship out from a dock." He grinned. "Those who want you will welcome you all the more when you do get ... wherever you choose to go." He set his chair back down on all four legs. "I may have to make the final decisions but your preferences will be taken into consideration. I owe you that much, Talents."

Thian and Rojer exchanged surprised glances at his deference.

In line with that generosity, Jeff Raven managed, in a manner as near to coercion as he ever came, to get the Raven-Lyons all home at the same time. He got David of Betelgeuse to release his T-1 son, Perry, to take charge of Clarf Tower, borrowing Yeshuk from the Sef Tower until Perry became comfortable with the peculiarities of the planet.

Perry hasn't dealt with enough Mrdini yet and he'll need to, Jeff told the Betelgeuse T-1. *You won't let him have your damned Tower until you're moldy so he might as well have some variety in his life.*

Jeff then made extravagant use of pressure to get Clancy

Sparrow and Rhodri Eagle leaves of absence and had Damia invite them to Aurigae. He also suggested to his daughter that Asia Eagle could use some Tower engineering work experience with Xexo and wasn't it time for Zara to get a break from her arduous training under the T-1 Healer Elizara? Damia was so eager to have all her children home again at once, especially Rojer, that she would have struck a deal with a Hiver.

You're matchmaking again, Jeff Raven, his wife accused him.

How can you say that when all these young people will be 'porting off to distant star systems and not see each other for years.

That doesn't matter if they are only a thought away from each other, does it, Jeff Raven!

Jeff grinned and firmed up all the private arrangements before he called in his administrative assistant, Gollee Gren, to see exactly which Talents suited which of the many other assignments he had to fill. At least, he thought gratefully, he had more available options than Peter Reidinger, his predecessor, had ever had, with all the new generation of kith and kin growing splendidly and strongly into their Talents. Now, if the High Council would get its joint act together, he'd know where he needed the heavy-weights of his corps. Once again he thanked the ghosts of all the Earth Primes who had managed to keep Federated Teleport and Telepath autonomous and apolitical.

A-what? asked a laughing voice and Gollee Gren, his dark, close-cropped hair showing a sprinkling of silver, entered the spacious office.

"I always do what's best for my Talents," Jeff said in a gruff voice, mimicking his predecessor, Peter Reidinger, so perfectly that Gollee grinned even more broadly.

"So what's best for whom this time, Jeff?"

Jeff steepled his fingers briefly, pressing them against his lips. Neither mimicry nor laughter was present when he answered. "I hope we'll see that they've been able to make the proper choices."

By the time Damia had settled all her guests, she almost wished that they could have come singly, with a good day between arrivals, so she could fully savor each return. She'd worried most of all about Rojer, returning without Gil and Kat to a house full of 'Dinis. The moment the capsule arrived with the brothers and Flavia, she "reached out" for Rojer. He was steeling himself but foremost in his mind was an eagerness to be home. No sooner was that carrier down, than Laria, Tip, Huf and Kincaid Dano arrived. The dust in the Tower yard hadn't settled when Zara, with Pal and Dis, 'ported in.

Morag, Kaltia, Ewain and Petra, plus their 'Dinis, were dancing up and down with the excitement of having their "famous" brothers and sisters back on Aurigae. Xexo and Keylarion were trying to keep order but the Tower yard was in minor chaos as the younger children kept running from one to the other sibling, 'Dinis dizzy from following.

Like a hard knock on a painful bruise, Damia felt Rojer respond to energetic greetings from Kaltia's and Ewain's 'Dinis. They were so caught up in the general elation that none of them remembered to give Rojer the time or space to initiate contact. Damia was all set to abandon protocol and 'port down to intervene when she felt the sudden shift of emotion in his mind. Then he was lifting Petra up in his arms—Rojer had got taller all of a sudden and muscled up, Damia noted, testing the strength of him—while Big and Sil affectionately flapped against legs which surely had got longer. Any reluctance or hesitation dissolved in the warmth of affectionate kisses and pats showered on him by his totally unselfconscious youngest sister and her friends.

"He'll be fine, Damia," Afra said gently. "This was perhaps the best way to get over that hump." He held her briefly in his arms, kissed her tenderly and released her. He peered out the Tower window and a fatuous grin spread across his face. "A bit overwhelming even if they are all ours."

"Mostly ours," Damia corrected him, as she noticed that Flavia and Kincaid Dano were being introduced and as warmly welcomed. She hurried down the stairs to add hers.

Parental embraces were perhaps more restrained but just as heartfelt. Damia tried not to hug Rojer any harder or longer than she did Thian, Laria and Zara but she *had* to know.

I am all right, Mother, he said on a very thin line to her. *Really, coming home is going to work out.* "GOOD TO SEE TRP AND FLK ONCE MORE." And Roger bowed to his parents' 'Dinis.

Surprising everyone, Trp and Flk bowed very low to Rojer, their poll eyes almost touching the ground. Then each held out one upper limb to him which he obediently grasped. Silently, as they began to lead him toward the path to the house, all the other 'Dinis, even Petra's, fell into step behind.

I'm still all right, Mother, Rojer said, so she turned to speak with Flavia and Kincaid and introduce them to Xexo and Keylarion.

"Shall we all move up to the house then?" Damia said. "Don't hang on your brother, Ewain. Yes, Petra, Zara can certainly see how much you've grown. C'mon now, all of you, we'll adjourn to the house."

"Noisy lot. No manners whatever," Afra said, staring

hard at Kaltia and Morag, who were determined to monopolize their oldest sister. Then he turned to Kincaid. "Earth Prime told me that there were some unusual aspects to your recent tour of duty with Squadron C."

"Even if you had help from other Talents, it was asking a great deal too much," Damia said, having deftly assessed the young man's fatigue. "The Navy treats Talents far too off-handedly. We are *not* stevedores," she added with some heat.

Mother! Laria said on a very thin line. *Let Father handle him. As T-2 to T-2. What Kincaid doesn't need is another brain-browsing T-1.*

Oh? Were you a little clumsy, dear? asked her father.

"No," Laria continued aloud, "but we're suckers when someone asks us if Talents can do this or that, in just that tone of voice that forces us to prove we *can*. Frankly, the labels 'performing bear' or 'pack mule' are becoming more appropriate than 'stevedore.' "

"Laria!" Damia exclaimed, half-laughing, half-astounded by the comment. Then she frowned, glancing ahead at Rojer, being . . . "herded," the term came to her mind, toward the house. And . . . She had a compelling urge to run forward, to be *with* Rojer. Then Zara caught her by the arm.

I feel it, too, Mother, Zara said. *But it is not for us to be present.*

What are you two talking about? Afra asked.

I'm not at all sure, Damia replied, trying to reconcile the 'Dinis' odd actions with the growing sense that some extraordinary event was about to happen. *This morning when I told Fok that everyone was coming, it asked if I meant Rojer also. Then it muttered about suitable reparation and an apology for the length of time it had taken.*

Laria strode up beside her mother and Zara, her face twisted with concern, one hand absently rubbing her diaphragm as if to relieve a tension there. "Mother, I've the oddest sensation . . ."

"I, too," Flavia said, equally puzzled.

"Well, Fok and Tip have been cooking up something, Mom," Morag said. "They've been acting funny and I can't get *why* out of Fip and Kim. But all the 'Dinis're almighty pleased with themselves, whatever it is they're doing."

Every one of the Talented family by now was touched, and wondering about the strange imminence. From the puzzled, almost wary, expressions of Flavia and Kincaid, the atmosphere was affecting them.

"There are moments when I wish I had a touch of prescience," Damia said, lengthening her strides just short of a run.

"And what the hell do you think this is, then?" Thian asked, grinning at his mother.

She shot him a reproving look. "It's too nebulous to be useful!"

They were in sight of the front terrace of the house, Rojer already halfway up the steps, surrounded by various sizes of 'Dinis. Then he halted.

A blast of totally unshielded astonished emotion stopped everyone midstep but this was followed by such joy that everyone also broke into vicarious smiles, until Damia, Laria, Zara and Morag began to cry. The four of them ran forward so that they could see what prompted such a cascade of feelings, followed by the remainder of the family and its guests.

The 'Dinis had ranged themselves on the top step, their colors bright with their own joy. On the porch Rojer was on his knees, his arms about two 'Dinis, clasping first one, then the other tightly to him, caressing each before snagging them together against him.

It's Gil and Kat come back to me! Mother! Dad! Every-one. I've got my 'Dinis back. Young still but they are *Grl and Ktg! They are!*

It took time to sort it all out, even with the full cooper-ation of Trp and Flk, the elder 'Dinis of the household, and occasional comments from Tip, Huf, Mur and Dip. No Human had ever been allowed into a hibernatory. Al-though it was understood that this was where Mrdini pro-creation occurred, the process of gestation was not understood.

"I'm not confident that I do even now," Damia said when Trp and Flk had done their best to explain.

"Like the amoeba, splitting apart, Mother," Zara said. "Or, like a Human zygote splitting in two to form identical twins *in utero*. Not quite like . . ."

"Thank you, Zara," Damia said, but she patted her daughter's hand to apologize for stemming a xenobiolog-ical lecture. Zara didn't take offense.

The "time" problem had been due to the necessity of checking back through hibernatory records to discover which pairings had originally produced Grl and Ktg. They were not from the same "split," for a "split" only pro-duced one new Mrdini. So both sets of original parents had had to be contacted and brought to the Aurigaean hibernatory at the appropriate time and a new "split" of the same elements as the original Grl and Ktg had to be "programmed" which, Flk said, was an intense form of meditation to "urge similar traits" to occur in the new form. With this sort of procreation, no worthwhile "per-sons" were totally lost, but could be retrieved by encour-aging a "split" by the same two Mrdini which had produced the original. Those who had gone on the line to preserve their elders on long voyages were therefore not "lost," but their living was deferred.

"Oh!" Laria said at one point during the explanations. "So that was what those symbols on Prtglm's capsule meant. Nothing of *it* would be allowed back into the procreative cycle. Wow! What a punishment!"

"That also explains why the Mrdini grieved so when ships were lost to the Hivers," Thian said.

"NO, THN," Flk said, "THOSE ON THE SUICIDE SHIPS WERE SPECIALLY CHOSEN BECAUSE THEIR COMPONENTS WERE AVAILABLE FOR RE-CREATION. MRDINI ARE NOT WASTEFUL."

"THEN THAT ALSO EXPLAINS WHY MRDINI CAN BE BRAVER THAN HUMANS AND MAKE THE SACRIFICE OF DEATH," Thian added, nodding with relief at his comprehension of this facet. "MRDINIS DO NOT REALLY DIE. THEY CAN BE REPLICATED."

"NOT REPLICATED," Flk said firmly. "NOT THE SAME PROCESS. MRDINI LIVES ARE NOT REPLICATED. THEY ARE REPRODUCED."

"WHATEVER!" Damia said with a shaky laugh. "BUT COULD NOT YOU HAVE TOLD RJR THAT HE HAD NOT LOST GRL AND KTG. HE HAS MOURNED THEM."

"THAT, TOO, IS NECESSARY," Tri said without apology. "MRDINI MAKE A SPECIAL DISPENSATION FOR RJR. HONOR REQUIRED IT. AND TIME. WHAT HAS BEEN SAID REMAINS WITHIN THIS FAMILY."

"OF COURSE," Afra answered, inclining his whole body forward in acceptance of that requirement. "A SIGNAL HONOR FOR US ALL. TRULY AN INESTIMABLE HONOR."

"Speaking as a healer," Zara said, "it certainly does clear up a lot of crazy theories." Then she sighed. "Well, *I* know and, while it is privileged knowledge, it is a privilege for me to *know* it." She stroked her 'Dinis, Pal and Dis, who were wedged in on either side of her. "JUST SEE THAT IT DOESN'T HAPPEN TO YOU TWO!"

"NOT LIKELY TO," replied Pal, waving its forearms and wriggling its digits.

"This whole family is high!" Damia said with some asperity, but her grin broke out again. Once more, she had to brush tears of joy from her eyes. Just seeing the radiant look on Rojer's face was enough to set her off again. "Now, let us all try for some decorum."

Afra rose with an air of renewed vigor. "And resort to a few practical matters. Hunters are needed to fill the pots for tonight's feast. Who'll go out?"

They were all willing, so Damia showed the guests to their rooms while her children found their own much as they had left them and changed into riding gear. When all reassembled, Afra divided them into smaller groups, excusing Rojer so he could spend uninterrupted time with his 'Dinis.

Thian chose Flavia to come with him, Ewain and Kaltia. Afra and Damia took Morag and Petra who proudly informed Kincaid that she was a crack shot with her slingshot. That left Laria, Zara and Kincaid.

"Ever ridden?" Laria asked Kincaid.

"Ridden what?" Kincaid replied uncertainly.

"Ponies, small horses."

"Oh, animal riding. Yes, somewhat," he said and Laria beckoned him to follow her to the stables.

"Can I join you two?" Zara asked.

"Sure," Laria said without hesitation. *Saki's mine!* she roared after her siblings who were already in the stable.

Who'd dare take her with you around?

Laria thought that muffled response came from Rojer, for it had the ring of an elated personality.

Is he yours, sister? Zara asked on a thin line.

Kincaid? He's not for either of us, dear. And you, a

healer, to miss it! And careful, Zara, 'cause I know you can't resist a healering "look." He was as near burned-out emotionally as I've ever touched. *What* does *Navy do to the empathic?*

Emotional burn-out? Zara asked sharply, her healer's instinct alert.

Plus considerable strain on a T-2's abilities. I think *he's healing but if you could, at your deftest, slip in and check, I'd be relieved, Zar,* Laria said gratefully. *I'm speaking as Kincaid's Prime.*

Zara nodded as she slipped the headpiece over her pony's ears while Laria found a saddle suitable for Kincaid's size. She found it very good indeed to be surrounded by ponies; grateful to see that the oldest were still vigorous and whinnied anxiously against being left behind. The entire complement was needed to mount the hunters, with three spares taken on lead ropes in high hopes of bringing back much game.

Kincaid eschewed slingshot and bow and arrow, choosing a small-bore rifle and ammunition for it as if he knew what he was about. Laria was rather surprised to see Flavia take bow and arrow. She also saw the grin on Thian's face.

As each hunting party was armed and mounted, they moved off in preferred directions. Laria decided on an eastern route, to the foothills. With only her parents, the four younger kids and the 'Dinis, there wouldn't have been much call to go too far from home for scurriers, rabbits and the small plump-breasted avians that nested nearer by. Although Laria had thoughtfully chosen a steady mount for him, Kincaid's "somewhat" was near enough to the level of her own abilities that her respect for him went up another notch. She raised her arm, signaling a faster gait, and kneed Saki into a ground-covering canter, a rock-

ing gait that required little more than balance for a rider.
She heard the other two ponies pick up to the same gait.
A surreptitious glance showed her Kincaid, easily sitting
into the canter and grinning with pleasure.

He was also a good shot, as he proved when their approach flushed a covey of avians from their hedges. He
got two brace of them, each neatly shot through the head.
Zara had also chosen a rifle but she went after the scurriers, which broke cover when Kincaid's shots startled them.
Laria got three rabbits, two scurriers and even one avian
hen in that first stop.

"No one's been hunting this way in a long while," she
said to her sister as they bagged their catch.

"When was the last time you were home?" asked Zara
with a bit of a snort. "This always was the route you preferred."

"Yes, but you'd think someone would have tried to keep
the game down all over the hills."

"Do you always hunt for your table?" Kincaid asked,
handing over the birds he had retrieved.

"Uh-huh!" the sisters said in unison and all three
laughed.

"When we were younger, we used to take our 'Dinis
with us . . ." Zara began.

"They were small enough to ride pillion then . . ." Laria
continued.

". . . And didn't consider it beneath their dignity to grab
a stirrup leather to get up the hills."

"Ah . . ." Kincaid began tentatively, "what *did* happen
to your brother's original 'Dinis? I've only caught
snatches and I'd rather not misinterpret."

Laria and Zara exchanged glances and begged his pardon.

"Apologies, Kincaid," Laria said, taking the initiative.

She related the incident quickly, trying not to let her emotions color the facts. Neither sister expected his bitter reaction.

"Bad enough to try that sort of coercion on someone of full age and your own species, but to subject a kid . . ." He flushed, thinking he might have belittled their brother's abilities. "I admit that I like Clarf far more than I thought I would, even in the short time I've been at your Tower, Laria, but I haven't changed my mind about naval practices at all." He looked down at the ground, at the pattern he was scuffing in the thick moss. "You'll never know how grateful I was to be transferred back to the company of *civilians*!"

Zara touched Laria's wrist, where the riding glove left her hand bare, and Laria "heard" the message: *This bears investigation. The problem's festering. I'll do it when he sleeps.*

"Grateful, are you?" Laria said with a light laugh. "I haven't half worked you yet, Kincaid. You may wish to transfer back to the Navy."

He looked her squarely in the eyes, his jaw set at an obstinate angle. "No, I wouldn't. Not ever." He turned and, with a respectable vault, was astride his pony. "Have we got a large enough bag?"

"Only if you're feeling the saddle," Laria said with a challenging grin.

The hunt's good for him, Zara said tightly.

"I'll feel the saddle tomorrow," Kincaid said with a rueful grin as he kneed his pony forward to follow the nearly overgrown path, "but let's get on with the hunt."

The hunt had been so enthusiastically pursued by all participants that Damia decided, as the 'Dinis helped them dress down the results, that they probably wouldn't need to hunt for the rest of the week. She sent Zara out with Petra and their 'Dinis to pull vegetables to go with the evening meal and set Rojer and Ewain and their 'Dinis to dig tubers. With her friends, Laria began to make a dessert while Flavia watched in fascination as Tip and Huf measured ingredients, set out appropriate pots and pans. Thian took Kincaid back to the stable to feed and secure the stableyard creatures. Kincaid enjoyed the chore, having missed working with tamed creatures while on his naval assignment.

There turned out to be time enough for a quick swim before dinner and there was more aquatic rough stuff than energetic laps of the large pool.

By dinner, Rojer's joy had settled to a glow and the new Gil and Kat had acquired enough orientation, between his efforts and those of the other 'Dinis, to appear quite comfortable at the large table. If, at first, they were clumsy with unfamiliar utensils, they learned with amazing speed and obviously enjoyed the meal.

Leaving children and guests to clear the table and cleanse the dishes, Damia and Afra settled in the lounge to have a quiet liqueur, watch the sun set over the sea, and get a few words with their 'Dinis.

"TELL US PLEASE," Damia asked Trp and Flk, "HOW MA-TURE ARE THE NEW KTG AND GRL?"

"OLDER THAN THE FIRST BECAUSE THE IMMATURE WOULD NOT BE ABLE TO ACCOMPANY RJR USEFULLY."

"CAN YOU TELL US HOW THIS WAS ACCOMPLISHED? WE DO NOT PRY . . ." Damia left the thought hanging.

Fok resettled itself right next to Damia, laying one upper hand on her arm, stroking its head against her shoulder.

"DM IS TOO GOOD A FRIEND TO PRY. IT WAS PART OF MEDITA-TION THAT THESE BE MORE MATURE. THIS REQUIRES VERY

CAREFUL ATTENTION TO DETAILS NOT USUALLY REFINED SO EARLY. HALF-GROWN KTG AND GRL ARE BUT NOT MORE GROWN THAN CAN ABSORB NECESSARY DATA NOW THAT RJR IS OLDER TOO."

"DO YOU *KNOW* HOW MUCH THIS MEANS TO US AS WELL AS RJR?" Damia said and, although she knew perfectly well there wasn't an ounce of telepathy in Mrdinis, she exuded gratitude and knew that Afra did, too.

"WE KNOW. ALL MRDINI KNOW. THE REGRET IS THAT TIME HAD TO GO SO SLOWLY FOR RJR. SUCCESS HAD TO BE ACHIEVED OR DISAPPOINTMENT WOULD MAR RJR FOR ALL TIME."

"YES," Afra said slowly, "TO HAVE RAISED HIS HOPES PREMATURELY WOULD HAVE CAUSED MUCH MORE PAIN. YOU WERE WISE."

"YES, WE WERE VERY WISE," Trp said with such a smug tone in its voice that both Damia and Afra burst out laughing at its uncharacteristic arrogance.

Then the chores were finished and Damia and Afra were joined by children, guests and 'Dinis. It made for rather a full room, but a very happy one.

The next day, to shake out the kinks caused by riding after a long absence from the sport, Thian, Laria, Zara and the two guests took an easy hack to another part of the foothills. Rojer grinned at their stiffness for he'd been riding regularly on Deneb and he had other plans for his day. Afterwards Thian and Laria gave Flavia and Kincaid a tour of Aurigae City, the 'Dini village, where they caught a fleeting glimpse of Rojer, Kat and Gil making a formal call on the inhabitants.

"WILL RJR KNOW WHO . . ." Laria couldn't resist asking Tip.

"NEVER KNOW. WE DON'T. WE KNOW IT WAS DONE. THAT IS ENOUGH."

Well, you would ask, Thian said when he saw the chagrined look on his sister's face from the brusque reply.

There was no harm in asking, she said with a sniff. *Otherwise how would I know that there is a limit to the knowledge they have of the process? They aren't offended.*

No, they're not. They know us too well for that.

Thank goodness. Sometimes . . . and Laria halted, closing off her thought.

Thian nudged her. *Hey, it's me, your brother.*

Laria gave him a sideways look. *If I could analogize the nebulous I would, but I can't. When I can figure out the question I need to ask, I'll bring it to you, and Zara.* There was a sad and perplexed tone to Laria's mental voice that Thian had never heard before from his practical, sensible sister.

Not Mother or Dad?

Laria gave a little laugh. *When I know enough to ask, I might. But I think you and Zara might know better.*

I'm highly complimented. Thian tousled his sister's hair. She was tall but he had centimeters on her.

"Hey, what gives you the right to mess me up?" she demanded in mock outrage. Their mental exchange had taken so little time their guests could not have been aware of discourtesy or such a tight colloquy.

"Hey, I'm bigger'n you now, sis. I got the right!" Thian said, grinning back. He noticed Flavia and Kincaid exchanging amused glances. "Where to now? A view of the open mines? A fascinating scenic tour of the river? Ah, I know. Breakfast was a long time ago and there's a great place where they've fresh crustaceans I'll bet neither of our guests have ever had a chance to eat!"

"Gotcha!"

"I'd rather you didn't use that word around me, sis," Thian said, having had to catch his breath at the shaft of remembered fear and terror the innocent vernacular phrase produced in him.

"Ooops, sorry, Thi," and Laria was full of remorse. Once again they inadvertently excluded their guests and smiled apologies.

"Maybe if you spoke of it to us who will understand as others can't . . . ?" Flavia asked, peering up into Thian's pale face.

Thian knew himself to be tempted by Flavia's obvious concern but he also caught the wariness in Kincaid, a rigid seizing of muscles in the man's body that made him loath to add to whatever burden Kincaid already coped with. For Thian was as perceptive as Zara about the T-2. So he made himself grin.

"You would understand, Flavia," he said, lightly and briefly touching her shoulder, "and so would Dano, but at another time. Laria just caught me unawares."

They ate fish of all kinds as well as the fresh crustaceans and Laria put in an order for ten kilos of frozen shellfish to be sent on to Clarf.

"I'd forgot how much I liked 'em," she said as they turned back toward the Tower. She took a meandering course, turning the sled just beyond the main mining complexes and into the next level of hills.

"You wouldn't know there was a highly industrialized city just a hill away," Flavia said, as Laria slowed the sled so they could all enjoy the panorama.

It was late summer on Aurigae and the ground vines were beginning to turn color, rivaling what flowering shrubs and plants still bloomed.

"This is a pretty time of year, too," Laria said with a sigh.

She was now accustomed to Clarf's heat, but the crisp air of Iota Aurigae and the softness of its primary's distant

light were subtly soothing, relaxing. But then this was
home and all that the term implied: familiar, safe, comfort-
ing, pleasant. Even Kincaid seemed easier in himself, his
attitude languid. Flavia, on the other hand, was eagerly ab-
sorbing all the views, glancing all around her, or peering
down as they passed over some particularly lovely setting.
Thian had a droll smile on his face as he watched the
Altairian.

She is lovely, Laria said on a thin line.

No question of that, Thian replied easily and his smile
broadened a trifle.

Grandfather?

I'd hate to surrender easily to his manipulations.

Is that fair to Flavia?

*I don't know. She's pretty cool. I can't get past her pub-
lic mind.*

Have you tried?

Ethics are involved, Lar.

In love and war, all's fair, isn't it?

*This is neither love nor war, sister dear. Speaking of
which, how come Kincaid Dano got posted to Clarf?*

*As to that, I couldn't get on with that wretched
Clarissia. She was even worse than Stierlman and proved
'Diniphobic to the point of acute embarrassment for the
Tower. I can't keep breaking up Yoshuk and Nesrun . . .*

They are a pairing, then?

Far's I know.

How's Kincaid working out?

*As well as could be expected with someone as mentally
fatigued as he is. But he's improving.*

Laria had been skimming quite low and had set the
sled's speed at almost a walking pace so that Flavia could
enjoy the landscape. She was ascending a shrub-covered
hill when all of a sudden a large flock of avians sprang up

in front of the sled. In an effort to avoid unnecessary slaughter, Laria hauled the sled sideways, but in doing so, unbalanced her passengers so they slid to the port side. What with the sled's slow forward speed and the proximity of the hill, the imbalance tilted the sled out of control. The humans grabbed at the lighter 'Dinis to keep them from tumbling overboard, but they were, in turn, overbalanced and fell over the side. Laria caught Tip's arm, saw that Kincaid had Huf, and had to leave Thian and Flavia to manage his 'Dinis. They all 'ported safely away as the sled plowed its nose into the hillside.

Setting Tip down on its feet, Laria regarded the sled, its motor still running, with stunned surprise.

"I didn't think I was that out of practice," she said, shaking her head. "After all, I do a great deal of sledding about on Clarf and Vanteer prefers me to drive him."

The motor cut suddenly, with a loud discharge from its exhaust tubes which blew back a noxious smell.

"Hoooo," and Thian waved the reek off.

"Everyone's okay?" Laria asked, looking about her.

"I must say you lay on unusual entertainments for guests," Kincaid said.

Laria flushed. "I probably did overcompensate for the flock but they make such a mess if they get sucked into the intake."

Kincaid laughed. "Don't get me wrong, Laria. I'm not objecting. A relief to know that emergency reflexes are in working order."

Thian, followed by his 'Dinis, walked over to the tilted sled, peering at the underside.

"How bad's the damage, Thi?" Laria asked, not quite sure of Kincaid's jest.

"You did a lot worse when you were learning to fly . . ."

"Isthian Lyon, I never put a single . . ."

Thian laughed and suddenly the sled backed out of the trench it had dug in the shrubs and soil and settled on as even a keel as the rough ground permitted. Flavia and Kincaid joined him so that Laria broke out of her outraged pose and sprinted the few meters to join them.

"Shouldn't've overbalanced like that," Thian said.

"No, this model isn't supposed to, is it," Kincaid said and opened the access panel.

"D'you think it'll restart?" Laria asked.

"Probably," Kincaid said, "but I think there's something wrong with the fuel lines or there wouldn't have been that backfire."

"I'll check the intakes," Thian said and levered himself down for a good look at the hooded opening on the starboard side of the sled.

"Good heavens, Thian, why not just 'look'?" Flavia asked.

"More fun to tinker when I have the chance," Thian said, his voice muffled by his position. "Yeah, flight pinions clogging this one. Check the other, will you? Laria? Flavia?"

Flavia made a sound of disgust, totally out of character with her elegant exterior. She deposited a bloodied clump beside the mess Thian had extracted.

"Couldn't we just 'port back to the Tower?" she asked.

"What?" Laria asked, "and admit that we came a cropper?"

"Any tools on board?" Kincaid asked, holding up a very greasy-looking object.

"I doubt it," Laria said. "This sled's only used for short hops. The big sled has a full kit, of course."

"No one's using it today, are they?" Thian asked.

"I don't think so." Laria concentrated, "found" the mass

of the big sled in its garage, "located" the tool kit, and 'ported it to a spot by Kincaid's feet.

"Thanks," he said and, opening the metal locker, began to search for the tool he needed. "No rags?" he asked querulously.

"Here!" Laria dumped a pile, scavenged from the bin her mother generally kept them in, beside the tool kit.

Flavia watched another moment and then, turning, leisurely began to venture from the scene of the crash to examine the clumps of little blooms.

"Any toxic plants I should be aware of?" she asked Laria.

"None," Laria replied absently, more interested in Kincaid, the mechanic, for he went about cleaning the component with a competent air.

Thian cleared all the intake openings.

"That's done, but I don't think that was the whole problem. Xexo usually keeps this serviced," he said with a frown.

"Xexo usually does but we don't know when he did it last and Mother said Morag's allowed to drive now."

"Hey, that's not fair," Thian cried with mock indignation. "We were at least fifteen before we were allowed and she's only thirteen!"

Laria grinned at her brother. "I suspect they may miss us and have had to revise a few directives now they're down on staff. Besides, Morag's capable."

"I think we have to get to the fuel injection and clear the line," Kincaid said.

"That's underneath," Laria said, pointing to the bottom of the sled.

"No problem!" The two men said it simultaneously, grinned at each other, and the sled slowly rose to a suitable height to allow them to work easily on its underside.

She could see Flavia off in the distance, picking wild flowers, occasionally holding a bloom up for inspection and smelling it for scent. Not many had any aroma, but none that Laria could see in the immediate area were the stinkweeds which had a reek that could linger in nasal passages for days.

"I'll hold the sled up if that'll free you up to do the nitty-gritty," she offered, leaning comfortably against a boulder. "Vanteer says that helps him no end."

"Oh, well," Thian said in reply to her offer, "if you want to feel part of the team . . ."

She took over the "lift" and the men "removed" the bolts holding the panel, slipping it to one side where it hovered as a receptacle for the pieces they began to remove to get at the line.

"Can't you just 'see' into it, Thian?" Laria asked. "You've spent the last couple of weeks 'looking' inside pipes and conduits, haven't you?"

"Not quite the same thing, Laria," Thian said with an obvious exercise of patience. "This is hands-on stuff."

"Ah!" Kincaid had given a moderate tug to a hose and it had not only come away in his hand but disintegrated. "I didn't pull that hard!" he said in surprise, looking at the mess and the fuel that spilled down his hand.

"But that's the faulty part," Thian said. "Completely perished. Where does Xexo keep his spares, Laria? Can you remember?"

"I couldn't but Roj would know."

Thian grimaced. "I'd hate to interrupt him . . ."

"Well, it's that or admit to Xexo we crashed," Laria said.

"What's wrong with that?" asked Flavia, returning. Then she began to laugh. "Xexo's a T-8. You could be in and out of his mind before he knew you were there."

Laria and Thian exchanged thoughtful looks and then began to grin at each other. Thian chuckled and scratched his cheek with a dirty finger. "Old habits surface when you least expect them."

"You're not *that* old, Thian," Flavia remarked, thoroughly amused.

Holding the damaged hose line by each end, Thian could be seen to concentrate on it briefly. Then a second length of similar but brand-new hose appeared.

Laria cheered, then said ruefully, "I suppose it'll be my job to tell Xexo who messed up his inventory."

"Leave him a docket. That keeps everything in order."

The sled was quickly repaired. Kincaid even straightened the ding in the prow. "While we're about general repairs."

They were all in good spirits on the way back, Laria giving Thian the drive since she wanted to name the blooms in Flavia's bouquet of wild flowers.

The first week passed very quickly in all kinds of leisure pursuits that the Talented enjoyed as ordinary people. Laria and Kincaid went to the mixed school the younger Lyons attended to speak to both Human and Mrdini students about working on Clarf. Although Kincaid begged off, Thian and Rojer were also in demand in secondary-level classes, describing their adventures with the two Squadrons. With his 'Dinis back, Rojer had no trouble taking part with discreet evasions. Afterwards they told the dinner table that they might have made the service seem a bit too adventurous for some of the young people.

"Navy is actively recruiting," Afra said. "It's a good career if they don't fancy staying on here."

Damia smiled fatuously at her mate, knowing the experiences with his own family which had generated such tolerance. What he did not ask his sons was if they had decided which duty they would take on their return to work.

Flavia was included in an evening appearance when the exploration of the Hive ship was discussed with miners and engineers of both species, eager to have firsthand information on the matter. They also wanted to know if the great new long-cruise Nebula-class ship had been completed. Thian wasn't sure but said he suspected it would soon be launched. Its bulk had been noticeable in the working orbit it maintained about the Phobos Moon Base. No launch date had been mentioned and the disappointment of the men who had supplied the metals to build it was palpable.

"Is it because this planet is so new," Flavia asked Damia on the way back to the Lyon home, "that everyone seems so . . . so relaxed with their Talents?"

Damia had to think about her answer. "Well, the Tower is perhaps more important to Aurigaeans since it's still mainly a mining planet, and so much is imported. Also, even when I was here by myself, before my marriage to Afra, I was always accessible. Our children have grown up with their children—mine always ran wild on their ponies—their 'Dinis with ours." She gave a sigh. "I'll be sorry to see Aurigae spreading out and losing the closeness we've so enjoyed!"

"I'm lucky I've had a chance to see it," Flavia said, her tone envious.

Damia laid a light finger on Flavia's arm. "You would be welcome here any time."

"That is very kind of you." Flavia ducked her head so that her expression was obscured.

Don't! Afra said sternly to his wife.

Really, Afra! As if I'd ignore protocol with someone we barely know.

Someone I think you'd like to know better.

She could hear the teasing in his mental tone. *Kincaid has shown more interest in her than Thian.*

Kincaid is not interested in women, Damia. Or hadn't you caught that?

Damia managed *not* to gasp in surprise. She was rarely caught out. *And Laria . . .*

She twigged that the day he arrived but she likes *him very much. That friendship already means a lot to him.*

I must say the choice astonishes me. Surely Dad knew that about him . . .

Of course he did, but Kincaid's worth salvaging and Laria's so stable that she'd do that and give him a breathing space. Kincaid has more need of a real friend than a lover and she'd have the support personality she needs.

She also needs a man of her own. Damia's tone was adamant!

She's only twenty-three, dear heart.

I'd had her *and* Thian *by her age.*

She has an entirely different personality, darling, and Afra's tone was teasing again, *and your needs do not match. Now our Zara, who has also tagged Kincaid quite accurately, says he was in the midst of a destructive three-sided relationship that added more stress to a difficult enough assignment. He can relax at Clarf and heal—all the injured parts. Laria has her own soothing effect on people which is why Jeff tried such difficult ones as Stierlman and Clarissia at Clarf.*

Tried? Damia shot a flash of anger at her father's manipulative ploys.

Afra laughed. *I think your father understands and appreciates Laria far more than even we do.*

That remark both annoyed and mollified Damia. *So how long must Laria wait to fulfill herself?* she asked with some traces of indignation.

I have a suspicion that Laria only needs to look a little closer to those she already knows.

Yoshuk?

Vanteer.

Really?

I'm guessing but you'll have noticed how often his name came up.

Damia thought about that on and off during the evening. She hadn't met the Clarf Tower engineer, although she would have preferred a higher Talent than 6 for Laria. But that hadn't, apparently, all that much to do with inheriting the genes that produced T-1s in totally unexpected families. Like Flavia ... like the Rowan and Jeff Raven, for that matter.

The second week T-2 Clancy Sparrow, Lieutenant Senior Grade Rhodri Eagle and his youngest sister, Asia, the recently graduated honors engineer, arrived. None of them had been as far out as Iota Aurigae, even though they laughingly claimed Deneb IV was almost as remote in its quadrant of the inhabited galaxy.

Roddie, once the bane of the young Raven-Lyons' adolescence, had improved beyond belief. Clancy, having so recently worked with Thian, Rojer and Flavia, eased himself into the household and asked permission to do some hunting if that was all right. Instantly he had Morag, Kaltia and Ewain begging their parents to be his guide. Permission was granted and the three younger Raven-Lyons swept their cousin to the stables.

Despite all the efforts of Damia, Laria and Afra to welcome and reassure Asia, she was stiff with uncertainty and so afraid to say or do something "wrong." She didn't even complain when half the household slithers decided to investigate her slender body where she sat, rigid on the stool on which she had seated herself, eschewing a large number of more comfortable, empty chairs.

Petra regarded Asia for a moment and then briskly walked up to her and unwound all the slithers.

"Next time *say* that you don't like winding things crawling all over you," Petra said, rather disgusted that anyone would put up with such inconvenience. She ignored Asia's deep crimson blushing and, cocking her head, added: "D'you mind cats?"

"Oh no," Asia hastily said.

"That's a relief. What about Darbuls?"

Asia gulped. "What *are* Darbuls?" she asked in such a low, meek voice that Petra gawked at her for a moment before summoning one of the canine-like creatures. "Oh, they're not bad either," Asia said hastily, apparently trying to redeem herself in Petra's eyes for being so silly about the slithers.

"I'll tell the Coonies they're to watch out for you," Petra said with all the brash authority of a confident six-year-old. As she went off to do just that, she said to her parents: *Someone here ought to* do *something positive about this Asia girl. She doesn't know how to complain properly. The first Talent I've ever met with* that *problem.*

Petra's right. That one needs some major sorting out, Zara said to her mother, though her mental tone dripped with disgust for such abject self-effacement. *Why on earth didn't she peel the slithers off if their clinging was so abhorrent to her?*

And why didn't we notice her distress before Petra did? Damia responded, annoyed with herself that she had misinterpreted Asia's quietness for courtesy.

She's used *to being ignored, isn't she?* Zara said after a moment's thought.

Being the tenth of a big and noisy family that could produce Roddie would result in that posture, Damia said. And sighed. *None of you allowed yourselves to be ignored for any length of time. Asia might be soothing company.*

Zara gave her mother an odd glance to see if Damia was teasing, or serious.

A bit of both, dear.

She's pretty, too, Zara remarked, *if you look at the bones of her, though that outfit is not the best style for someone with bones to show off . . . well, that'd follow the personality problem. However, if she'd do a little* something *with herself . . .*

You're right, she is *pretty, though I doubt she's as delicate as she appears. The Eagles are a physically strong family. Afra, we must do what we can with this child,* Damia told her husband. *She's got some Talent but she's even locked that up as tight as hot-weather seed pod in snow.*

Before any of them could stop him, Rojer walked up to Asia, took her by the hand and hauled her shrinking self up from the stool.

"I want you to meet my 'Dinis. I got the new improved models when I got home. Since you're here to learn a few things from Xexo, I'll just take you along and do the introductions. You'll like Xexo," Rojer said as he hauled his reluctant victim beside him. "C'mon, now, Asia. I don't want to hear a single moan of 'Oh, I can't do this' out of you, d'you hear me?" *Stay out of this, Zara, Asia's mine!* And, as he left the room with the girl, he shot a stern warning at his sister over Asia's head. And a second one at his mother. *I know you two ladies too well! You keep away.*

Berated from such an unusual source, Zara and Damia exchanged bemused glances and grinned as they "heard" Rojer telling Asia all about the puzzle and how many pieces he had part credit for fitting together when all the engineers on Alliance worlds were trying to reconstruct the Great Sphere.

"Of course, that was before we all snitched Refugee out from under the Hivers' noses."

"Is our Rojer smitten?" Afra asked quietly of his womenfolk.

"I'm not quite sure . . ." Damia replied.

"Well on the way to it, if you ask me," Zara said with a knowing sniff. "Deciding to protect someone who appears defenseless can lead to a meaningful relationship. Provided, of course, it doesn't lead to an unsuitable overprotectiveness that inhibits the less-confident party."

Damia grinned at her suddenly authoritative young daughter who was only just in control of her own hormones and burgeoning womanliness.

And don't even think *like that about me, Mother,* Zara said with some asperity. *I've learned a great deal, a very great deal, from Elizara and Isthia in the past three years. I'm qualified on first-level psychotherapy and Asia's problem is not that complex.*

Leave Asia alone. She doesn't need *two more mothers!* came Rojer's acid rejoinder.

Do as he says, Afra suggested, casting a mildly stern glance at wife and daughter.

Rhodri had changed into a very elegant leisure suit, remarking that it was a relief to be out of uniform as he passed his host and hostess. He took Zara by the arm and insinuated them both neatly into the group, comprised of Flavia, Laria, Thian, and Keylarion, the Tower expediter.

Later it was he who suggested they roll up the rugs and

dance. If he danced more with Flavia than the Lyon girls, he also danced three times with Damia, two slow dances with Asia, one each with Morag and Kaltia and a boisterous polka with Petra, a dance which he insisted was well within the scope of the 'Dinis and shortly had them cavorting as wildly as he and Petra.

And he's Asia's older brother? was Zara's enigmatic comment.

People come in all shapes and forms, Afra said, even mentally breathless from his exertions with Damia as his polka partner. Then he smiled broadly at Petra's prim curtsy when Rojer took her hand for a waltz, the next dance on the tape of assorted musics.

Was or was not Petra 'porting half the time Rhodri was flinging her about? Damia asked, mopping her perspiring face with one hand while she worked a fan with the other.

I doubt it. She's as agile as a slither anyhow. Afra sank to one of the chairs pulled to the side of the large room and 'ported himself a long cool drink of water.

There were all kinds of wines, beers and assorted spirits set out on the refreshment table. While a medium strong, cold Aurigaean beer would have been appropriate, Afra was already charged with the heady ambience in which young, high spirits devoted themselves to fun dancing.

Asia was not allowed to sit by herself. Either Rojer or Xexo, who had suddenly presented himself for the family evening—he was more often involved with ailing mechanical objects—sat or danced with her. Apparently she didn't like the more exuberant dances and that preference was catered to. But, if she sat a dance out, Rojer, Xexo and one of the Coonies—to keep the slithers away, so Petra had informed him—were with her.

Afra would have been delighted to dance with her, for he too deplored her lack of self-esteem and confidence. He also had the thought that the rambunctiousness of his family might be too overpowering for her, being similar to what she contended with in her own home. He would have danced with her, as he had with Flavia, Damia and each of his daughters, but she reacted so negatively to his approach that he pretended to be winded and sat down beside her, emanating as much reassurance and kindliness as he could without her awareness. But she was closed down too tightly even for his gentle pervasions.

The next morning, he and Damia attended to their Tower duties, though Keylarion moved carefully and admitted to aching muscles from so much dancing. Xexo was all businesslike, announcing that Rojer and Asia were with him, learning more about Tower requirements. Teleportations and telepathic messages were both light so that the Tower could be put "on call" and its resident Talents returned to the house to find a sleepy Clancy being fed by Morag and her 'Dinis. Roddie had "asked" for a bucket of coffee which Petra had insisted she was able to bring, with her 'Dinis carrying cup, sweetener and milk. Denebians were known to drink quantities of milk even in their mature years.

Clancy, Damia began on a tight line to the T-2, *are you awake enough to talk about Asia?*

Clancy gave his hostess a quick and not at all sleepy look before resuming that pose. *There have been times when I've suspected that our Asia puts on an act . . .*

That's no *act, Clancy . . .*

. . . No, it's been borne in on me that it's for real. And how could I let such a thing happen to my sweetest cousin? Clancy sighed, took another sip of coffee and smiled gratefully at Morag, who presented him with a cooked breakfast of gargantuan proportions. *It just happened. You know what Roddie's like—well, there were thir-*

teen others in the house, too, and I suspect Aunt Alicia was relieved to have even one who was quiet and content to do things on her own, and responsible enough not to need much supervision. Asia's always been responsible, and quiet, and self-effacing. It's only after not *seeing her for a while—and hearing how Roj has been going on about "negligence" and "deprivation" that I realized that she* was *deprived and neglected. Only what's to do now? She's smart as she can be, got enough Talent to get along most places. She used to repair all the machinery at our place as well as Aunt Alicia's. We kids used to tease her that she'd rather play with machinery than play with us.* He grimaced.

"Doesn't it taste good, Clancy?" Morag asked anxiously.

"Breakfast tastes real good, Morag m'darling. It's that my feet are killing me from all the dancing last night." His grin reassured Morag.

"Are you really my cousin?" she demanded, half of him and half of her parents.

"Second or third cousin, I believe," Clancy said, plowing his way through the eggs, potatoes, beans, grilled tomatoes and fungi on his plate.

"And do you really have to report back to Blundell in just six more days?"

Clancy, she's thirteen! Damia said on a tight line as she recognized the adolescent symptoms in her daughter.

Don't think I don't regret that, Damia. You've mothered a brood of heartbreakers, so you have, and it's not fair on poor mortals like us Denebian backwater boonies.

Backwater? Boonies? Then Damia burst out laughing, knowing that Clancy would handle Morag's crush gently. *Don't ever let my father hear you say that!*

It's your father I learned the words from, but I'd never have the gall to repeat them near your mother!

Roddie appeared next and it was his intention to swim off the exertions of the evening before and that seemed like such a good idea that the heated pool was crowded by the time the last Lyon arose.

"Thought you'd like to hear what else happened," Roddie said to Rojer, Thian and Flavia after brunch, when they found themselves more or less alone in the lounge area.

"Like what?" Thian asked.

Roddie grinned. "Our queen's hatched up a lot more specialty creatures and, while I don't know for sure, I'd say she was assembling a crew to help her fly Refugee out of her vile durance." He paused, waited a beat, and then went on. "She's a lot more active, too, and sends the scurriers out on all kinds of errands. Some of the new hatchings are the kind that would go down the conduits and pipe lines I understand connect the Refugee. And she's got a couple of big bruisers we couldn't quite figure out a need for. They're not true males so it isn't a mating she's after. She's also started planting . . . of all things . . . the seeds and pips she's saved from her food. Used her own dung to plant 'em in. Got herself a trio to take care of the garden, too."

"What sort of things is she growing?" Flavia asked.

"Broadleaf plants," said Roddie with a significant wink and nod.

"That's going to be one disappointed female," Thian said with a thin smile.

"Counting on hatched eggs isn't wise," Rojer said.

"No, no, you mean don't count your eggs until they're hatched," Thian said.

"Uh-uh," Roddie put in, waggling an index finger.

"You've both got it wrong. It's putting all your eggs in one basket."

"What are you talking about?" Laria asked, joining them.

Each one answered simultaneously. "Eggs!" "Chickens!" "Expectations!"

Rojer looked about him, concerned. "Where'd Asia get to?" When no one knew, he went to the kitchen. "Mother, you seen Asia?"

"Xexo has her," Damia said, and added to Rojer's disappearing form. "She *is* here to learn Tower engineering, you know."

CHAPTER
SIX

THE last day of their holiday Rojer, Thian and Flavia were asked to attend the Tower for a conference with Earth Prime.

Thian wondered if Rojer felt as odd as he did, to be sitting on their own, on their parents' couches. The generator silence, too, was unusual, but then a link between Primes did not require the use of the gestalt. That fact gave Thian a certain glow of satisfaction—probably about to be blasted by whatever his grandfather had in mind for him.

Isthian Lyon, Rojer Lyon, Flavia Bastianmajani, Jeff Raven said, stating the official nature of the interview, *I know I offered you choice in your next assignments but there have been some unusual developments. I heard that groan, Thian.*

Yes, sir, so what's happened? They've canceled the pursuit, and Thian felt a wave of almost prescient dread that that was what Jeff Raven would say, and he *knew* that to discontinue the search right now could only have serious repercussions in future generations when the Hive imperative sent yet more Sphere ships forth from their colonial fastnesses, looking for more M-5 worlds to colonize.

The Washington . . .

The who? Thian thought he was familiar with the names of all the major Alliance ships. Rojer raised eyebrows and shoulders, puzzled, too.

The Washington *is the Nebula-class battlewagon that the Alliance has built, mainly from Aurigaean metals, I might add,* Jeff replied with a droll tone to his voice, *and* that's *not yet to be public knowledge. As I was saying, the* Washington *has been assigned as flagship, with an escort of six Galaxy class and four destroyers, all armed with the new Hive-hull–piercing missiles. There're two more spheres to be tracked down.* Jeff paused, allowing his listeners to absorb that. *Then there's a second expedition, equally as important to the High Council, by the way, as the* Washington's *mission, to explore and evaluate the M-5–class worlds which the Hivers bypassed and any more that are identified. Squadron B's got a five-year mission and has been assigned an additional lightweight destroyer craft. The* Genesee's *got a new captain; there's a completely new complement on the AS* KTTS, *and Captain Brikowski of the* Beijing, *plus whoever's sitting in the captain's chairs of the smaller craft.*

Wow! Rojer said.

Sir, I'm ready to go to the Washington, *if they'll have me,* Thian said with quiet reserve.

HAVE YOU, Thian lad? You're top of the list. Ashiant's been bumped up to command the Washington. *Told that paper-asshole of a base Commandant that Ashiant had asked particularly for you.*

He did? Thian could not restrain his elation and had a foolish grin of utter delight on his face.

Captain Spktm also implied that it would not budge the LSTS *out of orbit unless you're on the* Washington *as Prime.*

Wow! Rojer repeated, amusement at his brother's reaction turning to respect.

I hope you can think of saying something more than "Wow," Rojer, when I inform you that you are also to be part of the Prime team on the Washington.

Me, sir? After . . .

That's better. Yes, you, sir. Your conduct during the KTTS *incident met with approval in many 'Dini quarters. And then there's the expertise you displayed during the debriefing of Operation Illuminate.*

After that? Rojer's eyes went so wide that Flavia grinned at his astonishment.

"I told you you did well and you didn't believe me."

Quiet, Flavia, I'm getting to your appointment. Let me add here, Primes, that I never expected FT&T would have to supply naval ships with personnel. But the distances covered and the lengths of these current voyages, as well as the need to maintain close contact, require the services only Primes can offer the Navy. You will not be under naval authority and I have specified that a Prime on a Navy ship has rank equal to the ship's captain.

We do? Rojer was delighted at that.

"Don't let it to go your head, Roj," Thian said aloud.

I won't, but it's nice to know.

They all heard a chuckle from Earth Prime. *I didn't get as much argument as I thought I might. AND I expect you lot to be cognizant of the fact that you ARE to conduct yourselves at all times with the same probity and discretion a captain uses.*

Yes, sir. Even Flavia's reply was suitably ingratiating.

I'm assigning the Pursuit Squadron two Primes because

I am never going to leave my people open to the problems that you boys both faced. Bearing on that problem and preventing any sort of a repetition, I want you to give me the names of support personnel, Talents by preference, whom you would like to have, either overtly or covertly, on your staff. There is always the possibility that you might have to mobilize additional support.

Lieutenant Commander Semirame Kloo, Thian said immediately.

Clancy Sparrow, Rojer said at the same time.

Lieutenant Alison Anne Greevy from the Vadim, Thian added.

Good choices, all three. Especially Greevy, Thian, or had you heard that she's been taking extracurricular training in 'Dini diseases and problems and she was to be transferred to the Washington *in any case. The* Washington *will have a mixed crew.*

Thian had had only the briefest note from Greevy, in which she had said she was "okay, and busy. Hoped he was, both." He was inordinately pleased that she had the initiative to extend her abilities. He'd have to tell her that while *he* had kept his promise, she'd outmaneuvered him. He looked forward even more now to being on the same ship with her again.

I may send along some others who would have various duties, but they will make themselves known to you. Thian, as the elder, you are nominally in charge but I believe that you two brothers work well together anyhow so I anticipate . . . and Jeff paused just briefly to emphasize his point *. . . no discord.*

Now, Flavia, I would like you to undertake the leadership of Talents in the Exploration Squadron. I know you have been in several Towers so you might know the specialists you'd like to have with you. I'll do my best to re-

*assign them to you for this mission—if they're willing.
Tower experience would be helpful, but Talents in biology,
engineering and sociological fields would augment the
specialists already slated to join that expedition.*

I'd like Zara, Asia and . . .

You'd like Zara and Asia?

Thian and Rojer managed to suppress their glee that
Flavia had totally surprised their grandsire.

*Yes, Earth Prime. Zara has first-level therapy qualifica-
tions which would be invaluable on a long cruise. She can
undertake further medical education with whatever medical personnel is aboard. Asia took honors, you know, in
mechanical engineering, just two points below Rojer.
Travel would be invaluable to personal development and
self-confidence. She would be the responsibility of both
Zara and myself. I would also like Rhodri Eagle, whose
talents as a liaison officer are wasted on a queen who's
going nowhere, and Morgelle of Betelgeuse because she's
got archeological credits.*

I didn't know that, and there was still a slightly bemused
tone to Jeff Raven's voice.

That doesn't surprise me, considering her situation, and
Flavia's tone was terse.

*Your selections are excellent, well thought out, Flavia,
and I don't think those appointments will cause much trouble.* His mental tone held more than a tinge of amusement
and satisfaction. *The newly appointed captain of the* Columbia, *which is Squadron B's flagship, is one Vestapia
Soligen and, while her crew is as usual mixed, she requested a female Prime if that was possible.*

*There are also two men of my acquaintance who would
be most helpful, a T-3 and a T-6,* Flavia said in a bland
tone. But her eyes sparkled at Thian and Roger who were
grinning broad encouragement at her.

Their names?

The T-3 is my brother, Mallen, and the T-6 is my cousin, Jesper Ornigo, who has 'Dinis and is keenly interested in alien civilizations, though it has been more hobby than practice . . .

Understandably . . .

Both are Altairians, and currently in positions which could be filled by anyone of the same Talent rating.

Never let it be said, Flavia, that I stood in the way of someone else's nepotism.

I beg your pardon, sir?

"Family joke," Thian and Rojer chorused while Jeff repeated it telepathically. That set them all laughing.

There is a serious aspect of this initial briefing, my young friends. I have laid down certain conditions on your assignments that must be upheld no matter what the circumstances: your duties are strictly outlined in the FT&T Charter and you are definitely aboard as civilian specialists and non-combatants. With the possible exception of launching the sort of surveillance probes Rojer used on Xh-33, you may give no more assistance than that to any explorations or contact, no matter what the provocation, up to and including the saving of lives. Any "projects" beyond the ordinary despatch of your duties must be discussed with me and I will answer the commanders involved.

You may not like it, but you will preserve your own skins first, although, as Thian was once instructed, you will do your best to rescue whichever other essential personnel are designated by the captains. The Navy is supposed to be able to fend for itself.

Flavia, all you Talents are to be escorted at all times while on a planetary surface. Special suiting has been developed for Talents that might reduce the sting-pzzt of proximity to Hiver artifacts and I hope the material proves effective.

A final caution—the launch of the Washington *has already taken place and she is well outside our system at this moment.*

They were afraid of demonstrations, sir? Thian asked.

Around the biggest holograph ever attempted, and Jeff's voice was amused but with a grim edge. *So common sense prevailed over ceremony and, should you hear that the* Washington *was blown up by isolationists, ignore it. You are, however, not to discuss your assignments with anyone, even your parents. Orders are being cut for the additional personnel requested. Rhodri and Clarence will receive ordinary Tower-hour communications, as will Zara and Asia. And the others will be contacted through proper channels. You three will report for transport to your respective postings at 0800 Aurigaean time tomorrow. Enjoy your last day dirtside.*

Before any of the three could even thank Jeff Raven, his contact was broken.

"That's just like him, too," Thian said with a grimace of chagrin. "He plops exactly what you've dreamed of in your lap and bounces off before you can thank him."

"Maybe," Rojer suggested with unusual ambivalence, "we *won't* thank him in the long run. That damned Operation Illuminate ought to have been a snap and it turned out to be a hangover from the Spanish Inquisition."

"The what?" asked Flavia.

"Never mind, Flavia," Rojer replied, grinning. "And I want to thank *you* for wanting Zara and Asia along. I really didn't fancy them on a pursuit mission . . . ."

"I'll work their butts off," Flavia said, being quite serious as she rose from her couch. Then she grinned. "I thought it was worth a try, but I never believed Earth

Prime would let me have them. *And* Mallen and Jes. They're both in such stultifying jobs and I *know* they're capable of much more. And if that's nepotism, I really don't care!" She gave her head a sharp nod.

"Good on you, Flavia," Thian said. "And now, let's assume slightly lugubrious expressions and *try* hard to enjoy these last hours before the booms of hard work and long separation fall on our innocent heads."

Rojer made a derisive noise.

"It *is* going to be hard work at that," Flavia said and started down the Tower steps.

The two brothers rolled their eyes at her pragmatism and, taking the steps three at a time, reached the ground level before she did. Rojer opened the door while Thian waved Flavia through it with an exaggerated flourish of hand, arm and leg.

"Great stars above!" Rojer said, stopping so short that Flavia nearly bumped into him. "Whaddawe tell the parents?"

"What's to tell? Our leave of absence is over. Grandfather is having us report to Blundell Cube at 0800 tomorrow," Thian said in an airy tone and started down the outer Tower steps. "Hi, Asia, has Xexo let you get your hands oily yet?"

"Yes, he did," the slender girl said with an air of startled delight on her face. "I greased and lubed one of the backup turbines. Xexo made me do it by myself. Though I had the manual open all the time!"

"As you should when working with unfamiliar machinery," Rojer said, but grinned so proudly down at her that, for once, she didn't retreat into her usual shyness. "Which one? The 8-32-XR? Or the 184-QJ?"

"The QJ," she said equably. "It's not that great a model but Xexo says it's given very good service with a minimum of trouble."

"That's all to the good when you don't have easy access to spare parts."

"You know very well that you'd have to *make* spare parts for the QJ," she said, tilting her head up to Rojer with a grin for his forgetfulness.

"And have done, now you mention it."

Asia cocked her head at him, a smile wanting to appear on her lips. "Did you have good news?"

"Yes," and Rojer turned to both Thian and Flavia for support since her question took him a bit unawares, "I'd guess you'd say we have." He heaved a resigned sigh. "But vacation's over."

"Back to Blundell Cube in the morning," Thian said in his easy fashion. "Done your lesson? Let's all go swim!"

If, occasionally, their parents regarded them oddly as departure preparations were undertaken, the newly gazetted trio managed to keep shields up and excitement down to an acceptable level. There had been a bit of a flurry from Damia to know that Asia as well as Zara and Clancy were to report to Blundell. Rhodri was surprised but delighted to get orders from his superiors to report to the Navy Base for reassignment.

A last long ride at sunset brought what Afra jokingly called the "Raven-Lyon cavalry" back with appetites capable of dealing with the masses of food that had been prepared. Even Petra was allowed a sip of the sparkling wine that was served as a special accompaniment to the feast. The evening was so convivial that even Kincaid appeared totally relaxed and smiled more often. It was, of course, possible that Rojer filled Asia's glass more often than necessary but she, too, beamed happily about and laughed at every joke, even the ones she didn't quite understand, which Rojer would then explain quietly in her ear.

During the week, her willingness to relax the tight control she held over her mind had verified her T-4 status. Toward the end of the evening, though, as she realized this was the last night of such a marvelous holiday, she began to brood with such intensity that Rojer very privately told her that the best was yet to come and she'd have to be patient until tomorrow. Between the unaccustomed wine and reassurance, Asia fell asleep, leaning against Rojer's shoulder before anyone, even he, noticed.

I'll take very good care of her for you, Rojer, Flavia said when she noticed him sitting unnaturally still, so as not to disturb his sleeping companion.

Am I that obvious? Rojer asked.

Well, not obvious to her, at any rate, Flavia said with a ripple of laughter. *Right now you're good for her. . . .*

And when she gets more confidence and "finds" herself . . . Rojer's tone held a cynical and skeptical note.

I know it's trite, but she'll only be a thought away. You certainly can reinforce your position. If the relationship is to grow, it will. And I personally think it will. She's already improved a hundred percent since she came to Aurigae.

As far as everyone was concerned, 0800 came earlier than usual to Iota Aurigae the next morning, but all the travelers were fed, packed and gathered at the personnel carriers minutes before the appointed time. And the generators were up to maximum.

Dad says he has something special in mind for you, Thian and Rojer, Damia said as her sons and Flavia made themselves comfortable in the carrier, the boys' 'Dinis secure in their smaller slings.

He loves to have something special for us, Thian said

with a resigned groan. *If you're born into this family, you're likely to tour the galaxy.*

You're only ever a thought away, Afra put in. *Ready?*

Steady! Go! Rojer couldn't resist saying, and heard his parents' laugh as his "go" was perfectly timed with the 'port.

Thian and Rojer were only allowed to help Flavia out of the capsule before Earth Prime announced they were to be sped to the *Washington* where it had already passed out of the Sol system. Jeff Raven, bringing them up to speed on the so-called *Washington* riots, said that the scope of the demonstration had proven the wisdom of all the precautions.

There had been numerous attempts to damage the hologram—missiles exploding on target but doing the massive hull no damage "because of its unusual construction and tough design which proved that it was advanced enough to go against even a Hive Sphere." Adherents, trying to protect that launch, had been as numerous as the protestors and nearly as cunning in their attempts to protect the great state-of-the-art ship.

We managed quite a show for all when the Washington *was duly christened by Gktmglnt and Admiral Mekturian, down to the firing of thrusters to disengage from the building gantries and then the inner rockets to begin its majestic voyage of pursuit.*

Grandfather, I didn't know you were poetic!

I'm quoting, Thian, replied Jeff.

Who staged the effects? Rojer wanted to know.

Everyone got in the act, Jeff said, slightly smug. *Haven't had that much fun since your grandmother and I took on the Hiver scouts over Deneb more than a quarter of a century ago. You'll like the* Washington. *Once you learn your way around her. Your first task, however, is to get her the hell out to the poor destroyer the* Maine, *which was left behind by C Squadron to keep on the Hiver's trail. D Squadron left her behind because the two Hiver ships split up. You'll have to bring the other ships of Squadron A in one at a time over the next twenty-four hours. Even with all the help the Prime merge can give you, that's going to be an exhausting task. Flavia, Zara, Asia and every Prime in the family are ready to assist, so don't hang about. You'll enjoy your luxury quarters. The* Washington's *quite a beauty.*

Grandfather wasn't kidding, was he? Rojer said to Thian as they climbed out of their carrier into a hangar four times the size of any other one, including the commodious one on the Refugee.

"Permission to come aboard, Captain," Thian said, nudging Rojer sharply with his elbow, because he'd seen who was in the welcoming committee. *Ashiant himself. Brother, are we getting the treatment!*

"Permission to come aboard, Captain Ashiant," Rojer blurted out.

"Permission granted, Primes, and very glad to have you two aboard," Ashiant said, stepping forward as Thian and Rojer stood on the deck. He then helped the 'Dinis scramble out. "The rest of your team is reported on its way so we can get the *Washington . . .*" and there was great satisfaction and pride in Ashiant's voice as he named his new command, "out to where she's supposed to be most effective."

"GREAT PLEASURE TO SERVE WITH YOU AGAIN, CAPTAIN SPKTM," both Rojer and Thian said to the large 'Dini, to whom their friends were making proper obeisance.

"THIS ONE ASKED FOR YOU, THN, RJR. WITH YOUR HELP WE

WILL OVERCOME," Captain Spktm replied, bending its poll eye in a complimentarily flattering fashion.

"Prime Thian, you will notice a few friendly faces have followed me to the *Washington*, but we'll leave that until dinner, when we've made the initial push," Ashiant went on.

He can't wait, can he? Rojer said in private amusement to his brother.

Nor can we, added Earth Prime. *Work now, play later, boys.*

Another carrier was deposited in the cradle beside theirs. Clancy Sparrow sprang out, repeating the traditional request to board. Ashiant welcomed him and Clancy's 'Dinis made their courtesies to Spktm.

As Captain Ashiant nodded to ratings standing nearby to handle the duffels of the new arrivals, he gestured for the Talents to follow him and Captain Spktm, Clancy bringing up the rear.

"You'll want to learn the intricacies of the *Washington*'s many decks and facilities, Primes . . ." and he gave Thian a long look.

"I was afraid you'd hold that against me forever, Captain Ashiant," Thian said with a broad grin.

"Well, it made naval history," and Ashiant turned to Rojer. "Has your brother ever told you how much protocol he shattered the first hour he was aboard my old command?"

"Sir, you should have heard what Dad had to say about it, and he's not even Navy," Rojer said mendaciously but with a broad smile.

"It's good to know *you* will not try to outdo him."

"Me, sir, no, sir. *That's* not what I do best."

"And what do you do best, Prime Rojer?"

"Classified, sir."

Ashiant regarded Rojer with the same cynical look he had once leveled at Thian.

"I see that this trip is going to be instructive . . . for *all* of us," and there was warning in that mild remark.

There was only the one short walk to a turbo-lift and then another dog-leg down a carpeted corridor clearly in officer territory before Ashiant stopped at a double door, guarded by two marines who immediately braced to attention.

"These accommodations were specifically designed for the use of Talents, Primes, so if you'll press the palms . . ." and Ashiant nodded to the security pad. Thian, Rojer and Clancy laid their hands on it.

"Sir, you will need access, too," Thian said, "she's your ship."

Ashiant nodded and placed his palm on the pad as well. "I appreciate the courtesy."

Then Thian pressed once again and the double doors slid apart. With considerably more poise than they were inwardly feeling, the young men walked into a large lounge, the captains following.

"This is sinfully luxurious," Thian said, glancing around at the appointments of the room. Doors, slightly ajar on either side of the lounge, showed sleeping accommodations, but there were two doors in front of them that were not open, and one set catercornered on the left-hand side.

Now Ashiant strode across the lounge. "This," and he opened it with a palm pressed to the door's pad, "is your *Washington* Tower, if you will, and this," he opened the second room, "a ready room, while that," and now he pointed to the catercornered one, "is the access corridor to the bridge. So you're right on top of everything."

"This is all much more than we had any right to expect, Captain," Thian said, making a bow of appreciation.

"Earth Prime's orders," Ashiant replied with an expressionless face, which altered to a smiling one. "No more than you deserve for the services you supply an entire fleet. If you'll assemble the rest of the team you have aboard immediately," and he gestured to the intercom system in the Tower room, "we can get going."

"Right, sir," Thian said.

"Just leave those duffels there, lads," Clancy said as the ratings arrived with their luggage.

"If you'll proceed to the bridge, sir," Thian added, opening that door, "we'll organize the advance. Oh, sir, who's the *Washington*'s engineering officer?"

Ashiant regarded him with surprise. "Tikele, of course." He pointed to the screen. "When you've the chance, check the roster. I brought as many of my officers with me as I could."

Captain Spktm followed Ashiant, murmuring that it would join its own ship when the Primes were free to 'port it there.

"Rojer can oblige you right now, sir, as I imagine you'd prefer to be on the *LSTS* on her jump," Thian said, giving his first order in his new position.

"Sure can, Captain, if you will be good enough to return to the hangar and your carrier," Rojer said, and strode to the Tower room. *Boy, have we landed in gravy, bro?*

WHAT? And Thian 'ported in beside Rojer, peering around the place.

Enough nonsense! said Earth Prime, his tone slightly peevish.

Rojer slid onto the couch beside him, which happened to have been made to his height so he settled comfortably in it. Clancy and Thian took two of the remaining six couches and settled themselves.

As soon as Rojer had 'ported the Mrdini captain to its

Constellation-class ship, Thian took him into the merge, then Clancy, and announced the merge's readiness to proceed.

First came Jeff Raven, assuming the focus position while the Rowan slipped in right beside him. Sublimated in her mind, Thian recognized Flavia, Zara, Asia, the undistinguishable current complement of both the Blundell Cube and Callisto Tower, then the familiar touches of his parents arrived, Laria and Kincaid, David of Betelgeuse, the T-2s of Altair, Capella and Procyon Primes, his Uncle Jeran and Aunt Ceran and even the only faintly familiar touch of his Uncle Ezro on Vega . . . and other Talents as the teleportation force gathered more strength than it had ever before had and launched the immense bulk of the *Washington* in a long-drawn breath to where the tiny mote of the *Maine* patiently followed the strong ion traces of a Hive sphere's course.

Then one by one, the other vessels—two Constellation class, four of the Galaxy and four destroyers—were 'ported fluently to take their assigned positions in the fleet. Despite the restrictions of the merge, Thian activated the forward screens in their Tower room and saw, no longer quite a mote, but decidedly small in comparison, the lean shape of the *Maine*. He wondered if her crew were aware of their mighty neighbors but he was too integral to the merge to inquire.

Abruptly, most of the merge, having acquitted their part of this gargantuan transportation, disengaged. Only the Earth-Callisto element remained.

Thian, you can tell the Maine *now,* that merge said, *that they are relieved of their duty.* The merge was amused. *Captain's name is Bremerton.*

Still elated by the contact with so many energies, Thian had no trouble making the contact. Bremerton's mind was

wide open with the relief he was experiencing at the arrival of his replacements.

Eleven ships at once? was Bremerton's half-stunned,
half-exultant response. Thian had the distinct impression
of sudden physical movement along with peripheral mental jolts of relief and joy. *Oh, my God, you are. Fleet's
here! Look lively. Fleet's here. Open a channel to the*
Washington, *Sparks. We're about to be relieved!*

*Captain Bremerton, we can 'port you back to Base as
soon as you're ready,* Thian said. *Though I hate to rush
you, sir, the merge is on-line and waiting.*

Clancy was nearest those controls so he cut on the
bridge screen. Despite a crisply neat shipsuit, the tired face
of a relatively young captain was visible on the *Washington's* main com screen, saluting smartly.

"Clark Bremerton, Captain Ashiant, and my respects."
His face developed a broad smile comprised of respect,
awe and amazement. "I'm sending my log over for your
records but I can't say that anything unusual has happened,
sir. No deviation is noted in the ion trail since the split-up
three weeks ago and the Hiver we're following hasn't altered speed."

"Good work, Captain. I won't keep you as I imagine
you, the crew and the *Maine* are looking forward to
home."

"Indeed we are, sir," was the heartfelt response.

"Your log's been transferred. On your way, *Maine.*"

Ashiant saluted smartly and the salute was being returned by an obviously grateful Bremerton when his image
on the forward screen faded.

"Your turn, Primes," Ashiant said into the chair com.

And about time. Thian heard the unmistakable voice of
his grandmother Rowan. *All this naval pomp and circumstance is time-consuming.*

Thian felt the pressure of the merge in his mind and the *Maine* disappeared. So did the constriction of the merge. Beside him, Rojer gave an exaggerated sigh of relief while Clancy stretched until his sinews cracked.

"Do we know where we *are*?" Clancy asked.

"Since I'm the engineer," Rojer began and slipped off the couch and over to the console. It was so shiningly new, not so much as a scratch on any surface but, it was also familiar, and he had their main screen showing the vista before them: an expanse of stars of all variations in color and pulsation.

"Far, far away from every star we know and recognize," was Clancy's thoughtful comment.

All three were startled at a discreet rap on the door.

"Come in."

"Lieutenant Senior Grade Greevy reporting for duty, Primes, and I've taken the liberty of ordering peppers for you."

Alison Anne was appropriately solemn-faced as she advanced with the tray of tall drinks which she presented first to Thian, managing a sly wink before she served his brother and Clancy.

"Good thinking, Lieutenant, and congratulations," Thian said formally, then grinned. "Alison's taken courses in 'Dini health care, Rojer, Clancy . . ."

"Yes, while waiting for you to perform your first duties," Greevy said, still very much in a dignified naval attitude, "I've had the chance to meet all your 'Dinis. So has Commander Kloo . . ."

"Rame's here?" Rojer cried and, careful not to slop the drink from his glass, he made his way to the lounge, where Semirame Kloo snapped him a salute before her face broke into a proud and grateful grin.

"I can't thank you guys enough. Del Falco turned piss-

ant with a vengeance when you skivved off," she said,
"which made him difficult enough until Clancy was
yanked off, too. When the Admiral discovered his destination, the shit really got recirculated. I was clenching my
teeth in expectation of where he'd land next when I got
my orders. I don't think anyone's ever cleared the Phobos
Base as fast as I did. And to the *Washington*, of all assignments! D'you guys have any idea how many people hate
my guts now?"

"And we don't bloody care," Clancy said, swinging
Semirame up and around before he put her down on her
feet again.

Still grinning, she pulled her tunic straight, because she
was wearing the same formal uniform that the medic was.

"Then you've already been on the *Washington* a week?"
Thian asked. When she nodded, still grinning, he asked
who else Ashiant had brought of his *Vadim* officers.

"I haven't met even half my own watch yet," Rame
said, "but I know for sure he brought his engineering officer, Yuri Tikele, Ailsah Vandermeer as first officer and
Commander Fadh Ah Min as weapons, plus quite a few of
the *Vadim*'s chief petty officers, too."

"Not his number one? Commander Germys?"

Rame grinned. "He got booted up to captain on the
Vadim."

"Commander Exeter's here in sick bay," Alison Greevy
said, "and we've a Mrdini unit, because this is a mixed
crew, and I'm liaison." She added that with a grin of pride.

I always said you were cleverer than you knew, Greevy,
Thian said.

And you kept your promise.

Only because you *added an element that made it absolutely possible.*

With due ceremony, Rame then handed a disk to Thian.

"I'm told you're officially the head of the Talent facility, Prime Thian, and I personally received this from Earth Prime Raven with instructions to give it into your keeping. It's for you three only: a listing of all the Talents in this fleet. A handful *are* known to their superiors as possessing *some* Talent, but they're mostly higher than the grade they're listed as. Some have come aboard in minor capacities with T-2 and T-3 qualifications. I respectfully suggest that you either 'port them to this lounge privately or allow me or Lieutenant Greevy to make contact. A code word for all Talents to open their minds to you has been set up throughout the Fleet. That's in the orders, too, and every one of us has been primed to response, though Earth Prime told me that *we* don't know what the word is.

"On an open frequency, the code word 'Saki' will alert us to be on guard, for you and whoever else is named after that code."

"Now," and Alison took a step forward, "peppers not withstanding, Misters Prime, or is that Prime Misters, or what?"

"I'm not a Prime," Clancy said with a grin.

"In here, we're informal, but if you've got to use titles, Prime'll do," Thian said.

Alison cocked her head slightly. "I heard—scuttlebutt, mind you—that you got captain's rank."

"I," Thian responded with a broad smirk, "was told that, humble civilians though all Talents are, T-1s are considered as holding a rank similar to that of a ship's captain."

"But that doesn't mean we're captains," Rojer said, finishing the explanation.

"So a T-2 like me would be equal to a lieutenant commander?" Clancy asked.

Thian shrugged. "Why not?"

"You did well ... Clarence," Semirame Kloo said, arching her eyebrows.

"I've got the Talent, kid."

"What I started to say," Alison began in a stern tone, "is that peppers notwithstanding, you Primes have a captains' dinner tonight, and that's captains plural plus all first officers so that's a mess of people. So you Primes get some rest. That was a big push you just made. Even Rame and I felt it, didn't we?" She looked toward the shorter commander for verification and got an answering grin.

"We're fine," Rojer said negligently.

"That's because you've never been to a captains' dinner, coz," said Clancy and glanced around at the half-open door. "Which is mine?"

Rame shrugged. "Whichever—since you're informal here."

"Haven't you ..." and Clancy stopped, gesturing vaguely at the room doors.

She shook her head. "I'm quartered nearby but Alison's down in sick bay. Now, you guys sack out! C'mon or they'll never stop talking."

Greevy managed one more sly wink at Thian as the door slid shut behind her.

"Eeney, meeney, miney mo!" and Rojer's finger ended up pointing at the middle door on the port side of the lounge.

Thian grabbed his duffel and made for the top room on the other side as Clancy made for the nearest starboard one.

Thian noted with approval that this was a proper bedroom, though there were storage units under the double bed, and wardrobes, as well as private shower and toilet. He didn't feel fatigued at all until he had dutifully lain down. Almost as if there'd been a subliminal command, he fell instantly and deeply asleep.

CHAPTER
SEVEN

THE captain's captains' dinner was every bit as formal as Thian, Rojer and Clancy dreaded. Captain Ashiant made good use of their fluency and acquaintanceship with Mrdinis and each had a 'Dini on either side. Opposite them were Humans and it was permissible to talk across the table from time to time.

Captain Ashiant sat at the head of the table, with Spktm, now captain of 'Dini Constellation *LSTS*, on his right and Thian on Spktm's right with the 'Dini first officer, Mgl, from the Galaxy *KLTL* as his other partner. Rojer was across from his brother with the 'Dini Galaxy-class commander, Ktpl of the *KLTS*, on one side and AS *LSTS*'s first officer, Tlpl, on the other. All four 'Dinis were quite conversable so there was no problem for the brothers. They both 'pathed messages of encouragement to Clancy who was seated at the bottom of the table between the 'Dini destroyer captain and a Galaxy-class number one. But Clancy was also seated across from one of the three women, a very attractive commander. The captain of the destroyer *Athene* was seated beyond Rojer and the third woman, another first officer, was beyond Thian by two places. Clancy quipped back that he was better off than they.

The food was good and each species treated to specialties designed to satisfy different palates. The wines were excellent and Spktm obviously relished the yellow beverage it was served, though the first officer, Tlpl, drank only water.

The dinner went on and on, with numerous courses, and much conversational time between each. Then Thian began to appreciate the ulterior motive of such a lengthy and seemingly formal affair. By the end of it, every one of the top-ranking officers had had a chance to assess each other, and the Primes, either by direct conversation or by observation.

When the final course of savories had been finished, and after-dinner beverages had been replenished, the stewards withdrew, the double doors swooshing shut, and Captain Ashiant rose.

"Captains, Primes and commanders, while we are still far enough away from the Hivers' objective, wherever that may be," Ashiant began, and received a few chuckles, "I suggest that you take advantage of the lull to personally inspect the new facilities aboard the *Washington*. I know that the two Constellation-class ships have had the new weapons systems installed and so has the *Solidarity*, but we must all be aware of how these missiles can be effectively used. *If* we need to employ them."

"WHY HAVE THEM IF NOT TO USE THEM," Ktpl asked bluntly.

Ashiant leveled a glance at Ktpl. "OUR ORDERS ARE WRITTEN SO THERE IS ONLY ONE MEANING, CAPTAIN KTPL." He glanced around to be sure that all the Humans had understood his 'Dini reply. While Thian noted that Ashiant's command of the 'Dini language had improved in accent and fluency, he wasn't surprised when the captain continued in slow and well-enunciated Basic. "The Alliance High Council has spoken in these orders and guides us all in the performance of the objectives of this mission. We have the greatest fleet ever to set out across this galaxy. We will accomplish its aim: to be sure the remaining Hive spheres do not destroy life forms, do not begin two new colonies. When that is done, as you all know, this fleet is to separate and investigate other G-type star systems with M-5 planets that have been bypassed. And establish their condition. Five years have been allotted to these tasks. Let us drink to success, captains, Primes and commanders."

Solemnly all rose and the toast was repeated by Human and 'Dini alike.

Thian rather hoped that this ended the evening but the diners left the long table and congregated in smaller groups: some officers renewing acquaintances while others solemnly discussed details.

"Don't turn," said a low voice behind him and, recognizing Ashiant's tone, Thian complied. "Would you be good enough to 'port me to your quarters for breakfast tomorrow morning, Thian? Raven said you'd know me well enough to find me wherever I am on a ship, even the size of this one."

Thian bent his head, appearing to smooth down his hair as he murmured his reply. "I can if you really require such security, sir."

"This once, I do."

Ashiant immediately drifted away, raising his voice to address Captain Cheseman of the *Solidarity*. Thian was still puzzling over that request when Clancy wandered up to him to say that they could politely leave any time, now that two of the captains had bid Ashiant a polite farewell.

Thian "told" Clancy about Ashiant's request. "Why should a captain, a fleet commander, have to resort to such tactics, Clancy?" Thian asked, uneasy about subterfuge.

"Doubtless he'll tell us tomorrow morning at breakfast," Clancy said, not at all perturbed. "And that's going to come soon enough," he added, glancing at the digital which flashed 0235 at them. "At 0645."

"I'll just secure this door," Rojer said, waving his hand across the inner door pad. "I never *knew* a dinner could last this long and everyone—well, nearly everyone—still be stone-cold sober."

Having set his internal alarm, Thian was awake at precisely 0630, showered and dressed by 0642. He found Clancy in the lounge ahead of him with a table for four loaded with covered dishes.

"Thanks!"

"Know my way about a ship's galley better'n you would."

"Nonsense," said Rojer, yawning as he joined them, his short hair still wet and soaking the neck of his fresh shipsuit. "You took a good few peeks into those stewards' minds last night so you'd know the exact layout and when not to freak 'em out of their minds, 'porting stuff up here."

Clancy dismissed that accusation with a wave of his hand. "Thian, time!" Clancy said as the digital went from 0644 to 0645.

Thian easily located Captain Ashiant, whose quarters were on the same deck and not far away, but the man had had no warning to set down the cup he'd been drinking from when Thian transported him. He glanced quickly to be sure the liquid hadn't spilled from the cup and seemed mildly astonished that it showed no ripple of its recent transplantation.

"Damned smooth, Thian lad, damned smooth," he said and then gestured for Clancy to stand down from attention. "In these quarters, Sparrow, Talents don't stand on ceremony."

"Thank you, sir," Clancy said with one of his irrepressible grins. "Have some more breakfast, Captain?"

Simultaneously, a chair was pulled back from the table and covers whisked off the hot food they had concealed.

"Humph," Ashiant remarked with a wry smile for each of the young men, "breakfast in here could get to be a pleasant habit."

"Any time, sir," Thian and Rojer chorused.

Ashiant laughed. "I doubt you mean that, lads, so I'll give advance notice."

They were all seated when Ashiant handed Thian a slender four-centimeter square.

"From Jeff Raven. It's his authorization for you lads to keep your minds' ears on general . . . and I do mean general . . . morale."

Trying to hide his distaste for that aspect of a Talent's ability, Thian carefully placed the square in his breast pocket.

"You don't like it, lad," and Ashiant included Rojer and Clancy in his quick glance round the table, "and I don't like to have to ask you to do it, but you know the trouble we had with the *Washington* launch. If it hadn't been a hologram, some of those missiles would have inflicted sufficient damage to keep her from being launched."

Thian hadn't known that but Clancy nodded complete understanding.

"There *are* dissidents aboard then?" Thian asked, beginning to appreciate the need for Talented surveillance.

Ashiant gave him a sardonic grin. "We know who *most* of them are. It's the ones we didn't or couldn't identify— the sleepers—and we have to assume that there *are* some. You wouldn't have had any reason to know that the subversive elements have tried to sabotage the *Washington* from the moment her keel plate was laid—as much as you can lay anything in space. She was built in sections, you know, as if she were four smaller ships of a revolutionary new design." Ashiant grinned. "By the time we had those sections connected, we could *then* mount the sort of security so that her outfitting could be completed without too much risk of implanted remotes.

"Now, I'm not asking you lads to 'spy' in the old- fashioned melodramatic way. I'm certainly not asking you to delve into anyone's private mind—unless you have bloody good reason to do so or my specific orders for such an action," and Ashiant swung a thick forefinger to include all three, "but I am asking you to liaise with all the Talents available on all Human ships and have them keep on the alert for any anomalies, strange behaviors, oddities, and report them to you. If your 'Dinis can legitimately mix with the crews of the five 'Dinis ships, that would help, too."

"You're expecting trouble from our Allies?" Thian asked, since the 'Dinis were the last ones he'd expect to sabotage the expedition.

Ashiant nodded once, not looking at Rojer. "We don't want a repetition of the Xh-33 either, Prime."

"No, sir, Captain Ashiant," Rojer said with more vehe- mence than he intended, "we don't!"

"I don't expect any problems immediately. This is likely to be a long, long journey. That's why I felt that *now* was the most appropriate time for me to make you aware of this aspect of your duties. Even in this, you are non-combatants and, as your boss'll tell you, it is compatible, in this instance, with Talent ethics. I'll have more of that toast, if you please, Sparrow." As he buttered it, he added, "The more often you're seen—beginning today—in all parts of the *Washington*, and on the other ships, either singly or as a group—the sooner that sort of habit will become so established no one will find it odd. Rojer, you'll find immense puzzles on one or another cargo deck on the six Human ships. We're having intership contests of all sorts, including VR endurance rides," and he grinned briefly at their surprise. "The other excuse Jeff Raven concocted was that every crewman or woman has the right to send a private message home." When Rojer rolled his eyes, Ashiant chuckled. "I know we've six thousand crew on the *Washington* alone but there're families aboard, so that drastically cuts the number who might use the privilege. Nevertheless some'll be too shy to deliver them here," and he jerked his head toward the doors, "but that'll be one excuse for you to circulate frequently." He glanced up at the digital. "Any questions? I've got to be back in my quarters, finishing my breakfast, by 0710."

"Yes, Captain," Thian said. "Who are the priority personnel we must rescue in the unlikely event of an emergency?"

"Me," Ashiant said with an amused snort. "Contrary to naval history, the captains of every vessel, especially and including the 'Dinis, plus as many first officers as possible, any Talents 5 and above, your 'Dinis, Commander Tikele and Commander Yngocelen . . ."

"Where's he?" Rojer interrupted, remembering Yngie with affection.

"On the *Genesee*, and he'll be delighted to see you, Lyon. So, as one of your first duties, figure out which each of you'll be responsible for. As you know, the *Washington* carries six scouts . . ."

"But there're only three of us," Rojer said in some consternation.

"There are also three other T-2s whom you've yet to meet, Primes, so count them in your calculations. Scouts can accommodate fifteen easily, twenty cramped. Most of the *Washington* pods are built for fifty persons each: for one hundred on the family decks. Constellation pods hold thirty . . ."

"We'll take care of the disposition, sir," Thian said, noting the time on the digital.

"We'll have the usual drills," Ashiant said, rising then. "You can practice then." He nodded to Thian.

"Sir?" and Rojer solemnly handed him the cup he had come with.

"Good lad!"

Cup in hand, a friendly and amused grin on his face, Ashiant was 'ported back to his own quarters.

"Talk about security . . ." Clancy said, dramatically wiping his face with his napkin.

"Actually, it's a sound idea," Rojer replied.

The door chime sounded, almost imperiously.

"Whoops," Clancy said and hastened to disable the inside lock, allowing the door to slide open to admit a puzzled Semirame Kloo. She regarded her palm.

"I thought I was keyed in to that pad."

"Rojer, I told you we didn't need to enable an inner lock on the *Washington*," Thian said with a hint of pique in his voice.

"Sorry about that, Rame. Coffee?" the culprit asked, holding up the thermal pot.

Thus began the first of many long days on the way to their distant and unknown goals.

*   *   *

Flavia, with her team—Asia, Zara, Mallen and Jes—arrived at Clarf Tower for a conference with Kincaid. Flavia had checked with Laria whether or not Kincaid would object or could expand on his initial report.

He certainly doesn't object, Flavia, was Laria's reply, *and I don't know whether he doesn't want to expand on the reports or it's the* time *when he wrote those reports that bothers him.*

We don't have *to . . .*

No, and Laria's negative came out as a slow mental drawl, *I think it might do him the world of good to have to speak of those days. He's much easier in himself now, you know.*

That's good to hear. He's a very likable person.

I know. Laria's brief comment had echoes that set Flavia wondering about Laria's feelings about Kincaid. *I caught that, Flavia Bastianmajani, and I'm his* friend. *I really like him.*

He's lucky, then.

I'm the one who's lucky. I'll catch you tomorrow then at 1400 your time. That'll put you here in the cool, cool dawn of Clarf's autumnal day.

Laria's facetiousness made Flavia even more thoughtful, but that exchange she could keep to herself and did. Zara's enthusiasm for practicing her qualifications could well extend to her oldest sister and that, in Flavia's mind, would be totally improper. Flavia's opinion of Laria was quite high and, whatever her relationship was with Kincaid, it was a very private matter. As all such matters should be.

"This is cool?" Flavia asked Lionasha, her forehead beaded with sweat from the short walk up to Clarf Tower in the crepuscular dawn light. Behind her, Zara, Asia, Jes and Mallen were also finding the closeness of the sultry air uncomfortable.

"Yes, rather," Lionasha said with the cheerfulness of someone thoroughly accustomed to the vagaries of the local climate. "When are you joining your expedition?"

"More or less as soon as we've had a chance to confirm details with Kincaid."

Lionasha nodded. "He really enjoyed himself at Aurigae," the tawny woman said.

"We all had a great time," Zara said, ending in a sigh. "It'll be months, years maybe, before we'll get back."

"Homesick already?" Mallen Bastianmajani asked in a teasing "elder brother" tone.

"I've never been homesick in my life," Zara replied smartly, "but I miss the things I can do there that you don't have anywhere else in the Alliance."

"That's part of homesickness," Mallen said, shooting a glance at his older sister to see if he was laying it on a bit thick. He enjoyed teasing Zara Raven-Lyon: she gave back as good as she got.

Jesper's long legs carried him to the door into the Tower first and it opened for him, a whoosh of cooler air wafting out.

"Oh, my word! What a relief!"

"For now!" Lionasha said with a rueful smile, "but we have to turn the temperature up in here if anyone's going outside or they'd collapse."

"Hmm, yes, or heat stroke . . ."

Laria, with Kincaid at her heels, came down from the Tower room and there were wide and happy grins, renewing the acquaintances established on Aurigae, while Flavia introduced Mallen and Jesper.

"This way," Laria said, taking charge and, with a nod for Lionasha to assume the Tower watch, led her guests

into the living quarters. Refreshments awaited them there
and the 'Dinis served them cooling drinks and finger foods
before they settled into the comfortable chairs and
couches.

"I don't know if you're aware that this scientifically
based expedition does not have full support of the Council," Flavia said.

"That may be luckier than you know," Laria replied.
"There is great curiosity here on Clarf, especially if some
of the planets can be cleared for *our* colonization." She
grinned. "Any disruptive problems?"

"Not for us," Zara said crisply and wrinkling her nose
with disgust. "But some crew members got mauled when
the list of ships in Squadron B was posted."

Asia sort of squinched herself down in the couch corner
she had chosen and stopped eating her snack.

"So we began our duties," Flavia said with a rueful
grin, "by 'porting sailors out of brawls and safely aboard."

"Their families had to be sent to protected enclaves,"
Asia added.

As that was the first information Asia had ever volunteered in her presence, Laria paid close attention and sent
a strong reassurance to the girl. Though Zara was younger
by several years, Asia seemed the junior.

"Rather silly, isn't it, though," Laria said, "as if the
families had anything to do with the orders. And why the
fuss over Squadron B's goals? It's scientific, not combat-
ive."

"Well, there had been quite an organization formed,"
Mallen began, "to prevent the *Washington* from being
formally launched. So there was a lot of undissipated anger and resentment which was then turned on perfectly innocent targets: the nearest being crews of the second

squadron. The dissenters got bilked out of blowing up the *Washington*," Mallen said with a grimace for such folly.

"And even that was only a hologram," Zara added. "Biggest one ever attempted."

"So's the *Washington*. Ship, that is," said Mallen who'd been impressed by the cover operation as well as the immensity of the newest Fleet addition.

"So, what can I do to help your ... ah ... scientific venture? Kincaid said with a wry smile, looking from one expedition member to the next, his glance sliding quickly away from the shy Asia. "I'd've thought the probe files would be sufficient."

"They show what you *saw*, Kincaid," Flavia said slowly. "But everything we see we interpret from our own experience. As you're telempathic, did you have further reactions that wouldn't have been taped?"

Kincaid regarded her for a moment with a very blank expression, but then tension left his long frame and he smiled ruefully.

"There isn't any empathy possible between Humans and the Hivers, and little between Humans and 'Dinis, no matter how close we are to our 'Dini friends." His Nil and Plus were busy talking to the visiting 'Dinis, their low voices an almost melodic descant to the Human conversations.

Zara smiled at him. "Tell us what we don't know, Kincaid."

"Zara!" Flavia called her to order. "What were your impressions, your reactions to what you saw, particularly on the deserted planets?"

"I deplored the waste of valuable colonial property," Kincaid said, slightly flippant. Then leaned forward. "The first one . . ."

"Marengo . . ."

"Is that what they ended up naming it? Ah, well, it had once been reasonably successful. Agriculture not quite as extensive as I understand it was on Xh-33, and I think I was surprised that there wasn't more . . ." He paused and regarded Flavia. "Is this what you mean?"

"Yes, yes, exactly."

"Why?"

"I don't know," she answered honestly. "It just seems sensible to gather as much information as possible from available sources."

"You're it," Zara said, grinning.

"I wasn't the only Talent in the merge that searched," Kincaid said in a voice gone suddenly harsh.

"But you're down as the only T-2 and the merge focus . . ." Zara began, "surely . . ."

"I can only give you *my* impressions," Kincaid interrupted her.

Leave it, Zara, Laria said on a tight line to her sister as she spoke aloud. "Even those would give some insights . . . For instance, you've never mentioned any . . . any detritus in the buildings you scanned."

"Detritus?" Kincaid gave a snort. "You mean bodies? Not on Marcngo. Too old."

"That's another fact I needed to know," Flavia said, grinning with relief. "So many people assume—and that's a major problem with the dissenters who are sure our 'interference' is going to make *them* the next victims—that ALL Hive colonies have been successful, ipso facto."

"We have to find out *why* those that failed, failed," Zara said. "And why Hive Central didn't know? Or didn't care? Or what? I mean, you said the second one looked—"

"Waterloo . . ." Flavia supplied.

"Thanks, the Waterloo planet looked as if it had started out okay and was then abandoned. So what happened?"

Kincaid frowned slightly. "Yes, I wondered about that one, since the Hive colony ship was still in orbit. Even with the plastic probes, I approached both ship and planet very carefully. Spatially, the Waterloo system wasn't far from Marengo. Had the Marengo group merely switched to the Waterloo planet?"

"We don't have all that much substantive detail," Mallen said, "but the 'Dini do maintain that the Hivers haven't changed their modus operandi in centuries. Comparing the installations on Xh-33 with those on Marengo and Waterloo shows that they use the same general structures and agricultural schemes—at least on those three planets."

"And on the other two I probed," Kincaid said, relaxed enough now to lean forward, elbows on his knees, hands clasped together. "They pick sites well inland, as if they don't like, or maybe are even afraid of, large bodies of water."

"They irrigate fields . . ." Zara put in.

"I want to see what sort of hydro pumping units they have . . ." Asia put in. "Did you see any?"

Kincaid smiled at her. "Asia, I wouldn't know a pump unless it had a big sign written all over it—*Pump!* But where agricultural activity had been started, there were irrigation ditches which I can recognize. On the ecologically poor planet, the third one, Talavera, these were just straight gutters of some material, full of leaves or dirt and sand. Very sad to see. Very desolate."

"But nothing to show why the planet was ecologically slain?"

Kincaid shook his head. "If the Hivers fumigate every planet they want to colonize, they may not restore the necessary ecological balance. If it can be saved, it'd be a lovely place," and his face took on a wistful expression.

"We'll damn well try!" Zara said and made a face at Jesper when she saw him regarding her with a slightly supercilious expression. "You just wait and see."

"Are you going there first?" Kincaid asked with a hint of eagerness in his voice.

"That's the plan," Flavia said.

He leaned forward more urgently. "But that system's very close to the one the Hivers are active on."

"Don't worry, Kincaid," Flavia replied with a confident smile, sending him a mental reassurance as well.

With an impatient gesture, he waved that off. "That planet's dangerous. They've a ship. And you'd be in range of their scouts."

"Squadron B's armed with the new missiles, Kincaid," Mallen said, though he did not dismiss Kincaid's obvious alarm. "And the complement includes one of the fast 'Dini destroyers."

"What bothered you so about that planet, Kincaid?" Laria asked in a conversational tone.

He glanced over at her, took a long breath and expelled it.

Flavia was empathic enough to pick up his rising anxiety, and to know that Laria was deftly calming him and carefully shielding his reaction. A quick touch at Zara, and Flavia realized that the highly empathic young therapist had been diverted. Zara would mean no harm, but Kincaid had not completely recovered from whatever had depleted both mental and physical resources.

"The frantic activity, the almost desperate urgency with which the Hive creatures pursued what, for any other culture, would be done with ... energy ... but not such frenetic turmoil."

"Was it the spring of the planet's year?" Jes asked.

"No. I would have understood that!" Kincaid shook his head and began twisting his hands together.

"I know what bothered you," Zara exclaimed, bouncing on her chair. "The sting-pzzt!"

"The what?" Kincaid stared at her and then, almost accusingly, at Laria when she began to laugh.

"No one would have known to tell you, dear friend," Laria said, briefly laying her hand on his shoulder, "but all Talents get a curious reaction from proximity to Hivers and especially Hive metals and artifacts. We named it 'sting-pzzt' because that's the way it echoes in our heads. It leaves a nasty, an unmistakably metallic taste in the back of the throat and tends to make Talents very irritable!" To everyone's surprise, Laria then tousled his hair, laughing with relief. "Going through all those Hive buildings and ending up on an active Hive world, you had a massive overdose of it."

"Sting-pzzt?" Apparently oblivious to the hair-mussing, Kincaid repeated the term in a witless fashion, obviously trying to relate it to his experiences. "The taste I had ruined anything I ate, which was bad enough to start with . . . and I was certainly . . . irritable . . ."

"And a good bit beyond mere 'irritable,' I'd say," Laria remarked. "What a stupid I've been not to have seen what's been bothering you. You must have thought you were going mad with the reactions."

"Yes," and both Kincaid's expression and his tone echoed his amazement, "yes, I did think I was going insane." He looked at the other Talents. "And you've all experienced the same reactions?"

"Not me," said Jes and Mallen shook his head but both Zara and Asia emphatically reassured him.

"We summered on Deneb, you know," Zara said, "and even if our parents and aunts and uncles and cousins had already found most of the Hive metals from the original two scout ships that got strewn over the planet, we'd occasionally smell out a piece or two."

Kincaid turned to Flavia. "But you were at the Base going through the Refugee . . ."

"Not *inside* it, Kincaid," she said, smiling. "We've been supplied with some protective clothing that's supposed to reduce the sting-pzzt effect on Talents. We'll tell you how well it works."

"I could just kick myself," Laria was saying, wallowing in remorse about such an oversight on her part. "Small wonder you had such a miserable time of it, Kincaid."

Don't overdo it, sis, Zara said on a thin line to her older sister. *But it's sure taking the angst out of him. A deep one is your Kincaid.*

He's not my *Kincaid, Zara, and never likely to be.*

More's the pity, sis. He's got a real nice aura. But Vanteer, for all he's a rover, is more your style.

Vanteer? Zara Raven-Lyon, you stop therapizing me, right this instant! D'you understand me?

Before Zara realized how angry she had made her sister, she found herself out in the dawn heat by the multiple carrier.

I can take a hint, she said apologetically. *Laria? I'm sorry. Really I am. And I'm going to be gone for ages.*

Good, was the unequivocal reply. *Oh, all right. I forgive you but don't try that sort of stunt around me again. Understand!*

Yes.

You don't do meekness well. The others are coming.

The complex doors slid apart and the rest of Zara's team moved quickly through the warming air to the capsule, eager to be away before Clarf's sun rose to give them a more intense sample of its power.

Zara's natural buoyancy sustained her during the awkward moment when the others joined her inside the capsule.

Good luck . . . all of you! Keep in touch! said Laria. *Granddad says I'm to put you aboard the* Vadim.

Thanks, Zara, Kincaid added.

Then the capsule was 'ported to join the Second Expeditionary Force and Squadron B, which hurtled on its way to Talavera, third planet of the Tau Ceti VI system.

When the generators wound down from thrusting the large carrier to the point where David of Betelgeuse and his son, Perry, could 'port it the rest of the way, Kincaid sat up and slid his feet to the floor. Keenly aware that Zara's revelation about the sting-pzzt had been a breakthrough point for her Tower partner, Laria pushed herself upright and faced him.

"There should have been some sort of announcement about such a reaction to Hiver stuff, shouldn't there, Laria?" he asked in a reasonable tone of voice.

Behind that, Laria could almost hear his mind shouting with relief, a boiling anger that he hadn't been briefed on that one very important detail and a roiling of other ancillary regrets and recriminations he might never vocalize.

"The sting-pzzt . . ."

Mild words to describe the effect the damned stuff has on the unsuspecting! His mental tone was savage.

Shut up and listen, "Kincaid," and Laria ended up speaking aloud in the tone of a teacher whose pupil continually interrupts. Kincaid gritted his teeth and glared at her. ". . . has been until very recently limited to Deneb, which is the only Human planet to have received Hiver attentions. Probably the only one that ever fought back successfully. True, all the Primes involved were aware of it when my grandparents focused the two merges that destroyed the Hive ship. But over the ensuing decades, no one has, thankfully, had much contact with Hivers.

"You," and she pointed her finger at him, "were by way of being an experiment in FT&T communication possibilities when your Squadron was diverted to follow one of the outbound spheres. It wasn't anticipated that you would be asked to probe Hiver-occupied planets and the Fleet still doesn't half-believe sting-pzzt is valid. Then there was so much going on, what with the Great Sphere being found, then the queen pod—when, it is true," she held up her hand when he had a cogent interruption to make, "more people became aware of this reaction, but not anyone directly in touch with Squadron C. Granted?" He nodded, his anger slowly subsiding, but not, Laria noticed, some of his other confused and roiling emotions. "Then the Xh-33 happened and the focus was off Squadron C until Earth Prime reassigned you here.

"When you arrived, you were in no condition for any debriefing, so it never occurred to me you didn't know, hadn't taken into consideration, the good ol' sting-pzzt that gives every Talent the willies."

"I thought I was going crazy as well as everything else," he said, holding their eye contact.

"I'm not just your Tower chief, Kincaid. I'm your friend. So are Lionasha and Vanteer, because we're already a team. Much more so than we were with those two misfits my grandfather thought I'd be able to work with." Laria gave an indignant huff.

"I'm not a misfit?" Kincaid asked drolly.

"You can be as gay as Dick's hatband in your private life, but you *fit* so much better with me, Lio and Van that we've done everything we can to ease you in ..."

"Even to taking me to Aurigae?"

Laria caught the thread of indignant suspicion and made a face at him.

"You needed a change and were well enough to *enjoy* a vacation. It was Granddad's idea, not mine. And he was trying not to be too obvious with his matchmaking."

Kincaid sat straight up in protest. "He knows I'm homo."

Laria laughed. "Sure he does. We all do, but he wanted Flavia paired with Thian and I could have told him she was far more interested in Jesper Ornigo."

Wry humor caught the edges of Kincaid's thin lips. "I figured she already had calculated on someone other than Thian."

"Flavia's calculating?"

Kincaid grinned at her surprise. "In a nice quiet way, Flavia Bastianmajani knows exactly what she wants and she'll find the best way to achieve it. But you'd want that in a T-1."

"I need it in my T-2, Kincaid Dano. Do I have it? Will you give me the friendly support I need to do my job on this stinking hot planet amid aliens I mostly admire and sometimes fear, because sometimes their alienness overwhelms the Human in me? Will you grab me and shake me out of doing something stupid? Will you be *my* good friend?"

Kincaid rose to his feet, held out his hands to her and lifted her to her feet. As he looked down at her, Laria saw flickering emotions: incredulity, surprise, gratitude and something less definable which made her feel grateful and quite humble.

"I can be your friend, Laria," he said, oddly sad, "and I could wish there was more to share with you."

Surprising her even further on a day of many unusual events, he embraced her, one hand pulling her head to rest against his cheek. *Then* she knew the full story of what had happened to him during the voyage, how he had been emotionally abused in a contest of two very strong-willed men who had thought more of denying the other of his company than of how their passion battle was wracking him who admired them both.

She tightened one arm about his shoulders and, with the other, pressed his head into her cheek. She doubted even Elizara, for all her skill, could completely heal Kincaid's wounded and tormented psyche. But she was here and he was wide open so she could *try*! And did.

They released each other by degrees, for the rapport had been a complete sharing.

"Vanteer may be a rover, Laria, and love many women fervently but not forever. But he would come back to *you* time and again because you would never hold him. Now, if Humans could do a 'Dini split and produce a male you, it would be the best of all conclusions," Kincaid went on, finally slipping his fingers out of hers, "but we haven't even figured out how to clone so I will continue to admire, respect, and love you as my very good friend."

The generators began to spin, recalling them to the day's duties.

"Damned sting-pzzt!" Kincaid muttered as he stretched out again on the couch.

"It really is the most appalling nuisance," Laria idly agreed, aware of the new tranquillity in her partner and much relieved to know that he was finding balance.

One Constellation, two Galaxy-class ships and two speedy destroyers now comprised Squadron B for Back-track. Captain Vestapia Soligen was Squadron Commander and captained the *Columbia*; Hyner Steverice, the *Valparaiso*; Li Hsiang, the destroyer *Valiant*; while Captain

Hptml had the *KMTM* and an unusual bronze-colored Mrdini, Klml, had the 'Dini destroyer-equivalent, the *KVS.*

Captain Soligen, her science officer and two more of the specialists welcomed the Talent contingent aboard with proper ceremony. The *Columbia*'s captain was not what Flavia had half-expected, considering her request for female Primes. Flavia told herself to find out why at some convenient moment. Now she found herself instantly liking the woman: Soligen's face was unlined and pleasant though certainly not a pretty one. She had wide-spaced light eyes which seemed to alter between blue or green, under sharply arched dark brows. Her figure in the ubiquitous shipsuit was trim and athletic without losing essential femininity. Flavia recognized behind the "pleasant" expression a strong personality and a shrewd mind. She grinned, without showing her teeth, as she acknowledged the introductions to Asia and Zara, Rhodri Eagle, Mallen Bastianmajani and Jesper Ornigo.

"Glad to have you aboard, ladies, gentlemen, lieutenant. Let me introduce my science officer, Wayla Gegarian: she's also my official 'Dini interpreter. I've never been able to advance from garble to greeting . . ."

"Captain," Zara said instantly, her hands on the sloping shoulders of Pal and Dis, "my 'Dinis are top-notch tutors. There's nothing they like better than a real challenge to their abilities."

"We teach you . . ." Pal began.

"You understand all you need to hear . . ." Dis put in.

"More important, all you need to say," Pal finished.

Her science officer smothered a cough and the captain raised her eyebrows, her light eyes sparkling bluely.

"I like . . . personages who accept challenges," she replied. "And," she pointed a finger at Dis and Pal who wiggled with pleasure, "I warn you, I'll be a challenge. But I'm determined to try. There's ..."

Flavia caught her almost say something else and veto it.

"... There's plenty of time, despite the almighty push we got out this far, for me to learn a few phrases and understand more."

Then the tall lean man, who had been rocking impatiently from side to side, shoved a hand at Flavia which she gracefully ignored by dropping her carisak, which he graciously retrieved from the deck and handed to a yeoman, obviously on hand to manage impedimenta.

"I'm Dr. Tru Blairik, team biologist. This is my assistant who's the team archivist as well, Mialla Evshenk."

I keep telling Tru that Talents don't make casual physical contacts, Mialla said, as she smiled and bowed slightly from the waist to acknowledge the introduction. "There are more of us, but you'll have plenty of time to get to know which is who. We're delighted to have Talents to help." *Not that I'm likely to be much but I thought I'd see if you can hear me. I'm not strong.*

Strong enough, and greetings, Mialla, Flavia responded. "Nice to meet you, Evshenk."

"There'll be drinks in my quarters this evening at 1930, Primes, gentlemen," the captain was announcing. "Wayla'll take you to your quarters."

"We could ..." Blairik offered.

"Anyone but you, Tru," Mialla said in a gentle tease.

"Be advised," the captain said ruefully. "My electronics officer's designing a special locator for Dr. Blairik."

"You won't need that," Zara said, "with us aboard. I could find Dr. Blairik anywhere."

He gave Zara such a blank stare that it bordered on the hostile.

"Absolutely discreet, I assure you."

But Zara's assurances were no more welcome than her original suggestion.

Leave it, Zara, Flavia said. "In any case, locators should be available for use on any planetary excursions."

"Indeed they will, considering the number of experts and guards needed to do any significant exploration," Captain Soligen said briskly, "the distances to be covered and the fact that your Talents," and she smiled to show she was making a play on the word, "cannot be spread too thin."

There was a brief silence while Zara coped with the embarrassment of her gaffe, which Asia broke.

"I'm a qualified engineer," she said in such a timorous voice that Dr. Blairik regarded her with surprise, "and, if it wouldn't upset anything, I might be able to help with the fabrication."

"Your help would be very welcome, Prime . . ."

"I'm not Prime, only a 4," Asia corrected Wayla Gegarian in her apologetic way.

"Four, three, five or six, the chief will welcome a qualified engineer," Gegarian replied heartily.

"So I'll leave you in Gegarian's capable hands then," the captain said and departed in a brisk fashion.

"Sakers, Perley," Wayla said, gesturing toward the luggage, which was quickly gathered up even as Wayla led the party from the hangar bay.

"We'll see you again at dinner," Blairik said.

"We're all rather pleased," Wayla said as they made their way to a lift, "with the way the *Columbia*'s been refitted. Done up in jig time, I'll tell you. Almost didn't recognize the old tub," she went on with the affectionate insults of a fond and long-term association.

"We heard there was trouble . . ." Flavia began tentatively.

It wouldn't have taken much Talent to "hear" the fury and indignation that came out as a blast from the science officer. The emotions were quickly controlled before Wayla Gegarian answered calmly enough.

"Whole thing was stupid and badly handled—by the Shore Police, too. Good thing we have marines. We'd only minor injuries and the families who had come to see us off got the worst of it. Despicable, useless sort of violence. Didn't change our leaving, though I devoutly hope they'll be gladder to see us return! Here we are. Just down this corridor."

The odors of fresh paint and the dyes of new carpeting were unmistakable.

"Is blue the captain's favorite color?" Zara asked, her ebullience returned.

"Actually, green," Wayla said with a grin, "but blue's traditional for officer territory. Here we are," and she had all of them register their handprints on the door pad.

"We haven't taken someone else's place, have we?" asked Asia uneasily.

"Not at all," Wayla said, so promptly that Asia's uncertainty was set to rest. "Like I said, the ship was refitted with this expedition in mind, so shielded quarters were arranged. Maybe not as roomy as those on the *Washington* but not shabby, and definitely suitable for Talents."

Remembering her brief tour on the *Genesee*, Flavia was quite certain of that: a generous lounge with workstations that could be recessed into the walls or the tables, and six private sleeping rooms. One end of the room was paneled off into screens: a central large one with three smaller on either side. A semicircle of six reclinable chairs faced this.

"I think everything in here is self-explanatory, but you do have a meal dispenser behind this panel," Wayla said, indicating the opaque dark brown panel. "Just settle in and use the door call panel if you need any assistance." She glanced at Rhodri, who grinned back.

"What they don't know, I'll teach 'em," he said, and her smile lingered on him as she took one final backward look as the door panel closed behind her.

"Made a conquest already, have you, Rhodri?"

Rhodri shrugged and winked at Jes and Mallen. "Hell, we've just got aboard, coz. And there're two other Human ships we haven't even cased. If no one minds, I'll take this one," he said and, grabbing his duffel from those the yeomen had stacked inside, mumbled a cheerful tune as he settled in.

Flavia realized quickly enough that her sojourn on the *Genesee* had been no prelude to this voyage. Not only did the Talents have messages and courier services to perform, they had to sit in on long briefings and lectures with the expedition teams, and satisfy the marine commander, Kwan Keiser-Tau, that they were physically fit and were knowledgeable about hand weapons. He'd been a trifle put out when all six Talents showed arms proficiency in the Master class.

"You guys using Talent?" he said, jutting out his head and jaw in a suspicious pose.

Zara laughed. "I come from Aurigae, Major. I've been hunting small game all my life. Easier to use reflexes than Talent to hit those stationary targets."

He turned from Zara to Flavia, his mistrust still plain.

"I hail from Altair, also a pioneer planet, Major."

"None of us are city bred, Major," Mallen said, shifting his position so he was nearer Asia. He had already adroitly intercepted criticism of the shy girl on several occasions.

"And I come from Deneb," Asia said, enough aware of

the discreet support to take advantage of it from time to time.

"Let me reassure you, Major, you need not concern yourselves with *our* safety," Mallen continued with a slightly conciliatory smile. "The dedicated scientists aboard, however, are seldom aware of externals and can be quite focused on their enthusiasms. Feel free to call on our support to maintain their safety whenever necessary."

"My orders are to guard the *lot* of you"—and Major Keiser-Tau did not much relish these orders.

"Well, then, now that you've checked us out," Zara said, "work the others and let us get on . . ."

Watch your manners, Zara, Flavia said.

". . . with our duties," she finished with no perceptible pause. "I must meet with my 'Dinis, who are tutoring Captain Soligen," she added, and, making a careful show of snapping the safety on the weapon she was holding, stowed it in the correct rack. *Frankly, I think she's language-deaf!*

When Squadron B was close enough to the beacon left by Squadron C, Flavia suggested to the captain that they could speed the voyage up by several weeks if they tried a merge.

"I'd remain on the *Columbia*, put Rhodri on the *KMTM*, Mallen on the *Valparaiso*, Asia on the *Valiant* and Zara and her 'Dinis on the *KVS*, and with a merge of all available Talents of lesser ratings, we can reach the Talavera beacon, cutting off two weeks."

"That won't cause you undue strain?" Soligen asked, though she clearly liked the notion.

"Not with the generator gestalt available to us," Flavia said, her expression confident and reassuring.

Vestapia Soligen fingered her lower lip for a long,

thoughtful moment. "Why put Zara on the *KVS*? Wouldn't she be needed on one of the larger vessels?"

"I think it is wiser to place Zara and her 'Dinis on a ship that is so ready and . . . eager . . . to meet opposition," Flavia said. "Zara could stop Klml's ship cold. Asia's told her how."

Soligen chuckled. "So Klml's . . . attitude hadn't escaped you?"

"Captain Klml's attitude was noted by Lieutenant Eagle on his first meeting. He's reasonably sure that the moment the system is in range, the *KVS* will detour. He thinks it's had private orders to that effect. There hasn't been a real Mrdini strike against a live Hiver in far too long to promote any color to prominence."

"Run that last statement past me again, Flavia?"

"You will have noted that 'Dini hides are many different shades. The color denotes a clan relationship. All 'Dinis in a color, therefore, gain prestige if one of their color achieves merit."

"In this instance, blowing up a Hiver sphere even if they go with it?"

"That's about it."

"I guess we should be glad that the ethnic groups in Human history that considered suicide for whatever cause they espoused an honorable end have now been thoroughly integrated," the captain said in a tart voice, "or isolated on worlds where that kind of prejudice is limited to that population."

Flavia nodded agreement. "The 'Dinis do find our insistence on caution and safety as odd as we find their willingness to self-destruct."

"I wonder how much of a chance the *KVS*'d have to take out that Sphere?"

"Captain?" Flavia was astonished at such speculation.

The captain chuckled. "The Fleet's been a passive force a long time, Flavia. I suppose you've also noticed the average mean age of my crew, rating and officer, is younger than on most ships of this class?"

"I had." That accounted for the fact that Asia was suddenly developing poise and the self-confidence that comes from being popular with her peers.

"No matter how we conduct this Hiver campaign, Prime, we're going to have to learn new techniques and some will prove fatal. Maybe not as suicidal as what the *KVS* might have in mind, but certainly more daring than the usual tactics."

"Maybe the *Columbia*'s in the wrong squadron if that's your thinking, ma'am."

The captain's eyes were ice-green as she gave the Talent a long look.

"Where do you—personally—stand on that ground?"

"I come from a planet that is barely settled. I'm used to hunting to feed my family. There are times when aggression is required, but certainly not courted. However, I would feel privileged to serve with you on one that might test my theories, too."

"Theories?" The captain leaned forward with obvious interest.

Flavia smiled and dismissed the question. "Right now, let us pass the immediate danger point, keeping the *KVS* *with* the Squadron. I am obliged to inform you that this sort of maneuver is not specifically mentioned in the parameters of my assignment to Squadron B."

"I didn't think it was. I'd call it 'bending' to exigencies, myself, and it will be noted in my log as a means to the end of saving a planet. I'll hope we can do without too much such 'bending' but . . ."

"I would consider any reasonable request, Captain."

"I appreciate that, Prime. So let this 'portation be duly authorized and executed. I'd rather explain this than how a valuable Alliance ship defected. How soon before you can effect this ... bypass?"

"Within the hour."

Vestapia Soligen regarded Flavia with open admiration and a genuine relief dominated her public mind. So, the captain had entertained the same notions Rhodri had voiced.

"The sooner the better!"

Transferring the Talents to their designated ships, revving generators to their highest effective performance level and alerting every talent on the Human ships was all done within the specified hour.

First, Flavia sent her mind ahead to locate the identifiable pulsations and small mass of the beacon. Then she called for each of her Talents to gather the lesser ones into the individual merges before she integrated first Rhodri, then Jesper, Mallen, and Asia and finally the fine strong blaze of Talent that was Zara.

Let's get there! Flavia said, seizing the exact peak of the generated power for the gestalt.

We've got here! was Zara's exultant response a second later.

When Zara was 'ported back on the *Columbia*, she made straight for Vestapia's ready room and requested an interview.

"Ma'am, Captain Klml definitely would've defected. It's a bit upset at being where it never expected to arrive in the first place and in the second place, isn't too happy to have been denied 'honorable action.' Klml's words. My 'Dinis say that it's raging that it has been assigned to such a ... well, there isn't really a Basic equivalent but ..." Zara shrugged her inadequacy.

"Bunch of spineless slugs?" Vestapia suggested.

"That's close," she replied though there was little levity in her tone. "So I took the liberty of reminding Klml that this planet had the priority. I get the distinct impression its orders differ from yours."

"In that, Prime, you demonstrate an astute understanding of a classified situation. Do I make myself clear?"

"You do, Captain."

"See that it remains classified. And, by the way, Flavia has seen the matter clearly but I would rather the others do not."

"They already may but they won't talk about it."

"We should make an appropriate orbit in three days max. I shall require Captain Klml to make the initial landing, hopefully defusing a lot of pent-up resentment. I don't think there's a chance there're any Hivers left alive down there but you never know. And since Klml is so eager to meet the enemy, let us give him first go."

Zara hesitated, then grinned. "You did know that your marines would prefer to claim that distinction?"

"They can gain ancestral merit by guarding the scientists everywhere they need to go."

"Yes, ma'am. Did you wish me to convey your orders to Captain Klml?"

"Please, since I can barely manage 'good morning and do you require supplies.' But even that much is progress for me."

"Dis and Pal remark most favorably on your progress."

"Well, they're the only ones. You know, I'd've sworn Mrdinis were pessimists."

"Only those raised on Clarf. Can I leave now?"

"Yes, but if your 'Dinis can, keep in touch with our wily Captain Klml."

"You just bet they will."

*   *   *

By dint of careful compliments and skillful innuendo—
not easy in the straightforward 'Dini language—Rhodri
managed to imply that Klml would be the first Mrdini captain to ever set foot on a Hive colony planet. That fact
alone helped soothe Klml's wounded pride and damaged
honor.

"Smart thinking, Rhodri," Flavia as well as Vestapia
Soligen told him when he reported on that successful interview. "I hope Major Keiser-Tau will not feel his prerogative has been usurped."

The captain smiled. "Keiser-Tau will keep his thoughts
to himself—fortunately. He is not looking forward to
keeping tabs on scientists."

"Oh, I'm supposed to be down testing those locator buttons with Asia and Lieutenant Ismail," Flavia said. "If
you'll excuse me . . ." and she departed without waiting
for permission.

"Talking 'Dini makes my throat very dry," the captain
said, rising from her desk and going to the dispenser.

"Mine, too," Rhodri said, in the circumstances not
above confirming the reason behind her hospitality.

Zara reported hearing the major swear by several god
figures she didn't know existed in Alliance space, but he
desisted the moment he was aware of her presence in the
repairs shop.

"He's been briefing his men with every single tape
available in the *Columbia*'s library on what they might expect, landing on a Hiver planet," she went on.

Rhodri grinned. "That was predictable," was all he said.

"Captain said he doesn't like escorting scientists about.
They tend to get themselves lost or in dangerous situations
which 'sensible' people would avoid."

"We'll have locator buttons," Asia said with quiet pride. "Sadler . . . I mean, Lieutenant Ismail . . . has set up a very efficient assembly line of off-duty personnel."

"Like you?" Rhodri grinned affectionately. "No wonder we never see much of you, sis," he added kindly, ruffling her hair.

"I do wish you'd stop that, Roddie," she said with far more exasperation than she had ever displayed.

"Sure, sure!" Rhodri snatched his hand away as if it burned. "Don't get your knickers in a twist!"

"Mine aren't!" she retorted with such a sly look that Rhodri unaccountably flushed, causing Zara to demand whom he fancied.

"None of your damned business," he said and, going into his room, slammed the automatic door forcefully across the opening.

No speculations at this time, Flavia told Zara firmly. "When will we get these locator buttons, Asia?"

"They're being distributed now to everyone who's to be landed," Asia said, having retreated to her customary unassuming behavior.

"Well, it'll be a relief to get on with what we were sent here for," Flavia said, and no one in the lounge disagreed.

The actual landing was somewhat of an anticlimax although the state of the planet caused immediate uproar in the scientific corps. Sensor readings had indicated that the ozone layer was undamaged, which had been a major concern to the ecologists and added to the puzzle of its barrenness. Rivers and lakes, as well as several large seas, seemed to be in good order, life forms visible if unidentifiable. There was still topsoil, but unless plants could be coaxed to grow, it would sift away in the winds. On the higher ground, erosion was already obvious.

Avidly watched on remote relays, the 'Dinis landed in smart array and secured the main Hive installation. Its huge expanse, covering over three acres, was found to be empty of everything save windblown debris. Klml had its crew mapping the site and measuring both interior and exterior, plotting the different levels and sections and sending the results up to the waiting teams. When the tunnels were discovered, Klml itself led the exploratory team. Flavia was asked to 'port down more supplies and was very glad that she would not be included in this Operation Illuminate. All but one tunnel dead-ended and the completed one was connected with the smaller building ten kilometers from the original—and probably headquarters—building.

Between the two there were signs of attempts to cultivate the land: even plastic-lined reservoirs for water and several hundred meters of irrigation channel.

When Captain Klml was satisfied that no living enemy was apparent, it allowed "others," meaning the Humans, to come down. Despite Flavia's offers of teleportation, multipurpose shuttles were used as these would provide ground transport, not best accomplished by 'portation, which tended to go from Point A to any designated Point B. The Talents were asked to 'port down sensitive instrumentation once the base camp was established.

Where the Talents were undeniably indispensable was to see if the panels in the queens' quarters which Klml had located were still operational. Flavia, Rhodri and Zara slid down the connecting links in the main building while Asia, assiduously accompanied by Lieutenant Ismail and a detachment of marines, went off to the second building. Mallen and Jesper Ornigo went with whichever group thought it might require Talented help.

"They really don't alter their structures much," Flavia said when the three Talents picked themselves up off the dusty floor of chambers that so closely resembled the queens' quarters on Refugee. Dust had filtered in a thin film over the "foot" panels but the upper ones had been installed high enough to be covered by only a light layer. Rhodri and Flavia were tall enough to brush this off.

"First left-hand panel's exactly the same," Rhodri said, peering at what his hand light revealed. "But these—are different."

"You'd expect that, wouldn't you," Zara asked with some asperity. "This is a ground operation. So what do we do now?"

"Try to start it up: that panel's the same and I brought mock-ups," Rhodri said, removing from his thigh pocket a handful of triangular-tipped wands which approximated the shape of a queen's palps. He handed some to Flavia and Zara.

"I'm not damned tall enough," Zara muttered.

"Nor am I," Flavia said with some disgust.

"There're plenty of boxes the right size . . ." and Rhodri pilfered rigid crates from the supply depot for the two women.

"D'you remember the sequence that started the ship, Flavia?"

"Engraved on my retina," Flavia said, arranging three wands in her fingers on each hand in a triangular pattern. When she got them right, by using a light application of telekinesis, she inserted them in the apertures in the sequence she remembered.

A flickering illumination started—and also a near riot from the unprepared 'Dini crewmen still exploring the facility. The light, if one could call it that, lasted long enough for the power source to be found, and the dessicated remains of one queen and nine attendants.

When the corpses had been examined—such pieces as

permitted examination of any kind because most disintegrated into dust at the lightest touch—the generally accepted opinion was that death was caused by starvation. Then the arguments began: had only one queen been installed on the planet? That wasn't the usual procedure. Or had only this one been left by others which had escaped to a more hospitable planet? Had she died before or after their leaving? But fields had been plowed and seeds sown: a second building had been prepared and a tunnel connecting it to the first, a tunnel large enough for a queen to traverse. The enigmas quite outweighed the matters confirmed.

Only the queens seemed to have special quarters, though tubes and tunnels connected with what appeared to be large spaces where harvests were processed and stored. Egg tubes opened into each of the queens' quarters.

"Work, work, work, work," Zara muttered under her breath when the xenob Yakamasura went into a long explanation of the possible societal structure of the Hivers. "No other ethic but work."

"And conquest," Rhodri murmured back. "Don't forget conquest!"

"A change is as good as a rest!"

Continuing an orderly investigation, the scientists sampled and examined everything from the dust, to the underlying layers of clay and stone, to the dessicated fragments of vegetation that were found and brought in. Then they moved further away from the now sizable base camp, inspecting the dying vegetation, tree-like as well as groundcover. Bushes, shrubs, hedges, plants, large vines, grassoids: all were dead or dying right up to the snow level on the mountain ranges of the continental mass. It was on the higher slopes that scattered piles of skeletals, the remains of various species, were found, as if the creatures—whatever they had been—had sought sanctuary in the highest place away from the predators, and whatever means was used to destroy the planet's indigenous life forms.

The large preliminary Reformation dome was constructed over what ecologist Rovenery Mordmann considered to be a suitable site for an ecological jump-start. When both Human and 'Dini airborne investigations returned from the borders of the continental mass, he could be heard bewailing the fact that no life forms, not so much as ground-burrowing insects, beetles or worms, however insignificant, could be found. His wails took on the form of constant cursings of the Hivers for the murder of this world.

"All right, so the land's dead, but what about the seas?" Captain Soligen asked during an evening session which had consisted of too many Mordmann dirges and nothing of a positive nature whatsoever.

"The seas?" Mordmann regarded her with utter astonishment. "It's the *land* that the Hivers infest, ma'am."

"And it's the *seas* they never bother with," Zara reminded him. "Nor any water. We're drinking river water, although there's a rather noxious sulphuric aftertaste . . ."

"The seas . . . the waters . . ." Without a single backward glance at the meeting he was precipitously leaving, Mordmann departed and very shortly all heard an airsled taking off.

"I kept trying to tell him," the xeno, Yakamasura, said sorrowfully, "but he said it was the land that mattered."

"It is so possible to miss the obvious," Flavia said soothingly.

Hope for the revivification of Talavera improved considerably when it was found that the waters—seas, rivers, lakes, streams—were by no means as ecologically reduced as the land, though poor in quantity and quality. Mordmann pronounced that the planet's balance could be restored and they would immediately initiate several combinations that might suit. Whatever creatures had lived here before had had different basic requirements for there were significant basic constituents lacking in the soil: chitin, selenium, most of the rare earths and a paucity of calcium, though quantities of that would have been available from sea creatures. Lack of chitin alone would have been a problem for Hivers, since the captive queen ate substances rich with that compound.

Mordmann delayed departure from Talavera as long as he could, to be sure at least one of the domes showed some signs that seeds were prospering in the revived soil.

"One undeniable fact we have learned," Mordmann said at his most pontifical as his group settled into the shuttle carrying them back to the ship.

"And what is that?" Captain Soligen asked, knowing what she might be letting them all in for.

"That the Hiver policy of fumigation of all life forms from the planets they wish to colonize often results in benefits that are more short-term than they anticipate. I suspect they lose half the planets they find to just such a Pyrrhic program." Then, looking excessively pleased with himself, he folded his hands on his incipient paunch and said nothing more on the short voyage back to the *Columbia*.

The installations on the second former colony, Marengo, were more numerous, extending in all directions towards the mountain ranges. The fields had been assiduously cultivated for a substantial number of decades. Analysis of the dirt once again showed the lack of certain rare earths and minerals: chitin, Vitamins A and E, most of the rare earths and selenium, although sulphur was present in quantity. Whatever indigenous life forms had lived in Marengo had disappeared without trace though its vegetation, lush and vigorous on the highlands the Hivers had not yet tamed, suggested that perhaps no land creatures had as yet evolved in this almost Pleistocene era.

Rhodri reported to Captain Soligen that the Mrdini ship was unlikely to follow the rest of the Squadron tamely to the next M-5.

"There's a Hive ship orbiting Waterloo and I shan't want it attacking ours," Vestapia said, frowning.

"Ma'am?" When Captain Soligen gestured for Flavia to continue, she said, "I think we might be able to pull the same trick here as we did with Xh-33."

"Trick? Blow the orbiting ship up?" The captain snorted.

"No, steal it," Flavia said. "We don't, of course, know if the ship is occupied. The one at Xh-33 certainly wasn't. If it is, we can also use Hiver tactics and gas the maintenance crew."

"As I remember the report," Vestapia said in what Rhodri now privately termed her "captain's tone," "the gas was so corrosive, it took the entire voyage back to Phobos Moon Base to clear the stuff."

"There are other gases available . . ."

"You know that Klml's out for Hiver blood . . ."

"What would be on the ship would be the specialist types, maintaining cables and conduits and suchlike. Only queens control the ship. It's a queen Klml wants to fight, not her workers."

"I doubt we can supply Klml a queen," Vestapia said sourly, "but I sure wish we could end that problem. I didn't realize . . . No matter," and she broke off what she'd started to say with a dismissing wave.

Rhodri "heard" what Vestapia didn't say because her

mind had been vivid with it: ". . . how blood-thirsty Mrdinis really are." Quick contact with Flavia told him she'd caught that, too.

"Klml," Vestapia continued, "will get another first, the chance to invade a Hiver ship, and that ought to give its color some sort of glory, shouldn't it?"

"It'll help," Rhodri agreed. He was seated on the edge of her desk, hoping to get this planning session over with so he could enjoy another sort of planning. He caught Flavia's look at his informal position and decided discretion should reign. He took to a meditative pacing.

"Certainly," Flavia said, "we know the inside of the sphere well enough to know where to 'port Captain Klml's crew aboard to secure the ship. Klml can do whatever it likes to what might be on board and that'd be another coup. Then we steal it. The Waterloo Hivers will be stuck on that planet and we can take care of them when . . . when it's been decided what's to be done with Hiver colonies."

Vestapia spent one more moment looking at Flavia's elegant features before she started to laugh.

"Think of the honor Klml's color would gain by bringing back a Hiver ship under its own power."

"Could they do that?"

"If there's enough fuel on board and with a little instruction from us on how to manipulate the instrument panel, yes," Rhodri said, beaming because he found Flavia's idea as outrageous as the captain did. "Only we'd better have a chance to splash 'Dini insignia all over the ship, if we don't want it fired on during its way back. If you wish, ma'am, I'll explain all this to Captain Hptml on the *KMTM*. It's most anxious that the *KVS* does not go off half-cocked. *KMTM* would have to rescue it . . . if it could.

And the Captain's mortally afraid of putting us, as well as its color, in jeopardy over Klml's dreams of bravura."

"So, we take a page out of the *Genesee*'s log?"

"It worked."

The captain considered again. "Only this time, I think we permit the *KVS* to use its speed and skill and bombard the planet's defenses. That is, of course"—and she held up her hand—"if we find they have the same capabilities discovered at Xh-33."

"Why should the Hivers alter their time-soldered habits?" Rhodri asked.

"This time," Flavia said, "*we* will clear *our* actions with Earth Prime."

"Of course," Vestapia Soligen agreed suavely, her light eyes as green as Rhodri'd ever seen them.

"That'll be great," he remarked later in their quarters, rubbing his hands together in anticipation.

"I'll get Jeff Raven's permission," Flavia said, and left the two together. Which was exactly what both Rhodri and the captain wanted at that moment. Impending action had the fringe benefit of arousing other basic instincts as well.

Flavia's contact with Jeff received the necessary permission to duplicate—with the exercise of all due caution as far as the Talents were concerned—the successful tactics of the *Genesee*.

"That's no fun," Zara complained. "We'll be observers—as always."

"Yes, but I'll beat cousin Clancy into action," Rhodri said, delighted with that fact.

"Action?"

"All right, close encounter because, brat, we're much closer to our objective . . ."

"We're weeks away," she corrected him.

"But mere weeks instead of more months like the main attack units."

"We may have received permission," Flavia said, "but who knows if Klml'll buy the plan? It's one frustrated Mrdini and all of us remember what happened to Rojer."

"That's exactly why nothing remotely similar will be allowed to happen this time," said Zara in a hard, icy, vindictive tone that startled those who heard it.

Jes broke the silence with his question. "Is the main Fleet closing on the Hiver at all?"

"Earth Prime wouldn't say, precisely," Flavia answered him, a slight frown creasing her usually smooth brow, "but I sensed something . . ."

"Then Grandfather wanted you to," Zara said quickly. "So what did you sense?"

Flavia considered this for a long moment. "Triumph, I think."

"Damn!" Rhodri said. "They may be moving in for the kill before we can get to Waterloo."

"Unlikely, because I've already located the Waterloo beacon Kincaid so kindly set in place." She smiled as her team reacted with jubilation. Except for Asia.

"I don't see why everyone is so happy to be pulling primary-school tricks on the Hivers. Especially you, Zara."

Zara flushed. "I'll never live that moment down, will I? But you saw what Hivers did to Talavera—ruined a perfectly good planet. And damned near ruined Marengo the same way. They don't *deserve* to colonize their backyards."

"Which went nova!" Asia said but her expression was less vehement. "They must be good for something. Everyone and everything I know is."

"Try as I will," Flavia said after a long pause, "I cannot

find 'good' in a life form that deliberately annihilates all other life forms so that it can dominate a world for the sole purpose of multiplying itself to the point where it must find yet another world to fumigate and repeat the process."

Asia was so quiet and exuded such a depression that Zara approached her, delicately smoothing the fine hair back from her face.

"They're great farmers," she said softly.

"If that ability could be directed into proper channels . . ." Flavia began.

"No one else would ever have to crop-farm," Jesper finished.

"If only there was a way to get that across to them . . ." Mallen added.

"However, we have other plans to make now," Flavia said, "based on the information we have managed to gather about this enigmatic species and their modus operandi. It does seem a pity, though, that we can't communicate and form a collaborative effort."

"That'll be the day!" Zara managed the last words.

CHAPTER
EIGHT

T HE weeks had moved into months as the main fleet continued to follow the increasingly strong ion trail of the Hiver 2. Squadron D plodded on along after Hiver 1 which had diverted spatially down and towards the "arm" of the Milky Way.

Clancy Sparrow proved to have many inventive ways to keep boredom at bay, such as a lottery to guess the particle strength of the trail at the end of each week. The lottery also gave him and Rojer the chance to meet most of the other Talents, covert and open, on the *Washington*.

"We've got quite a few T-3s on board," they told Thian and ran down their mental lists, with descriptions.

"All'll answer to the code word now," said Rojer, who had done most of the implanting.

"One way or another," and Clancy grinned.

Another notion was to give names to the G-type systems which the Hivers ignored. An official name was drawn later from those that had been sent in from the squadron-wide competition. Kloo joined Clancy and Rojer 'porting over to other ships to explain the procedure and, in that way, managed to meet more Talents and pick up a few new ones.

"I don't know how much help I'd be to you," a T-4 chef said to Rojer in the captain's galley of the *Genesee*. "To my knowledge, the only things I have any control over are professional problems."

"What, for instance?" Rojer had asked, propping one hip on the corner of a worktop and eyeing cakes the chef was icing with deft movements of his spatula.

"I never cut myself," and he paused to regard his handiwork. "Fat never spatters on me. I've never dropped a hot pan or baking tray—and I've handled plenty without so much as a burn blister. That's why they call me Lucky Louie."

Amused and intrigued, Rojer leaned back against the counter behind him. "Anything else?"

"Well, I've never broken a bone," and the round-faced man grinned, "lost a fight or a card game. I don't play them no more. Didn't think it was fair if I always won."

Rojer took that opportunity to grip the man's shoulder in an expression of approval for such probity, and caught the unmistakable touch of Lucky Louie's mind so that he could bring him to a merge should that be necessary.

"His soufflés and cakes never fall either," muttered another galley crewman as Rojer left, but the tone was good-naturedly envious.

On the destroyer *Athene*, Semirame Kloo "discovered" an unexpected Talent in one of the electricians who had an extraordinary record of avoiding accidents in a somewhat dangerous job. Chief Petty Officer Lea Day had always chalked that up to the fact that she was careful and never attempted a repair unless she'd thoroughly looked over any schematics. She was vastly surprised to test out as a T-4 kinetic.

"But I've never *heard* anything in my skull," CPO Day told Kloo, her expression perplexed.

Thian, Kloo said, *I've just found us another T-4 kinetic. CPO Lea Day* says *she's never heard anything in her skull.*

Chief Day, Thian promptly said, *just nod your head to Commander Kloo if you're hearing me?*

Chief Day's brown eyes protruded from her skull as she obediently nodded. Then she leaned toward Rame Kloo and whispered. "Who was that?"

"Prime Thian Raven-Lyon."

"But he's on the *Washington*!"

"He's also a T-1 and made me hear him, too. Now, Chief, with a kinetic Talent like yours, we may need to contact you for help real soon."

"What kind of help?" the chief was dubious as well as anxious.

"Nothing beyond your abilities, Chief, but if Prime Thian calls you, put down whatever you're doing and just let yourself go."

"Go? How?"

Kloo relaxed her entire body, hands draped on her thighs, shoulders and chest collapsed.

"That's all I gotta do?"

"That's right. Your being relaxed helps Thian tap your kinetic energy."

"*That's* what I got? Kinetic energy?"

"Which is why you've been able to turn aside electrical jolts that would have injured you."

"But how'd I know how to do it?"

Kloo was getting very good at proving her next point. She sprang at Lea Day, who immediately assumed a defensive stance.

"Like that, basically," Kloo said, stepping back. "A basic survival instinct. Only your brain clicks in with its kinetic whammy." She rose and shook hands with Chief Day, who had a good strong grip with fingers calloused from work. That was the next to the last step of preparation. "If you hear the word 'Saki' in your head, stop what you're doing and relax."

"Saki!" The chief nodded. "What if I'm not near a chair?"

Kloo laughed. "Don't tell me, Chief, you can't relax any damned time you have the chance!"

"Aye, sir."

The science officers had other puzzles, concerning why the Hivers rejected so many systems. Were they already inhabited by Hivers? Or uninhabitable? Had any of them, by any remote chance, once held off a Hiver advance, too? The skeptics thought this area of space far too remote to have received much Hiver attention. Others argued that the very fact that the Hive ship was going so far from its original homeworld proved it had investigated all the intervening systems and either occupied them or found them useless.

To settle some of these arguments—which often proved agitated—Captain Ashiant initiated a program for the fast scout ships which the *Washington* carried. Whenever an M-5 system was observed, the scouts—using a different crew each time—departed their mother ship for quick discreet surveys.

For these, Ashiant asked the assistance of the Talents, who were as glad to have some excitement as any other crew member. Thian always took Lieutenant Senior Grade Alison Greevy with him; Rojer favored a T-3 ensign from Engineering, Cyra Charteris; while Clancy needed to have two augment his T-2 abilities. Invariably he chose Semirame Kloo and the only other T-3, one of the gunnery officers, Targia Upland. An attractive girl, her nickname of "Target" was respect for her professional competence and a knowledge of antique and archaic weapons.

When the scout was close enough for the Talents to deploy the undetectable plastic units, the relevant planet within the system was probed. Four Hiver colonies were discovered out of twenty worlds surveyed, two with sphere ships in orbit and the usual debris. Once Hiver possession was noted, the scout ship was under the strictest orders to leave the system immediately. Detection had to be avoided. Hivers often worked moons and other planets for mineral deposits. An argument arose over how the Hivers would know a system of theirs had been invaded, when they had no intersystem communications and their planet-based sensors had, as shown by the Xh-33, limited range.

"Let us not *assume* what has not been established beyond doubt," Captain Ashiant reminded those captains and first officers who attended his weekly updates. "There are still panels on the Refugee whose function is unknown."

That was the standard warning every scout captain impressed on his or her crew before the scout departed on an exploratory mission.

Every week the star charts were upgraded by such side trips and new primaries were added, including an unusual binary-sun system that fascinated all the astronomy buffs.

After the second Hiver occupation was discovered, the *Vadim*'s new captain, Pat Shepherd, brought up the suggestion that a multi-tasked beacon be set up near the heliopause of Hiver systems: to warn any passing Alliance ship of Hivers, and to record any out-goings, in which case a message capsule would be released to speed back to Alliance space where any Prime would soon "hear" its shriek and retrieve it. After the Denebian Penetration, every Alliance system had installed a device that could identify the Hiver sting-pzzt and emit a warning.

A contest to design such a device was circulated through the Fleet and small mechanically oriented groups vied with each other to come up with the successful design. The winning design group came from the *Washington*, because Rojer and Commander Tikele worked all the hours of the week to win the competition. Then the design was distributed among the machine shops of all the ships to ensure a sufficient supply.

Uninhabited M-5 planets were examined in more detail: one had an indigenous life form which was already using primitive tools and had controlled fires. That system was duly put off limits. Several planets, despite appropriate atmospheres and distribution of land mass to sea, did not appear viable for Human or Mrdini occupation, showing high levels of radiation, too much seismic activity or other anomalies.

"Well, such conditions would account for some of the bypasses," Captain Ashiant said at one of the weekly "brass" meetings which included the Talents. "One thing puzzles me. How did the Hivers know which to bypass? If we have probes, what do the Hivers use to obtain the same information? They surely must. Did anyone ever discover if Deneb had been probed by a Hiver mechanism?" He turned to Clancy.

"Sir, the Denebian Penetration happened long before my birth. My uncle who lived through those days never mentioned a probe, but then Deneb was pretty primitive in those days. And who was expecting visitors from outer space?"

"But did you not as a youngling on Deneb recover quantities of Hiver materials?" asked Captain Spktm.

"Yes sir, indeed, we all did," and Clancy indicated

Thian and Rojer, "and the Navy installation on Deneb is still trying to fit the pieces together." He grinned.

"Probes usually return to the sender to deliver the information they've acquired," Rojer added.

"True, true," Ashiant said, fingering his jawline as he often did.

"Flavia Bastianmajani recently sent us a message," Thian went on, "that the first of the occupied Hive systems showed a total breakdown which hasn't yet been fully analyzed. The xenobs and biologists have an unconfirmed opinion that the planet was deficient in some element or elements which are vital to Hive survival. So, if they do use a probe, it doesn't tell them all they need to know."

"So there are discrepancies in their colonial program," Captain Germys of the *Genesee* remarked in his dry fashion. "That's encouraging."

"And they avoid some planets that are fine for us."

"But if that colony failed, what sort of information do the Hiver probes seek?" asked Germys's first officer, Beckin Watusa, a very tall and very dark-skinned man.

"Well, one we saw was mainly islands, some good-sized, but no large land masses," said Selig Derynic of the destroyer *Comanche*. "So perhaps that's one of their criteria—large continents."

"They probe for suitable atmospheres as well, since two they've bypassed showed hydrogen-nitrogen imbalances," Vandermeer said.

"No," Captain Prlm of the *KLTL* said emphatically, its usually smooth fur ruffling, a sign of agitation, "the probe finds out how much and what kind of life had to be 'fumigated.' "

"Then let us be thankful for whatever limitations their probes, if they use them, report," Ashiant said briskly. "We can at least propose a few colonial sites for the Alliance."

"So far nothing we have discovered explains why they have ranged so far, especially now," Spktm said in an almost lugubrious tone, echoing some of the pessimism Prlm displayed.

"I would have thought that obvious, sir," Ashiant replied courteously. "Their homeworld was lost to the nova. They must be seeking an alternate."

"That must not happen!" Spktm said, bringing both upper hands hard down on the table, the percussion felt by everyone touching it.

"That is the purpose of this squadron, Captain," Ashiant said as resolutely. "And, especially, the reason the *Washington* was conceived and built!"

"And the Hivers built their Great Sphere to establish a new homeworld," Thian said. "Could it be in all the volume of space they, and we, have explored, they have not yet found a similar one? And that's why they have ranged so far, and looked in as many directions as they have?"

"You give the Hivers credit for emotions which they do not have," Spktm said, its poll eye swiveling to give Thian the full glare.

"Now, a moment, Spktm," Ashiant said, raising one hand, "the Prime has a valid point. Wouldn't Mrdinis, deprived of Clarf, search for one as near to what they'd lost as could be found?"

Spktm's fur ruffled further, and so did Prlm's and the other two 'Dini captains seated around the table. Thian inwardly groaned at his tactless remark. Exuding as much pacifying empathy as he could, he followed Ashiant's lead.

"MRDINIS HAVE LONG HISTORICAL KNOWLEDGE THAT HIVERS FOLLOW INSTINCT WHICH HAS NOT CHANGED, HONORED SIR, AND THAT IS, ABOVE ALL, SURVIVAL OF THEIR KIND. THEIR SPECIES MUST HAVE HAD A VERY UNUSUAL HOMEWORLD TO HAVE ALLOWED THEM TO BECOME DOMINANT. THAT WORLD IS GONE.

SURVIVAL OF THEIR SPECIES REQUIRES THEM TO FIND ITS LIKE.
THAT IS WHAT THIS ONE MEANT. PARDON THE OFFENSE THIS ONE
HAS UNWITTINGLY CAUSED THE HONORED SPKTM."

The 'Dini captain's fur began to settle, and so did
Prlm's. Thian felt the wave of relief from his fellow humans that the Mrdinis were mollified by his explanation.

"So they haven't found it. And, by my honor, I hope
they don't," Cheseman of the *Solidarity* said, "but give us
a little hope, Captain Spktm. Do we even know what their
primary's spectrum was like before it went nova?"

Both Spktm and Thian, who had reached the area where
the dead star was still cooling, shook their heads.

"Bluntly, no," Thian said.

"We've got a helluva lot of space to check out," Captain
Cheseman of the *Solidarity* said, made gloomy by the
sheer magnitude of the task facing them. "Five years
won't be long enough!"

"But a lustrum makes a start, gentlemen," Ashiant said,
adopting a firmly positive tone, "and let us not discount
what we have managed to accomplish in the past two
years. We may have been forced by circumstances to explore further than any previous program for either of our
species but we have already discovered enough new
worlds to support members of the Alliance for thousands
of generations to come.

"Let me come back to the point that there may be a
more specific goal for these Hive Spheres—finding a new
homeworld under a sun similar to the original one. I certainly don't know what spectro-analytical means the Hivers possess," and Ashiant attempted to inject some humor,
"but I'd like our astrogation officers to start checking the
spectrums of all G-type stars, however far away they are,
on the off chance that it's a certain type they're hunting,
not just any G-type system with M-5 planets."

Even the Mrdinis saw the merit of that suggestion and the meeting ended with considerably more enthusiasm and purpose than it initially had. Ashiant later confided to Thian that there'd been some very tricky moments but he was positive they were onto a line of investigation that was going to prove invaluable.

"Certainly it's giving us another purpose while we're tracking that damned Sphere to wherever it's going. What odds would you take that it *has* a definite primary objective?"

Thian regarded Ashiant for a moment before letting out a startled guffaw. For one moment, Ashiant glared at him and then, realizing what he had said, joined Thian in a much-needed laugh.

"In line with that, sir," Thian said, still shaking with laughter, "maybe I ought to contact Flavia. Squadron B's been to quite a few systems now, too. Maybe they can throw some light on the matter."

"Light on the matter?" Ashiant echoed and enjoyed another chuckle. "I needed that, Lyon. That was a hairy moment there . . ."

"You mean, of course, when all the 'Dini fur started to ruffle up?"

That set them both off again until Ashiant, huffing and coughing, pulled himself back to sobriety, but his eyes still twinkled and he continued to grin.

"Actually, sir, even a process of elimination, based on what types of G-stars they ignore, might help us establish the criteria they're looking for. Even minute differences—the period of variability, sunspot cycles, size—in a G-type primary can have incalculable effects on the satellites in its system. It certainly has proved so in species adaptations.

"On another subject, Captain—which I didn't have time to pass on to you before the meeting—Flavia's message this morning contains some interesting items. The first being that they, too, have devised a beacon to be set outside any Hive-suspect M-5 system: to warn vessels off and to send a message back to the nearest Prime to warn of any outgoing Sphere."

"Great minds, huh?"

"I've received specs, sir. Captain Soligen thought you might like to glance over them in case they have modifications we could use." Thian handed over the hard copy and the software. "Or the other way round," he added tactfully.

"Indeed and we will," Ashiant replied as he glanced through the material. "Though the one your brother and Tikele designed seems to be similar."

"Flavia also informed me that, with Earth Prime's express permission, they are going to approach the Hive-occupied planet."

Ashiant gave him a hard stare.

"There are good reasons to take the chance," and Thian grinned, "the main of them being to give the *KVS* under Captain Klml the opportunity to pull the *Genesee* ploy."

"Steal another Hiver ship?" Ashiant said, almost exploding. "Whatever do we need with *another* one?"

Thian chuckled, as much at the captain's reaction as the one which would surely await the triumphantly returning crew aboard it.

"Captain Klml is of the new Mrdini generation which hasn't seen much direct contact of the kind that allows a color to gain prestige . . ."

"Damned untried young scuts," Ashiant murmured, shifting restlessly in his chair, "they could precipitate more trouble . . ." Then he cleared his throat as he remembered all too vividly the morning's near breach between Human and 'Dini. "Ah, well, I suppose fighting's more recent in their culture than . . . Is 'counting coup' the action I mean . . ."

"I've heard the phrase," Thian replied, not remembering where or in what connection.

"Go on. Tell me how this 'Dini plans to gain prestige so I'll know how to prevent it in this squadron."

"First Flavia got Earth Prime's permission. And I assure you, as Flavia did me, that Captain Soligen would not contemplate such a move unless she was very sure of success."

"Well," and Ashiant simmered down, "Vesta's one helluva fine captain, even if she does have some odd ideas of opting for young and virtually untried crew. I assume all you Primes are restricted by the same rules?"

"Yes, sir!"

"Then let me know the outcome of the . . . what did you call it . . ."

"The *Genesee* ploy."

"Osullivan must be pleased by that. Too bad he's stuck at a desk now. And how is Captain Klml intending to get its prize back to our occupied space?"

"Flavia seemed to feel the captain would be able to do so under the ship's power. We were able to establish the disposition of certain controls on the panel. She's known them. And we know what fuel is used . . ."

"That's fine until the damned thing gets in more traveled space . . ."

Thian nodded, grinning. "I believe the plan is to decorate the sphere with 'Dini designs to let all and sundry know who is bringing this one in."

"Do ask your Prime to send out an all-ship warning. Wouldn't do to have a trigger-happy missile crew trying out the new weaponry on a 'friendly' hostile vessel! And can you get onto the proper authorities to forward all documentation on known G-star variations, whether the planetary systems have been explored or not. It may well be that the tedious process of elimination will provide the information we need."

When Thian, who had always prided himself on his eidetic memory, found himself confusing figures of the very complicated spectro-analyses of G-type stars within an hour, he traded off with Rojer. Clancy was about to have to take a turn when Jeff Raven decided his T-1 and T-2 staff had better things to do with their time than mentally transfer such complex data. So the rest of the material from Human astronomical files was 'ported out. Laria 'ported even more from the Mrdini libraries.

Everyone's pretty excited about the theory here, she told her brother. *You sound in good form, Thi. Things going well for you, Roj and Clancy?*

Why? D'you miss us? he asked teasingly.

Oddly enough, I think I do, she said.

How's Kincaid?

Kincaid is in fine form, brother! Then there was a ripple in her mental tone that signified a giggle. *Vanteer, too.* Then she signed off, leaving him to digest that information just as the cargo officer announced the arrival of a small pod from Clarf Tower.

The comparative analysis of G-type stars continued until a special board had to be set up for that information alone. Each ship in the Fleet wanted to access files to support their own theories and constant, lengthy ship-to-ship conversations were interfering with necessary operational messages.

Over the next few weeks, although neither Thian nor Ashiant had mentioned the *Genesee* ploy, most of the Fleet knew that it either was about to happen or had happened. The news that the maneuver had been successful, that the

KVS had destroyed the space field of the Hivers at Waterloo as well as the three scout ships that had tried to launch from the planet, was anticlimatic but gave an excuse for considerable celebration on all eleven ships.

Barely had they recovered from that than the *Washington*'s sensors picked up a reading that suggested the Hiver they were pursuing had sent out its scouts. The target was a G-type sun which the Alliance had first thought the Hiver would, once more, pass by since its spectro-analysis didn't seem that promising.

Instantly crews were scrambled to the *Washington*'s fast scouts and Thian ordered Rojer to accompany the *Revere*, commanded by Captain Vergoin.

You'll get yourself in a pod the moment there's trouble, Thian told his brother.

Aw, Thi ... Rojer began and then, remembering his grandfather's stern warnings, subsided. *Yeah, I will, but what about the destroyers? Who's going to keep Prl and Ktpl in check when they get close to the Hiver?*

Captain Spktm. It's transferred its command to its first officer and is on board the KLTS.

Spktm does mean business.

We all mean business!

Thian sent Clancy, with a similar reminder about saving his Talented skin, to one of the two Human-crewed destroyers. All four larger ships were ordered to shift themselves at top speed after the lighter, faster vessels. The Nebula, the two Constellations and the four Galaxy-class would need more time to attain the requisite speed to catch up and support any action.

We're ahead of the Hiver scouts, Rojer told his brother several days later, *and they didn't even see us coming in on the ecliptic.* His tone was one of high good spirits. *Are those Hiver queens so utterly oblivious to anything but their goals? Are they so arrogant they think they're totally invulnerable?*

Until they came to Deneb, they were, Thian remarked drolly. *Have the astronomers come up with any more data on the primary?*

Checking sunspot activity and running another one on uvl and irl emissions, and naturally probes have been released on orbital sweeps of the planet. Lots of lush vegetation is reported and some clearly visible seismic activity, good blue seas and a chain of large lakes across the main continental mass we've already identified on the night side. Smallish ice-covered polar regions but that's normal—so's the ozone layer. Can't find any signs of civilization, no large habitations, no fires—apart from a forest fire raging in the midwest. Ah, but indigenous critters, running straight for the nearest body of water. Least that's what the science officer says such a cloud of dust could mean.

Could the fire have been set by the Hivers? Thian asked.

Doubt it! Their scouts are just about inside the orbit of the fifth planet, your typical ringed giant.

"Your brother's reporting in?" Ashiant asked from the seat he had taken behind Thian's couch.

Thian gestured for the captain to come around; he hated reporting to thin air. He repeated verbatim what Rojer had said.

"Too much potential to leave to the Hivers for any reason," Ashiant said, which was Thian's opinion as well. The captain opened communications with the bridge. "Primary's spectrum matches to within .0356 of Sol?"

Thian pondered that as well as Ashiant. "Hivers never came near Earth, sir. They *did* try to colonize Sef, though, and Sef's primary is very much like Sol."

"Enough to make it the sun system they're searching for as a new homeworld?" Ashiant shook his head. "I'd haz-

ard the guess that they might just need to replenish supplies. They haven't stopped anywhere . . ." He bent over
the com unit. "Ailsah, based on the examination of the
supplies stored on Refugee and the estimated size of those
Hiver crews that the 'Dinis extrapolated, tell me if they'd
be running close to empty?"

"You suspect this might be only a supply run?"

"It's a possibility but I'll need the figures first." Ashiant
grinned, rubbing his hands together in anticipation. "How
long before the main Fleet can intercept the Sphere?"

"Seven hours, sir, but she appears to be slowing down.
That *would* be consonant with a resupply action. We know
Hiver scout ships have plenty of range but they may also
want to conserve fuel—if they're still in search mode. The
LSTS just confirmed that speed reduction and has asked
for battle dispositions of the destroyers."

Thian could hear just the minute pulse of excitement in
the First Officer's calm voice.

"First, order all ships to be alert for any sign that the
Hiver has detected our approach. I've never quite believed
the 'Dini report on Hiver sensor range. Anyway, Prime,
ask your brother to pass my order on to Captain Vergoin
to release low level probes. We might as well establish if
it's just animals or potential sentients we're about to save
from Hive attentions."

The bridge rang through again. "The *KLTL*, the *Vadim*,
the *Solidarity*, and the *Genesee* are asking for you."

"I'll be right with them momentarily, First." When the
channel was closed, Ashiant inhaled a deep breath. "I almost look forward to discovering if those new missiles
will be effective against a Hiver." He gave Thian a wry
grin. "Do I let the 'Dinis do the honors, Thian?"

Sensing in that rare moment of Ashiant's candor more
than the simple question, Thian smiled reassuringly.

"I don't think 'let' is operational, sir, but it'll be a triumph for us all. We'll have reduced by one more ship their chance of finding that new homeworld they're desperate to have: that new base from which they can multiply the problems we've already got in containing them. Then there's only the one ship Squadron D's following and *then* we really will have reduced Hiver threat to manageable proportions."

Ashiant gave a short bark of a laugh. "Manageable, Prime?" He laughed sardonically again. "When we're discovering that the odds are one in five that any M-5 planet on our way out here has a Hiver colony on it?" Ashiant threw out his hands in exasperation.

"Even that's a good deal more than we knew before 'Dinis ran across those three Hivers."

"Damn!" And Ashiant rammed one fist into the other palm. "I'd feel it more of an accomplishment if this system *was* the one the Hivers *have* been so desperately searching for."

"Put it this way, sir, it's one more they won't occupy, even briefly!"

"Good point, Prime. I could almost feel sorry for our prey."

"I won't tell anyone I heard you say that, Captain," Thian said with a grin as he prepared to 'path the new orders to his brother as well as a warning of the Hiver's slowing.

The Hiver scouts never got closer to the lush planet than its outer moon. Nor were they quite so unaware of an opposing force as their directness suggested. As the *Washington*'s scouts moved out of a planetary orbit to intercept them, the Hivers split in a well-calculated distraction even as they initiated a terrific barrage at the scouts before the larger destroyers could move into firing range to shield them.

Thian, if I'm not loud, listen harder. I'm in a pod. Vergoin had two yeomen stuffing me and my 'Dinis in here as soon as we began closing with the Hivers. Rojer sounded far more indignant than scared.

Main screen's magnified to show the blasts. Any damage?

Minor's all I can tell. I've got the pod's com unit on but I'm not catching all the . . . Wait a minute . . .

Rojer? ROJER?

Don't bother me now, brother. I've work to do!

Thian kept bothering Rojer with constant demands for answers. In between those, he 'pathed Clancy, who was no more available to his requests for information than Rojer. Infuriated with a disobedience that amounted to downright mutiny, he charged onto the *Washington*'s bridge where the intense atmosphere reminded him that he might be intruding and he half turned to leave. Then he saw that the main screen of the bridge gave far larger, clearer details of the battle than the one above his couch. What he saw also made him realize exactly what essential work Rojer and Clancy were doing in deflecting a virtual onslaught of Hiver missiles. Definitely he could tell Earth Prime that this was self-defense: if the *Revere* took a mortal blow, the Hiver scouts could pick off the pods one by one before the evacuees could get out of range. Rojer had shown good sense with his deflection policy!

The main batteries of the Sphere began to open up on the seven Alliance ships which had deployed themselves to prevent the Hiver scouts from escaping while the Nebula and the two Constellations were converging on the Sphere. One advantage of the round design was that batteries could be fired in any direction. Thian knew from the Refugee just how much firepower the Hiver had.

"Look, sir," Vandermeer said, "the Hiver's wasting ammunition as usual. She isn't within range of our ships."

"The scouts are."

"But her missiles are missing although . . . Sir, Ensign Upland is of the opinion that the detonation of those missiles could cause shock waves almost as dangerous to scout ship hulls as a direct hit."

"My compliments to Ensign Upland," Ashiant said, nodding his head briefly in acknowledgment of the information. Then, under his breath, he muttered: "When I get those two Talents, I'll skin 'em, I'll keelhaul them." Thian and the nearer bridge officers heard him. "But they *are* managing to deflect incoming rockets. Tikele, how soon before we are in range of the Sphere?"

"Twenty-two minutes."

"Why doesn't Ktpl use the ones it's got on the *KLTS*?"

"I believe the captain's maneuvering her into position now, sir," Tikele responded. "And two of our scouts are protecting her. She's got to be on target, on those fuel tanks, and in range . . . she's . . . she's fired both, sir."

Unbelievably one of the Hiver's scouts managed to get between the Sphere and the missiles, which penetrated it, sticking out port and starboard.

"Like a scurrier skewered on arrows," Thian murmured.

Then the blast occurred, an orange-red eruption of force which hurtled the *KLTS* backward like a leaf in a storm. Somehow the flanking scouts had peeled away, and although they were scudded further from their original positions, they did not appear to have taken much damage. The *KLTS* patently had. As 'Dini ships still did not carry pods, it was impossible to estimate how many of its crew survived.

ROJER! CLANCY! FOR THE LOVE OF HEAVEN, ANSWER ME, Thian roared, catching the gestalt of the *Washington*'s generators to reach his targets.

I'm okay, Thian. But I had to bounce missiles. Just like Granddad did when the Hiver attacked Deneb.

Not the same at all, Rojer! CLANCY?

I can hear you, I can hear you. Over the ringing in my ears. Were we ever lucky! Kloo's a damned fine pilot.

"Thian?" Ashiant called urgently. "Can you get in touch with either of your Talents and ask them to check the status of the *KLTS*? The other destroyers must hold their positions to contain the Sphere."

"Yes, sir." *Rojer, you've 'Dinis. Ashiant's ordering Vergoin and the* Revere *to aid the* KLTS *and assess their condition. You do the liaising . . .*

Clancy's ship better come with us—the Hiver scouts are moving in for the kill and we'll have to bounce some more . . .

That that was what the two *Washington* scouts were doing was obvious, while the three destroyers slung medium-sized missiles on the two remaining Hiver scouts, all the time inching closer to the Sphere.

"We've just reached the maximum range of the new missiles, Captain," Vandermeer announced.

"Signal the Galaxy-class ships to assume Formation C and begin firing as soon as they are in maximum range. The Sphere must be distracted from the destroyers."

She's some mother, this one, Thian distinctly heard someone say. It could have been any one on the bridge, even Ashiant, dropping his mind shields in the excitement of battle.

The first of the new missiles the *Washington* launched was not that far off its target but exploded on contact with a large fragment of the Hiver's scout. The next three, one from the *Washington* and the others from the *Solidarity* and the *Athene*, penetrated the Sphere as easily as a sharp knife cuts through soft fruit.

"One, two," began Ashiant under his breath, *"three,"* and he was joined by Vandermeer, "FOUR," and it was practically a chorus. No one got to "five." The Hiver disintegrated by quadrants, like skin being peeled off a round fruit from top to bottom. Then the fireball blossomed and its furnace expanded, melting all in its white hot circle.

The *KLTL* peeled off to follow one Hiver scout and the *Franklin* went after the other.

With ordinary communications opened again now the enemy was routed, Captain Ktpl was able to send its regards to the *Washington*. Its voice was shaky but proud of being aboard the ship that had fired the first missile against the enemy. The *KLTS* had taken a lot of damage from the blast concussion: many 'Dinis were dead and injured. Some compartments had had to be closed against the vacuum without knowing if they had been occupied.

Thian did not have time to find either Rojer or Clancy to give them the dressing down they so richly deserved for disobeying orders in spite of the life-saving success of that violation. By the time he spotted them, some of his anger had dissipated. They were across the *Washington* cargo hold, which had been turned into an auxiliary 'Dini sick bay, doing much the same sort of emergency use of telekinesis he was: "lifting" the injured into beds, onto gurneys. Rojer was helping Medic Sblipk among the 'Dinis injured, with Gil and Kat rushing about on errands. Clancy was working among the Human wounded.

We'll all have a little talk, later, Rojer, Clancy, Thian said in a cold voice.

Sure thing, bro. When there's a little more free time . . .

Don't get cocky with me, Rojer Raven-Lyon!

Who? Me? Cocky? After what I just went through, bro? That was almost . . . almost worse than the KTTS, *Thi.*

His brother's words, unrepentant though they were, cooled Thian still further but he'd have to tell Earth Prime about their escapade. He was responsible for all the Talents on this expedition and somehow he had failed to make them obey orders they *knew* they mustn't ignore. If he'd had to tell his mother and father that Rojer had . . .

"Hey, Thi," said a soft voice in his ear, and he felt a touch on his shoulder, "you need rest, honey." Greevy looked up at him, her blue eyes anxious, though her face was as tired as his. He and his 'Dinis had been working with her, using kinesis to help her use her healing skills.

"If I rest, you do, too, Lieutenant Senior Grade," he said sternly.

She glanced over the now orderly ward, where 'Dinis were immersed in tubs of restorative fluids, or wrapped in bandages of various colors, repairing damaged tissues, wounds, burns and breaks. 'Dinis endured discomfort better than Humans did, Thian thought, and wondered if that was a species differentiation, rather than stoicism.

"Ah, here comes the new watch," Greevy said with relief that came out close to a sob.

Thian leaned back against the nearest support and "listened" for his brother. Rojer was asleep—Thian couldn't tell where—and so was Clancy. He'd get them both tomorrow . . . when he'd had enough sleep.

"Thian," and Greevy caught him by the hand and pulled him around the corner. "You got enough energy left to 'port us to my room?"

He put weary arms around her, his head resting on hers, and 'ported them to her quarters on the level below. She palmed the door lock and they collapsed in each other's arms onto the bed, asleep almost before they had stretched out on the horizontal surface.

*　　*　　*

"You realize that that Hiver ship, even with its three scouts, hadn't a chance," Rojer said, blithely tucking into a huge meal in their quarters late that next afternoon. "Operation Overkill, that's what it was."

"Need I remind you how many 'Dinis died in the *KLTS*?" Thian said, glaring at his brother.

He had read the riot act to both Rojer and Clancy for "endangering" their lives which were far too valuable to be risked. He could also point to the minor cuts and contusions which both had suffered when their respective ships had maneuvered abruptly or suffered concussive buffeting: those could as easily have been mortal wounds.

"I'm not that slow, Thian," Rojer replied indignantly, "even if I didn't manage to keep my balance through all the bumps and grinds the *Revere* did. But you should have seen some of the others. I 'ported when I could."

"I got most of mine," and Clancy fingered the long proskin dressing down one side of his face, the splint on his left arm, the sealed wound on the right, and managed a benevolent expression, "buffering someone else's impact."

"Besides which, big brother," Rojer said, hands on his belt and an intense frown on his face, "if either of us *had* made use of the escape pods, you'd really have had bad news to send home. It only occurred to me when I was stuck in it that the damned pod was the most dangerous place to be! *I* was at Xh-33, remember, and I *watched* the queens' pods get blown out of the sky the way we'd pick off avians! Any one of the Hiver scouts could have made a real killing . . . of *pods*!"

"We also saved both the *Revere* and the *Franklin* from being made into sieves," Clancy reminded Thian, "or smashed flat. Shielding the ships shielded *us* and it's really only a very minor variation of our standing orders from Uncle Jeff." He grinned engagingly. "Just a larger escape pod."

"I'll have to *tell* him what you did!" Thian was not about to let them get away without reprimand.

"Go right ahead!" Clancy said, his grin broader, "but *I* heard that both Spktm and Ashiant are mentioning our defensive action as the main reason casualties were minimal. Although I do now appreciate why the Mrdinis had to consider suicide attacks! There can't be much room on those scouts with all those heavy missiles they fire off. And that Sphere wasn't going to give up short of total destruction!"

Thian could never stay angry long, not in the presence of Clancy, though he continued to feel an irritable frustration, especially as the two young heroes tossed off their actions as nothing out of the ordinary for Talents of their abilities. That almost annoyed Thian more.

"I think," Greevy told him when they met for a quiet meal in the medics' mess room, "that you're a little jealous, maybe, Thian, that you weren't in on the action?"

"Me? Jealous?" He regarded Alison Anne, startled. He'd never thought of himself as a jealous person for any reason.

Her blue eyes twinkled up at him. "Jealous of things or people, no, Thian. But jealous, a little perhaps, of prestige."

"Are you sure you're still T-5?"

"Probably not," she said airily with a delighted sigh, "but I *am* an empath and very empathic for you." She reached across the small table and stroked the back of his hand lightly, a contact that conveyed more than empathy. "I've picked up as much from you Talent-wise as I have about treating 'Dinis from Medic Sblipk. More perhaps," and her eyes laughed at him over the rim of her cup. "You had the hard part—watching, waiting, hoping. Do Talents pray?" This was said with such an ingenuous expression that Thian felt his aggravation and frustration dissolve. "Besides which," she went on, teasing him, "you saw action long before they did, on the Great Sphere."

Thian made a face at her. "*That* little fracas was not against live Hivers."

"The difference is immaterial, Thian. And it was far more dangerous than what your brother and cousin did."

Thian faithfully forwarded Captain Ashiant's detailed report of the encounter and decided, when he could not help but "feel" Jeff Raven's furious reaction to the heroism of Rojer and Clancy, that he could safely leave any further discipline to Earth Prime and Callisto Prime, and possibly both Aurigaeans. Righteous anger often ripened with waiting.

Thian was called back by Earth Prime later to receive the official commendations and replies from the Alliance and High Council as well as new orders.

The Fleet was now to join Squadron D, using all available Talent to make the 'portation, and track down the third Sphere with all possible speed. There was great weight being given to the theory that the three spheres had been looking for a particular G-type star, as close a replica to the one which had turned nova as possible. The High Council did not care to wait until the remaining Sphere found such a star and a new homeworld planet.

Once that Hive Sphere had been dealt with, the Fleet was to return, making in-depth surveys of all potentially habitable planets and disabling Hiver colonies, using the *Genesee* ploy whenever possible to remove Sphere ships from use.

"What's the High Council after, might I ask?" Ashiant inquired of Thian in an agitated fashion. "A fleet of Sphere ships? We've got more than we need right now. We should blow 'em up. Save time and effort."

"Use 'em as decoys?" Thian threw out as a possible solution.

"I think this 'know your enemy and you can defeat him easier' is going a bit too far."

"Perhaps I misinterpreted, sir," Thian said, running over the wording in his mind. "Disabling the Hiver colonies could merely mean making certain they had no further space capabilities. Shall I reconfirm?"

"Please do."

I doubt the High Council meant to bring more Spheres back, Jeff Raven said, but his tone was uncertain. *But with 'Dinis you'd never know, would you? I'll get back to you.*

When he did, he was chuckling. *Seems the 'Dinis would like to have an intact Sphere for each of their colonial worlds as trophies. Admiral Mekturian pointed out that the two operational ones presently in our possession could be displayed wherever necessary. I will never understand 'Dini logic or honor. The Admiral is more sensible and re- peats that the Fleet is to destroy Hiver space-travel capa- bilities until other remedies can be effected to prevent their colonial aggrandizement.*

Other remedies?

That's what's being discussed. There's a powerful lobby that would prevent the Alliance, and not just the Human element, from doing unto the Hivers as they have done to others. Why reduce ourselves to their level?

What else could *be done, Granddad? Not,* Thian added hastily, *that I believe the annihilation of any species could be justified.*

Ah, now, Thian, the discussions are ongoing and heated. Both Gktmglnt and Admiral Mekturian are insisting that nothing be engraved in granite until both investigatory units, the Main Fleet and Squadron B, have returned from their voyages, laden, we hope, with information enough to suggest a sensible, humane *and 'dinified course of action.*

If we've to stop and investigate every bloody M-5 system on the way back, sir, Thian began . . .

By then some form of common sense might have resulted from the current shambles. Once more I am relieved that FT&T is involved only in the mechanics, rather than the politics, of this issue. And, there was definite amusement in Jeff Raven's tone, *as a messenger, I am too far removed from those I deliver them to, to suffer the fate often meted out to the bearers of adverse replies. So, grandson, I say unto you, bring back as much information as you possibly can about the bright new worlds that have not been Hiverized and can give the hot-blooded another focus for their energies.*

Wouldn't a colonial explosion be following Hiver tactics?

Really, Thian, your sense of proportion is slightly skewed by distance. Humans and 'Dinis respect other life forms and any planet bearing identifiable sentients is to be scratched off the list. Oh, but put up one of those warning beacons that'll inform the Alliance of incoming Hive traffic. There're still a lot of those damned Spheres loose in this galaxy.

The official segments of that long exchange were duly reported to Captain Ashiant and then repeated to the other captains and first officers, in Basic and in 'Dini, so that there could be no misunderstanding of either directive.

Thian excused himself then, to give the brass the chance to discuss the orders privately.

Outside the Talents' quarters, the corridors of the *Washington* still echoed muted sounds of celebration although the Nebula-class ship was now swinging around the rescued planet on its way out of the system. Thian knew that the science officers would be busy at every available station, recording whatever scrap of surface information could be learned during the circumnavigation. Probes had returned with samples which would be analyzed and assayed. He watched as the planet turned under him even as the *Washington* turned round the planet to the original sight he had had . . . had it only been two days before? The forest fire had gone out, doused by a rain system which, unfortunately, resulted in smoke obscuring that area, so the cause of the conflagration remained a mystery. The creatures which had fled the fire were now browsing by the lake which had saved them. None appeared to be more than a variety of large ruminants, grazers, and several equally big predators, and none acted with any sentience.

"And not a single creature will ever know or care about the fate we saved them from," Greevy said softly from the open door to his room. When she had come off duty the night before, they'd done some private celebrating. All her patients would recover and she was no longer fearful for the progress of several of the 'Dini burn victims.

Thian held out his arm and she came across on bare feet to stand in under it. She liked the fact that she fitted just there. He closed his arm and pulled her against him.

"Are we on our way out of this system, Thi?" she asked, noticing the rotation.

He nodded. "Orders came in. If that door opens, be prepared to get 'ported back in."

She started to release him and he pulled her back against him.

"All the brass's there and they've a lot of talking to do, so I don't think we need worry. Besides, Alison Anne," and he looked down at her, "I'd rather stop playing hide-and-seek . . ."

"Thian, you know perfectly that your folks will have someone better in mind for you than a T-5 empath who's . . ."

Thian put one finger across her lips. "Don't you poor-mouth yourself in my hearing, Lieutenant Senior Grade, sir, ma'am!"

"Look, you were a raw kid . . ."

I'm no raw kid now, Alison Anne Greevy, Thian said, turning to pull her full against him and pushing her head up to catch her lovely blue eyes, *and I have far more need of a comfortable T-5 empath whom I happen to love, respect and admire for certain earthy and caring qualities I haven't found anywhere else. If we can still stand each other's company at the end of this mission, I'd say we had a good chance of enjoying a good life together. And I'll probably opt for full service as a Naval Prime. I'd be the first . . . if I can talk Granddad into creating the position.*

Alison could and often did shield her thoughts from him but not the wistful hope in her eyes.

"If you're thinking of Flavia Bastianmajani, don't," he said and kissed her, loving her with mind, heart and soul. "She had other ideas even when we first met."

"She did?"

Thian threw his head back, laughing at her indignation. "She's probably as assiduously pursuing her own way as I have been mine!"

"A trained T-1 like Flavia?"

"Sometimes, Alison Anne, you astound me."

"Well, I like to be able to do just that, I can tell you, Prime Isthian Lyon, sir."

"Good. Come, astound me now. I think I've some free time to fill."

When Thian was called, late that evening, to make contact with Earth Prime, it was to ask permission to exchange the damaged Mrdini destroyer *KLTS* with the *KLLM* currently in Squadron D. That was agreed, though the other two ships comprising the Squadron were to be sent back to be refitted.

I'm told there's an adequate brig on board the Valparaiso, *so you can send those dissidents back and rid yourself of unnecessary baggage,* Earth Prime added.

Thian had not liked that aspect of his responsibilities but it was now no secret that several attempts had been made to tamper with the *Washington*'s missile guidance systems. Suspects had been interrogated by the NI officers, with Thian watching in a covert observation booth. In all but one case his Talent wasn't needed and in that one, he had felt both distress and pity that the ensign, a young woman of otherwise impeccable record in her duties in the engine complex of the *Washington*, felt it her duty to Humankind to destroy the first of the Nebula-class design because a ship that huge and powerful was against the wishes of the God her native planet revered.

How she had slipped through the careful screening of any candidate to the Space Academy became the subject of a dedicated search of both Naval Intelligence and the medical board. She was placed in the brig under maximum surveillance. She protested vehemently about the "paid," godless saboteurs that also occupied the accommodation. *They* complained because she prayed both loud and long, trying to bring them to see the "light" and save their "souls." Only bouts of laryngitis silenced her. And that, according to the officer in charge of the facility, never lasted long enough.

All the Fleet elements were now making their majestic way out of the system so blithely unaware of its escape from annihilation. One day a developing sentient species might wonder about the ring of debris about the outer moon.

In their ready room, Thian, Rojer and Clancy were tot-

ing up the potential power they could access to 'port the
Fleet to Squadron D's present location.

"Well, it's not that far," Rojer was saying in an attempt
to encourage himself. Gil and Kat were lounging on the
couch beside him, playing one of the finger games that often absorbed them, with a piece of colored string.

"With ninety T-2s and -3s to spread out, plus the sixty
4s—and don't forget they're mainly kinetics, too—
strategically placed . . ."

"There's none on any of the 'Dini ships," Clancy reminded them.

"So we haul them over last . . ."

"That wouldn't sit well," Rojer said. "Look, Thian, you
and Clancy haul the *Washington.* Give me ten 2s and
twenty 3s and I'll 'port Spktm. It's the mass of the *Washington* that's going to be the worst to 'port. Even Constellations are easy after that."

"Or, I stay here in the *Washington* and send to you."

"Who's the T-2 on Squadron D?" Clancy asked.

Thian and Rojer gave him a weary look. "Stierlman!"

"Oh!"

Rojer lifted one shoulder in a shrug. "He hasn't lost
anything sent him . . . yet."

"Well, we sure don't aim the *Washington* at him all of
a sudden," Thian said.

Semirame Kloo and Alison Anne arrived, off duty now,
and Thian absently 'ported in more drinks and finger foods
for them.

"It's getting the experienced Talents in the right places
to buffer the new ones who'll never have had a chance to
merge."

"Then whyn't you do a drill merge first?" Kloo said
with a wicked grin at Thian in memory of a certain mock
drill she'd pulled.

"Who? How? What?" Thian asked although he mind-touched his approval of her suggestion.

She tapped out a sequence on the terminal and a spatial view of the disposition of the Fleet came on screen. She sniffed, and tapped at the destroyers in flank positions. "Change 'em over. Switch the *Athene* with the *Comanche*. Just as an exercise." Then she chuckled mischievously. "See how long it takes the crews to figure out what happened. Could be a bit of fun."

"I think," Thian said, standing up, "I'd better check such a Fleet maneuver with Captain Ashiant." He was grinning with sheer devilment as he asked Ashiant for an immediate interview.

"More trouble, Thian?" Ashiant demanded, striding into the Talents' ready room almost as soon as he had broken off the call.

"No, sir, not trouble, just sorting out how to make the jump to join Squadron D with most efficient use of the Talents we've got. I'd like to have a trial merge and, say, switch the *Athene* with the *Comanche*."

"And see how long it takes them to realize they've been moved," Rojer couldn't resist adding.

Ashiant looked from brother to brother, his broad face expressionless, hands behind his back. "Might prove salutary at that. Proceed."

Thian waited a moment.

"Oh, I'd like to remain here," Ashiant added and then grinned, the cloth of his shipsuit beginning to wrinkle with his slow chuckle.

Immediately the two Primes swung onto their couches. "We'll try it, merging with just the Talents on each of the destroyers," Thian explained. "Me with *Athene* and Rojer with the *Comanche*."

"No prior warning?" Ashiant asked.

"Just the code word. Ready when you are, Rojer."

Three, two, one, SAKI, the brothers broadcasted, and instantly felt the response of Talents: scrambling a little to obey the unexpected and unusual summons.

Switch!

Captain Ashiant, Commander Kloo, Lieutenant SG Greevy, and T-2 Clancy Sparrow stared at the display on the screen.

"Caught it!" Ashiant cried in triumph, clapping his hands together. "No more than a ripple. Now, let's see how . . ."

"Captain Ashiant, there's been a fluctuation of some kind around the *Athene* and . . ." Vandermeer's voice broke off. "Sir, would you come to the bridge, please?"

"On my way, First." He turned back to the Talents just as the bridge door swooshed open, twisted his thumb upwards in an approving gesture and unexpectedly winked.

"Captain, it's very odd, and I don't know how it could have happened," the Talents heard a perplexed Vandermeer saying, "but I could have sworn the *Athene* was in the starboard flank position . . ."

"Incoming message from the *Athene*, sir . . ." the com officer announced.

"Full marks to the *Athene* bridge crew, First," Ashiant said in a calm voice, rippling with an undertone that the Talents had no problems identifying as suppressed amusement.

"Incoming query from the *Comanche*, sir . . ."

"Tell them to hold their current new positions. A drill has been in progress. Full security was in force. Put the *Comanche* on . . . Ah, Captain Derynic, your bridge crew needs a bit of sharpening. The *Athene* reported the change of position a full two minutes before you did. I want every crew fully alert. We may have defeated one Hive Sphere but we've another one we know of out there, and we still are not positive they have no intercolonial communications of a nature we have yet to understand. Yours is the conn, First."

Ashiant returned to the Talent ready room. Once inside and the door closed, he enjoyed a hearty chuckle.

"I think that's a drill that's proved more efficacious than most I've ordered," he said, coughing a bit into his hand as he finished his laugh. "Did it prove conclusive for you as well, Primes?"

"Yes, indeed," Rojer and Thian chorused.

"With a little more practice none of 'em will hesitate," Thian added. "Now, sir, our problem becomes more a matter of protocol: which captain's ship goes first of the bigger ones. We've just proved we can swap destroyers with only their indigenous Talent merging."

"It's the mass that's the problem?"

"Not as much as whose nose'll be out of joint by being left to last."

"That's no problem at all, Primes," Ashiant said. "I'll give the orders and they'll be followed. Captain Spktm on the *LSTS* goes first, then Captain Germys and the *Genesee*. I'd want all the destroyers next, then the rest of the Galaxics, and the *Washington* last. How does that sound?"

"Fine, sir. We'll need to rearrange some Talents to more critical positions . . ."

"Any way you need 'em . . ."

"And it'll take two days to complete the 'portation."

"That all?" Ashiant seemed mildly surprised.

Thian wasn't sure if the surprise was favorable or not.

"With respect, sir," Commander Kloo said, "the mass to be 'ported is considerable."

"I wasn't complaining, Kloo." Ashiant turned to Thian. "There *is* a Talent along with Squadron D, isn't there? To give you an assist?"

"Yes, sir, we'll be in contact with him as soon as we've rearranged personnel. That'll take the rest of today."

Ashiant nodded and returned to his bridge, leaving the Talents gazing at each other in puzzlement.

"I don't think he really understands what's involved," Alison Anne said thoughtfully.

"I'm not at all that sure I do, either," Thian said. He gave himself a shake and briskly started compiling lists of which key Talents would have to be moved and to which ship.

When Thian made contact, the mind of T-2 Stierlman on board Squadron D's Galaxy-class ship, the *Valparaiso*, exhibited such surprise and consternation at the task to be performed that Thian immediately deleted the man from his range of key links. Stierlman's job at his end only required holding a firm mental tone as a beacon. The very mention of the proposed merge weakened Stierlman's touch to the tentativeness of a Tower novice. Thian's sister, Petra, would have been of more use. How had Laria stood the man's indecisiveness for as long as she had?

The distance, Prime, it's the distances involved, Stierlman rabbited on. *They keep getting longer and longer. We've no right to intrude so far from our homeworlds. We really don't. They're so far away.*

Then you'll be relieved to hear that the Valparaiso *is scheduled to be returned to Phobos Base for refitting.*

She is? And I can return with her? Hope strengthened his mental touch.

Most certainly. I would insist on it, Stierlman. You've been on such a long tour. Thian gritted his teeth as he 'pathed that reassurance, but he needed Stierlman able to operate for just two more days.

But how will we get back? We're such a long way out. Oh, no problem, Stierlman. This fleet's Talent-heavy, which wasn't accurate even though Thian felt that he'd re-assigned the right people to the right positions. *We'll be with you tomorrow. What's your current time?*

Ah . . . oh . . . 1635.

Inform Captain Steverice that the Constellation-class AS LSTS, Captain Spktm, will be 'ported to join you at 0800 your time tomorrow.

What do I have to do? A thin line of barely contained fear trembled in the mental voice.

Nothing, Stierlman, Thian said kindly. *You're already there and we've only to join you.*

Two days later "we've only" was a choice of words that Thian regretted. There'd been no mishaps with any of the 'portations but it had been a draining process for the T-1s and T-2s who bore the brunt of each merge. The fact that each merge had different components also added to the strain on the merge foci. The second day, after a hasty conference, Thian 'ported back specially selected 3s and 4s from those whose ships had already joined Squadron D. Rojer had gone to the *LSTS* to strengthen future links, since Stierlman was useless. Thian had reluctantly sent Al-ison Anne on the *Genesee* with orders for her to report to the *Valparaiso* and find out what was wrong with Stierlman.

He had occasion to wonder if he shouldn't perhaps have brought the *Washington* across first and managed from there. But he had no cogent reason why that would have worked better. Especially once he managed the final and major merge that 'ported the Nebula-class ship.

Now, if anyone wakes either Roj or myself for any rea-son short of a Hiver fleet materializing in front of us, I'll kill 'im. So help me, I . . . Thian sighed with immense re-lief as his heavy, hurting head touched the softness of his pillow and was immediately asleep.

CHAPTER
NINE

THOUGH Alison Anne swore herself blind that Thian had slept fourteen hours without moving, that his 'Dinis had been up and about and eaten and were giving their usual tutorials, Thian was positive he had only just put his head to the pillow when she shook him awake.

"I am sorry, Thian, honey, but Rojer says you've got to talk to Earth Prime, too. It's real urgent." She separated the last words to emphasize them, her face so bad-news-blank that he didn't want to "look" in his present half-conscious state. He drank the stimulant beverage she handed him, grateful that it was cool enough to drink off quickly.

He grabbed the clean shipsuit she handed him and, slipping his feet into the soft-soled shoes he preferred, strode across the lounge to the ready room. He had worked the kinks out of his shoulders and his neck by the time the door opened for him. Both Rojer and Clancy were on their couches; Semirame Kloo leaned against the wall, arms crossed on her chest, watching their faces, which were blank with concentration. She glanced briefly away from them as Thian entered and jerked her head for him to take his place fast.

He had already picked up the thread of mental message which the two were receiving.

... inform the captains to prepare. I know the missiles are heavy work but you're going to need all you can stuff on board ... Thian! Good morning, said Earth Prime, aware of his entry into the discussion. *Briefly, I'll repeat what I've detailed to Rojer and Clancy. Those warning beacons the Squadrons have been setting in the heliopause of Hive-occupied worlds are going off, one after another. Captain Soligen informs us that Squadron B is in pursuit of two and worried about another one or two coming up behind them. With only two Galaxy-class and two destroyers, one of them minus significant numbers of its ordinary complement, she is not really equipped to tackle two or more Hivers and their complement of over-armed scouts. Nor does she have the new Hive-hull–piercing missiles.*

Did that mad 'Dini captain set off in the captured Sphere? Thian thought with a groan. *Did Captain Klml have any armament? Did Flavia tell it where we figured the missile controls were?*

Easy, Thian. Flavia and the others 'ported Klml into Clarf space a week ago. Laria says it arrived, scared the short hairs off half the 'Dini population, but let's deal with your current situation. Thian had never heard quite that tone of voice from his grandfather before and concentrated on this briefing. *With alarms going off all over the Alliance, the High Council is reluctant to send additional units to support you, despite the fact that you'll obviously have a fight on your hands even with the two squadrons already in your quadrant. But, before you give Captain Ashiant the good*

*news, can you give me any information on this totally unex-
pected mobilization of Spheres? High Council is . . . rather
. . . upset, you might say.* Thian grinned, reassured by that
flicker of Earth Prime's usual wry delivery. *What's this Rojer
was telling me about a new homeworld sun?*

*That looks a much more valid theory now that the Hiv-
ers have reacted. I'm also afraid that the theory that Hivers do not have communications just got knocked down a
wormhole.*

Jeff sounded as if he'd let off a long whistle of amazement. *The High Council is going to be scared shitless.*

*Not as badly as I am, sir. This Fleet sets beacons, too,
you know, and Commander Kloo just handed me a note
which confirms that those four beacons have gone off.
With the two or three Captain Soligen can account for, we
can now add another four, AND the one we're chasing.*

*Seven, possibly eight? And they can communicate with
each other? Why now?* Jeff sounded exasperated.

*I think, sir, we've made the mistake of presuming too
much about the Hivers.*

Obviously. Let's get back to this homeworld theory.

*The Hivers' homeworld sun went nova. They sent out
the three Hive Spheres to find the right sort of primary
with an M-5 planet to replace what they'd lost. The way
we're seeing it now is that the original three Spheres the
'Dinis came across were an advance group, spreading out
to look for just the right primary, which is why they
bypassed so many likely colonial M-5s. The Great Sphere
was following with everything else needed to set up the
new base. So let's operate on the theory—because I don't
want to presume anything I can't prove about the Hivers—
that this Sphere Three is the lucky one and has located the
primary they want with the sort of planet they need. They
are either inviting others to come see and/or want addi-*

tional groups to secure the world. Or, and I like this possibility less, Three knows it's being pursued and has broadcast for assistance, it being the last exploratory ship left. Or all of them!

Oh! There was a pause while Jeff Raven assimilated that information. *Well, we—the Alliance—certainly can't let them establish a new home base. Look, inform Captain Ashiant of the situation within the Alliance. Assure him that we will supply whatever new missiles and material you can 'port out there but he's got to make do with the two Fleet elements in the quadrant. The High Council is adamant that all other Fleet units remain deployed within the Alliance to counteract any Hive intrusions. I'll do all I can, personally and professionally, to help you, Thian.*

Thank you, sir.

Damn it, boy, I didn't think I was letting you, any of you, in for a WAR! Jeff sounded more indignant than alarmed for their sakes.

Sir, we won't let you down!

Remember this, Primes, and Clancy, and I've said this to Flavia, you Talents are to preserve yourselves!

That we will, you may be sure of it. Thian put a good deal of strength in that assurance.

I'd better be, was Jeff Raven's final word.

Rojer and Clancy regarded Thian with sardonic expressions as they all sat at the end of that 'pathing.

"And how are we going to do *that*, bro," Rojer asked, "when we know the mortality rate of escape pods in a Hive encounter?"

Thian started to chuckle, then his amusement so overcame him that he fell to one side on the couch while the others regarded him as if he'd lost his wits.

"Rojer . . . you should . . . know . . . what's so funny.

You did it yourself." *We use a variant of the* Genesee *ploy! It's the only logical course of action! Hell, we know the insides of a Sphere ship like we know a Tower. All we have to do is get close enough. And not all that close either.*

Semirame Kloo was actually the first to perceive what Thian was thinking and stared at him with an awed expression. "That's no way to fight a war, Thian Raven-Lyon!"

"Who was it said that all's fair in love and war! Hell's bells, Rame, why should more than the enemy die in a war they started?"

"The 'Dini won't look at it quite the same way," Clancy reminded him. "They achieve *honor* destroying Hiver ships."

Thian dismissed that. "They still have the scouts to take out. That'll give them glory enough. If I knew the insides of a scout as well as I do a Sphere, we might be able to work out something inside 'em, too."

"D'you think Ashiant will go along with this bright plan of yours?" Kloo asked skeptically.

"Well, I think it'd be best if we let them all steam a bit. It wouldn't do for me to act, as Grandmother says, like a cocky kid. But didn't the 'Dinis approach us to form a mutual protection Alliance because we managed to defeat the Sphere with no casualties on our side?"

"What was it you said to Granddad, Thi?" Rojer asked, cocking his head at his brother. "About presuming something we don't *know* for sure?"

"For one thing, Thian," Clancy put in, "using our kinesis to shield against Hiver missiles has a finite limit ... our individual strengths. I'll be frank. I'd about run out of the energy to keep up the necessary gestalt on the *Franklin* before the engagement ended."

Rojer nodded.

"Shielding ought not to be so great a problem. Look,

let's inform Captain Ashiant. Even my solution's going to need more naval tactics than I know."

"Glad to hear you admit it, Thi," said Kloo with approval. "But if I grasped your plan properly, it'd save a hellacious amount of lives!"

Ashiant heard the report with a blank expression but the way his eyes blinked rapidly from time to time and the way they moved over items on his desk told Thian, who knew him the best, that he was already mulling over available options. At the point where Thian said that the High Council was keeping all additional units in Alliance space, he grimaced and "hmmmd" deep in his throat.

"I can understand that," he said, allowing the words to emerge on a long expelled breath. "We shall first take Earth Prime up on his offer to send us more missiles and whatever other supplies on which the Fleet needs topping up." He taped the connection to the bridge. "Mr. Wasiq, please call a red emergency session of all captains, first officers, gunnery and commissary personnel. The Primes will be standing by to 'port carriers to the *Washington*. Vandermeer, clear the landing bay and be ready to receive Human and 'Dini visitors appropriately."

Having given the necessary preliminary orders, Ashiant sat very still, not even steepling his fingers as he sometimes did, his eyes unfocused but, if Thian couldn't read the thoughts, he was aware of intense mental activity.

Abruptly Ashiant rose and, with an odd explosion of breath from his slightly opened mouth, pulled the blouse of his shipsuit down.

"We have quite a job of work ahead of us, don't we?"

Thian nodded. Rojer, Clancy and Kloo shot Thian curious glances but he ignored them.

"Rojer, would you be kind enough to discover from

Captain Soligen's Primes, what course setting she's currently on in her pursuit of the two Spheres? If she knows which systems they emerged from, and where the third one might come from?" Then he looked at Thian. "Has Squadron B been informed of the total picture?"

"Earth Prime was not specific on that point, sir."

Ashiant nodded. "Then tell her, Rojer, and, as tactfully as possible, ask her to refrain from taking direct action. I think we have presumed too much from too little substantiated information . . ." Ashiant missed the look Thian received from the others, ". . . but from all the 'Dinis know, a Sphere rarely initiates space attacks. Let us hope they are, as has been their *custom*, single-minded in their current mission."

Ashiant began to pace then, hands behind his back.

"We don't yet *know* if their comparable primary has been discovered, do we? How far ahead could you 'port a scout, Prime?"

"Using the mass of the Third Sphere as one reference point, we could possibly send it that much further beyond as the distance between our current position and the Sphere's."

We've never done anything like that, *Thian,* Rojer said, his mind tone aghast with consternation.

I think we may have to do a lot of things that haven't been done before, Roj. But I know *we could manage that.*

The exchange was so brief that Thian did not miss Ashiant's reply.

"We might be in a tactically superior position if we could establish exactly where the Sphere is headed. I know I would feel a considerable relief if that could be ascertained."

"Excuse me, sir," Kloo said, "but we don't even know

what *they're* looking for. How would we be able to find what they haven't?"

"Since we now have a sizable file on what they haven't wanted, perhaps any G-star registering odd fluctuations or variations or sun-spot activity, or aberrations not listed, would be worth staking out. This Third Sphere . . ."—and for the first time since receiving news of the unfavorable developments, Captain Ashiant vented agitation. "Bells! Gentlemen, this is Operation Number Three. So, Number Three will undoubtedly have to make a course correction at some point. If advance scouts—we'd best deploy all we have . . ." and he paused to look queryingly at Thian, who nodded with more energy than he felt for such a project, "we will be in a better position to cover possible objectives. Kloo, you'll command the *Revere* and, when you assemble your crew, include Lieutenant Commander Langio—she's the best astrogator—and whatever other personnel might be useful in that aspect. I'll have to let other captains have their byte on selections but you're mine."

Kloo looked briefly toward Clancy but caught Thian's quick head shake and, saluting, retired from the room.

The com unit buzzed then. "Sir," said the com officer, Eki Wasiq, "we've replies from everyone and most are ready to lift on the 'go' from the Primes."

Ashiant nodded to the three Talents. "I'll want all three of you at this strategy conference, too."

Do we know what we're getting ourselves in for, bro? Rojer asked, echoing the sentiments Clancy held clear to be seen as the three jogged back to their ready room.

No, but we've done pretty well so far, handling matters as they come, haven't we? Thian said with a grin as he swung his feet up on the couch and began to lean into the generators for gestalt. He would use as much artificial help as he could, to spare his energies for what he was undoubtedly to be saddled with all too soon. *And I'm just as scared as you are.*

Neither Prime was at all surprised when their 'Dinis entered the room and settled beside them as if on guard.

"Who're we to pick up first, Mr. Wasiq?" Thian asked. "Give them to us in batches of threes, please."

"Ah, well, Spktm, Prlm and Ktpl sound awful eager . . ."

"Is there a 'Dini officer available to greet them properly?"

"Aye, sir."

Take 'em in order, Thian said to Rojer and Clancy and reached out to grasp the 'Dini carrier from the Constellation *LSTS.*

"All in neatly, Thian," Wasiq said, a note of relief in his voice. "Next are Captains Shepherd, Cheseman, and Germys."

All were on board within fifteen minutes and, as the Talents rose from their couches, Alison Anne appeared with a tray of high-protein bars and more stimulants.

"I told Commander Exeter that you'd need watching," she said, glaring at the three, "and you will! Even your 'Dinis know something big's up."

They don't know the half of it, do they? Thian said, grinning as he grabbed up some of the bars and deposited them in his thigh pockets and drained the beverage. Rojer and Clancy followed his example. "Greevy," he added, grasping her elbow, so she'd at least get an empathic reading the urgency of the day, "get in touch with all T-2s and T-3s and have them alert and ready for unexpected duties."

Do I use the code?

Not yet. We've got the strategy meeting to get through first . . . But if any 2s and 3s are slated for one of the scouts—Rame can have her choice, but I'll want to clear on anyone else first. I'll need the best of kinetics here.

Alison Anne nodded in response and, while Thian would have liked a quick embrace from her to sustain him, he approved of her moving immediately to carry out his orders.

Rojer, make that 'path to Flavia and find out what the captain wanted to know from Captain Soligen.

Right. It won't take long. I don't want to miss a moment of this meeting.

Rojer arrived with that information and gave it to Captain Ashiant just as Thian began repeating the message 'pathed to him by Earth Prime, along with Captain Soligen's situation. The three Primes settled back then, to wait until the initial reaction was over and Captain Ashiant called for comments on appropriate tactics. As Thian listened to opinions, options and, more importantly, the almost overconfident optimism of Humans, he was half-sorry that the recent skirmish with the Second Sphere and its scouts had ended so successfully. Everyone had recovered from the original scare. Confidence was useful—in moderation. Presumption, and the Mrdini commanders were worst in the area, could lead to disaster.

"Prime Thian!" His name jolted him out of his contemplation.

"Sir?" and he swiveled in his chair to face Captain Shepherd of the *Vadim*.

"Did you identify any communications facility on the control board of the Refugee?"

"No, sir, but there was a lot of sort of end-of-the-row positions whose function had not been identified at the conclusion of our assignment."

"Can you find out if such a function has now been recognized?"

"I will query Earth Prime on that point, sir." And when

Captain Shepherd looked as if he expected Thian to perform his contact then and there, he added, "With respect, Captain, Prime's time is at a premium within the Alliance so I was asked to collect all pertinent data for one sending."

"Oh! Yes, I quite understand, though that should be a priority question," the older man said, his prominent eyebrows nearly touching over the bridge of his nose as he fumed quietly over the delay.

"Indeed it is, sir, and I'm certain High Council has the Phobos Base working all the hours of a day to discover what and how."

"What good would that do, Shepherd?" Cheseman asked bluntly. "We wouldn't have the foggiest what they were saying even if we did access their communications frequency."

Shepherd considered that but refused to concede. "We'd at least know *when* they were contacting each other, and, if we could determine the direction, be warned from what other quadrants we might expect additional units to join Number Three. I'll be candid, Cheseman, Ashiant, one Sphere posed enough problems. We may have the state-of-the-art missiles which have now proven effective, but the possibility of eight . . . or more . . . such ships, plus twenty-four of those overkill scouts, makes a formidable adversary."

"We have reinforcements . . ." Germys began, pausing to frown at the ensign who entered as discreetly as possible to give Ashiant a note.

Shepherd took advantage of that pause and sprang in with: ". . . who are themselves not in a favorable situation, with a possible third Sphere coming up their ass. And what's this, Ashiant, about sending the scouts out *ahead* of Number Three, to *try* to find the one G-star in I don't know how many astronomical lengths ahead of us that these Spheres could be homing in on? If that is what they're doing? And what is their sudden mass mobilization all about? Frankly, I think they're assembling a punitive force to despatch this Fleet and end its threat to their colonial expansionism!"

"Captain," and Spktm rose to its full height, "what the Hivers do now has never been seen in the two hundreds of years that we have been opposing them. We Mrdini find ourselves in accord with the theory that the three Spheres and the Great Sphere went in search of a homeworld to replace the one that was burned up. It is regrettable that the specific nature of that primary is unknown . . ."

Ashiant rose, bowing apologies to Spktm for an interruption in its peroration. "As to that, honored captain, the specific nature of the Hive primary *is* known." He smiled as everyone eagerly awaited his next words, and waved the note in his hand. "As you know, we've been examining the systems which the Hivers have bypassed, but one of our bright young astronomically inclined ensigns, Cyra Charteris, hit on the notion of examining tapes from the astronomical files of the Hive quadrant and comparing them with those taken by your good self, Spktm, while at the nova site. We now know that primary's spectrum signature!"

His ringing voice echoed in the brief silence. Then everyone began to talk at once.

"Then I see no bar at all to sending the scouts out to home in on that star before Number Three can," Shepherd said, almost shouting to be heard.

"We approve," Spktm said, raising its voice over the second spate of excitement. "But," and it raised its flipper-like arm, its digits displaying in a fan-like motion, "there are still eight Spheres to be disabled, preferably before any reach this star. They would fight more fiercely than ever before to protect it. And to deny us the way to such a reverent destination."

"They will fight with madness never seen," Prlm said. "Even the new missiles might not work."

"They'll work, all right," Thian said, suddenly rising to attract everyone's attention, "if they're *put* where they will do the most damage and *that* is a Talent we possess!"

That momentary silence was broken by a burst of laughter from Commander Yngocelen of the *Vadim.*

"Thian Lyon, you have made my day!" And he gave a triumphant whoop of delight, jumping to his feet. "Don't you all *see* what the Prime proposes? I mean, with that technique, it doesn't matter a hoot in hell how many Spheres come after us, they get a missile where it'll do the most good and boom!" He clapped his hands together and then extended his arms outward. "This is the *Genesee* ploy in a new guise. And it means we don't even have to get in range of any Sphere to destroy it. We'll only need to know *where* it is! Thian, Rojer and Clancy here plant the missile—hey, it doesn't even have to be a missile . . ."

"Which actually wouldn't fit in a Sphere engine room . . ." Rojer remarked, grinning at Yngocelen's enthusiasm.

". . . Whatever," and Yngie flicked that minor detail away with one long-fingered hand. "The package can be delivered and the Sphere is history!"

"BUT THAT IS NOT THE WAY MRDINIS FIGHT HIVE SHIPS," said Captain Ktpl of the Galaxy-class *KLTS.* Its fur ruffled in agitation and it looked across to Spktm who was still on its feet, glancing from one Human speaker to another.

"MOST RESPECTED SIR," Thian said first to Spktm and, bowing, to Ktpl, "MRDINIS SOUGHT HUMAN AID BECAUSE WE DESTROYED A HIVE SPHERE WITH NO LOSS OF LIFE AMONG US. NO HUMAN BLOOD WAS SPILT. TOO MUCH MRDINI BLOOD HAS BEEN SPILT IN TWO HUNDREDS OF YEARS. NOW IS THE TIME TO END THAT WASTE OF COLOR'S BLOOD AND SPEND YOUR TIME

FINDING NEW WORLDS ON WHICH TO LIVE AT PEACE. YOU SOME-
TIMES FIND OUR CAUTION COWARDLY . . ." A rumble of
protest from as many Human throats as Mrdini briefly in-
terrupted him. "BUT WE HUMANS DO NOT RE-CREATE AS
MRDINIS MAY SO WE ARE CAREFUL OF THE ONE LIFE WE HAVE."
Thian wondered whether he had overstepped the bounds to
interject that fact but he had to assume all Mrdinis of
Skptm's, and probably Prlm's, status would know of the
re-creation of Kat and Gil. "THERE WILL BE FIGHTING
ENOUGH TO SATISFY HONOR BUT FEWER DEATHS TO CAUSE
GRIEF. LET US HUMANS DO WHAT YOU SOUGHT US OUT TO DO—
DESTROY THE HIVER THREAT WITH THE LEAST POSSIBLE LOSS
OF ALLIANCE MEMBERS."

The few Human captains and commanders who had not
followed all his impassioned speech were quickly given its
gist. Even Shepherd looked approving. Spktm bowed to
Thian from its mid-section with great dignity and resumed
its chair, thus acknowledging Thian's points.

Hey, bro, good points!

Thian, you're marvelous, came Alison Anne's comment.

I'm with you, Lyon, was Kloo's enthusiastic acknowledgment.

*This is supposed to be a high-level top-secret strategy
meeting but, Kloo, kiss that ensign of yours who had the
wits to compare astronomical tapes!*

Not quite. I'll leave that for you . . . or Rojer!

Ashiant rose and banged the gavel to restore order.

"I observe that most of us here are in accord with Prime
Lyon's excellent suggestions, although I'm sure he'll be the
first to admit that we haven't solved *all* the tactical problems
facing us. But our priorities are now clearly defined.
Yngocelen, figure out what sort of payload would be needed
to destroy a sphere if 'ported into the engine room?"

"I'd need a few details but, considering the fuel Hive

ships use, a rather compact package of the right stuff would set off a fuel reaction nothing could stop." The gunnery officer was unable to stop grinning at such a satisfactory prospect.

"Do we have the requisite components on board?"

"Sir, I believe we do."

"That's all well. Our Talents need to reserve their energies for exportation rather than importations." Ashiant's little witticism took a moment to sink in but Rojer caught it and gave a laugh which he tried to smother behind both hands. A few more chuckles allowed Ashiant to grin in response. "So, I've preempted the *Revere* for my scout crew; you gentlemen had best decide on how to man the other five scouts the *Washington* carries so we can implement the next task on our list—finding the damned star now we know what its spectrum is."

Thian took that opportunity to lean towards Ashiant.

"Sir, if I may excuse myself briefly to inform Captain Soligen of the diy . . ."

"The diy, Prime?"

"Yes, sir, the destroy-it-yourself. . . . Captain Soligen will be very anxious to deal with those three Spheres as soon as possible . . . and she should. Who knows how many more we'll have to deal with! She's got the Talent to get the . . . ah . . . exportations . . ."

A flicker of a smile crossed Ashiant's face. "By all means, inform her of the strategy, Prime. And also inform Earth Prime. Some of those anxious boots back in Alliance territory can take the byte and use it themselves to good advantage."

"I'll ask about communications, too, sir."

Ashiant flicked his hand to speed Thian on his message round.

Stay, Rojer, Clancy, and keep our end up!

*   *   *

Thian made contact with Flavia on the *Columbia*.

Didn't Rojer give you the course headings? We'll let you know the moment they alter, Flavia began, somewhat startled to have two contacts in such a brief time.

No, we got that and the ones you're chasing are on the same heading Number Three is. However, I've got good news. Can you get Captain Soligen in with you so you can voice to her what I'm about to say? She can think up her questions as we go along.

She happens to be in here right now, Thian, so go ahead.

Flavia, you know how a Genesee *ploy works? Well, we've got a variant to try on the Spheres fore and aft of you. Are the ones you're pursuing very far ahead?*

No, and Vesta's closing the gap daily. I once thought Klml was trigger-happy, but sight of two strong ion trails have altered not only Hptml until its poll eye's gone fuchsia, but Captains Steverice and Hsiang are nearly as blood-thirsty. They want those Spheres worse than Klml wanted the one it got. And I'll bet that's one bad-tempered 'Dini on Clarf, thinking of what it's missing here. So what's this variant on the Genesee *gambit?*

When Thian had explained, he could hear her startled exclamation—and possibly an echo from Captain Soligen. And the relief that flooded her mind. She'd been trying to sound so cool and composed. Now he realized that she'd been as scared as he had been until he figured out the advantage Talent was giving both elements of the Fleet. Indeed, the entire Alliance.

What did you just say to Flavia, Thian? Zara demanded. *She's sounding like she's in pain but she's grinning as if you proposed or something.*

I didn't propose marriage, little sister, but listen.

By the time he had explained the stratagem, her mind was focusing tight on his words.

Thian, that's marvelous news, Flavia said. *You can't hear how everyone is cheering.*

Now, let's not celebrate prematurely. I don't want anyone presuming *we've got the upper hand . . .*

What else would you call it, Thian? Flavia demanded. *We've skills they don't have and never will have, given their mind set.*

There's still the scouts to contend with, and who knows how many other Sphere ships will come on course. And the Hivers do communicate together on some level . . .

What good would that do us, Thian? Flavia replied. *None of us know what medium they use for communication.*

The queen made sounds, Zara said, an odd note in her mental tone. *There were tapes and tapes made of her clicks and stutters and glottal stops. I know I'm in a minority, but I still feel sorry for that one and I'm not ashamed of myself for it.*

Nor should you be ashamed of a genuine act of empathic kindness, Thian replied firmly, sensing Zara's curious ambivalence. She had, after all, saved the queen once without ever understanding how she knew why she felt so compelled to act. *Did anyone ever make any sense out of those sounds, Zara?* Thian asked kindly.

Noooo, Zara admitted in a melancholic tone, then more briskly: *Have any of you bright boys figured out the frequency on which they communicate?*

Thian chuckled. *I'll bet they're swarming the Refugee right now trying to figure that out. Probably going over the one Klml brought back to Clarf. Look, I've got to tell Granddad all this, and get him off the hook, with the Alliance in a state of utter panic. One of us will get back to*

*you as soon as Commander Yngocelen's figured out the
specifications of the surprise package.*

You know, it's so strange how things work out, Thian,
Flavia said. *If we hadn't worked on the Refugee, we'd
never be able to do what we are about to do.*

Though Thian felt the same reverent awe that she expressed, he could never have stated it. He was glad that she
could.

*And if Rojer hadn't been forced aboard the Xh-33, we'd
not have had a useful strategy,* Thian added.

Oh, someone would have thought of something else.

Well, there're more minds to merge this time round.

By the Cluster, Thian, against how many Spheres?
Flavia sounded aghast at that prospect. *It's just as well
there're more sensible alternatives available!*

She broke off contact then and her final indignant remark left him chuckling. He wasn't chuckling by the time
his grandfather, very much Earth Prime throughout the
lengthy interview, had winkled every scrap of all the conversations Thian had overheard in the *Washington*'s ready
room, and had Thian repeat his reply to Spktm—rhetoric
which made Thian squirm on the couch as he recited it.
Verbatim it sounded more pompous and impassioned than
it had when the phrases and ideas had just formed in his
mind and issued from his mouth.

Then there was that long pause before Jeff spoke again,
more Granddad than Prime.

*I concur with Flavia, Thian lad. There has been a re-
markable inevitability, starting at Deneb years ago, that
leads inexorably to this confrontation. Perhaps the Hivers
had had warnings as far back as Deneb that their sun
would turn nova. You may be sure the High Council will
be relieved to hear of this turn of events. Not to mention
every other frightened citizen of this Alliance. And grateful*

*to you and that young astronomer . . . what was his name?
You didn't mention it.*

Her *name is Cyra Charteris.*

*Thank you. If Ashiant doesn't give her a field promotion,
she'll get official word of one very soon. So get on with
the workings and keep me up to speed. Or let Clancy make
the contact if it's just information. Spare yourself as much
as possible. You're in the catbird seat out there, boy. How
do you like it?*

No more than you ever did, sir. But I'm here.

And I . . . am here for you, Thian.

Thian never knew until much later who decided the de-
ployment of the *Washington*'s scouts, but the three Talents,
with a little help from three T-2s brought into the ready
room for this mass 'portation, got the six scouts into their
assigned positions.

None of the Talents liked using Number Three as the
reference point—they all caught the heavy sting-pzzt—but
they got the scouts safely past that obstacle without
alerting the Sphere to their passage.

Yngocelen had the help of every other munitions expert
in the Fleet. Late that night, when he came to the Tower
ready room so he could be present while Thian passed the
requisite instructions to Captain Soligen, he told the Talents that it took more time to hear everyone's theories than
it did to make up sufficient "surprise packages."

"We made a lot more than I hope we'll ever need,"
Yngocelen said, shrugging his bony shoulders and grinning. "But hell, once we got started, we kinda just continued. They're compact, handy little mothers!" He grinned
again and then yawned.

"Don't do that," Thian said, answering yawn with yawn
as he slipped onto the couch.

Oh I'm so glad to hear from you, Thian, Flavia said. *We've got three behind us unless our sensors are seeing triple . . .*

Don't fret. Is Captain Soligen nearby? And your gunnery officer?

I called Rhodri. He can take down the information and save you more effort. You're tired.

Never mind. Link with Rhodri so he can ask any relevant questions. Here's the way Yngocelen's made the surprise package.

Hey, coz, came the unmistakable tones of Rhodri Eagle, *that is one neat little dealie. We've got everything on board, too. Ah, Captain just arrived. I'll see if she has any queries.*

Oh, Thian, will *this work?* Flavia was trying very hard to maintain her usual composure.

These men know what they're doing with explosives. And we know how to deliver. Remember where there're all those connecting pipes in Refugee's engine room, Flavia?

Yes, yes, I do.

That's where you plant it. Detonation can be set just before you 'port it. Yngie suggests no more than five seconds because it just might be noticed. They see better in the dark than we do.

I've got that. Captain Soligen sends you her most profound thanks and Lieutenant Commander Searles says it's neat, easily assembled, and he's just left to do it. Vesta says she's going to do the ones behind us first. She says it makes her nervous having those things rolling up our backsides.

I'd agree. Clancy's taking the first watch so let him know what happens.

There was a brief pause when Thian knew that Flavia had not yet broken the contact.

Good luck, Thian Lyon!

Good luck right back at you, Flavia Bastianmajani! And give Rhodri a chance to help 'port. He'll never stop bragging but that'd be better than his complaining he was left out.

I had actually decided to bring him in on it. Flavia's mental tone held a ripple of amusement.

While Thian slept, curled around Alison Anne, with Mur and Dip snuggled against his back, he had good dreams. And while he slept, Flavia, with assists from Rhodri and her brother—Zara flatly refused to have anything to do with the 'portations—delivered the packages.

"She said," Clancy reported to Thian over breakfast, "that everyone joined the countdowns and saw the distant bursts that marked the destruction. Captain Soligen reports all four Spheres removed and she's running at top speed to join us. Flavia said that Earth Prime was delighted." He waited a beat, ducking his head, his expression full of chagrin. "I thought we should have waited until you were awake and could do the honors. Rojer spoke out, too, but once Yngie had assembled the bombs, Spktm couldn't wait to see if they'd work, so Captain Ashiant ordered us to despatch 'em."

"What're you looking like that for, then, coz? You didn't muff the job, did you?"

"Hell, no!" Clancy said on a nervous laugh, *but I really think it was totally unfair for you not to be able to plant one.*

Thian gave Clancy an affectionate clout on the shoulder. "So long as you left Number Three for me . . ." and he fixed his cousin with a stern stare.

Clancy raised his hands and recoiled slightly at the thought of such perfidy.

"Okay, then! Relax. So long as Number Three's *mine*!"

"Only because Captain Ashiant wants to be *sure*," said Rojer, joining them then, "it leads us to the right star."

" 'Twinkle, twinkle, little star / Tell me, please, which one you are!' " Clancy said, grinning with devilment.

The two Primes groaned in unison.

"Any word on which?" Thian asked.

"Not yet, but we've got six scouts doing broad sweeps and it can't take forever . . . If Number Two had to stop to resupply, Number Three must be running low, too."

"Maybe she did," Clancy said. "Wasiq had been running through D's log tapes and found that they had lost the trail for about three weeks and had to trawl around to pick it up again."

"Stierlman never mentioned that."

"Well, it's in the official log."

"Bet Ashiant was furious." Thian said, cursing Stierlman.

"With Captain Steverice, not Stierlman. At least they found the ion trail again."

Thian sighed. "How far behind Number Three are we hanging?"

"Far enough so there's no chance of any *known* sensors picking us up on Number Three."

"But, if they *do* have communications . . ."

"Look, bro, the spheres that got blown up wouldn't have had time to send a click, clack or clatter!"

"A lack of communications from ships known to have been operable and following Number Three would make the rest of them suspicious," Thian said, running an impatient hand through his hair, and hauling back into place the white lock that was always falling in his eyes.

"Ashiant feels the same way," Clancy said and then shrugged. "But they won't know *what* took 'em out. I'd say great uncle is making sure none leave Alliance space.

Ashiant ordered the *KLTR* and the *Comanche* to hang back and sweep for any late arrivals."

"So, it's a waiting game again, is it?" Thian said.

"Looks that way," Clancy replied.

"We can always pass the time making up a few more packages, Thi," Rojer suggested. "We don't *know* how many Hiver colonies there are, or how many spheres lurk on our way to Paradise Regained."

The *Franklin*, crewed by a mixture from the *Vadim* and the Galaxy *KLTS*, discovered Number Three's destination: a youngish G-type star, matching the original Hiver primary within .0378 disparity in its spectrum, which the astrogators considered close enough. It had eleven planets, two of them with the suitable atmospheres and the correct proportion of land mass to sea that Hivers preferred, in the M-5 and M-6 positions. The Sphere would shortly have to make a course alteration if this were, indeed, the primary it sought.

Tension mounted in the Fleet when reports from Captain Soligen that she had "surprised" another sphere coming up behind her added to the dismay of those wanting to reach confrontation.

Captain Ashiant broadcast shipwide that as soon as Number Three made a course correction to approach the heliopause of its target system, they would intercept it. As a precaution, he asked Thian to arrange the 'portation of Captain Spktm and the *LSTS* and two Galaxy-class, the *KLTL* and the *Vadim*, and the destroyers, the *KLTR* and the *Comanche*, in case Number Three sent her three scouts out ahead of her to confirm the suitability of the system. He recalled the furthest-ranging scouts but let the *Franklin* and the *Revere* remain with the task force.

Jeff Raven reported phenomenal success with the *Genesee* ploy, and Captain Osullivan was reassigned to one of the newly commissioned Constellation-class ships to play an active part in the defense of the Alliance. His old crew toasted their former captain with considerable enthusiasm, with Captain Germys springing for the beverages served. If Rojer looked a little smug, since it was he who had actually originated the *Genesee* ploy, no one who knew that denied him that right.

Since Zara remained "unavailable" for the offensive maneuver, Captain Soligen redeployed her Squadron to cover a larger area of space. Asia and Mallen Bastianmajani were transferred to the *KMTM* and Rhodri and Jes to the *Valparaiso:* the two Galaxy-class ships hung slightly back of the *Columbia*'s center and she was guarded by the two destroyers as she maintained her course following the ion trail of Number Three, the main Fleet ahead of her.

Only one more Sphere ship met its end under their aegis but, to the chagrin of the main Fleet, it gave Squadron B an impressive total without a single casualty.

"Number Three's slowed," Ashiant said over the com unit to the Talents. "She's hanging outside the heliopause. Ah, now she's deploying her scouts. Could she have sensor readings of our forward elements?"

"Whether she has or not, sir, will it make any difference how she receives the package?" Thian asked, striding toward his couch. *This one's mine, remember!*

Gee, can't we watch? Rojer asked in a pesky kid-brother voice.

"Commander Yngocelen here, Prime Thian, package is ready to go."

"Thank you, Commander." Thian settled himself, caught the gestalt of the generators, "found" the explosive package where it sat on the floor of the landing bay, sent his mind ahead to the darkness of Number Three's engine room, the macaroni junction of tubes and pipes, and 'ported the package there.

One ... and Rojer had jumped to the terminal to activate the forward view screen.

"Two," Thian said, racing on long legs to the bridge door. When he got there, Ashiant was saying "Three." The bridge crew, eyes on the main view screen, chorused "Four!"

Rojer, Clancy, four 'Dinis and Alison Anne crowded at the entrance as everyone said "Five!"

The screen showed the vivid blossoming of the distant explosion, tiny though it was at this distance. The screen cleared more rapidly than perhaps the watchers could wish at this moment of ultimate triumph, but the after-image of that dramatic climax to a long search would be remembered often in the mind's eye. No one felt like cheering, but there were sighs of relief to be heard around the bridge and thoughtful expressions on every face.

"Mr. Wasiq, check with the *LSTS* to see if the scouts got away," Ashiant said, breaking the silence. Other muted sounds on the bridge indicated the resumption of normal duties.

"Sir, Captain Spktm and the other ships have engaged two of the scouts, the third was caught in the blast destroying Number Three. The captain believes that the scouts received some damage ..."

"With no Minds to guide them, of course they have," Thian murmured.

"... and the *Vadim* and the *KLTL* have launched a barrage. Sir, Captain Spktm reports the demolition of both remaining scouts."

"Operation Number Three completed," Ashiant said quietly.

As Thian lay on the couch, readying himself to report Captain Ashiant's words to Earth Prime, he felt none of the sense of triumph he had anticipated. Relief was the dominant emotion, relief from tension, strain, apprehension, uncertainty. *This* phase of the centuries-long struggle against Hiver aggrandizement no longer threatened the Alliance. But there were all those other Hive planets, and who knew how many spheres waiting until their populations had swelled to the point where yet another planet would have to be "prepared" to receive the Hive species. That could be his job for the rest of his life: finding all those myriad colonies.

Not necessarily, Thian, came his grandfather's voice softly in his mind. *Though I'm sure you could pick whatever Prime opportunity you choose.*

You know Number Three's gone?

I read that. I also perceived your state of mind and on that you have my most sincere compliments. You are a credit to our calling and to your family. A war where only the enemy dies!

Thian was startled to hear his own phrase repeated, though the thought would have occurred to more than one person who disliked unnecessary violence.

We have won this part of the war, Thian lad, but only this part. If it gives your mind any ease, a great many people, wise and simple, are trying to find out how to control the population pressure on Hive worlds, in that way reducing the species' need to colonize, eliminating their aggressiveness.

Either is preferable to their solution for life on other planets, Thian said.

War-weary, are you?

Weary, yes, sir.

How about finding new worlds Humans and 'Dinis can live on, either together or by the species?

There are a couple of hot-sun worlds the 'Dinis can have all to themselves, sir. I gather that we are to explore all possible colonial systems on our way back?

Yes, those are the official orders to relay to Captain Ashiant, plus his promotion to admiral.

Thian grinned, feeling pleasure at such a task pushing back the various types of relief that had dominated his present mood.

Meanwhile, the sociologists and bios and xenobs and all the rest of that stratum of reparational specialists will be using the data the Fleet has amassed to see if we can't come up with a solution to containing, but not necessarily restricting, Hivers to their current colonies.

Zara would like that part especially.

There was a beat of a pause. *Yes, I suspect with her ambivalence, she would, and she may join them in that research, especially if she's a burden on Captain Soligen and Flavia.*

You might, sir, transfer Rojer to the Columbia *if you reassign Zara to a research situation.*

The little Asia enters into that suggestion?

She does.

Well, the degree of cousinship is not a detriment, and Thian thought his grandfather sounded mildly pleased and surprised. *Hmm. Both Squadrons will now be assigned colonial explorations but . . . I see no reason to put the boy through any more emotional stress than he's already had. He* likes *Asia that much?*

Sir, he's very protective of her. Either a steady dose will cure him or it will consolidate his current interest.

You don't like Asia? This was definitely Grandfather talking.

She's sweet and engaging and, when she's out of shy mode, she can be fun but . . .

She's not your type.

In a word, yes. And, Grandfather, I've got my own plans.

So I understand, Thian. And we approve.

Abruptly, although a chuckle echoed distantly, Jeff Raven had broken the contact.

ROJER! CLANCY! Thian shouted. *Did either of you mention . . .*

YOU THINK WE'RE CRAZY! The two Talents answered in unison and Rojer burst in the door to the Tower room, glaring at Thian that he'd believe him guilty of such an indiscretion.

Then how the hell does Grandfather know about Alison Anne?

Rojer shrugged. "How the hell does Grandfather know half of what he does? He just does, and what did he just tell you? Thanks, maybe?"

Don't be cocky, boy, Thian said, with a grin and a punch on his brother's arm as he passed him on his way to Captain Ashiant's ready room down the hall.

Well, give us a clue, wontcha? Clancy added his complaint to Rojer's.

Thian heaved a sigh as he knocked politely on the captain's door. *Just listen in. I get so tired of having to repeat things . . .* "Captain Ashiant, the compliments of Earth Prime, who forwards the deep thanks and appreciation of the High Council and all Alliance citizens for the speedy settlement of this threat to our civilizations."

Ashiant regarded Thian for a long moment.

"Is that really what he said they said?"

"Well, sir, if not, that's how it should have been phrased. Earth Prime is deeply relieved that, as he did say, this is a war where only the enemy died."

"Not quite, but near enough to make it a valid comment," Ashiant said, nodding acceptance.

Then Thian grinned broadly. "I've also the happy duty to inform you that you have just been promoted to the rank of admiral in recognition of your services."

"Prime, I don't take kindly to practical jokes."

"No joke, sir, not to you, Captain Ashiant."

"Admiral, hmmm?" and Ashiant swung his chair around so that, when Thian next saw his face, it was as composed as ever, save for a brief upward slant of the corner of his mouth. He tugged at the blouse of his shipsuit. "That's rather good news and certainly an honor."

"Aye, aye, Admiral, sir, an honor to your family, your color and everyone serving under you."

"If you don't mind, Prime, I think we had best wait until this has been officially confirmed, but I thank you for apprising me of it."

There was another polite tap on the door, but First Officer Vandermeer did not even wait for Ashiant's response before she entered, holding out the usual documents carrier.

"This just 'ported in, sir, and it's addressed to 'Admiral Ashiant'! Sir!" Face wreathed in a broad and happy smile, she handed him the narrow carrier with her left hand while snapping him one definitely high-class salute.

"Well," Ashiant said, uncapping the cylinder and taking out the tightly rolled official document, "well," and he unrolled it, "well, and so it says."

"May I be the first to congratulate you, Admiral Ashiant?" Vandermeer said, tears of pride in the corners of her eyes.

"Why, that's splendid news, Admiral Ashiant," Thian said quickly, stepping forward and holding out his hand. "I'm honored to be present on such a felicitous occasion. My sincerest congratulations, Admiral Ashiant, for a well-deserved promotion!"

Ashiant cocked a sardonic eyebrow at the Prime, but there was no way Thian would have deflated Vandermeer's moment.

The news was all over the ship before Thian finished the further report and the orders he was to relay from Earth Prime. It didn't matter that Rojer and Clancy had been instrumental in its dissemination. The promotion was official and everyone went about their duties grinning: Ashiant was a popular man.

"So, our orders are to make our quadrants of this great galaxy safe for us harmless Human and 'Dini colonists," Rojer said when they were all back in their quarters. Thian was grooming Mur and Dip, a pleasant task he enjoyed but had had little time to do.

"We signed up for a five-year mission," Thian reminded him.

"That could have some dangerous moments, too," Clancy said in a hopeful tone. "But Cousin Raven's correct. There's a lot more to be done to see if we can't alter the Hivers sufficiently to reduce the threat they pose."

"Did those boffins at Phobos Base discover how to communicate with the Spheres?" Rojer asked, remembering that unresolved line of endeavor.

"Who knows? We destroyed all the Spheres they could have talked to. But there's got to be some way to establish contact. Communication might even explain to them—in a much nicer way—that what they're doing isn't currently acceptable social behavior," Clancy said facetiously. "That would settle the problem and we'll divvy the available M-5s equally among us."

"Only the Hivers would want to be more equal than the rest of us," Rojer said. "They breed faster."

*   *   *

By evening everyone knew of Ashiant's promotion and he had to tour the messes on all the nearby ships to take the toasts due his new rank. When Alison Anne got off duty, Rojer insisted that he could as easily 'port the Admiral wherever he needed to go, so Thian should go enjoy dinner with Greevy and Clancy.

"You know, don't you," Alison said, a certain remonstrating tone in her voice as she fixed Thian with what she called her "nurse glare," "that *you* should have had the promotion? You're the one that thought of the idea that got Ashiant his promotion."

"Come on, now, honey," Thian said, putting his fingers on her mouth and trying to make it curve up into a smile. "Ashiant deserves his admiral stars. Don't deny him."

"But does *he* realize that without you Primes," and she included Clancy in her gaze and rattled her fingers at Rojer in the ready room, "he'd be in deep kimchee right now with Spheres doing billiard balls with him the eight ball."

"Honey," and Thian's voice rose above her unexpected championship of Talents. He patted the chair beside him for her to take. "We're all in the same boat, win or lose. We did win, if that's what killing all your enemies is about." With a deft snake of his arm, he pulled her to his lap, though her body resisted him, tense and unrepentant. He kissed the nape of her neck and felt her give just a little. "Look at it from my point of view, hon. I'm just not supposed to be a combatant at all. I'm supposed to 'port and 'path and that's all I did."

"Yes, but that's what won the war for Ashiant . . ."

". . . and all of us, love. And that's the only time in my life I hope I'll have to do *that*! Don't you?"

He tried to turn her head toward him so he could look her in the eye. And then, those tactics unsuccessful, he tried another one.

I've asked Grandfather to send Rojer to the Columbia
and Asia. *He's really missing her. . . .*

"Oh, did you, Thian darling!" She was suddenly supple
in his arms again and twisted to put hers around his neck.

Neither noticed Clancy's discreet withdrawal, with Mur
and Dip, through the ready room.

"Oh, what a marvelous idea. I mean, we've still got
years of this mission and I think Rojer's really and truly in
love with her . . ."

Thian was more interested in cuddling Alison's pliable
form than her opinions about his brother's love.

I know it hasn't come up between us recently, he said,
kissing her lovingly to end the unprofitable conversation,
*but isn't it nice to be able to talk together the way we are
and still be able to kiss?*

Hmmm, was her response as he picked her up in his
arms and, deftly managing to maintain firm contact on her
mouth, carried her toward their room.

Grandfather also approves of us, you know, he said.

She broke the kiss and stared at him, wide blue eyes incredulous. "The Prime of Earth approves of *meeee?*"

*With reference to your complaint about who should get
the credit for all this, as long as I have you, Alison Anne
Greevy, I won't complain.*

I guess, she said in a dreamy contemplative voice as he
laid her gently on the bed, *maybe I did have just the tiniest
bit of precog when I first met you . . .*

*Did you now? And what did your precognitive Talent
tell you?*

That I'd be doing this with you a long time!